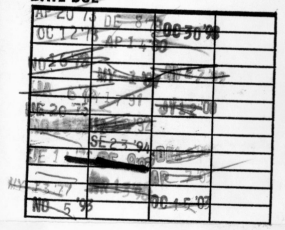

Books by Joyce Carol Oates

The Edge of Impossibility:
  TRAGIC FORMS IN LITERATURE
Wonderland
The Wheel of Love
Them
Expensive People
A Garden of Earthly Delights
Upon the Sweeping Flood
With Shuddering Fall
By the North Gate
Anonymous Sins (poems)
Love and Its Derangements (poems)

On the Marriage of a Virgin

Waking along in a multitude of loves when morning's light
Surprised in the opening of her nightlong eyes
His golden yesterday asleep upon the iris
And this day's sun leapt up the sky out of her thighs
Was miraculous virginity old as loaves and fishes,
Though the moment of a miracle is unending lightning
And the shipyards of Galilee's footprints hide a navy of doves.

No longer will the vibrations of the sun desire on
Her deepsea pillow where once she married alone,
Her heart all ears and eyes, lips catching the avalanche
Of the golden ghost who ringed with his streams her mercury bone,
Who under the lids of her windows hoisted his golden luggage,
For a man sleeps where fire leapt down and she learns through his arm
That other sun, the jealous coursing of the unrivalled blood.

                                        DYLAN THOMAS

Marriages
and Infidelities

SHORT STORIES BY

Joyce Carol Oates

THE VANGUARD PRESS, NEW YORK

Second Printing

Copyright, ©, 1968, 1969, 1970, 1971, 1972, by Joyce Carol Oates

Ltd., Toronto

cation may be

by any means,

ocopy, recording,

otherwise,

blisher, except by

a reviewer who may wish to quote brief passages
in connection with a review for a newspaper,
magazine, radio, or television.

Library of Congress Catalogue Card Number: 72–83348
SBN 8149–0718–0
Manufactured in the United States of America

Designer: Ernst Reichl

ACKNOWLEDGMENTS   "The Sacred Marriage" was first published in
THE SOUTHERN REVIEW, Summer 1972.

"Puzzle" was first published in REDBOOK, November 1970.

"Love and Death" was first published in THE ATLANTIC MONTHLY, June
1970.

"29 Inventions" was first published in THE ANTIOCH REVIEW, Vol. 30, Nos.
3–4, Fall/Winter, 1970–71.

"Problems of Adjustment in Survivors of Natural/Unnatural Disasters" was
first published in THE BOSTON REVIEW OF THE ARTS, May 1972.

"By the River" was first published in DECEMBER, December 1968.

"Extraordinary Popular Delusions" was first published in THE VIRGINIA
QUARTERLY, Spring 1972.

"Stalking" was first published in THE NORTH AMERICAN REVIEW, June 1972.

"Scenes of Passion and Despair" was first published in SHENANDOAH, Summer 1971.

"Plot" was first published in THE PARIS REVIEW, Summer 1971.

"The Children" was first published in THE TRANSATLANTIC REVIEW, January
1969.

"Happy Onion" was first published in THE ANTIOCH REVIEW, Winter 1972.

"Normal Love" was first published in THE ATLANTIC MONTHLY, January
1971.

"Stray Children" was first published in SALMAGUNDI, Winter 1971.

"Wednesday's Child" (as "Wednesday") was first published in ESQUIRE,
August 1970.

"Loving . . . Losing . . . Loving a Man" was first published in THE
SOUTHERN REVIEW, Autumn 1971.

"Did You Ever Slip on Red Blood?" was first published in HARPER'S, April
1972.

"The Metamorphosis" (as "Others' Dreams") was first published in THE
NEW AMERICAN REVIEW, November 1971.

"Where I Lived and What I Lived For" was first published in THE VIR-
GINIA QUARTERLY, Autumn 1970.

"The Lady With the Pet Dog" was first published in PARTISAN REVIEW,
Spring 1972.

"The Spiral" was first published in SHENANDOAH, Winter 1969.

"The Turn of the Screw" was first published in THE IOWA REVIEW, Vol. 2,
No. 2.

"The Dead" was first published in MCCALL'S, July 1971.

"Nightmusic" was first published in MUNDUS ARTIUM, July 1972. Vol. 5,
Nos. 1 and 2.

for Robert Phillips
            "brillig"

Contents

The Sacred Marriage, 3

Puzzle, 37

Love and Death, 55

29 Inventions, 83

Problems of Adjustment in Survivors
    of Natural/Unnatural Disasters, 101

By the River, 127

Extraordinary Popular Delusions, 148

Stalking, 171

Scenes of Passion and Despair, 180

Plot, 194

The Children, 216

Happy Onion, 237

Normal Love, 260

Stray Children, 278

Wednesday's Child, 302

Loving
Losing } *a Man*, 319
Loving

Did You Ever Slip on Red Blood?, 338

The Metamorphosis, 361

Where I Lived, and What I Lived For, 379

The Lady with the Pet Dog, 390

The Spiral, 412

The Turn of the Screw, 433

The Dead, 453

Nightmusic, 489

Marriage and Infidelities

The Sacred Marriage

I

Howard Dean reached the outskirts of Mouth-of-Lowmoor, West Virginia, at about four-thirty on a warm autumn afternoon, after having driven most of the day. Route 77 had been ascending steadily into the mountains. Now he found himself driving along a ridge on this two-lane mountain road, his hands fastened firmly to the steering wheel, while his eyes kept drifting off to the right to stare down into a valley. He could not help himself, this scene was so beautiful—the valley was placid, marked by filmy, misty divisions between fields, and all the fields were the same uniform, dull, sweet green. A kind of paradise. Another world. It surprised him that there were so many white houses in this part of the country. Surely the coats of white paint wore out in a year or two? . . . He was pleased that people in these valleys and foothills should take the trouble to paint their houses white.

The altitude had begun to affect his ears. He parked at the side of the road and got out, so that he could look down into the valley. His eyes had been aching for the last hour, from the glare of driving on this sunny October day, and from his need to see everything clearly, closely. He was a man not accustomed to beauty. Rarely out of the city, rarely out of his routine of work, he felt a little giddy with the excitement of this trip, like a child. He wanted to see everything.

Silence. The countryside was silent. To his right the land fell steeply to a small, shallow creek, and to pastureland, where uncertain white dots grazed—they must be sheep, so motionless! The first farm in sight had a red barn so dulled by the haze in the air that it seemed no more than a smudge. Beyond it, a white house. Then there was a confused ridge of trees—then another stream, or a small road, and two more houses, both white. Maybe one of them was a church. Far off to the right, nearly hidden behind more trees, were several white structures that Howard guessed were large barns, one of them a long white rectangle showing no depth at this distance, another an even longer metal-gray rectangle hardly visible; Howard had to squint to make it out. Beyond was another dense ridge of trees, then the slope of a hill that gradually became a mountain. He was so high, standing here, he believed he could gaze right across the valley to the top of the mountain range, eying it levelly, in a sense as an equal. But probably he was not so high. It was like being in a two-passenger plane, gifted with sudden intimate scenes of the countryside and yet in constant, whimsical danger. . . .

Excited, Howard returned to his car and drove on to Mouth-of-Lowmoor. To his right the valley continued in its sleepy beauty, mute and understated, its wildest autumn colors blunted by the distance, placid as a water color by an artist who mixed all his colors with brown. It was a very human, miniature landscape, diminished, yet remote and unfathomable. It was hypnotic. Even the occasional stretches of automobile dumps, and bedsprings and mattresses and other junk thrown down into shallow creek beds and ditches, were somehow attractive. Howard didn't dare drive more than fifteen miles an hour on this road. To his left a wall of rock rose jaggedly, sometimes falling back to show fierce little plunging streams of water that looked cold as ice, gushing white, noisy. Howard felt he was being hypnotized, and this thought somehow pleased him.

In Mouth-of-Lowmoor he passed a small local motel called the Four Star Motel, and made a mental note of it; he would probably stay there tonight. But he wanted to see the Pearce home before he checked in. *The Pearce home.* . . . He had already studied many times the map Pearce's widow had sent him, and now he took it out of his pocket and unfolded it, anxious that he should not miss Lydia Street. It evidently ran perpendicular to Route 77, which had become Lowmoor Street. The town was like many small towns he had been passing that day. Unsurprising, not exactly disappointing. He drove over a narrow bridge and, still descending, on an incline that made his heart flutter, he began to pass house after house, all of them small, plain, painted white, with no room between them for driveways. Many automobiles were parked at the curb; some looked like junked cars. Children played in the street. They hurried out of his way. One small boy pointed at Howard's license plate and shouted something, as if an out-of-state license plate were an extraordinary sight.

He drove through the center of Mouth-of-Lowmoor at a quarter to five, according to the clock of an old-fashioned bank. The downtown area was very old, shabby. A drugstore with a flashy white tile façade caught his eye, but otherwise the buildings were all made of weathered red brick. Howard drove on, watching for Lydia Street. Yes, it came up soon, just past the big "X" Pearce's widow had made on the map . . . the "X" stood for a large warehouse, now abandoned, that he "couldn't miss," and indeed he couldn't miss it. This monstrous building had been constructed on the bank of an untidy, foul-smelling little river,

which something had stained to a bright, festive rust color. Howard turned obediently to the right here, and drove for about two
miles on Lydia Street. He passed through a crowded neighborhood of frame houses, then small and dowdy brick houses; then,
near the edge of town, he found himself in a neighborhood of
larger homes. And then, at the very end of Lydia Street . . .
the Pearce home itself, a small mansion, a Victorian house of
three stories that was rather shocking at first, monstrous and
gaunt, arrogant and ugly, all drab red brick, with abortive spires
and cupolas, and white trim that had begun to peel. . . . Howard
stared at the house. So this was it, after all, the Pearce home.
. . . It was so plain and arrogant and *real*.

The front yard was circled by a wrought-iron fence with a lopsided gate. The yard was thick with unmowed grass in spots,
while in other spots ground showed bare and dusty. A few colorful chickens were pecking in the dirt. Chickens? Howard believed they might be bantam roosters. They were prim and energetic. A black cat lay sunning itself on the house's front stoop.
The verandah was crowded with wicker chairs that looked old
and unused; a few were tipped toward the porch railing and balanced against it, as if bowing toward the street. The windows of
the house were extremely high and narrow, framed by shutters
that gave a displeased, frowning appearance to the place. Blinds
had been pulled down halfway.

So Connell Pearce had lived here?

Howard stared at this house, not knowing if he thought it
monstrous or attractive. He himself lived in Madison, Wisconsin, in an ordinary apartment building, fairly attractive but for-
gettable; in fact, Howard easily forgot it and carried around with
him, in the back of his mind, the idea that he still lived with his
parents in the East, or maybe nowhere at all. It did not matter
much to him where he lived. But Connell Pearce had planned
his homes so carefully, he had contrived such a mystique of
places—even the names of places—that this house in Mouth-of-

Lowmoor must have been chosen for a purpose. A decade before, Pearce had written, in a book called *Psalms and Runes:*

> *We become*
> *the places we inhabit*
> *our faces grow transparent*
> *as their names, frail*
> *with holy surprise*

Howard drove by the house and then saw, with a smile of discovery, that the place extended far back from the street, that, in fact, it was a small farm. There was a large red barn, and a smaller barn adjacent to it, and a barren, rutty space in which discarded farm implements lay. Between the house—which looked enormous when seen from the side—and the barns there was a garden, all yellow and gold and orange with a few splotches of white and red, and, bordering it on two sides, great scrawny sunflowers. The garden looked dusty, dreamy, hypnotic as the valley. Howard braked to a stop and stared in wonder. The autumn air was fragrant, slightly acrid. He had never seen a house like this, the combination of a dignified old mansion and a small, slovenly farm, so casually yoked together. It was here that Connell Pearce had lived the last year of his life. . . .

A woman came out of the side door of the house, dressed in green. She was some distance from Howard and did not glance toward the street. She went back into the garden; Howard could not see her face, but he knew that she must be Pearce's widow. A pang of excitement shot through him. He did not dare remain here, so he drove back to the Four Star Motel. . . . There he rented a room with walls of concrete blocks and a bed that smelled damp and sour. But he was very pleased.

First, he must telephone Mrs. Pearce and set up an appointment for the morning. No, *first* he must unpack and get his things in order. He must get his thoughts in order. His first

words would be very important when he spoke to her. He must
not make a poor impression. For hours he had labored over the
wording of the letter he had sent her. . . . *First* he must calm
down, calm himself down. He might telephone his fiancée back
in Madison. Her name was Joan. She was divorced from a man
Howard had never met, had a two-year-old girl, and was a secretary to one of the deans at the university. She was a nervous,
unhappy, confused young woman, sometimes morbidly depend-
ent upon Howard, and other times quite indifferent to him—according to her moods. It was Howard's belief that she needed
him, and her need for him was a responsibility he accepted gratefully, because he was, after all, absolutely free, uncommitted,
still awaiting, at the age of thirty-seven, the event that might
change his life and give it value. He picked up the telephone
receiver to call Joan, but then hesitated . . . he recalled
Pearce's widow, stepping out of the side door, unaware of him, in
her green dress, a young woman unknown to him, going to work
in the garden. . . .

The single photograph Howard had seen of Pearce's wife had
not shown her face clearly. She and Connell were standing in
glaring sunshine; in Spain somewhere, hardly a year ago. According to something Howard had read, she was twenty years
younger than Pearce, evidently a very attractive woman—like
the other women Pearce had loved and brought into his life. But
she had no reality for Howard, who had hardly thought of her
until today: she was simply a presence, a medium between himself and the dead poet.

He dialed the number she had given him and waited, nervously, as the telephone rang on the other end.

When he contemplated himself—Howard Dean—he often
thought of himself as a man making a telephone call, a man not
yet connected with his party, though given over to this party,
suspended, no longer safe in the privacy of his own silence, yet
not absorbed in the conversation that lay ahead. People made him
uneasy, frightened him, yet he was drawn to them, wanting to

please them. His fiancée, who had not exactly promised she would marry him, sometimes frightened him too; so did her little girl, whose stepfather he might well become. Howard's colleagues at the university frightened him, though he knew they admired him. They were good men, though troublesome, troubled, impulsive, if you became acquainted with their personal lives, yet fine men if you kept at a distance. Several of his colleagues were brilliant, distinguished scholars. Howard himself was the author of three books that had been well received, but they embarrassed him because he had not felt exactly equal to his ambitious subjects. He always seemed to choose ambitious subjects. His new project was a critical biography of Connell Pearce that had begun as a modest work of research and criticism, something he thought he could handle; then it turned out that Pearce had published hundreds of poems, many of them uncollected, forgotten, in literally every significant magazine in the United States and England; he had even written in Spanish for *Revista de Occidente*. Pearce's terrible energy, his prolificacy, had alarmed Howard, who felt like a child compared to him. It was frightening to realize the immense differences between men.

He had been thinking about this project for several years. Gradually he had come to feel that he, Howard Dean, was destined to present Pearce to the world, which would never discover or adequately appreciate Pearce by itself. He could not wait for someone else to do it. Howard had written three books that had not pleased him, though he had worked at them with love and fierce dedication, even in bouts of sickness and spiritual depression; but they had not been really important enough to draw upon the energy and capacity for patient, complete devotion he knew he possessed. Connell Pearce's poetry would be different. It was great poetry, important poetry. For the last twenty years Howard had been aware of it, aware of Pearce as his contemporary in these confused, unserious, tragic times, Pearce in book after book leading the way for Howard and others of his generation, explaining their fates to them, joking with them, giving them courage, startling them, annoying them, reducing them at times to shame—Howard had been aware of Connell Peace at a distance, living out a parallel life, a presence, not ghostly but very solid, substantial, the kind of transparent substance Howard had once attributed to God. So long as Pearce lived, there had been a kind of promise, a suspension to the present; it was interpreted by Pearce, and then Howard and their generation could accept it.

But Pearce had died.

Howard had come upon the obituary in the *New York Times* one morning, unprepared to see Pearce's photograph there. The news story had been about eight inches long. Pearce had died suddenly in a small West Virginia town Howard had never heard of before, survived only by his wife of two months. Death by natural causes. Biographical information was scanty. The exact cause of death was not mentioned, though there were to be rumors, later, about suicide. Howard had gulped for air, as if part of himself had died. In a sense he had never recovered from the shock of turning the newspaper page and coming across that obituary.

He had always thought, dimly, that someday he might have met Connell Pearce and that they might have become friends. Might have had something to say to each other. To offer each other. Howard was like a man in perpetual suspension—standing forever with a telephone receiver pressed to his ear, waiting, waiting patiently for someone to speak to him, to call him by name.

As soon as Pearce died, testimonial notices and brief, enthusiastic essays began to appear. A national newsmagazine printed a full-page photograph of Pearce—a slightly outdated photograph that showed the poet in his late thirties, dark-browed, brooding, with fine curved mouth and ironic eyes. His publishers reissued his most popular book, *The Fate of Animals*. An acquaintance of Howard's at Harvard, a man he knew to be coldly opportunistic, announced his intention of getting hold of whatever papers Pearce had left behind; evidently he wrote a number of letters to

Pearce's young widow, but the letters went unanswered. Howard had been terrified that this man might actually get through to her. He himself had not wanted to write immediately, out of respect for the recent death and because of his own timidity, but finally in midsummer he composed a very long, pleading letter, accompanied by offprints of the two essays he had already published on Pearce and copies of his three books. He had not dared to hope that Pearce's widow would reply; his letter had been so shameless—

. . . There is a prose-poem of your husband's that contains the lines, *We woke out of adolescence to discover that there is nothing private in the senses. Why not die, then? We are on exhibit. But, why not live? We are not doomed to private fates.* When I first read these lines I felt a tremendous shock. I can't explain my feeling. I don't know if I brought this feeling to the poem, which exposed it, or if the poem—I mean, your husband—entirely created it as I read. *The Fate of Animals* was the first book of your husband's I read, and I think it changed my life. I realize later books of his are more thoughtful, yes. He has created brilliant books. This is what I want to say, to make clear out of all this confusion: your husband has partly created me. Without his work I would not be the person I am. You have a right to ask who this person is—this inconsequential Howard Dean—a man of young middle age who has always been, even as a child, middle-aged!—a person of no importance, really, but insignificant as I am I know that without the poetry of Connell Pearce I might not have survived until now. Connell Pearce has allowed us all to see how he survived, how he carried himself through this mess of America since 1963, and through his own private hells. He has shown us how. He has managed to create a sense of destiny, personal destiny, out of this chaos, and he has made us see that it is not sentimental to believe in something, that it is not simply the pious who have hope of being saved. . . .

While other men's letters went unanswered, Howard's letter was answered at once. A chaste, perfectly typed note invited him down to investigate the papers Pearce had left. He could stay a week if he wanted. A week! Howard had been astonished at his good fortune. How had his single letter, written feverishly, with an almost adolescent yearning, managed to get through to Pearce's widow? It had somehow touched her, like a seed fertilizing an egg, so swiftly, so accidentally, yet by immutable design— a single seed, a single egg, while billions of other seeds had been helpless, wasted, sterile. . . .

The telephone was answered at the other end of the line.

2

He was a few minutes early for the ten-o'clock appointment, so he waited in his car, several houses down from the Pearce home. He wondered at the distance he had come—the distance of miles and years. Connell Pearce had brought him here. He owed this morning to Pearce, who had written: *We gain everything by asking only for another morning.*

Pearce had helped him mature. By dying, Pearce had shown him the way to die—otherwise death might have seemed to Howard unimaginable.

But he didn't want to think of death this morning. He went to the house, let himself in through the rusty lopsided gate, his heart beating with apprehension. He noticed that the heavy front door was surrounded by windows of stained glass, a little faded, outlined by puttylike, stark strips of black.

The door was opened and a woman appeared, smiling at him. Howard stared at her. She was a very young woman, yes, as he had expected, but extremely beautiful. . . . It was something of a shock, a bad shock. She introduced herself and shook his hand, and Howard responded dully, staring at the woman's heart-shaped, girlish, pretty face, a face that looked unnaturally pretty. It was out of place here; it was inappropriate. Her dark hair curved in curls and tendrils toward her face, framing it.

She seemed unaware of Howard's confusion. She showed him inside the vestibule, offered to take his briefcase from him, asked about the drive down. And the motel: was it satisfactory? Howard glanced shyly at her and saw that she was wearing a green dress. A leaf-colored green that stood out too brightly in this faded room. In honor of his visit, maybe, she had looped several strands of amber beads around her neck. Howard had never thought much about her before, and he was now forced to acknowledge her existence, her disturbing reality. As she spoke with a smile about the town, its peacefulness, the fact that she knew no one here, Howard cast his mind about for information he must have read about her: she was about twenty-five, from a city somewhere in New York. Otherwise nothing. A blank.

In reply to one of her questions, Howard heard himself saying: "I . . . I'm so grateful for this. . . . I could hardly sleep last night. . . ."

She smiled deeply at this, deeply and slowly, as if it were the perfect thing to say. "Let me show you through the house. Connell loved this house," she said. They were in a kind of parlor, with a single long sofa of some neutral beige color, rather shabby, and an easy chair, and chairs pushed back against the wall, two tables pushed back against the wall also, old-fashioned floor lamps with tassels and ornate shades, a typical Victorian household. Howard could not help but see that the aged wooden floors had not been properly buffed and polished. Near the windows were large, awkward cabinets that had obviously been constructed to hide radiators; they were painted a light green that did not harmonize with the rest of the room.

On the wall was an old photograph of a man with dark mustaches and complicated dark hair. He looked like a general, in a costume. Pearce's wife saw Howard staring at this picture and said, quickly, "That isn't anyone important—I mean, it isn't an ancestor of Connell's. It's just an old picture that came along with the house."

She led him through the dining room, a long, musty, shadowed room with a heavy chandelier that was too fancy, even a little vulgar, though Howard guessed it was very expensive. The massive mahogany sideboard was mirrored. On top of it were two rows of crystal goblets, covered with a fine film of dust. "We didn't use this room often," Pearce's widow said, leading him into the kitchen—a ghastly old-fashioned room with a huge stained sink, in fact two sinks, both stained with rust gone green around its edges. A large ugly stove. A series of cupboards without doors, so that the stacks of plates and glasses and cups—hanging coyly, at a slant, on little white hooks—were exposed. Howard marveled at all the china. The woman picked up a plate and showed it to him, as if pleased at his interest. It was good china, but its rose-bud and vine design, on a blank white background, seemed to Howard trite and disappointing.

"Connell bought the entire house, the household and all its furnishings," the woman said. "We didn't have anything of our own. He said this was his inheritance—all this."

Her name was Emilia. He would have to force himself to call her that. She was simple in manner, gracious, in absolute control of the situation, aware of his nervousness—the calmer she was, the more nervous he felt—and therefore gentle toward him, even a little apologetic. She might have been in charge of a treasure so enviable that she must apologize for it.

"Yes. It's very nice," Howard said.

In a small breakfast room, obviously unused, Emilia had him look out the window as she chattered about the "farm." The bantam roosters were right outside. "Connell loved to hear them crow in the early morning, he loved to be awakened that way," she said. He did not want to look at her. He wondered what her life must be now; Pearce had been dead seven months.

She was leading him through another room, a kind of pantry with glassed-in cupboards that rose all the way to the ceiling, where the molding was discolored. The wallpaper in this room was a strange, rather oppressive mixture of gray and blue. "This house was meant to be run by a staff of servants," Emilia said.

"It's far too big for two people. We've closed off a number of rooms because the furnace isn't very good and it saves on heat. . . ."

"Whom did you buy it from?" Howard asked politely.

"The widow of a man named Nesbitt. Horace Nesbitt. He was supposed to have been Lowmoor's richest citizen, a banker."

"I wondered why . . . I mean, why your husband decided to move here. . . . He lived all over the world, and I gathered from reading his poetry that he loved Spain and New Mexico . . ." Howard said.

"Yes, he lived all over the world," Emilia said, with a shy, proud smile, "but he wanted to return here because he was born in this area. Just a few miles outside Lowmoor." She looked levelly at Howard, smiling. There was an innocent frankness to her, an artless regality, as if she were in charge of a historical site, in charge of the careful recitation of events now past. She carried herself with an easy, confident grace, conscious of her responsibility and yet not burdened by it. She even spoke slowly, as if she knew Howard would want to remember everything she said. "Connell didn't tell very many people where he was born. He even kept his age a secret. But he was born on a farm about seven miles outside town. It belongs to other people now, his family is all scattered. They were very poor. Connell used to go for long walks out there, by the farm, but he said he had no sentimental attachment to it. He did have a certain feeling about the Nesbitt house," Emilia said. She was leading him along a corridor toward the rear of the house. Howard stared at her back; she seemed to be floating in a kind of dream, along this hazy ill-smelling hall, not really seeing it. She was speaking happily and a little breathlessly.

They entered a room that was a surprise to Howard—an open, airy, spacious sitting room, with an enormous floor-to-ceiling window and a fireplace made of fieldstone. "This is Connell's favorite room, I mean, it was—we used to have our meals here— We can have lunch here today," she said.

Howard stared at her, uncomprehending.

"We can? . . . Today? . . ."

"You and I. If you want lunch. If you want to stay for lunch," Emilia said.

"Why, that would be wonderful . . ." Howard said slowly.

He looked around the room, at the leather sofa, the massive round table, the piles of books and magazines and newspapers; it was so comfortable here, so human, in spite of the uneven and warped floorboards and the water stains on the ceiling, that he could not reconcile it with the rest of the house. For a moment he could not even remember where he was. A cat approached them, a large brute-faced black cat with mats of fur clumped together on his back. Emilia murmured something and stooped to stroke the cat. Howard watched her, imagining how those clumps of fur must feel—stiff, maybe sticky—

"Now I'll show you Connell's workroom," she said. She led him back into the corridor and up a very steep staircase. Howard could not keep his eyes from fastening upon her legs, the backs of her legs, her young, confident calves, the bare skin pale and even a little bluish. A delicate woman, in spite of her manner. She was talking over her shoulder to him. He was grateful for her talk. "Connell could work anywhere," Emilia was saying. "But he said this room was the best place he had ever discovered; it was the center of the world for him. . . ."

Howard entered the room, blinking. There were three tables, loaded with papers. Papers in stacks and in folders. Papers. Howard looked around in disbelief.

"Are all these . . . his papers? Did he leave all this?" he asked.

"Yes," Emilia said.

Howard's heart had begun to hammer. He could not quite believe what he was seeing.

Emilia said softly, "There are about thirty years of work here . . . old journals, and poems in manuscript form, notes for a novel and other books . . . hundreds of pages of notes and scribbling I can hardly make out," she said breathlessly, and gauging by a sideways glance the excitement Howard felt. "There must be several thousand pages here . . . it's so confusing, a chaos, the way he left things without any instructions, except there were certain people he didn't want to come here. . . . Near the end he had broken off with his editors and many of his friends. You probably know that? . . . In fact, the only things he never saved over the years were letters. Many people wrote to him, even famous people, but he threw the letters away after reading them. He didn't want to clutter up his life with other people. . . ."

"Are there poems here that haven't been published?" Howard asked.

"I don't know. I think so," Emilia said. "And there are early drafts of other poems. . . . Do you know a poem of his called 'Impulses'?"

"Of course," Howard said.

"I've come across sixty-seven different drafts of it." She spoke softly, not quite looking at Howard.

"Sixty-seven drafts? . . ."

"Yes."

"And there are poems that haven't been published. . . . Poems of Pearce's that haven't been published . . ." Howard said softly.

His heart had begun to pound violently. He felt that he had come to a sacred place. He had not deserved this place, but he had come here innocently, without selfishness or design.

"Are you happy?" Emilia whispered. "Is this what you wanted?"

"Yes. . . ."

"Did you think he would have left so much—so much no one knows about?"

"Never," Howard said. "No. I never dared to think—maybe a few letters, a few early drafts—"

He broke off, helplessly.

After a moment Emilia said, "Would you like to see our room —my room?"

She led him down the hall to a large dim bedroom. Howard drew in his breath cautiously. He smelled the odor of time and sorrow in this room, which was crowded with antique furniture. The bed had a canopy of some light silkish material; the curtains, held back by silken ties, were made of aged white lace. Underfoot was an Oriental rug that was still fairly handsome. The room's heavy furniture was decorated with whorls and small stunted spirals that looked as if they could never be rubbed clean.

On one wall were several photographs of Connell Pearce. They were all encased in antique frames. Howard was immediately attracted by these pictures, which showed Pearce in a number of attitudes—smiling dourly, unsmiling, taken by surprise in what must have been a garden, standing on a beach, the side of his face turned to the camera, indifferently. Emilia watched in her comforting silence while Howard went to examine the pictures. The one he favored was the same one that had been used by the newsmagazine—Pearce staring bluntly into the camera, unsmiling but not grim, his clear, dark eyes appearing all iris, as if blinded by a tremendous light or a deluge of sights. Howard, staring at that face, felt his own face tingle; he felt numb, as if he were being stared at in return. Pearce's teeth seemed to be gripping tighter, so that the muscles of his lean cheeks and jaws were defined, and a vein in his forehead seemed to stand out. Pearce was a strong, vital, very *visible* man—Howard felt, by contrast, rather transparent, even invisible.

"Did you take these pictures?" Howard asked.

"Me?" Emilia asked, startled. "No. I didn't know him then."

Howard noticed that the photographs showed Pearce at different periods in his life. He had changed slowly, going through a Western phase—when he lived alone in New Mexico for nearly three years, affecting a lean, tight, hungry, sardonic style—and a hectic citified phase, when he appeared in well-tailored clothes, knew many people, went about with a fanatic's enthusiasm for experience, and became involved with a number of women: "He used these women," someone had said of him, "but he did love them. He loved each one of them deeply." So far as Howard could judge, Pearce must have entered a final phase, this return to the mountains of West Virginia and the acquisition of someone else's "inheritance." . . .

When Howard turned back to Emilia his eyes were stinging with tears.

She noticed this, smiled quickly, took his hand, and led him out of the room. In the corridor the cat brushed against his legs.

"Did he—did he die in that room?" Howard asked.

"Yes, in that room," Emilia said.

She left him in Pearce's workroom while she went downstairs to prepare lunch. Alone, Howard went from table to table, picking up folders, batches of papers, putting them down again and picking up something else. . . . He still felt like weeping. He couldn't even remember when he had wept last. He examined a yellowed piece of paper covered with Pearce's handwriting—a poem scrawled in black ink—yes, a poem he recognized, though in another form. He put the poem down again as if he had touched something sacred. What was he to do with Pearce's papers? Would he be equal to them?

He was very excited. He looked out one of the narrow windows. In the distance the mountains were obscured by a faint, colorless fog. Below, the garden had begun to pick up light. The sun flowers were especially striking. Such grotesque flowers, stalks not quite erect but leaning forward a little, as if toward this house, as if anxious to peer in the windows, flowers with blanked-out burned-out brown faces! They were perfectly still, at attention, gazing toward Howard, as if they had once been men like him, now enchanted to coarse, ugly, goodhearted brutes.

3

After lunch Emilia took him outside. They left by the front door, as if Howard were too important a guest to go through the kitchen. In the vestibule Howard caught sight of a handful of letters on a table—his eyes narrowed with a jealous reflex—but of course she must receive letters like his every day, from men who wanted to come down here.

"Have very many people come to work with your husband's papers?" Howard asked.

Emilia gazed at him as if she were not certain of an answer. "No, not many," she said. After a moment she said, "He didn't want many."

They walked through the scrubby front lawn, with its patches of dry baked dirt and its patches of lush grass. Around the side of the house Howard had the feeling that he was passing over into another part of Pearce's life as he left the vicinity of the house and approached the barns. Here, the bantam roosters scattered, without alarm.

"He didn't want many men to know him," Emilia said.

She was extremely polite, almost exaggeratedly hospitable. During lunch she had shown Howard that exaggerated concern, that meticulous observation for small things—her guest's smallest wish—that characterizes genteel hostesses, or the slightly insane. He had appreciated that. Even now she stayed close to him: she had a habit of lightly touching his arm with her fingertips.

"It's a great honor for me to be here," Howard said.

She gazed at him with her liquid, languid dark eyes, as if listening closely to everything he said or might say or even thought, and at the same time listening closely to something else—a voice in her head, perhaps. Howard was fascinated by her.

They walked carefully through a maze of discarded farm things to look in the first barn—just empty stalls, scattered straw, an old half-pleasant smell of manure. Howard started into this barn, grateful to be seeing anything that had belonged to Pearce.

The larger barn was dusty and cavernous; spider webs dangled, broken, heavy with clumps of dust. "Connell wanted to buy some horses. He wanted to use this barn," Emilia said. They walked into the barn, lightly, almost on tiptoe. The place seemed unhuman, holy. Howard kept glancing up at the shadowy hayloft, and behind him at the opened door, as if he expected someone to be watching.

"It seems so quiet here. So lonely," Howard said.

"Yes. Connell didn't have any friends at the end of his life. Only me," Emilia said slowly. "He discarded his friends, one by one. He hated the idea of having people know him. . . . I really didn't know him myself," she said.

This startled Howard, though it was spoken in that same liquid, unemphatic voice. Even her hand, pressed lightly against his arm, was unemphatic.

"He married me in January, when he knew he was going to die. He decided between me and another woman, whose name I never found out . . . she's living in California now. Before that, I came down here to stay with him from time to time, when he wanted me. He would call me here. Then he'd send me away again. He didn't want anyone to know him, because he thought people would confuse him with his poetry. He just wanted the poetry. He didn't want himself—I mean—he didn't want to exist as himself, so that people would remember him."

Howard murmured agreement. He was becoming uneasy.

"You do think he was a great man?" Emilia asked.

"Yes."

"A really great man? A genius?"

"Yes. Certainly," Howard said at once.

She smiled at him. But the smile came after a moment's hesitation, as if from a distance. "Then we'll go out to his grave. He would want you to see his grave," she said.

Pearce was buried in a run-down Presbyterian cemetery not far away. At his grave Howard and Emilia stood in silence. Howard was disappointed with the ordinary headstone and the ragged condition of the grass. But the afternoon was hazy and mild, a beautiful day, and he felt with an almost violent certitude that he had come to the right place, that he was standing now in exactly the right place—right here, contemplating Connell Pearce's grave with the woman who had been married to him. Howard's aimless life was at last beginning to take shape.

Emilia was looking at him.

"Are you happy to be here?" she asked.

"Yes."

"He was a very strange man," she said slowly. "Dying excited him. He kept the details of his sickness to himself, a secret even from me—as if he were making up his own death, like a poem. I suppose that's how it might be: you die only once, a unique death. I don't know. But now that he is dead I don't seem so afraid of death . . . it's as if he went ahead of me, to explain it to me. . . ."

"I know what you mean," Howard said.

"Only after he was dead could I find out what his sickness was—cancer. He had forbidden his doctor to tell me before then. He was a very strange, wonderful man."

Howard nodded slowly.

She was watching him with a peculiar intense smile. Pushed by a kind of urgency, leaning toward him, she seemed unusually tense; her trivial prettiness had faded and Howard could not exactly see her face, not the contours of her face and her curly dark hair, these distractions that had annoyed him earlier. He seemed to be seeing only *her,* her self. He could feel her. She was saying softly, "If Connell touched someone with his fingertips he would know that person . . . he could absorb that person. . . . You felt a jolt, like a small electric shock, go through you and into him, passing out of you and into him, permanently. . . . That way he brought many different people into him, into his life. He told me that he had lived through many different people. Do you understand that?"

"I don't know. I don't think so," Howard said.

She smiled at him.

Driving back to the house, Howard tried to talk to Pearce's widow about other matters—he had become rather nervous now —and he heard his eager voice like a stranger's voice, echoing from unlikely corners of the air in an attempt to forestall his fate. Emilia kept glancing at him, with that smile. He felt that he was falling in love with her, and he had had little experience of love. He believed in love, but he did not understand it. His voice began to shake, though he tried to talk of mild things—the names of towns and cities in this state. "Some of the names are very beautiful," he said. "Bluefield, Ramage, Oceana, Appalachian. . . . And some of the names are very striking, mysterious, like Hungry Mother, Cobble, Danger, and Mud—there's a town called Mud, and another town called Odd—"

Emilia put her hand over his.

"Yes, I've heard of those names. Do you like the name Mouth-of-Lowmoor?" she asked.

"It's very beautiful. . . ."

"It is beautiful, yes," she said, with that sideways smile.

After a moment she said, "Do you want to stay here for a while? With me?"

Howard had begun to breathe quickly.

"I had planned on staying a week . . ." he said.

"Is there someone you have to get back to?"

"No. Yes. My job. But. . . ."

"Connell married me when he knew he was going to die. It was his only marriage. Are you married?"

"No."

"He saw me when we were both in Málaga. In southern Spain. I was with my first husband and he was alone, I think. He saw me in the lobby of my hotel. He left a letter for me. Do you know why he allowed me to fall in love with him?"

"Why?"

"Because he thought I was beautiful."

"You are beautiful."

"He thought so, *he* thought so," she said slowly. "It was his reason for approaching me. He always went after beautiful women, isn't that right?"

"It's supposed to be right," Howard said.

He was perspiring freely.

But why? In this woman's presence there was no need. No reason to be nervous. She showed no strain, hardly any consciousness of what she was saying. She spoke soothingly, lightly. Her fingers caressed Howard's as if she had known him a long time, as if she were perhaps his wife, the two of them returning now to that house as a wife and husband might return, without any haste.

They entered the front door.

"Do you want to come upstairs with me?" Emilia asked.

"What do you mean?"

"Do you want to love me?"

His mind seemed to contract, and then it brightened as if with a silent explosion: throwing light upon Howard himself, his physical body, his benign, fairly attractive face, his close-cut, unfashionable hair. He had not thought of himself for some time. Not his self, his body, his particular face: he had not thought about his personality for some time. He did not take himself seriously enough to worry about his personality, as other men did. He was too modest. He had too much serious work to do. But now the raw jagged outline of his skeleton seemed to be asserting itself. *Yes,* he was thinking, saying, *yes, of course—yes!*

They walked through the vestibule, where she took no notice of the letters on the table. "Don't you think you could love me?" she said.

"Yes," he said in a faint voice.

In that boxlike, crowded bedroom upstairs, made dimmer and more confused by Howard's excitement, this young woman put her arms around him sweetly and kissed him. Her face seemed to melt into his, it was so close. And how sweetly she moved, how easily she moved against him! He could hardly think. He felt his own face emerge as if out of a lifetime of slumber, hard-browed, darkening with blood.

They became lovers.

In the days that followed, Howard was to remember that afternoon, that love-making, with amazement: it had taken place so easily, with so little strain or self-consciousness, that it seemed like an event in a dream. He had always thought that reality— the reality of bodies—had to be coarse and grappling, and embarrassing. Certainly he had always been embarrassed. But Emilia was like a wife to him and there could be no embarrassment between husband and wife.

He went about touching his own face, as if discovering it for the first time. He was an attractive man, with clear brown eyes and a narrow, intelligent forehead. He was only thirty-seven, after all.

4

"You've never been married? Never?" she asked him.

"Never."

"You weren't in love?"

"Not really."

Her eyes, her mouth, were dreamily distorted to him, as if observed through a hazy medium. "Everyone should be in love," she said.

In the past, Howard had drifted into involvements with women that had begun with a certain lighthearted tone and progressed through periods of deep, intense sympathy, of serious, lengthy conversations, and then, declining sharply, inexplicably, to muffled accusations and tears, finally bitterness and tedium. A mysterious process. He had always felt himself apart from it, baffled and unable to control it. He could have loved and married any number of women, he supposed: he had never taken himself too seriously.

Emilia was exactly right. There was no discord between them, no self-consciousness. They seemed to have known each other for years. Though Howard knew that Connell Pearce had known this woman only a short while before his death, she seemed to be the woman constantly celebrated in his poems. Her essence, her sweet invisibility had been prophesied a decade before in one of Pearce's long, fragile love poems:

> *She draws in the very breath*
> *you exhale*
> *giddy with the fragrant unguessed-at soul*
> *in your man's body*

Howard said out loud, "I was unguessed-at. That's right. I never guessed myself."

"What do you mean?" Emilia laughed.

"I can't explain," he said happily.

He had moved out of the motel and into the house with Emilia, and he had decided to stay another week. His head rang with excitement! He began work each day at seven, sitting at Pearce's middle table, on an old dining-room chair with a loose back. There, he examined the Pearce manuscripts for hours at a time. It was all he could do to make himself go slowly, slowly. He wanted to snatch at everything, examine everything, as if disbelieving his good fortune; but he forced himself to proceed carefully. . . . He came across loose pages from diaries of Pearce's that dated back to the late thirties: his reactions to the work of poets he loved, especially Yeats, and his reactions to confusing personal relationships, which Howard could not figure out. There were aged notes scrawled on notebook paper, and drafts of poems—crude, faint shapes of poems that were to become great poems. Howard felt himself slipping into a daze, enchanted.

Overcome with emotion, he would push the chair back, get to his feet, stalk to the window . . . he would rub his face roughly and stare down into the autumn garden. Sometimes Emilia would be working out there, hoeing.

Emilia.

Howard felt as if he had already been living in this house for

part of his lifetime. He seemed to belong here. It was natural that
he live here, his things neatly hung in the closet in that bedroom,
his sleep faintly, gently disturbed by the roosters' crowing long
before dawn, his body sweetly perfumed by Emilia's love, which
made no demands upon him. He felt that he had been working
with the Pearce papers for many years. He felt at times lost in
this work, somehow mixed up with Pearce's manuscripts. For instance, had Connell Pearce written in pencil the first draft of that
beautiful poem, "Lying Awake," back in 1941, or had Howard
himself written it? . . .

Pearce had developed several styles of handwriting. Howard
admired the most recent style, its slanted, dignified letters, done
with a blunt-tipped fountain pen, and usually in black ink. Howard tried to copy that handwriting. He had found the pen Pearce
had used, and he practiced Pearce's signature until he believed
he could match it perfectly.

Connell Pearce. . . .

At night he lay with Pearce's wife in the canopied bed, beneath an old quilt that smelled of bittersweet dust. He spoke
with a quiet amazement of his good fortune, and he sensed how
this pleased her. "Usually a quest like mine ends in failure," he
said. "It turns out that the poet's manuscripts are lost, or useless,
or somehow disappointing. . . ."

"But Connell's are worth examining?"

"My God, yes," Howard said.

"I don't know much about his work," Emilia said. "I didn't
even know him well. . . ."

They had begun to whisper. Howard said, "But you loved him
very much? . . ."

"Yes." And she would clasp her arms around his neck, as if to
demonstrate her love. She was small-boned and conscious of
being a little too thin. "You won't love me if I lose any more
weight," she said. "I've got to start gaining weight again. Should
I become pregnant? What do you think?"

"Pregnant?"

"I've never been pregnant," she said.

Howard lay beside her, stunned. Then he heard himself saying, "Whatever you want."

He would bring her back home with him and marry her there. That was how this adventure would turn out: he would marry Connell Pearce's widow.

"Connell didn't want any children," Emilia whispered. "I think he wanted to elude everyone. That was why he came back here, where he didn't know anyone and no one knew him, where he had lived as a boy—because he could handle this part of the country like a boy, knowing the places to hide. He wanted me to love him, but he didn't want me to know him."

"You weren't lonely?"

"Yes, I was lonely," she said, but without resentment. "Of course I was lonely. I always will be. But I was his wife . . . I was the woman he married, out of all those women. . . ."

"Yes, that is something to be proud of," Howard said. "You were the only woman he didn't reject. And his only friend, in the end."

"I think you might have been a friend of his, if you had met him," Emilia said softly, as if to flatter him.

"I don't think so," he protested.

They were both grateful for the darkness of this room, which seemed to erase the distinctions between them, Emilia and Howard, and to draw the Pearce of those photographs nearer. The boundaries between the three of them became hazy.

Emilia said softly, "Connell believed that many things were possible in one lifetime. But you must force them to happen. I grew up in Albany, New York, where my father has an insurance company. I was always very happy. Always. I was always loved by my parents and by other people—friends—young men— people always loved me, for my face, I think. I don't want to sound vain. I'm afraid of vanity. But I know I have a nice face, and if you're a woman with a nice face many things can happen to you, things you never expect. . . . Connell left a letter for me in my mailbox at the hotel. My husband and I were going to leave the next day. But Connell left this letter for me, he picked me, he picked my face out of a crowd. . . . He taught me that anything can happen between people. If you can imagine it, then it can happen. It will happen. He taught me that the world is absolutely open, like a dream."

"But you were able to fall in love with him, in spite of that?"

"In spite of what?"

"The way he selected you."

"Of course. Any woman would have loved him," Emilia said. "There was never any question about that. There are certain men who understand that any woman can be made to love them, the only problem is whether they want these women. And then, how to get rid of them. As it turned out," she whispered, "he chose not to get rid of me. Off and on, yes, he sent me away, but he always called me back. He married me. Except I never really got to know him. . . ."

"Why not? Was he always working?"

"Yes, he worked constantly. Constantly. If he wasn't actually up in that room, he was thinking about his work. He imagined it all in his head before he wrote it down . . . I would see him standing, a strange, happy look to his face, as if he were hearing music from inside his head. . . . I never interrupted him at these times. I was happy to live with him and be his wife, I had no need to interrupt him."

"Where were you married?"

"In Charleston. Just a civil ceremony."

"Your parents didn't come down?"

"Oh, no. They were through with me. They were disgusted."

"Because of your living with Pearce?"

"Because I left my husband for him immediately. They never forgave me. I sympathize with them, but I had no choice. I had to go with Connell."

Howard was moved. He framed her small heart-shaped face in his hands. She was so docile, so *wifely*. "I think you'll like Madison," he said.

She pressed close against him and said nothing.

5

On the eleventh day of his visit here, Howard was at work puzzling out a sequence of notes for an "autobiographical novel" that were mixed in with notes for "religious parables and riddles" when he heard Emilia answer the door downstairs. Evidently someone had knocked.

Howard looked up from his work. He waited. Waited for the door to be closed and Emilia to return to the kitchen, where she was preparing dinner. But after a few minutes he heard voices. A man's voice, and Emilia's musical, nearly inaudible reply. . . .

Some time passed. At least ten minutes. Howard was too nervous to work, and when he heard footsteps on the stairs he had to fight the impulse to jump to his feet. He heard Emilia's light, gracious laughter, and a man's surprised, appreciative laugh that seemed to reflect hers, as in a mirror. They were approaching this room. Howard turned to face the door, feeling an unaccountable terror.

Emilia led a very tall freckled young man into the room. "Howard, I would like you to meet Felix Fraser. Felix is from the University of California."

Howard stood to shake hands with this man. Felix smiled shyly and with pleasure. His face was freckled, but a little sickly: his eyes were sparkling. Howard saw how the young man was making an effort not to stare gluttonously at the stacks of paper on the tables.

"From the University of California? . . ." Howard asked tightly.

"Riverside," the young man said.

"He has asked to do a study of Connell's early poems. The first drafts," Emilia said.

"I see," said Howard.

Felix was staring, transfixed, at the papers.

There was an awkward pause, and then Emilia said, "Howard has been working here for over a week. He plans on staying a few more days, but the two of you can work in the same room, can't you? Is that too difficult, for scholars?"

Howard was staring at Emilia.

"Is something wrong?" she asked.

Felix gave a little jump, thinking this question was directed at him. "Wrong? Of course not—no—"

"Of course not," Howard said.

He had to sit down again on the wobbly chair. His legs felt numb.

"I'm—I'm very happy to be here, and I—I'm anxious to begin work—" Felix Fraser said, gaping at all the papers. He was only about thirty years old. Very tall: six feet five at least. Attractive in a bony, gawky way. Not so attractive as Howard had come to be, but attractive.

"Where are you staying, Felix?" Howard asked.

"Something called the Four Star Motel. A dump, but it's convenient."

After a few more minutes Emilia led Felix away. Howard went to the door to listen, heard her lead Felix down the hall to the bedroom—the bedroom!—heard her say, "Connell loved this house—" Howard returned to the table and cradled his head in his hands. When he had spoken of Madison . . . when he had alluded to the two of them living there . . . hadn't she understood? He had not exactly spoken of marriage. Maybe he had failed to make his feelings clear?

He shoved Pearce's notes aside. Notes for an "autobiographical novel." . . . *What the hell does the world want with another autobiographical novel?* Howard wondered. Enough novels now. Too many novels. A living woman was worth more than a dead man's novel, any dead man's novel or his poetry or any poetry. That was a fact.

He could not believe this was happening to him.

When Felix left for the day, Howard went downstairs to confront Emilia.

"Why did you invite that man here?" he asked quietly.

"To work on Pearce's early poems," Emilia said. "The early drafts. He said he was very interested in—"

"Aren't we going to be married?"

"Married?"

"You and I, married?"

She stared at him. "I didn't know about that," she said, faltering guiltily. But her look was remote, hazy, fuzzy, as if all this were a misunderstanding she could not focus upon. She was still the meticulous hostess, gravely concerned for the small details that had to do with her guest's comfort, but not with her guest himself.

"You even spoke of becoming pregnant . . ." Howard said.

"Yes, but. . . ."

"But?"

"Yes, but not getting married. . . . Did I speak of getting married?" she asked, perplexed.

"And you invited him here. That Felix. That Fraser. You invited him here at the same time you were living with me. . . ."

"But you had planned to leave by now."

Howard clutched at his head. He wondered if he should strike her, as Pearce might have. Slap that face. Destroy that face. Howard's brain shuddered and seemed to go dead with his sudden hatred of her—that fussy, pretty little face, the vague, enlarged eyes, the well-loved mouth that had been kissed so much it seemed a little swollen.

"Then you aren't going to leave with me?" Howard asked.

"Leave here? Leave this house? How could I leave this house?" she asked. She came to stand before him, she opened her arms in a gesture of bewilderment. Open. Empty. Her girlish body offered itself to him. "What do you mean?"

"I want you to leave with me. We'll get married."

"Leave here?"

"Yes, leave here! You can come back with me to Madison. We'll work on the Pearce papers . . . we'll write a book about him, the two of us . . . but in the meantime the hell with him. . . ."

"You're crazy!"

She turned from him, angrily. Howard seized her arm. Again something shuddered in his brain. "Did you lie to me? Did you? It was all a lie? What the hell was it? A joke, a lie? A lie?"

She hesitated. Then she put her arms around him, pressed her face against his chest, and stood there, meekly, warmly, her body overwarm, silent. After a moment Howard began to stroke her hair. Her back. He felt his body going numb.

"Then you don't love me?" he whispered.

She pressed herself tightly against him and hid her face.

"You're never going to leave here? . . ."

She said nothing. After a while he released her. He stumbled out of the room, went back upstairs to the study. He couldn't work any longer, but he had nowhere else to go. What else was there to do? He stood for several minutes in the room, staring at nothing. He turned on the light. He went to the table and leafed through some notes, idly, nervously. Pearce's handwriting. Pearce's words. Pearce was not dead but still alive, more powerful than Howard. More attractive than Felix. Yes, Howard thought contemptuously, Pearce was certainly more attractive than Felix, with his freckles and anxious stoop; no woman would prefer him to Pearce! Never!

Howard leafed through the notes for the "religious parables and riddles." There were at least fifty pages of scrawled notes. Howard's body was stinging with little star-splashes of sweat breaking through his tense pores. He could not make sense of what had happened. It was a puzzle, a riddle. . . . In spite of his nervousness, he began reading, and after a while seated himself at the table. That was at eight in the evening. At a quarter to twelve he came across this:

Let us imagine X, the famous Spanish novelist, a nobleman. Born 1899. Must be born in the 19th century. Many adventures. Prison. A series of novels acclaimed by the world. X is handsome, aging, elegant, a dandy, something of a phony (his exaggerated Catholicism, his loyalty to Franco, etc.) Totally dedicated to his art. The language of this parable must suggest that—the transformation of a man into his art. Language that carries more than its own meaning. On edge. On the edge of poetry. Yes, X is about to die and wants to write the novel of his own life, extended beyond his life. In Madrid he selects a certain woman. He is a noble, dying old man, she is a very beautiful young woman. *She* is worthy of being his wife. And therefore he marries her, and she nurses him through his last illness, buries him, and blesses all the admirers of his art who come to her, or she alone retains X's divinity. *Her body. Her consecration.* A multitude of lovers come to her, lovers of X, and she blesses them without exception, in her constant virginity. . . .

Howard went to find Emilia. He thrust this paper at her. "This—have you read this? Do you know about this?"

"What?"

"Notes for a parable of his—"

"What parable?" She glanced at the paper. "I don't think so. No," she said. "Why are you so angry?"

Howard let the paper fall.

"I'm leaving," he said.

"Leaving? Tonight? But it's almost twelve o'clock—"

"I can't stay here."

"But why not?"

Howard moved away from her. She followed him into the bedroom. While he threw his things into his suitcase she said, perplexed, "But the mountain roads are dangerous at night. Why do you want to leave now? Mr. Fraser won't be here until tomorrow at eight. Why are you leaving? Are you unhappy? Are you disappointed with the manuscripts?" Howard crumpled a shirt and forced it into his suitcase. His fingers tingled with the desire to seize her, but there was no point to it. "But . . . will you promise to drive carefully? If there's fog in the mountains, will you promise to stop somewhere?" she asked.

"Yes. I promise."

"Why are you so angry?"

"Not angry," he said, shutting his suitcase.

She followed him downstairs and outside. "You didn't finish your work, did you? Are you going to come back sometime?"

"I don't know. Maybe."

"Were you happy, working here?"

"Yes."

"Were you happy with me?"

He threw the suitcase into the back of his car. When he turned on his headlights, immediate, hulking, flimsy shadows appeared in the driveway. Emilia was saying, "I still don't see why you have to leave tonight. It's time to go to bed. You're so strange." But she leaned in to kiss him good-by, companionably and chastely.

Howard drew away, frightened. "No. Good-by," he said.

He drove into the darkness, hoping he would not burst into tears. His mind kept imagining that room again, that bed . . . Emilia's face, her arms, her body. . . . And Pearce's photographs on the wall. That handsome disembodied face. Howard drove fast, into sheer absolute darkness. Wisps of fog drifted across the road. Very well, he might have an accident, might run off the twisting road. He didn't slow down. What the hell. He wanted to get away from that house. . . . He was agitated, depressed. Why should he continue living? He felt his face, his body, his very identity seeping back inside him, inside the amorphous shapelessness of his past.

He was becoming an ordinary man again.

The fog grew thicker. The mountain road kept looping giddily back and forth, his car easing giddily from left to right, right to left, as if in a dream, barely under his control. He was very tired. Depressed. Yet he did not really want to have an accident . . . he did not want to die. . . . His life was empty, a joke of a life. But he did not really want to die. After about fifteen miles he came to a motel, the Mountain View Travelers Lodge, where he decided to stay for the night. His room was unheated, but he slept. He had not slept so heavily for some time.

In the morning, on the road again and headed north to Charleston, he felt a little better. He contemplated the past twelve days and had to conclude that things weren't so bad. His depression began to lift. He had been betrayed, yes, but perhaps that was not important. He wasn't sure. If Howard Dean had been lied to, betrayed, what did that matter? The important thing was that he had seen the Pearce papers.

The sun rose. The fog was burned away. Howard's depression burned away, gradually, and by the time he came to the Ohio state line at Marietta it was nearly gone. He felt instead the same marvelous energy he had felt upon first seeing those piles of Pearce's unpublished, unguessed-at works. That was real. Yes, that was real, and whatever had happened to Howard was not very real. . . . It was not important. He thought about this and felt his old energy pour into him. He was going to bring Connell Pearce to the world's attention: that was his mission, the shape of his life. It was a sacred obligation and he was going to fulfill it.

He drove all day with a passion he could barely contain.

*P*uzzle

At the corner there is a bicycle rack with a few bicycles stuck in it. Several children stand around—the bicycle rack is outside a drugstore—tearing wrappers off popsicles. The popsicles are bright colors—orange, pink, green. The children's faces are bright. I feel a strange sensation rise in me as I approach them—will they look at me? Will they turn to look at me?

A big boy comes out of the drugstore and gets his bicycle. One of the smaller children follows him, whining, "Hey, Billy, Billy," it sounds like. "Gimme a ride back?" The boy waves him away without bothering to look around. The child stands on the sidewalk with his popsicle raised to his mouth and turned awkwardly, so that the inside of his wrist shows, pale, the bluish veins prominent. In this way the popsicle won't drip down his

arm. He sucks at it noisily. "Hey, Billy," he says in a high petulant whine, not loud enough for the boy to hear. He turns back.
The other children, arguing over something, have not noticed
me. This child notices me. He has a bright, sunburned face,
stained around the lips. His eyes are startled and shrewd. I feel a
sense of dizziness, a fear of fainting. *But I am not really here,* a
voice rises in me, assuring me, my own voice and yet detached
and innocent. The child stares at me. The popsicle in his hand
has begun to melt. He fastens his lips to it and sucks noisily at
it, staring at me.

He seems to know me. He knows something about me.

I hurry by him. It is a mistake for me to have come out this
morning—my mind is not right on such hot, muggy days. The
child, eying me, takes a few steps in my direction. I can hear his
lips sucking thirstily at the popsicle. Something must show on
my face or in the sudden urgency of my legs—I have to get away
from him, from that look of his—and he follows alongside me,
curiously, as if drawn to me, as if he has something to say that
the other children must not hear.

"What do you want?" I say nervously.

He says nothing.

"I don't know you. I don't know what you want." I hurry to
the drugstore. I have never seen this child before and he does not
know me. His face is a stranger's face. He is the child of strangers, people I would never meet. And yet there is something familiar about him—his face—a boy of about five, knowing, con-
demning, sly.

The popsicle is melting, running in a green watery streak
down his arm.

In the drugstore I realize that my body is wet with perspiration. The air around me is like my own body, like my breathing.
Very close to me, no relief. It will suffocate me. I don't look back
outside at that boy: I go over to the cosmetic counter where there
is a mirror. My face is pale and alarmed. Yet it is clear to me that
I am not really there, in the mirror or in this drugstore, hiding

from a child who seems to know me, to have a message for me, and yet who cannot know me because we are strangers . . . I am not really here at all, I am not hiding here.

Since last April I have had strange adventures.

Noises in the air converge upon me like flocks of birds. The birds are black, scrawny, invisible crows. Try to shoot a crow!— you have time only to raise the rifle and the crow is gone, invisible.

Many years ago, when I lived at home, my father and my brothers used to shoot crows. Once they gave me the rifle to shoot a crow, but I couldn't raise the barrel . . . I was afraid of raising the barrel and shooting. . . .

The noises in the air can't be frightened away. It is morning: I am cleaning the house. Beneath the noise of the vacuum cleaner there is another noise, not as constant, the sound of someone talking. Chattering, like a child. I try not to listen to it but then, suddenly, I switch off the vacuum cleaner with my foot and listen . . . but the chattering is gone. It has not been frightened away but it waits for me, patiently. When I turn on the cleaner it begins again, almost inaudible, a light chattering of words I can't make out. . . .

I rub furniture polish on the tables, on the arms and legs of chairs. I kneel on the floor to work. In the wood my own reflection is dark, vague. I would not be able to recognize myself. I am a married woman, a wife, an ex-mother, aged thirty. This is my house, I live here now. We lived in another house until a year ago, then we had to move here, to this particular house with a back yard that is unfenced and fades away into a field they haven't yet dug up. A big sign on the highway announces a new subdivision of homes to be built next year, but they haven't yet started digging the trees out . . . the field is nothing to look at, a few scrawny bushes and trees, mostly weeds, some piles of debris people have dumped there, and on the far end a large drainage ditch, dry now in October. It is a large, wide ditch that overflows with water in the spring, when everything is melting; now it is dry. I think it is dry—I don't drive by it, I take another street when I drive. But it would be dry now, in October.

I rub furniture polish onto the dull, nicked wood of our coffee table. The table does not need to be cleaned; it is already clean. But I polish it again, slowly, because it is only eleven o'clock in the morning and the day is very long. I work slowly. Everything moves slowly for me now. The cloth I use is from an old sheet of ours that wore out, a yellowed white sheet. As I rub the table a voice comes into my head. I think it is singing a song. *I am not really here. . . .* I polish the table's legs, slowly, frightened. *I am not really here.* Is this a song I heard somewhere but can't remember?

I am not really here.

All day I wait for the words to continue, to explain themselves. I believe that there are more words, waiting. The song must have more lines.

Side by side in my mind are two places: the place I live in now, this small house, and the place I lived in when I was a child. That house was a little bigger than this, with an attic two of my brothers slept in, but it was a poor house, falling apart. This house is too new to fall apart: it is on the corner of a street, at the end of a row of houses that are alike. One story, wood with brick on the front only, a garage, a picture window of moderate size. The brick is red. The rest of the house is painted white. In an airplane you would see this row of houses and other rows of houses, all alike. The streets are not yet paved; they will be paved next year. We are beside a highway that leads to the city twelve miles away. To the north of us are empty fields, waiting to be excavated so that more rows of houses can be built.

I am not really here.

There are large ditches around the fields, at the edge of our yards, cutting us off from the highway. The ditches are filled with leaves at this time of year. We played in a ditch back home

—I remember the weed-flowers, yellow and blue flowers, I remember the crickets and the frogs and the stink of scummy water. When we were very small we pretended the water in the ditch was a river; pretended to be afraid of it. In the winter the ditch water froze. We walked on it. I remember snowdrifts along the road—twelve feet high. The snowplows along the road at night, their revolving lights, big rusted plows lifted, partly suspended by chains. . . . Upper New York State, the foothills of the Adirondacks. Wild country. A small, wild city five miles from us, too much wind, too much snow.

Sitting here, in this house, hundreds of miles from that memory, I can define myself clearly. I am an adult, a wife. I live now in a climate where the snow doesn't drift in the roads; there are rarely snowplows. I am free of the bitterness of those winters and the prowling blue lights of the snowplows and the fact of my parents, whom I don't see.

The last time my husband and I quarreled and I left him, my mother said *He's no good, we always knew that*. Then when I went back to him she said I was crazy; said I could go to hell. Later, of course, she changed her mind. She wanted to make up. But I kept hearing her words, the anger in her words, and I wouldn't go back. I kept hearing her tell me *He's no good, we always knew that*. Her words got into me, ringing in my head. Something is always getting into a woman, giving her a shape, pushing her out of shape.

Sounds in the air slowly pushing us out of shape: like a great flock of birds.

I sit here in the living room, by the coffee table, unable to remember what I was doing. The rag stained with furniture polish—the bottle of dark polish on the floor. I must have been polishing the table again. The time is stuck at eleven-fifteen. Except for the noise of children playing outside, always children playing outside, there is nothing for me to hear. I must get up, get working. I must put on the radio. I must not think of my parents, of the time when I was their daughter. How does a daughter become a mother? How does a mother become turned inside-out again, back into being just a woman, a daughter?

I am not really here.

In the first days after Jackie died I could hear sounds vividly. The sound of traffic over on the highway—voices rising in the house next door—my husband's breathing. Sometimes he breathes heavily, grunting to himself. No reason for it. It is a puzzle to me, the sounds he makes when he thinks he is alone . . . his breath expelled in a kind of grunt as if he were pushing something from him. I could hear him in this house, the two of us living between the walls of this house, in a box. I heard him walking, I heard him out in the garage. I heard him drive into the driveway at night and I heard him slam the door of the car and I heard his footsteps on the gravel. In the kitchen he would bump into something and I would hear him mutter to himself.

He said to me, three days after the funeral, "Why don't you say something? I live here too."

Six years ago I walked around downtown wondering what to do. I wandered through the five-and-ten-cent stores, through the grubby little park, I sat in the old library and looked at magazines. The magazines had nothing to do with me. Time passed through my head, in and out of my head. I had become a married woman but nothing had happened to me. My husband worked for the siding company then, making good money. He had to climb ladders in the hot sun and nail siding onto houses and garages, his strong legs carrying him anywhere. Even then he was a big man. His face was tanned to an olivish dark, his eyes were light and jumpy in his face, his skin always looked a little greasy. When he grinned it was sudden, like a shout; like someone calling your name.

He had never been a child himself, he told me bitterly, because his parents were too old. He was the seventh child—coming at the end, for his parents' old age. But his father had died when he was two.

He had that dark face some men have—quizzical and dark but ready to grin—you must surprise them into grinning.

We met at a beach. Kids everywhere milling around, cars with their doors left open, seats too hot to sit on because of the sun. . . . Late Sunday afternoon. The odor of beer. The noise of radios. We were all in our bathing suits. I had been swimming and my long hair was piled on top of my head, I was a little dizzy from the heat, I kept giggling . . . he, my future husband, a man seven years older than I, kept fooling around on the beach, doing tricks. He was at the center of men like himself. Everyone liked him. He stood on his hands until the veins in his throat bulged . . . he brought his legs back down again, hard, spraying sand. . . . There was sand on his chest, drying in the matted dark hair. I felt the sharp angry pain of love for him in my own chest; deep in my chest.

The straps of my bathing suit left vivid pale lines on my shoulders, and the skin of my shoulders was burned to a bright red. I lay awake for nights after that Sunday, crying because of the sunburn, because I couldn't sleep.

We were married and he worked for a siding company. Then we moved out, after the trouble with my parents; we moved to another state. He worked for another siding company. The manager liked him, went out drinking with him. He made good money and kept saying that—*I'm making good money, right?* I walked downtown or sat on the edge of our bed, alone. I wanted to leave him. I did not love him. I loved him, yes, but he didn't love me. I loved him but I couldn't believe him, couldn't trust him, I wasn't ready for marriage, I couldn't stand his noises . . . his bullying . . . his plans for borrowing money and starting a company of his own. *I want to go in business for myself,* he kept saying. When I began to realize I must be pregnant, that it had happened to me at last, I did not want to tell him.

We had a fight and he moved out; threw his clothes in a suit-case and moved out.

In the back of my mind I loved him but I couldn't live with him. I wasn't ready to be married. I went to the movies in the afternoon and did not think about being married, about being pregnant. I did not think about myself at all. Pregnant? How could I be pregnant? My husband drove back and I went out to him; we went for a drive down along the river, not talking. I began to cry. He said nothing, his face was dark. I thought it was dark because of the blood held back, all the hatred he was hold-ing back.

"I'm going to have a baby," I said.

I did not look at him.

"A baby? . . ."

We lived then upstairs in the house on Sloan Street. He moved back in with me. Now the house is torn down, to make way for the new telephone building. This happened in 1963, in the summer. Jackie was born in April of 1964.

When he was three years old Jackie ran into the house crying. I asked, "What's happened? What's wrong?"

He showed me his bleeding hand—the palm of his hand had been scraped.

"How did you do that? It isn't bad! Did you hurt it on some-thing dirty?" I patted the blood away with a tissue. He stopped crying hard; he pressed against me with his wet face.

My husband said, coming into the kitchen, "Let's see what happened—"

He took Jackie's hand and stared down at it. Jackie's hand was very small in his; his own hand was not clean. He had been working on the lawn mower. "Should this be washed out or what?" he said, looking at me. "You think there's some germs in it?"

"I'd better wash it out."

I turned on the hot water.

"Maybe it should be sterilized. It should be washed out good," my husband said slowly. He stared down at Jackie's hand and for a few seconds he was silent. He loved Jackie very much; he was always afraid of Jackie getting hit by a car. Now Jackie tried to get away from him, uneasy. My husband looked strange, as if the sight of blood frightened him.

"I can wash it out. I'll put a bandage on it," I said.

He paid no attention to me. Instead, he turned on one of the electric burners of the stove, still holding Jackie's hand. "If it was something rusty . . . if it was some dirt, some filth, he could get very sick," my husband said. "The germs should be all killed."

"What? What are you going to do?"

"I know what to do," he said irritably, vaguely.

"All it needs is a bandage. . . ."

Jackie began to cry, afraid of his father. He tried to get away.

"Goddamn it, hold still! You want to get lockjaw or something? Why is this kid always crying?" He pulled Jackie to the stove and before I could stop him he pressed his palm down onto the burner—Jackie screamed, kicked, broke away—it was all over in a second.

"You're crazy! You burned him!" I cried.

My husband stared at me. Jackie was screaming, gasping for breath, he had backed away against the kitchen table. His screams rose higher and higher. My husband stared at him and at me, very pale.

"You're crazy!" I shouted at him.

I ran cold water for Jackie to stick his hand under. The burn was not bad—the stove hadn't been hot enough.

"I didn't mean to hurt him," my husband said slowly, "I . . . I don't know what. . . ."

"Putting his hand on the stove! God, you must be crazy!"

There was something pulsating in me, a bright, thrilling nerve

—I wanted to laugh in my husband's face, I wanted to claw at him, I wanted to gather Jackie up in my arms and run out of the house with him! I hated my husband and I was glad that he had made such a stupid mistake. I was glad he had burned Jackie and that Jackie was crying in my arms, pressing against me, terrified of his father.

"I don't know what I was thinking of," he said. His voice was vague and slow and surprised. "I didn't mean . . . I'm sorry. . . ."

"Don't scare him any more!"

"I'm sorry. I must be going crazy. . . ."

"Where did you ever get such an idea?"

He rubbed his hands violently across his face, across his eyes. "Jesus, I must be going crazy," he said.

"You're just lucky the stove wasn't hot."

Jackie kept crying, frightened. I took him into the bathroom and put a bandage on the cut—only a small scratch—no real burn at all.

We live in a boxlike house, a coup for people. My brothers had coops for rabbits back home. And, back home, we lived in a box-like house, a coop for people. I sit in this little house between the walls and think of that other house, where I was born, where I lived before I knew what would happen to me. I think about the puzzle I live in. My life is constructed like a series of boxes, rooms in which I did certain things. I then left the rooms and moved on to other rooms. Now I am in a particular room, between these walls, sitting on the sofa in front of the turned-off television set. My husband is late coming home from work and I think I am waiting for him.

At the cemetery the coffins are out of sight. On top of most of the graves there is a covering of grass; good. Nothing will heave up those coffins because they are buried quite deep. Nothing will pry them loose. They are little boxes, only big enough for one person.

My son had two fathers. One lived with us and the other lived away somewhere, a ghost-father, a stranger. I kept thinking of that other man. I remembered the day on the beach, the early days we went out together . . . sitting around in taverns, driving late at night. I hugged Jackie and thought about his other father, his real father. The man who lived in the house with us coughed in the bathroom every morning. He coughed violently, angrily. I could hear him: that coughing would tear out his insides.

My other husband, Jackie's other father, was a younger man. If he coughed, the coughing did not bend him in two, did not sound as if it were tearing at his insides.

I loved that man, but the man who lived with us, the man who slept with me, I hated. I did not hate him but I was afraid of him. I loved him sometimes, but most of the time I hated him. I wished he was dead. I said to Jackie, "Your father will be home soon so clean up that mess in the driveway. He'll give you hell." I walked through the house angrily, talking to myself. "Going into business for yourself . . . now you owe three thousand dollars . . . goddamn you, you should shoot yourself, you should drop dead!" I took Jackie with me when I drove out, the two of us alone together; sometimes I continued my argument with my husband, out in the car, laughing and sobbing so that Jackie was frightened of me.

"Your father is crazy! He's crazy! Why doesn't he die!" I cried.

Outside, children's cries. It is autumn now, six months since Jackie died. The cries are like a swarm of birds rushing at me. I press my hands against my ears but still the noise is with me, rushing at me. Children outside? Always children playing outside?

I run into the back bedroom, where it is dark. Shades pulled; everything closed up. Muggy air. Still a child is crying out in front of the house . . . my head pounds with his cries. Six months ago Joey Baxter, a boy who lives up the street, ran shouting to my back door. I saw him running from the field. He was running in a panic, crazily. He was shouting something to me but he couldn't even see me yet, in the house, watching him.

"The ditch!—" he was shouting.

I ran outside to meet him. His face was not a child's face.

It is October now and everything is rustling with wind and leaves. A child is crying outside. I hear the cries of children every day and I want to scream at them *No, I am not here, not really here, go home to your mothers!* But my hands, pressed against my ears, make me realize that I am losing my mind, I am going crazy, I must stop. I hold my pounding head between my hands, all that is myself, my soul, held panicked between my hands. I must not stay back here, hiding. I must see what is going on outside, I must be an adult, I must see if someone needs me. . . .

I run out the front door. Children by the curb, playing in the leaves. "What's wrong? Is someone hurt?" I ask them. The children break away guiltily and run across the street. But there is one child left behind, lying in the gutter, in a pile of leaves. . . . I kneel down beside him. They have covered him with leaves and rolled him around, a boy of about three. There are bits of leaves in his eyes, even. He cries helplessly. He seems blind, rubbing at his eyes with his fists, terrified. *Don't cry, don't cry like that!*

The other children have run away. This child is left behind, squirming in the dirty leaves, half-buried beneath them, gone blind. When he stares at me, sucking in his breath to scream, he does not seem to see me. When I try to help him up he kicks at me. His screams climb in my head until I have the crazy wish that they had really buried him, silenced him, stuffed leaves into his mouth. . . .

"Don't cry like that! I'm not your mother!"

Joey Baxter, in clothes too heavy for this warm April afternoon, is running to my back door. He and Jackie play together all the time. He runs shouting into the air. The back yard of our house has no fence but runs out into a field, and on the far edge of the field there are piles of lumber, concrete blocks, bricks, a drainage ditch. The ditch is swollen with water. Shading my eyes I can barely see it, the sun is so bright, and Joey's shouts make my vision blotch. Why is he shouting so?

Joey Baxter runs shouting to my back door.

Joey runs shouting from the field into our back yard.

Joey runs stumbling, shouting something to me.

"The ditch!—he fell in the ditch!" Joey shouts.

The drainage ditch has a twenty-four-inch pipe at one end, leading under the street. The grating in front of the pipe, they said, was pried off by children. But there was a grating there; a grating was definitely there at one time.

When the ditch is dry it is nothing to look at—lined with dead weeds, popsicle wrappers, junk. Nothing to catch the eye. The opening of the pipe is visible. It is dark and coated with last year's slime. It leads under the street, into darkness.

When the ditch is filled with water, when water rushes into it, the opening of the pipe is not visible. Branches and debris carried along by the rushing water are sucked into the pipe and out of sight, under the muddy street, vanished.

In the newspaper the contractor was quoted: *We definitely put a grating on that pipe. But children must have pried it off.*

He used to run out in front of cars on our street—once a driver stopped and came in to tell me. Jackie was hiding. I went looking for him and found him in the garage, hiding. He was giggling. Then he started to cry. I dragged him in the house and slammed the door and took him into the bathroom, my heart pounding, and there I could not think what I wanted to do—spank him? But I did not want to hurt him. I did not want him to cry. I knelt by him, hugging him, and the two of us cried together. "You shouldn't play in the street! What if you get hit by a car! What if something happens to you!"

He twisted into my arms, closer into my arms.

But he kept playing in the street; he played with other, older boys down by the row of new houses, crawling in the foundations, getting into trouble. He fell and cut himself, just beneath the chin, so that blood streamed down his neck and onto his shirt. . . . I wept over him, but I never punished him. All I could do was cry, bewildered and frightened.

"What are you trying to do? Are you trying to kill yourself?"

After he stopped crying we would lie together, the two of us, on the bed. My husband would not be home. We would lie together, quiet, on top of the bedspread, and I would touch his hot forehead until he fell asleep.

I never told my husband about these things. I was afraid of his anger.

Someone sent an envelope to me, my name and address printed in pencil, and inside was the clipping: BOY DROWNS IN DRAINAGE DITCH. No other message.

My husband and I go out with another couple, it is Saturday night, we end up at the usual place. We sit drinking. The other man eats potato chips and wipes his hands on his thighs, in a very good mood tonight. He works at Ford's, where my husband works now. He and my husband talk about men at work, about their foreman. The union. In the back of my husband's head are words he won't let out about how he hates this job, about how he is ashamed of it and of himself, losing so much money, being in debt. He had tried to start a siding company for himself but had lost it—too many bills, surprises, the weather, bad customers. But this couple doesn't know about that part of his life—they only know about the bad luck with Jackie, last spring. They never talk about it or about their own children with us.

Music is piped in from the bar. I can't hear the words but only the music. Then the words come out of my own head, surprising me. *I am not really here,* these words say. But I can't remember the rest of the song.

My husband's face is slack and heavy; Saturday night; he has worked for time-and-a-half pay today, until three o'clock in the afternoon. His skin is olive-tan, dark. Beneath his chin there is a roll of flesh, squeezed against his neck when he brings his chin back, talking. He and the other man smirk about some-one—a name I don't know—they drink beer—they settle them-selves in their chairs. There are three very sharp lines leading outward from my husband's eyes that I have not noticed before. Creases in his skin. He is squinting. He squints and rubs his hand across his face, up and down over his eyes, then lets his hand fall and laughs along with the other man.

The music clicks off but my own words keep on: I *am not really here.* I want to hear the next line of the song, I want des-perately to know what it is! *I am not really here.* But the words are stuck, they won't go any farther, I can't remember. . . . My husband and his friend are trying to remember something too. The name of a man who died? A heart attack in the plant? *I am not really here.* Watching them, pretending to listen to them, I think of Jackie and of how he would not have grown up to be a man like these men. I know that. Sucked into the pipe, carried along on that rushing, violent, filthy water, drowned and man-gled inside the pipe, his face smashed in, a five-year-old who would never have grown up into a man . . . he is with me here in the tavern as much as these three adults are with me. He is still with me. We are all present to one another like that—here and not here, remembered or not remembered. My husband breaks off, staring at me. He must see something awful in my face. Then he looks back to his friend again and the conversation continues. . . .

I am not really here.

We return home around two o'clock. We are reluctant to go home, a little afraid. I can hear my husband breathing hard. He grunts sometimes for no reason—doing something that takes no effort, like rolling up the car window. We go into the house where one light is burning, in the living room, and we are frightened to enter it. We do not look at each other. The house is filled with emptiness. With nothing. It is a kind of hole, smelling of damp, of nothing. You keep waiting for a noise. Something is going to happen, and yet it does not happen.

My husband opens the refrigerator and takes out a can of beer. "Sit down for a minute," he says.

The window beside him is dark and shows us both his reflection. If it were daylight we could see the back yard, the field, the heaps of debris, the line that is the drainage ditch, so far away.

My husband wipes his forehead with both hands. "Can't you sit down for a minute?" he says.

"I'm tired."

"I want to tell you something," he says slowly. When he expels his breath it is too loud, labored. His eyes are dull but the creases around them are sharp. He frightens me, sitting like this. It is not really my husband. It is not that other man, either, my real husband. It is no one at all. I am in the doorway, standing, and I can feel the warmth from the refrigerator, its slight vibrations. I think suddenly *He will want to leave me now.* . . .

"Before he—before it happened—the accident—just a few days before, I thought about it, that ditch. The ditch," he says quickly. "Not the pipe but the ditch. I didn't know about the pipe. I was driving by it, coming home the back way, where some kids were playing in the water, and I thought—Jesus, what if a kid falls in there and drowns, there'll be hell to pay for somebody, what if Jackie fools around there! But then I forgot about it—I don't know why—I just forgot about it."

He stares at me. I can feel the nausea in him.

"I forgot all about it. If I hadn't forgot he'd be alive now, wouldn't he?"

I look away from him. I put my hand out against the refrigerator; it is vibrating gently, invisibly. All the sounds of the house are normal. Now I will tell this man the things I must tell him. It is time. It is time for me to tell him of my hatred for him, and my love, and the terrible anger that has wanted to scream its way out of me for years, screaming into his face, into his body. It is time for me to tell him that the death was my fault. Jackie died because I wanted his father dead.

My husband turns abruptly in his chair, scraping the floor. "If we hadn't moved to this goddamn house, he wouldn't be dead. That was my fault. Moving here. He wouldn't be dead if we hadn't moved, would he?"

His face is anxious and sweaty, an aging face. I have an impulse to touch it—is it warm? What does it feel like to live behind that particular face? But I cannot move. The moment is too heavy upon me. I cannot believe that I am really here, listening to these words, that I am really here in this room, this kitchen, staring at a man I met on the beach so many years ago, another man. A stranger. This man, my husband, is getting heavy; his body is heavy and exhausted.

"It was my fault, wasn't it?" he says, questioning, staring at me.

"No."

"You want me to get out? I will. I don't blame you." His face is greasy. There are tears in his eyes.

I shake my head no, no. No. I go to him and put my arms around him, his head and his shoulders, and he presses himself against me, exhausted, hot, breathing hard. He hides his face against me and I can't see him. What is this puzzle of people!— what have they to do with one another? They can't help one another. They are better alone. Jackie did not die because my husband forgot about the ditch . . . he did not die because we had to move here, because my husband was a failure . . . he did not die because I wanted his father dead. There is no reason. He died.

But I can't think of it any longer—this puzzle we live in, the boxes, the walls, the hot dry sand that fell from my husband's body that Sunday, the pain of my loins, my backbone vivid with pain at that birth, that wonderful birth. And what came of it? A son, a death. Drowning. A drainage ditch. A small coffin.

How do these things come together—what do they mean? It is a puzzle I cannot understand. I am here in my husband's embrace, in the silence of our marriage, and there is nothing outside of this moment, this love I have been allotted, that I can understand.

*L*ove and Death

One February a man named Marshall Hughes returned to his hometown to visit his father, a widower. This is not really the beginning of the story, that is, not the true beginning; but it would be his idea of the beginning.

His father lived alone with an older sister, who was his housekeeper and nurse. His name was also Marshall; he had been "big Marshall" at one time; now it was Marshall, Jr., who was big and his father who was small, though perhaps that was just a trick of the light. "No, keep that shut," his father kept saying, wagging his fingers toward the window. "It hurts my eyes." He sat up in bed, or in a big armchair near the bed, reading newspapers. He was a sharp, petulant old man who still had money, coming in from sources he was secretive about. Good for him, Marshall thought, as if his father's financial stability protected them both from something; good, let him stay that way, let him die happy.

The family house was large and drafty, Victorian in style. It struck Marshall as the prototype for houses in the cartoons of certain sophisticated magazines—cartoons meaningful only to a generation that has abandoned such houses, with nostalgia. His wife could look back at such a family home too. Marshall and his wife were well matched, both intelligent and pleasant and accustomed to certain delicacies that are the result of money—money kept invisible, of course. They had both belonged to the same kind of social group; they had gone to the same kind of schools, had the same kind of teachers. They were bound together before they had even met by the queer pleasing network of names that made up their world. If Fran hadn't known Peter Applegate, the cousin of a friend of Marshall's, it was no surprise that she had known Gloria van Buren, who was the fiancée of another friend.

Marshall and Fran had been married for nine years in 1967, and they had three children. Marshall worked for a company that made electrical parts for other companies—an excellent business. And he needed to work, too, because the money that came to him and Fran from various sources was not enough to live on, no more than seven or eight thousand a year, and he felt a strange satisfaction at the thought of "having to work," because there was a kind of settledness in that thought, a sense of safety. They went to a Presbyterian church mainly for their children's sakes. And they lived in an excellent suburb in the Midwest, several hundred miles from their families and, it would seem, centuries beyond the influence of the past.

So Marshall went back to visit. His conscience nudged him, his wife said, "Why don't you? . . ." and he made up his mind to return, since his father wasn't well and it would be only a matter of time until the old man died. Marshall was worried that his father knew this. That was perhaps why his father kept saying sourly, "I'm going back to the office when the weather clears. This winter lasts too long."

"How is Dr. Fitzgerald?" Marshall said.

"Competent."

"Is his son doing well?"

"I wouldn't know about his son."

In such ways was Marshall's generation shouldered aside, squeezed out, ignored. Marshall, sensitive to his father's pride in himself and his power, never pursued any subjects that led to the forbidden subterranean world of time and mortality and death.

On the first evening of his visit he called Fran and was relieved to hear her voice—that cool, sane, immensely charming voice— that summoned up for him the elegant world of his home, his friends, his children, his wife. Whatever his father's people had achieved, there was none of the comfort of the new generation in it: its victories were grim, like its furniture. There was little joy in that generation. "How are the children?" Marshall asked over the telephone. Tears often stung his eyes when he called home from his business trips, asking about the children. He thought of them mainly when he was away; when he was home they somehow eluded his concern.

"Oh, they all miss you. They love you," Fran said.

"Tell them to be good."

There were odd embarrassed moments when he and Fran could not think of the next thing to say. This was not in spite of their politeness with each other but because of it.

"Please take care of yourself," Marshall said.

"Take care of your*self*," his wife answered.

The next morning he went out for a walk. He was prepared to see a decline in the neighborhood, but things weren't too bad. One or two of the old places were obviously vacant, another looked as if it must be a nursing home of some kind. He walked for quite a while. It was a mild, sunny day, suggesting spring. Marshall went all the way down to the post office, which looked smaller than he remembered; there were four windows inside but only one was open, so he had to stand in line, and he noticed a woman near the front of the line who looked familiar. He stared

at the back of her head. She wore a cloth coat of a cheap cut. A
flimsy pink scarf was tied about her hair, which was in no particular style, though bleached blond. Marshall himself wore a topcoat of a good, dark material, gloves, and his expensive shoes
were protected by rubbers. He was a tall, fairly handsome man of
about forty. When the woman turned away from the window he
caught his breath—yes, he did remember her.

She went over to one of the closed windows and set her purse
down on the counter, so that she could put stamps on some envelopes. He watched her. She had a thin, frail, careless profile, not
quite as he had remembered. He had remembered her as more
solid. She licked the stamps and put them on the envelopes, as
oblivious of anyone around her as if she were in her own home.
Marshall wondered whom she was writing to. He saw that her
coat was too short for her skirt, which hung down an inch or so
in an untidy way.

He kept watching her and thought surely she would notice
him. He was almost at the window when she picked up her purse
and turned to go, without seeing him. So there was nothing for
him to do but follow her—he didn't want to call after her, and he
didn't want her to get away. At the door he caught up with her
and said, "Hello, it's Cynthia, isn't it? Cynthia?"

She turned and stared at him. He saw that she recognized him,
and he saw also the sudden recoiling gesture, the half-demure
protestation, as if he had caught her at a bad moment. "Oh, Marshall," she said flatly. Her eyes were a cold, critical gray. "Marshall Hughes."

He laughed in embarrassment, breathlessly. "I was sure it was
you. . . ."

"Are you back home again?"

"I'm visiting."

The corners of her mouth turned up, but not in a smile. Her
lips were quite red. He was struck by the flat, blatant, tired look
she was giving him, a look that must have been defensive. Her
bleached hair, inside the scarf, had a festive and rather ludicrous

appearance, framing so cold a face. Several strands of hair had been combed down onto her forehead in a style that was a little too girlish for her. Her nose was long, as he had remembered it, giving her a slightly hungry, impatient look, her nostrils were thin, nervous, her mouth sharply and ironically defined, with the shadows of lines at its corners. It was an intelligent look somehow imposed upon an ordinarily pretty woman's frail, conventional face; her plucked, arched eyebrows could have belonged to any unstylish woman, but that mouth looked as if it might have something to say.

"Well, it was a surprise, seeing you. . . . I was sure it was you," Marshall said vaguely. He kept staring at her. The woman laughed in a short, humorless way, as if he had said something funny. "Do you still live around here? I mean—with your mother?"

"With my mother?" she laughed.

"Yes, I thought—I mean, weren't you living with her?" He was conscious of having said something stupid, having confused facts. She stared at him mockingly. "Well, where do you live? Nearby?"

"Yes, nearby," she said. Her irony was crude; he felt a pang of revulsion toward her.

"Well, how are you?" he asked.

"All right."

"I live in Kansas City now myself. My wife and I have three children."

"That's nice."

"And you, are you married?"

"I *was* married."

He tried to smile, wanting her to smile. There was something cruel about her mouth. He resented her coldness and the proud, indifferent way in which she kept him there, asking her questions. The very look of his clothes embarrassed him; she looked so shabby, so sad, and there was no failure of his own that he could offer her.

"Where are you going now?" he said suddenly.

"Back."

"Back? . . ."

"A few blocks away."

She moved toward the door. He followed, awkwardly. His eyes traveled down to the hem of her coat. There was something sloppy and intimate about that, something vulnerable. "Did you walk all the way down here from your father's house?" she said.

"Yes. It's a fine day for a walk."

They descended the steps. He had the idea she wanted to get away, and he was anxious to keep her with him. He had to think of something to say. Years ago they had been involved with each other casually, and he had forgotten her, and yet now he did not want her to get away; her indifference made him uneasy.

"Could I buy you some coffee? Or lunch?"

"It's too early for lunch."

"It's after eleven."

"I didn't get up till ten."

Again he experienced a slight tug of revulsion. He himself always got up at seven, never slept later. "Some coffee then, down the street?"

"All right."

They went to a small restaurant that Marshall believed he could remember. He felt a little awkward in it, in his topcoat and suit, but the woman sat down and unbuttoned her coat and let it fall over the back of her chair as if she were quite accustomed to the place. She wore a deep pink sweater that was too tight for her, and with the coat off she looked younger, more gentle. The sweater was cheap, its neck stretched and a little soiled, but it cast up onto her face a soft pink tone that was flattering.

"How have you been all these years?" Marshall said.

"I've gotten along."

"It was quite an accident, running into you. . . ."

"Yes," she said sarcastically. She was not yet smiling. Marshall was relieved when the waitress came to take their order. They were sitting across from each other at a small, wobbly table. The woman had not pulled her chair in, conscious of the smallness of the table, and so she sat back awkwardly. Marshall smiled at her. He folded his own coat neatly over a nearby chair, and with a deft neat movement that looked unplanned he pushed the table in toward her and drew his own chair up to it.

"Yes, it's quite a surprise," he said, rubbing his hands.

"Christ, do you have to keep saying that?"

"But I mean it." He flushed, as if embarrassed by her profanity. She had so much strength, mysterious strength, and he had none. Her eyes regarded him with an unsurprised, calculating look, a look he had never seen in any other woman, and he noticed with satisfaction that there were slight hollows beneath those eyes. She was about thirty-five now. In a few years she would age suddenly and there would be no strength then, none of this sullen independence. He could not understand why he had followed her out of the post office.

"Did you say you were married now?" he said.

"Who wants to know?"

"I do. I want to know," he said weakly.

"Maybe I am, what difference does it make? Maybe I kicked him out. It's the same old story—anyway, what difference does it make?"

"You certainly don't mean it makes no difference to you."

"No. I mean to you."

"But I care. I'm anxious to hear about you."

"Oh, Christ," she said. Her eyes moved about behind him with a remote, amused look, as if she were searching out someone to laugh with her over him. Marshall remembered that—he remembered this woman breaking off their conversation to gaze around in that stupid indifferent placid way, pretending she had better things to think about.

"How is your brother?" he said.

"Which one, Davey?" she said, more gently.

"Yes, what happened to him?"

"He's the same, he's married now. Working a night shift."

"And what about your mother?"

"Look, you know my mother died a long time ago. You know that."

Marshall frowned. He did not remember, and yet in a way he did remember. There was something sluggish about him. The woman leaned forward, crossing her arms at the wrists; her wrists were girlish and delicate. She said, "You certainly do remember. You're lying."

"What, lying?"

"You're lying." She smiled sourly. "Now tell me about your wife."

"But I want to talk about you."

She laughed. The waitress brought their coffee and Marshall resented the distraction. The woman said, "You want to talk about me? Why the hell about me? Do you have a cigarette?"

He took out his package of cigarettes at once, anxious to please her. She was so indifferent, so careless, that she might suddenly push her chair back and walk out, and he would not be able to run after her. Unwrapping the package, jerking the red cellophane strip around, he felt her eyes on his fingers and was nervous, thinking that there was something vaguely obscene about what he was doing. He finally got a cigarette to stick out and she took it. Lighting her cigarette was another awkward thing but at last it was accomplished. He felt strangely weak before her sullen, indifferent silence.

"So your brother is still in town?"

"Yes. You liked him, didn't you?" she said curiously.

"Why do you ask?"

"You liked him because he kept his nose out of our business. That was what you liked about him, and what you didn't like about my mother."

This stirred some memory in him; he nodded slowly. It would be better to agree.

"Your own mother, of course, was a bitch of another type. We won't mention her."

"You never saw my mother."

"I certainly did."

"When did you see her?"

"My God, you know very well—we saw her one day downtown, the two of us. We saw her with some other fat bitches, all dressed up, and you pointed her out to me. I remember that."

Marshall was a little shocked, but he made himself smile. "But if you only saw her. . . ."

"I knew all about her. You told me. And is your father still alive?"

"Yes."

"You're here visiting him?"

"Yes."

"How long are you going to stay?" But then she tapped ashes from the cigarette onto the floor, nervously, as if conscious of having said something wrong but not wanting to correct it.

"A few more days."

"Then you're going back—to Kansas City?"

"To St. Louis," he said slowly.

She smiled. "Oh, St. Louis, you live in St. Louis?"

He pushed the coffee cup aside, he had no desire for coffee. He watched her impatiently. "Well, never mind about that," he said. "What about you, are you married?"

"In a way."

"What does that mean?"

She shrugged her shoulders. With her thumb and two fingers she picked up the coffee cup, a precise little gesture of affectation that struck him. She was a pretty woman in spite of everything. There was something hungry and cynical about her, she had a way of looking steadily at him that no other woman had, yet still she was pretty in a way. Her hair was disheveled but clean, gleaming in the light from the window. He liked her hair. It was

vulgar, that color, and showed that she wasn't so clever after all
—what a phony color!—but still he liked it on her.

He said, "Your hair looks good."

She lifted one shoulder in a lazy gesture of indifference.

"You used to wear it long? . . ."

They sat for a while in silence. Then she said, "I have to leave
now." She spoke stubbornly, as if arguing. Marshall said, hardly
knowing what he would hear, "But where are you going?"
Home, she told him. He asked what that meant; whom did she
live with? She told him it was none of his business, was it? He
could feel his heartbeat quicken and he asked her the question
again. By herself, she said, she lived by herself; but she worked
in the evening and she had some things to do, she had to wash
things, go shopping. He asked her if he could come along. She
swore in a gentle, weary, unsurprised way, staring at him; she
shook her head. Marshall fumbled for the pack of cigarettes and
put them away nervously. The woman kept looking at him. He
felt guilty suddenly and had to fight down an impulse to look
over his shoulder, to see if anyone had heard.

They had met many years ago in a bar. She had been with one
crowd, he with another. He had been introduced to her, asked
her her name and telephone number, and a few days later had
called her up. She had lived then in a big ugly house, a very old
house. He remembered that house, and his shyness, and the girl's
carefully made-up, mocking face, and the very high heels of the
shoes she wore.

"No, I have to leave," she said.

He helped her with her coat and put on his own, not bothering
to button it. He caught up with her at the door.

"Where are you going now?"

"I told you, home."

"Where is that?"

"Close by." She looked sideways at him and smiled. "Do you
want to walk me there?"

Her apartment was in a six-story building, an old building.

Marshall had a vague impression of it but for some reason did not want to see more. He was in a hurry, his heartbeat was choked and rapid. On the stairs his feet ached to carry him up fast, faster than he was going. The woman kept glancing sideways at him, ironically. On the bannister her bare hand moved in jerks, a few inches at a time, and he watched this movement out of the corner of his eye.

At her door he watched as she put the key into the lock. This startled him, the way it went into the lock, forcing itself in and then quite at ease there, turning easily. He felt weak. She said, "You should go back down now, back down," indicating with a jerk of her head the stairs behind them.

"Couldn't I stay a while? Talk to you?"

"Oh, talk, what do you want to talk about? Talk!" she said in disgust.

"Could I see you later, then? Tonight?"

She had opened the door. She seemed impatient to get away, yet something made her linger; like him, she felt a peculiar tugging between them, an undefined force that would not release her. Marshall waited. He remembered her making him wait, in the old days, this sluttish girl who had nothing, really nothing, except what men like himself wanted to give her. Her profile, nearly overwhelmed by the bunch of blond hair that looked resilient and unreal as a dummy's wig, put him in mind of his wife's profile for an instant. But the two women were quite different. His wife had a healthy, wholesome, friendly face; she played golf with women like herself, she dressed with simple, excellent taste. What reminded him of her, in this woman, was no more than the fact that he was standing close to the woman. He had been close to few people in his life.

"Could I come in now? For a few minutes?"

He was perspiring, he was not himself. Her fingers, tapping impatiently on the doorknob, seemed to be tapping against his body, teasing him. He said, begging, "I won't stay long."

He had no impression of the room except that it was small.

Windows at one end with their shades drawn; mingled odors of food. He felt as if he had broken through to something, liberated and floating in a way he could not control. It was a strange feeling. All his life he had said silently to others, Let me alone, don't touch me, talk to me but don't touch me, because I'm afraid of— afraid of what? He was afraid, that was enough. He and his wife said this to each other, silently, Let me alone, don't touch me— Cynthia took off her coat angrily and looked around at him. "I don't know why the hell you're here. Do you think it's still fifteen years ago?"

This shocked him. "Fifteen years? Nothing ever happened— that long ago—" he said dizzily. He moved toward her. He put his arms around her, clumsy in his coat, and she stood there with a kind of contemptuous patience, a mockery of patience. "I don't think so much time went by—"

"All right."

"I've thought about you a great deal—"

"All right, sure."

"Could we go in there? Is that another room, could we go in there?"

"You'll have to give me some money."

"Yes."

"You used to give me money, right?"

"I don't know, yes, maybe—I don't remember. Did I give you money?" he asked, surprised. He thought about that. "No, I never gave you money. It wasn't like that."

"Certainly."

"I gave you money?"

"I was in love with you, sure, but I was never stupid," she said in her flat, amused voice. "What makes you think I'm stupid? Because I'm poor? Because I don't dress like your wife?"

"No, you're not stupid."

"Then give me some money, now."

He took out his wallet. He had the idea that she was degrading him in this manner, degrading herself, in order to block out the memory of their love together—that was all right, he understood her. She was protecting herself. He took out a number of bills and, smiling foolishly, handed them to her. She took them and began to smile too. "Yes, you gave me money," she said. "Otherwise why should I have bothered with you?"

They went into the other room. Marshall stopped thinking. When he began to think again, a while later, his mind was precise and he looked around the room as if memorizing it. And when they went back out into the larger room, the woman yawning and indifferent at his side, he looked around that room too. He saw the cheap modern furniture, blond wood and green cushions, a table with a formica top, flowered drapes, a worn-out rug. He felt dislocated and quite empty. The room was so ugly that it saddened him.

"Let me see you again. I want to see you again," he said.

"You can take me to dinner tonight."

"Dinner? Really?"

"Yes, dinner. Good-by."

He had to make excuses at home, saying he had met an old friend on his walk. When his aunt asked who this friend was, in her dry, suspicious spinster's voice, he really could not think of a name for several seconds. It was embarrassing. His father luckily paid no attention; he was reading newspapers. Marshall watched the old man, jealous of the attention he paid to all those papers while his son had traveled so far to see him. . . . He noticed the way the old man pursed his lips, reading, working his lips as if mumbling secret words to himself, flexing his jaws. There was something outlandish and too intimate, almost indecent, in the way he worked his lips. Marshall looked away. Then he looked back, fascinated. His father moved his narrow lips as he read, not shaping silent words, but simply out of habit, as a way of caressing himself.

Marshall called his wife again that afternoon. He asked how the children were, how Fran was. Fine, fine. But there was something—one of the boys had cut his leg. Out playing. No, he hadn't been pushed, it was just an accident. Marshall tried to keep talking and listening. It was easier to talk than to listen. His wife's voice was very far away; the book-lined study in which he sat seemed somehow very far away too, its indistinct walls confining the air of another, older time into which he had stepped accidentally. And he would step out of it again in a moment.

When he came to the woman's apartment that evening he was very nervous. She said, amused, "What's wrong with you? In the post office you were another person, now you're back to what you were fifteen years ago."

"But what was I fifteen years ago?"

"What you are now."

"But what is that?"

"I can't tell you. How can I describe you to yourself?"

They had dinner in a dark, ordinary restaurant. A big air-conditioning unit was perched up above them on the wall, silent and ominous; Marshall had the feeling that it was about to topple off and fall on them. He was very uneasy, very nervous. As they ate their dinner, uninteresting food he barely tasted, he kept asking her about what she had meant, earlier—"Did I really give you money?"

"Yes, of course."

"And you took it?"

"Why wouldn't I take it?"

"Do you remember how we met? The first time?"

"You came in a certain bar to make a telephone call. Your friends were outside, waiting. You saw me and asked me something—asked me for change for the telephone. You talked to me. Then you went out and told your friends to drive on without you, and you came back in, and the two of us went somewhere. . . ." She paused, thinking. "Yes. We went to this place I sometimes stayed in, a flat a friend of mine rented."

"But it wasn't that way at all," Marshall said quickly.

"No? How was it, then?"

"Didn't I call you up later? Didn't I get your telephone number?"

"Yes. You asked me for my number, after we went back to that flat."

"Only after that?"

"Yes, what do you think? Don't you remember?"

He stared at her. Slowly, reluctantly, he began to remember. She had been a thin girl in a black dress, trying to look older than she was. She had been sitting at a table near the telephone booth, in a corner. "So we went back to a flat? A friend of yours had a flat?"

"Yes. We only went there once."

"It wasn't someone else?"

"You mean, instead of you? There were other men, yes, but it was you as well, you were one of them."

"But you say we only went there once?"

"I lived at home then. I was with my family."

"Yes. I remember that, of course."

"You remember my mother?"

"Yes."

Her mother had screamed at him one day, a fat drunken woman who accused him of taking advantage of her daughter. Marshall had had to push her away, she had tried to strike him and scratch his face. . . . Yes, he remembered that fat bitch of a woman; he was glad she was dead.

"You were glad when she died," Cynthia said.

"I wouldn't say that. . . ."

"Yes, I would say it," Cynthia said flatly.

After dinner he said, "Why haven't you done more with yourself? Why are you still living in the same neighborhood after so long?"

"I don't have any ambitions."

"You never got married?"

"I didn't say that."

"Or have children? None of that?"

"But that isn't of any interest to you. You know that."

"What do you mean?"

"My real life isn't of any interest to you, it's nothing. What do you care if I did get married? All right, I did. Then it was ended, like that. No children. I'm not like people you know, I don't have any ambition. I don't care."

"It seems impossible. . . ."

"But I wouldn't want to be your wife. I wouldn't want that."

"You wouldn't want to marry me?"

She laughed. "No, I wouldn't. But I didn't mean that. I mean that I wouldn't want to be the woman who is your wife now—I wouldn't want to be that woman."

Marshall had to think for a moment, recalling his wife. His heart fluttered as if he were in danger.

"You are two very different people," he said slowly.

They went back to her apartment. Near as he could come to her, she always held him off, in a sense, observing him coldly. He could never get past the icy circle of her mind; she was always thinking about him, holding him apart from her. "What was your husband like?" he said. "Like anyone. An ordinary man," she said. "He didn't have money, did he?" he said. "Of course not," she said, "nobody has money except you." He wished he could see her face, to see what she meant by that.

He was reluctant to leave her; he wanted to stay all night, but his father would wonder about him; a vision of that ugly old mansion rose in his mind and made him stir guiltily. In the dark, it was difficult for him to know who he was. And yet it was a darkness that was not really unfamiliar.

She snapped on the light. "I hope that from now on we can be friends, and forget each other."

"Why should we forget each other?"

"But you forgot me before. You never sent me any money."

"I didn't know you wanted money."

"You must have known. Everyone wants money," she said,

without bothering to emphasize any of her words, just pronouncing them. He felt that she did not believe this, that it was nothing more than a means of holding him off. She had a strange face, this woman, an unhappy, brooding, and yet careless look that her make-up seemed to parody. He was uncomfortable, beneath her gaze. She might have been assessing any man, himself or a stranger, making no distinction between them.

"I can send you some money, when I get home."

She said nothing. Marshall went on, anxiously, "I want to ask you something before I leave. Why do you think I came over to you?"

"When, today? Or the first time?"

"Either time."

"Because you liked me, I suppose."

"But why . . . why do you think I like you?"

She shut her eyes wearily. "You mean, it seems crazy to you that you should be here? All right, yes, it is crazy. But I do know why you're here, as a matter of fact."

"Why?"

"Don't you know? Can't you guess?"

He felt a slight pang of terror, at the very softness of her voice. "What? What is it?"

"Do you remember what you said to me, the first time we met? I mean after we went back to that flat."

"No. What did I say?"

"You asked me my age, how long I had been doing that sort of thing. You asked me about the men I knew. You were very curious, very excited. Of course, you were a young man then—"

"And you were young too," he said nervously.

"Not in the same way. You were always pestering me then, back then—don't you remember?"

"I think you're mixing me up with someone else."

"Oh, hell," she laughed. "Go on home, then."

"No, please. Couldn't you be mixing me up with someone else?"

"I don't forget things. There was a time when I loved you, and this time is closed off from what came before and what came after, and I can look back at it and remember it perfectly. What's strange is that you don't remember it."

"But I want to remember it. . . ."

"You asked me about the other men. You came to see me all the time, it was crazy. You wrote me letters though we lived in the same city, you gave me presents—jewelry and clothes—you were always bothering me. You liked to tease me about those other men, you'd sit on the edge of the bed and ask me questions, lots of questions. Don't you remember that?"

"No," Marshall said dully. But even as he spoke he knew it was true, and a sense of revulsion and anger stirred inside him.

"What do you remember, then?"

"I asked you your telephone number and I called you up a few days later," he said, as if reciting something. "I went to your house—your brother was working on his car, in the driveway. You introduced me to your mother. I think it was a Sunday, Sunday afternoon."

"But we met on Saturday night."

"This was the next day. You introduced me to your mother."

"Did you like that?"

"I thought it was nice."

"But you must have known I did it to make fun. My mother was always drunk and I wanted to see how you'd act. Didn't you know that?"

Marshall was silent for a moment. Then he said, "But I don't remember any flat."

"Of course you remember."

"I think you're mixing me up with someone else."

"So, you called me up, you met my mother, what else?"

"And then . . . we started seeing each other."

"What did we do?"

"We went to movies, out to dinner. We went dancing." He thought about this, watching her uneasily. Then his mind cleared and he remembered that it was Fran he had done those things with.

"We went to rooms, to hotels," she said. "We drove around in your car."

"But you didn't seem to mind—"

"Why should I mind? You paid me."

"I remember that vaguely—"

"Vaguely, hell!"

She wanted him to leave but he was reluctant. He clutched at something: "But you lied to me too. You said you had to work tonight."

"Did I?"

"I think you said that."

"Yes, I work some evenings. I have a real job, I'm a hostess in a restaurant. But I took tonight off."

"For me?"

She shrugged her shoulders. Of course, he had given her money—but he did not think that was significant.

She saw him to the door. He turned to leave, his face burning. It seemed to him . . . that something was wrong, something was threatening. When he was out in the hall she said, in her low teasing voice, "Here's something else you won't remember either—how when we went out you talked to me about my life, how I was trapped, I had nowhere to go, no future—I'd get diseased or some maniac would kill me—You said you loved me, because I was just a tramp and my mother was a drunk and so on—and you really did love me, but you don't remember any of it."

He made up his mind not to see her again, and the rest of his visit was spent in the old house. He sat with his father while the old man read his papers, Marshall himself reading a newspaper, the two of them silent and bewitched by what they read, and quite oblivious of each other. Except from time to time Marshall glanced at his father and saw that queer silent smacking of his father's lips—again and again—and his very bowels seemed stirred by it, stirred to anger. He called Fran, as if in desperation. But her voice was distant and what she spoke of seemed trivial. He wondered whether, if he put the receiver down gently, he might cut her out of his life altogether.

But of course this was nonsense. He was frightened at himself, at such thoughts. He had never in his life had such thoughts before. . . . And he found himself recalling certain moments of his love-making with that other woman, when he had thought of the possibility of her being diseased and of the great risk he was taking. It excited him, to think of this risk. Yet that was all nonsense, all disgusting. He was anxious to return home again.

A strange thing: he began seeing things that weren't there. Or, rather, a foreign vision imposed itself upon them, distorting them violently. One day his aunt—a woman of over sixty, hefty, vague, sour, very religious—was cutting meat when he walked into the kitchen. He was eager to talk with someone. She was slicing pieces of raw meat off a large, fatty hunk, and something about her wet, bloodstained fingers, and the tender pink meat, and the flashing of the knife terrified him. He was almost sick. His aunt did not care to talk and so he passed on through to the breakfast room and so safely away. . . . And another time at dinner he watched his father finish a glass of water, lifting it to his mouth and drinking in rather audible gasps until nothing was left, and Marshall thought: in just that way do people make love. It was not a thought that made sense. But it flashed clearly through his mind as he watched his father empty the crystal goblet.

He was not going to call Cynthia, but on the last day he did. They talked vaguely as if they had nothing in common. "Now I'm leaving. I probably won't see you again," he said cautiously. She said, "Yes, good luck. I hope your father is well." The mention of his father startled him, for certainly she was thinking that he had to be back—didn't he?—when his father got worse, when his father died, he had to be back then and he'd call her up, wouldn't he? He was trapped. So he said irritably, "Of course he's well. And now I'm going back. You'll see—a person can do one thing and then do the opposite thing, it doesn't matter. I won't be seeing you again."

He arrived back home in time for a dinner party. Everything was confused, gaily muddled. He had to tell his wife about the visit while they dressed, the two of them already late, a little giddy with the prospect of a familiar excellent evening before them. Marshall felt good; he felt quite safe. He kept chatting to his wife about all sorts of things, and she in her turn chatted about the latest news, which friends she had had lunch with, who was in town. He was amazed at how rich and complex and yet safe this life was, out here.

It was several hours before he even remembered that woman. At about ten o'clock they went in to dinner, into an elegant dining room, and their host opened a bottle of wine. He worked at the cork, making jokes, and seemed to be looking at Marshall as if Marshall were somehow the main point of the joke. Marshall felt sweat break out on his body. He couldn't quite make out the joke, but he did watch with a kind of terror the man's fingers working at the cork. Something was straining for release, something threatened to spurt out—Then the moment passed, it was over. Wine was poured into glasses in an ordinary way and there was nothing behind it.

For more than a week he continued as his usual self, and then he had an overwhelming impulse to write to Cynthia. He was at his office and he used business stationery, with the firm's Kansas City address on it. Let her see it. He wanted to give her proof of how successful he was. He wrote her a long, aimless, unplanned letter. It was chatty and superficial. Rereading it, however, he saw that the letter was quite obviously a disguise for something left unsaid—but he did not know what that was.

She did not reply to it.

Angered, he wrote again. This time he typed out the letter, on the same stationery. He asked her specific questions, about her ex-husband, about her "present mode of living," about her plans for the future. This letter was five pages long, an inspired letter. Marshall had never been able to write letters to anyone and had always telephoned if he had anything to say, so he was both pleased and a little disturbed that he could write so much to that woman. She was so unimportant, after all.

He included in the letter a check for several hundred dollars, and this time she replied. She thanked him for the money and wrote a few more lines, just to be polite. He was enraged at this but did not know what he had expected. So he wrote again at once, ending his letter: "Write back. I want to hear anything you have to say. Tell me about your job, about your mother or anything."

As an afterthought he took some bills out of his wallet and slid them into the envelope. His fingers were shaking.

Her letter came a few weeks later. In ball-point ink she had written a few lines, mentioning the money. This was followed by a paragraph in pencil, evidently written at a later time, in which she did talk about her mother: "You both hated each other and yet you were curious about each other. She knew you had money and, who knows, she might end up with it herself—I'm sure that crossed her mind. And then, on the day she died, you had to hear everything about her and go right into her bedroom, though the poor woman had been in that bed a few hours before. And yet you two never really met except that one time and never talked to each other."

He read this and a fine dizzying film passed before his eyes. In such flat, blatant language, just as she spoke . . . what had she told him? Her mother's bedroom, what about that? He tried to remember but could not. Something seemed to be blocking his memory. So he wrote her again, careful to include a check this time (she had reproved him for sending money through the mail), and asked for more information. He waited eagerly for her to reply. But no reply came. He wondered if she had received the letter. He kept waiting, waiting for her to answer. When his wife mentioned that she had heard from a friend in Boston, Marshall turned to stare at her in amazement. Because it seemed to him that she was about to confront him with her knowledge of Cynthia, and he was excited not by the danger of his position but by the possibility of her having discovered a letter, having somehow intercepted it, and he would have allowed that if it meant he would at last hear from Cynthia. . . . But no, the letter was truly from a friend, no irony was intended.

He wrote Cynthia again, begging and demanding that she answer. He sent her another check, this time for a thousand dollars. Angry, frustrated, he believed that she was blackmailing him and that she was a criminal; she ought to be arrested and punished. Certainly she ought to be punished: she was a prostitute, taking money from men. He hated her for her power over him and thought of revenge he might take upon her. He would do something, yes. He did hate her. And yet when her letter arrived his heart pounded as if he were indeed in love.

She wrote: "You asked me about her room, about that apartment. You remember the living room—the ugly furniture, the religious junk on the walls. All right. My mother died of some kind of seizure while she was in bed. I went in and found her. Her face was awful, it was not her face at all or any human face. Her eyes were bulging. I went up to her and saw how it was, and so I went out to call the police. That night you came over. You wanted to take care of me, you said I must be very upset. You looked around the living room and asked me if you could see the bedroom. So I took you in. You were very quiet, you seemed sad. In that room you asked me about her, whether she'd known about me, how she had died, and you were very interested in hearing about it—because you hated her, I think that was the reason. Then you comforted me and put your arms around me, and you insisted that we make love in that bed. You insisted upon that. You begged me. I didn't care because a person can do one thing and then do the opposite, as you know. I didn't have a guilty conscience, because I had been good to my mother, so I didn't care. And while we were making love you asked me about her, about her eyes in particular, which had especially frightened me. Like what? What did she look like? you kept asking. Doesn't this all make you laugh now?"

He was sickened by that letter. "She's lying," he muttered, but at once he thought, "Yes, it was like that."

He reread the letter many times, as if hypnotized by it. He tried to get past the words and into that room again, into the man he had been, who had asked such things and had gotten such pleasure out of them, but what blocked him from entering into that man was not the gap of years between them but some terrified knowledge that he did not dare do that. He did not dare. Better for him to rip up the letter, forget it. Wasn't she blackmailing him already?

And he thought of the letters he had written her so recklessly. Certainly she could use them to blackmail him.

Feeling her power over him across the country, he began to send her things, to buy her off. He sent her some clothes, having them mailed from expensive shops. That ought to please her. And notes with checks enclosed now and then, anything to buy her off, shut her up. What was terrifying was that he had no way of knowing whether this would work, or whether his desperation would make her more bold. Suppose she wrote directly to his wife? Or went to see his father? He had given so much of himself to her, surrendered so much of his power, that she could destroy him if she wanted. And she never replied. What did her silence mean? He reread her letters again and again, lingering over the last one, sometimes lured into an erotic daze and unable to rouse himself—it was so vivid now, so real. Yes, he had certainly done that. He wanted very much to do it again. With Fran he was always too busy to talk, too tired to make love to her, and certainly this was a relief to her—she was not that kind of woman at all—yet his thoughts were preoccupied with his own body and its needs.

He thought, "When my father dies I'll have to go back."

But his father did not die. His father never wrote either. He had to depend for news upon his own telephone calls, put through every Sunday evening. But he kept calling, faithfully. He had become quite a dutiful son now, at the age of forty. And finally Fran said again, "Would you like to visit your father?"

He had overheard her talking with a woman friend one evening, about how hard it was for men to take their fathers' deaths. Fran had been assured that, according to Freud, it was the single most traumatic event in a man's life; therefore, with Marshall, she had to be as sympathetic as possible. His father was not dying yet, Marshall thought, but that seemed almost irrelevant. The old man would die someday . . . perhaps. He pretended to think it over, knowing all along that he would give in and take the trip. It had been nearly a year since the last visit.

Planning for it, he was overcome with a strange lassitude. He would sit in his office and daydreams forced themselves into his mind, as if he were being invaded by an alien, sordid force. He thought of that old flat—which he now remembered clearly—and its clutter: the dishes and underwear lying around, the stockings drying in the bathroom; he thought of Cynthia and what they had done together, which was not at all what he and Fran had ever done together; he thought of the money he had given that woman—it gave him pleasure to think of this—and, lingeringly, he thought of her mother's death, which seemed somehow to have taken place in the room with Cynthia and himself. He was tremendously excited by this. He did not understand it except to know that his body ached and seemed now to be the body of another man. It was hard to maneuver it, even to walk normally. He felt that at any moment he might take a false step, lunge off a sidewalk, bump someone. It was especially difficult to get through an evening with friends because, where once he had been able to imagine himself as a certain person, a successful business executive named Marshall Hughes, now he felt that his internal self had become impatient, as if waking from a long sleep, and might demand recognition.

The more his wife chatted about her friends and her bridge

circle, the more he felt that he loved her and could forget about her. When she talked about the children she was his wife, she belonged to him. She could never disturb him. Their affection was the affection of friends or companions, there was nothing passionate or brutal about it. He loved her. He hated that woman who was blackmailing him, and his body stirred at the thought of her, excited and furious at the same time. Yes, he had to have his revenge on her! He could not spend the rest of his life being blackmailed by a prostitute. . . . And yet, at this thought he would fall off into another of his disturbing dreams, recalling her, shaking his head at the memory of her hair and her plucked eyebrows—she was so common, really—and he had to urge himself awake to get where he was going, to do his work or to reply to his wife, who had begun to look at him a little strangely. So he decided to go back to visit his father.

He wanted to talk with her just once more, to say good-by. He would ask for his letters. Why should she have anything against him? He was prepared to write out one more check, a sizable check, and all she would have to do would be to return his indiscreet letters and promise to forget him . . . it disturbed him to think that she might not forget him. And yet it excited him. On the plane he sat rigid, thinking. It was not quite thinking, perhaps, but planning, groping, inching along as if with his fingers. Of his father he hardly thought; the old man could take care of himself. What did that old man, or any other old man, know of the terrible dangers of life? Marshall nearly wept to think that he had so many years to go before he drifted into the sanctity of old age and death, the final safety, far safer than his suburban life and marriage. "Those old bastards don't let us through. They block things up. They don't move along," he thought in anguish.

His body writhed at the thought of Cynthia, her silent stubborn face, all the secrets she possessed—and at the thought of her body too, which he did certainly hate for its power over him, and had always hated—but there was nothing he could do. His heart pounded strangely. The stewardess leaned over him and assured him that everything was fine, they would be landing soon. Her pretty, proper face reminded him of his wife's face and he was impatient to get rid of her. He did not want to be distracted.

At the airport he took a taxi out at once to her neighborhood. But, for some reason, he asked to be let out a few blocks away. His hands were shaking, he was quite terrified. The cab driver was silent, as if in the presence of a sick man. Marshall's palms were damp with sweat, his entire body was damp, he seemed in a kind of vague, outraged daze. He was both lunging forward and holding himself back. He did not think at all, except to say to himself: "I'll talk her out of it." He walked the several blocks quickly. Down on the sidewalk, he stood for a while staring up at her lighted windows. Again he thought of nothing, not really. His body seemed to be thinking for him. It was protecting all the people who stood behind him, his father, his family, the people who worked for him, the people who were his friends. After a while he went inside and up the stairs to her door. He knocked on it. The knocking echoed jarringly in his brain and he thought of all the letters he had written—so recklessly, and yet perhaps on purpose?—and he thought of the hours he had spent with that woman, losing himself in her, groveling in the darkness of her body and the mastery of her soiled, ugly life, and yet coming from her with no knowledge and no affection, nothing.

The door opened. A child of about twelve, a girl, leaned out and looked at him. "Whatdaya want?" she said.

"Who lives here?" Marshall said. "What—what happened to —Where is—?"

"You want my father?" the girl said.

"But—when did you move in here?"

"Last summer." The girl looked at him, chewing gum. She seemed to see something interesting in his face. "You looking for somebody else?"

He turned away. He began to weep. His breath came in great gulps, as if he had just saved himself from a terrible danger. Descending the stairs, he grasped the bannister and remembered the way she had held onto it, indifferently, lightly, and how, even then, he had wanted to reach over and snap her wrist. But it was better not to think of that. He would never think of it again, nor would he think of his having come to this apartment straight from the airport, drenched in sweat, his body stiffened and monstrous with desire; he would not think of that. When he felt better he called another taxi and went to his father's house.

The old man was about the same, perhaps getting senile. Not much change. He did not die for six years, and then his death was sudden. Marshall was nearly forty-seven at this time and his own health was unsteady, so he had an excuse not to go to his father's funeral. But no one in the family believed him, even Fran did not really believe him, and they held it against him all his life: he was a man who hadn't even bothered with his father's death.

29 *Inventions*

1

"I am dying. I am disappearing. I think about death all the time. Falling asleep I seem to be falling into death . . . dying. . . . I can hear my heartbeat moving away from me. It is inside me and yet moving away. This is a fact. I wake up suddenly and it comes back to me, beating hard. I get out of bed to take away this prize, this beating. I try to get away very quietly so that *he* won't hear me and wake up—if he hears me he sits up and says, *Where are you going? What do you want?* It is like an avalanche, the way he falls on me from his side of the bed."

2

I have not invented her, not all of her. Most of the words are hers. She is forever sitting forward in that chair—a cane-backed chair, very old—with the window to her right, all that glaring filmed-over glass, almost opaque with dirt. She is forever leaning forward to talk to my friend, a psychiatrist. To her I am a stenographer, a nurse, I am another woman and therefore not important. She doesn't bother to look at me. She is forever there in the clinic, deep in Detroit, buildings lying in rubble on either side of that five-story relic. *I am dying. I am disappearing.*

3

I have to invent her face because most of it is gone. The shock of her—the closeness of her to my friend—this unnerved me. I thought there was more distance between a psychiatrist and his patient. I was in disguise as a technician, taking notes for Dr. Geddes. Her face: young and yet not youthful. Premature lines on the forehead from too much frowning, too much fear for her departing heartbeat. She did have very light, fine blond hair. I remember that. She did nothing with it, just brushed it back behind her ears. A nervous habit: her hand darting to her forehead to brush away strands of hair. (Imaginary strands.) At one time—when she was in high school, maybe—she had a big mane of hair, a head of thick blond hair that cascaded down over her shoulders. I was taking notes. I pretended to take notes but really I was drawing faces on a pad. Dr. Geddes had said to me a few days before, *Do you want to encounter real life? Or are you afraid of it?*

4

Afraid.

5

When she began talking I couldn't take notes. Her words rushed out—no shame—it was too direct for me. Her heartbeat began to sound in the room. I could feel its vibrations. Why is that room so small? We were too close together, the three of us. I stared at her large, stunned, blank eyes, that were unseeing on me, and I couldn't take notes. It would have been a betrayal—one woman betraying another.

6

So I will invent most of her: her thinness, her shoulder bones showing through a tight yellow sweater, her hair combed back and fastened with bobby pins (the wrong color—brown and not blond bobby pins), her bare legs and their prickly, flushed look, her toes in open sandals grimy and careless, her purse a soiled yellow (some synthetic material, fake leather), lipstick. . . . No, she wasn't wearing lipstick. Her mouth was small and colorless and it surprised me, opening so desperately, letting out those words I can't forget: *I think about death all the time. Falling asleep I seem to be falling into death.*

7

She is leaning forward earnestly. A trickle of saliva in the corner of her mouth. Staring at my friend's face, the doctor's face, paying no attention to me. She is the kind of woman who thinks other women don't matter; so she won't look at me, I am just a nurse or a secretary, taking notes for the doctor. She never sees me. She only sees him—she stares at him hungrily, anxiously. She is younger than I am. She has a delicate, beautiful face, but the eyebrows are too blond, too faint, and the mouth colorless. It is a weak face, it is either shut tight in a frown or opened in a plea, pleading with the doctor: *If I could see my way clear to leave him. . . . He would like to kill me. . . .*

8

"He is always after me. He wants to make love every day, almost. I feel so tired. I want to get out of there. He lies on top of me and my head goes empty, my neck is ready to snap, I want to scream and scream. . . . And, oh, I always think of . . . I think of him dying too. . . . When he does that. . . . His face gets all twisted and I think of him dying and how I would be free then. . . . I think about running away and then maybe neither one of us would have to die. But I wake up at night and my heart is going like crazy, I'm all sweat and I'm so scared of dying, doctor, I'm scared of going crazy too—what if my heart stopped? It races fast and then it gets faint and goes away inside my ribs, it's like a radio station that is going away and you try to get it back again. . . ."

9

Dr. Geddes: thirty-five years old, a knobby, oblong face, thick eyebrows, dark hair, dark, clever, shrewd, listening eyes.

10

I park my car in a parking lot on Gratiot. The sign for the lot says PARK HERE 75¢. And then in very small letters it says "first half hour." I take the ticket from the attendant, a big black man. The street is busy—the sidewalks busy—people everywhere, cars, trucks, city buses, the smell of the city confining and cozy. It is all so predictable. I park my car and leave the keys inside, and hurry across to the building where he is waiting for me. It is in a block that will be razed for urban renewal. A new clinic will be built on top of all that rubble, lots of glass and concrete and mosaic decorations and plastic lounge chairs and television sets . . . in the center of it Dr. Geddes will stand with his arms folded, a saint.

11

I can see his face, but it is not the face I have described. It is not so clear. He is a fairly tall man and he walks in long, urgent strides. Has he any muscles? I don't know. His eyes are dark, yes. Shadowed and dark. He is thirty-five, I think, though sometimes he looks older. The girl must be ten years younger than he is, at least. Yet she stares at him so hungrily.

12

"If I could see my way clear to leave him. . . ."
She is vague, wispy, imploring. Her eyelids are strangely pink

there are small flakes on them, mixed in with her blond eye-lashes.

Silence.

"He is so heavy at night, in bed. I can't sleep. I think about dying, about sinking into mud or something. . . . I can feel my heart going away. . . . If he wakes up he gets mad."

Dr. Geddes at his desk. Smoking through all this. I am be-hind him, against the inner wall, out of sight. The three of us are very close together though. The room has a high ceiling and it is cracked. A calendar on the wall, but no one believes in the fu-ture. No one has bothered to turn the page over; the end of the month was last Friday. Time yawns here. Outside the window there is nothing. The girl's head moves sleepy and confused. She brushes a strand of hair back from her face. Dr. Geddes, my friend, shakes ashes from his cigarette into a black plastic ashtray.

He says, "And then what?"

"If he wakes up, you mean?"

"Yes, then what?"

"Oh, then . . . then we maybe argue . . . I don't know. . . . I pretend I have to go to the bathroom and hide in there until he falls asleep again. But if he doesn't fall asleep he gets up and. . . . I hate him, I wish he would let me alone. . . ."

"Why?"

She blinks at him. There are tiny flakes of skin on her eye-lashes; she must have a skin infection of some kind. "Why what?"

"Why do you want him to leave you alone?"

"Because. . . ."

13

I saw her out on the street once, walking fast. Long legs, blond hair bobbing about her face, lipstick, bracelets. In a hurry. She looked like a stranger, a girl of about twenty-five. She didn't no-tice me. I was alone, she was alone. Dr. Geddes was not in the city—this wasn't his day for volunteer work, charity work. He was in his own private office in Grosse Pointe, miles away. The girl didn't notice me, but if she had she would not have remembered me, because a woman does not matter to another woman. Her face was tight with frowning, very pale. Her head was filled with wild ideas, like weeds. Her long flaring legs. Her short skirt —I think it was white, and not very clean—her sandals, dirty toes—hair washed and curled and bouncing about her face. This is the girl some man, a husband, burrows into at night and would like to kill.

"Doctor, he wants to kill me. He said if I left him he would find me and kill me."

"Why?"

"Why what?"

"Why do you think he wants to kill you?"

"Because. . . ."

14

At the street corner she paused and turned to look at me. A full, ironic stare. I had just come out the back way from Hudson's, carrying one of their dark gray-green packages. She stared at me and her eyes narrowed a little in recognition. That small careful mouth. The slight arching of her back, one woman showing off her body to another. She stared at me. I hesitated, but she stood there, unmoving, while the light turned green and people moved out around her . . . I couldn't turn away, couldn't pretend I was someone else. I had to walk near her. Her lips moved away from her teeth in a small ironic smile. She whispered, "He doesn't love you! He loves me!"

She reached out and took hold of my wrist and dug her hard little nails into it.

15

I follow her home. She is not the way I remembered her. No, she is not that young—she is probably my age, she is thirty or more. Her hair is bleached. Dark brown at the roots. No, no, that can't be right—she wouldn't have blond eyebrows then, and she does have blond eyebrows; I remember that. Too blond. Flimsy and anemic, that kind of blond. So the hair isn't bleached. Erase that. Change that. A trim, wiry little body, thin wrists and ankles, a long unclean neck. A noble neck. I saw her on the street, I followed her home at a distance. . . . She didn't see me. If she saw me she would not have recognized me. She is in love with Dr. Geddes and never sees me, the nurse. I follow her home now, walking fast as she, keeping in time with her steps, one two three, one two three, swinging her arms, my arms are not free to swing, but my legs are as long and as eager as hers to take her out of this neighborhood, across John R. and a few blocks over, and into an apartment building.

I follow her up the stairs. I float up behind her. I am inside her skull: behind those flaky little moronic eyes! I put the key in the lock, open the door slowly, stealthily, I look around the cluttered kitchen to see if anyone is there. . . . Break-ins in this neighborhood, kids looking for loose change. Kids on dope. She enters the kitchen but does not yet close the door. If someone is hiding in the other room she'll have to get out fast. . . . I paint the kitchen white and then splatter the ceiling and walls with grease. Grease and dust. Designs of dirt like constellations. I tack that calendar on the wall with the pastel Virgin Mary on it, heart exposed, hand lifted in a blessing. I brush the girl's hair for her until it is bristling with electricity. She is a pretty young woman in spite of the frown lines. I walk her into the bathroom where there is a mirror and show her this face, her face. She stares at herself. She touches her face. *I am disappearing*, she says aloud.

16

I don't follow her home.

I saw her on the street but I didn't follow her. I released her. My heart gave a lunge of hatred, seeing her. She is more than ten years younger than he is, too young for him. She stares at him with her face like a water color, asking him to touch her, to kiss her, to smear her with his fingers. "I've got to leave him. I've got to get a divorce," she said last time, on Tuesday. A plea for help. The doctor smoked, frowned, thought about it. No. Not yet. Mustn't break up your family. Mustn't change your life. Too fast. Not now. Regret it later. Talk it over with him. Explain. *Yes, but he shoves me—shoves the table*—Talk to him. Explain. You are sore, you say, your body is sore from him; explain. Take a long bath. Sit in the tub. Warm water. Warm soapy water. Rest. Relax. *Yes, but he gets so mad*—Talk to him. Explain. No divorce. No change of life during counseling. And what about the children?

17

I didn't mention the children—

I invented her with bracelets, even loops of gold in her ears on that day, sandals, a short white skirt, a red pullover blouse, clean hair. All right. But she had two kids with her. Two boys. They looked very thin, thin chests, narrow shoulders. She was walking them fast—why so fast?—the yellow purse pressed against her ribs and her hand on the smaller boy's upper arm, guiding him. He looked panicked, that boy. Why was his mother making him walk so fast? The other boy ran a little ahead of them, in and around people, around a pile of debris at the curb, jumping out onto the curb to avoid a group of black kids, looping out around a parking meter and jumping back onto the sidewalk. Why was she hurrying them? I followed the three of them for a block, then gave up. Let her go. Let her go home and climb the stairs and unlock the door and herd the panting kids inside and rush into the bathroom where she can be alone, pressing her hand to her heart. *I am disappearing!* she cries out at her reflection in the mirror.

18

"They'll come with me. I want them with me."
"How will you support them?"

"Go on ADC."

"You wouldn't qualify."

"Go on welfare then."

"What is the advantage of leaving your husband right now?" She stares at Dr. Geddes. Thinking. Thinking.

"Why should you change your life so radically at this time? Aren't you making progress with me here?"

Staring at him. Thinking. Her eyes film over with panic. Dr. Geddes is wearing a white shirt with narrow blue stripes today, and a dark blue tie. He carries himself cautiously in this building, up the stairs with me—we never take the elevator.

"I don't know—I don't know—" the girl stammers, terrified.

If we got into the elevator together, the door would close upon us and we would be alone, alone together, in a box moving creakily up to the fourth floor of the Metropolitan Clinic. Alone together. No, it is better to take the stairs, which creak too.

Aren't you making progress with me here?

19

She isn't his only patient. I invented a vacuum around her, describing her as if she were his only patient. No. There are many more. I drive downtown on Tuesdays around ten, I go up to his office, I have been invited into his life. This office of his at the clinic is just a desk, a room with a desk, and in the corridor people are always milling around, most of them blacks. Most of his patients here are blacks, yes, but I wasn't interested in them. I picked the white woman to be interested in. I sat through an interview with a black of about forty, a black-purplish face, big nose, watery eyes, bad teeth. Dr. Geddes, fastidious and kind, behind his desk. The desk is small and battered. Other doctors use it. It is Dr. Geddes's on Tuesdays, until late afternoon; for all I know someone else comes in at night and uses it. The calendar isn't his—now someone has turned the page over. It is June. The black man with the bad teeth talked slowly, maddeningly, one morning back in April. I sat and listened. The note pad, the ball-

point pen. I stared at my own feet. The man talked about his
landlord and about a car he had bought. He kept repeating himself. I stopped listening and stared at my feet, afraid that Dr.
Geddes would sense I wasn't listening. *Do you want to encounter
real life?* he had said. Dr. Geddes (which is not his real name)
has the sardonic, weary look of doctors around here—they can't
cure anything, they can only wear themselves out; they turn sour
at the age of forty. But the black man did not interest me. A
woman came in next, a light-skinned black woman in her thirties—heavyset, perfumy, sociable. She wasn't right either. I
wanted someone else. Next came the blond girl, washed-out face
and hair, two kids, scrawny kids she'd brought along with her,
dirt lodged beneath her nails, the odor of panic about her. . . .

20

   "Aren't you making progress with me here?"
   "I don't know—"
   "What do you mean?"
   "I thought it would be—different—I mean, I need some help
with the law, if I get a divorce, I don't know what to do—Sometimes I slide out of bed and go in the bathroom to hide. I can't
stop crying. I'm afraid I'll go crazy. The kids sleep in the front
room so I can't go in there. Sometimes they wake up. Jeffy starts
bawling and then *he* wakes up and gets mad as hell. I want to
die, I guess. I don't want to live with him."
   "But we're making progress here, aren't we?"
   Progress here. Progress. Dr. Geddes eyes her suspiciously. He
doesn't want her to leave that husband. He wants her *there* with
him, in the bed, in the bathroom, barefoot at four in the morning, rubbing her fists into her sore pinkened eyes. . . .

21

   Her husband showed up one day, ten minutes after she arrived.
   His body was clumsy, propelled toward us. Somehow he had

gotten by the girl downstairs. His face was clumsy, flushed, furious. "You the doctor?" he yelled.

Danger.

Real life.

Dr. Geddes got to his feet at once. "You're—?"

The girl began to scream.

"You shut up! Shut it!" the man said to her.

"You're not supposed to be here! You followed me! Oh, you—you—" the girl screamed.

Everything came undone.

I got out of the way, pressed back against the wall. The girl jumped up, tried to run past her husband. He grabbed her. Dr. Geddes said quickly, nervously, "Wait a minute, please. Please. Wait a minute."

"Get the hell out of here, you!" cried the girl.

"You shut up!"

He started to drag her out but then, for some reason, released her. Maybe her screaming frightened him. The guard from downstairs, a policeman, came running up the stairs.

"I think everything is all right now, officer," Dr. Geddes said quickly.

The policeman was a young man. He stared at the husband. A sour smell to that husband—a sports shirt of green and black, designs like tropical vegetation—dark trousers bulging at the stomach. He hadn't shaved for a few days.

This man makes love to her? . . .

"I think it's all right now. Mrs. Pelletier will finish her hour with me . . . Mr. Pelletier can wait for her downstairs. . . ."

The husband was breathing hard.

"Mr. Pelletier? . . ." said Dr. Geddes.

He looked around, baffled. He was not accustomed to that name. Big bulging eyes. He is partly bald and yet his wife is so young; this dismays me. They have two children. She is trapped. She will never get free of him, never.

22

Dr. Geddes and I, standing together, in someone's home. A Saturday evening. We are standing together as if by accident, drawn away from the rest of the party.

"That girl . . . I keep thinking about that girl . . ." he whispers.

"Mrs. Pelletier?"

"I think about her all the time. I wonder. . . ."

I stare at him, surprised. I am leaning forward, eager and vacant.

"I wonder how she can live with him? A son of a bitch like that. . . ."

I want to cross this out; erase these words.

"It's happened before, a few times," he says, avoiding my look. "Falling in love with one of them. They get stuck in your head, their faces, and you can't forget them. . . ."

Then why do you tell her to stay with her husband?

23

Dr. Geddes and his wife, who is his age but looks older. Saturday evening. We are drawn together as if by accident. She moves her wrist watch nervously around her wrist, around and around. She eyes me, assessing me. Dr. Geddes is strained tonight—uneasy at parties. His sardonic look has taken over. His wife is wearing something golden—a disguise. The gold cloth casts its light up on her face. A handsome woman, glowing, gold, but aging. She stares at me. She has been drinking all afternoon. I don't have to invent her ironic glare, her loose wrist watch. Does she know about her husband and me?

She brings her hand around, balled into a fist, and strikes me on the shoulder!

I cry out. Everyone in the room is looking at us.

24

I park the car, take the ticket from the attendant, cross over to the clinic. Men are working next door. It is July, it is very hot. Dust explodes. Heat! Heat! It is a Tuesday. Girls in short dresses walk by slowly, looking at me: a white woman, maybe she has money in that purse? I hurry up the steps and into the foyer, holding my breath because of the smell—is it sewage? The girl at the desk recognizes me, the policeman recognizes me, everyone is very warm and tired. Up the stairs. To the landing: outside, another explosion of dust. Why am I here in this heat and confusion?

People are milling around. A baby is crying.

His wife didn't strike me that night, no. Nothing happened.

25

If you love her, why do you tell her to stay with her husband?

26

But he doesn't love her. I invented that. It is a plot if you imagine people in love—the lazy looping crisscrosses of love, blows, stares, tears. No. It doesn't happen. No love. People meet, touch, stare into one another's faces, shake their heads clear, move on, forget. It doesn't happen.

27

Yesterday he telephoned me. "Where were you on Tuesday?"

A man's attention, a man's stern staring eyes. A white shirt with narrow blue stripes. I run along the street with the two children, eager to be free, to get the hell away from everyone. . . . I will get a divorce. A divorce. All that talk about "divorce" was my own invention; the girl never said the word herself. They don't say that word. It is too legal for them, it means lawyers and the city courthouse and fees and papers, birth certificates, police, trouble. She wants to get the hell out but she doesn't want a divorce. I gave her the idea, the word. I was sitting there, blond and panicked, leaning forward but not staring at Dr. Geddes (who is an ordinary man) but at the woman sitting behind him taking notes. Was she a nurse? A secretary? That is the best chair in the room, back there. Outside there is an air hammer. It hammers inside your skull. It is like a heartbeat. But which heart is it—hers or mine? At first she complained about her heart beating too faintly, then too loudly. Which is which? Did I make it up, or did I forget something she said in between?

He telephoned me yesterday and said, "Are you coming down tomorrow?

I park the car, cross the street, go up the stairs. It is already after ten. The door is ajar and he is inside, at the desk. . . . I stand out in the corridor, watching him. Yes, an ordinary man. The face of a weak king. Sallow skin. Or is it the light? A baby is crying, a young white woman is talking sharply to the baby, rocking it in her arms. Do I love that man? Do I want to love him? I stand out in the corridor and my mind is wild with the noise from the baby and the construction next door and what sounds like an alarm clock ringing. It is only a telephone ringing, with a strange persistent ring. . . . Do I love him, am I jealous of him? Do I want him to die so that all this will be over? I am inventing him as I stand in the corridor, erasing one man and inventing another. I want to be free of him and of the girl and of her husband, who shoves her around.

Dr. Geddes glances up at me. He is startled. "What? . . . Come in!" he says, standing.

I enter the little office.

"She didn't show up today," he says, indicating the chair.

An empty chair facing him.

"She didn't telephone. Last time, you weren't here, she was talking pretty wild . . . I wonder. . . . I wonder what's going on. . . ."

"What did she say?"

"It was hard to make sense of it. One of her children got hit by a truck, he walked right into it—she said he was drugged, he was taking heroin. They took him to 'Receiving' and—"

"Taking heroin?"

"That's what she said. They took the boy to get stitched up, then on the way home her husband started fighting with her. She came in here looking worn out, I think she's taking something herself . . . she could hardly keep her eyes open. . . ."

"Her son is taking heroin? At that age?"

A haze seems to pass before my eyes. Dr. Geddes keeps on talking but I can't hear him.

"But what are you going to do?" I ask him.

"Well. . . ."

"Should you send a policeman over or something?"

"Well, no. I'll wait."

"How long? She's twenty minutes late."

"I mean I'll wait until next week."

"You don't think it's dangerous?"

"Why?"

"I mean with her—"

"That she might get hurt? Or hurt herself? No."

"But how can you be sure?"

"I'm reasonably sure."

"Don't they ever kill themselves, your patients?"

He shrugs his shoulders irritably.

"How would it affect you, if a patient killed himself?" I ask him.

"They do. Occasionally."

"How did it affect you?"

"I survived."

He smiles bitterly.

Someone is coming in—but it must be a mistake, it is a black woman with a very old man. They gape at us, apologize, back out.

"Why don't you sit down?" says my friend. "It's very hot outside, isn't it?"

I sit in the patient's chair.

I look across the battered little desk at Dr. Geddes. From here he looks different—his face more oblong, his nose a little lumpy. *I am dying. I am disappearing. Help me, please!*

28

The husband was picked up for murder. The wife was killed, stabbed with a kitchen knife. Dr. Geddes tells me all this when we meet by accident, months later. It is September. Dr. Geddes speaks quickly and professionally, as if he were dictating notes to me. *She never did come back,* he says. We stare over each other's shoulders. A terrible tension rises between us, stinging as sweat, but we do not acknowledge it. We do not look at each other. He goes on to talk about his busy, difficult schedule, and about the clinic. "Christ, it's one thing after another. . . . Did you read about the electricians' strike? The work will be held up indefinitely because of those goddamn unions."

29

September never came.

It is still July.

I sit in the patient's cane-backed chair and dream above the air hammer outside. One of the chair's legs is shorter than the others, or uneven somehow. The chair wobbles. Dr. Geddes and I stare at each other in silence. *I, I, I could make you happy! I am the only woman who could make you happy!* But it is not true. It is a lie I dream to myself, sitting here, alone with a man. . . . I will add five years to Dr. Geddes's face. Yes. He is really about forty; his youth is finished. Drained away. I will make his dark hair thinner, especially on the top. I will imagine small stiff whiskers in his ears, faunlike and coarse. Good. Look at that! He puts his hand against his chest, the upper part of his stomach. He has ulcers, this successful doctor. Psychiatrists' suicide rate is ten times that of the normal population. They die, they close their folders, they relinquish their practice to younger men, they die, they die, they stop listening, they stick their fingers in their ears and go deaf, the lights go out, the air hammer is disconnected, the electricians rush into the building and unhook everything, cut the wires, tear the telephone out by the roots.

The girl doesn't show up.

I sit in her chair and feel the heat all about me. I think.

Yes, I will erase Dr. Geddes too. It is a failure, our love. It didn't happen. No elevator; we always took the stairs, chastely. I will erase him too. He wasn't there that morning when I arrived, ten minutes late. The door to his office was closed and locked. I stood there, stunned. Why hadn't he come? He had just telephoned me the day before, to make sure I would meet him. What was wrong? . . . But he wasn't there. I wandered along the corridor, bewildered, hurt. I looked out the window at the skyline of Detroit, which is not a skyline but just buildings, gaseous and plain, pressed in close. Why hadn't he come? I stand there, alone, bewildered, feeling a little sick. . . .

No, he doesn't show up.

And the girl doesn't show up.

I wait a while. The corridor is noisy. A young man in shirt sleeves—one of the doctors—asks me whom I am waiting for. I am dressed too well for this place, but my manner is that of a victim.

Ten-thirty.

Quarter to eleven.

Well, it is finished. The end. My face is flushed with disappointment, humiliation. I am a woman who has been humiliated. I go downstairs and outside. I cross over to the parking lot and pay the attendant—he charges me $1.50, for nothing!—I get in my car. I sit there for a minute, staring over at the clinic. Maybe Dr. Geddes will appear, hurrying? . . .

Maybe the girl will appear? . . .

No one. Nothing. I am alone.

And so I erase them both, I kill them off. They are gone. They never existed. The next time I drive through this neighborhood the clinic itself will have been torn down: good riddance! In the sunlight the city itself is shimmering and unclear. The rubble vibrates, the pavement vibrates. Is that a crack in the street? The parking lot attendant's little cabin tilts suddenly, about a yard on one side. It is the end of this city. The city is caving in. The end of the world. I am erasing them all—erasing Detroit—the dust rises in puffing explosions to erase everything. Myself, I am dying. I am disappearing. I can hear my heartbeat moving away from me. I am a process that is dying, disappearing, moving away.

Of all of us, only you remain.

*P*roblems of Adjustment in Survivors of Natural / Unnatural Disasters

This is a picture of some mountains.

This is the road the people took, driving up—that's our car by the tree. The dog is in the back seat.

This is the same mountains but at night. That's the moon. The brush was still dirty from something else so the white got dirty and I couldn't fix it. The road is that black line like a ribbon. At night roads are black if they are real blacktop roads, but regular pavement is a light color and so is a dirt road like the one by our house. So I colored that wrong. I looked out my window last night to check and it was light-colored, not black. So that was a mistake.

That is a boy standing with his back to us. It isn't me, it's a boy I don't know. It's hard to paint hair. I meant that hair to be colored black but it doesn't look like hair on his head. It isn't me because my hair is brown. The boy's name is William. He's standing very still, listening for something—he knows someone is behind him. He knows something is going to hit him in a minute, on the back of his head. There will be screaming and blood. But he's afraid to turn around.

This is a picture of things falling down. The tops of the mountains are falling down like rain and rocks and parts of houses, and they all pile up at the bottom, where people are lying. You can't see the people because all that stuff is on top of them.

This is a picture of the boy, sitting at a table. I put his face smiling because he is eating breakfast and doesn't know the rock is going to come hit him on the back of the head.

I don't want to look at this one—this one is ugly—I had to cover up parts of it when I painted it and I couldn't do the face except for the mouth. The mouth is just a black hole. It would make a lot of noise, the hole in the face.

2

"The first one is of mountains," Sylvia said, holding a large poster-sized piece of paper for Donald to see. Donald took it from her and studied it, frowning: a crude water color of peaks and slopes, hardly more than angry, careless strokes done with a brush. The main colors were blue and brown. "Dr. Belitt said he was indifferent when he explained the paintings. His voice was flat and toneless. I told Dr. Belitt he was always that way with me, but Dr. Belitt said he could be quite excitable at times—but when he talked about the paintings he seemed to go dead. Do you see the car in the corner, at the bottom? Do you remember which car that's supposed to be?"

"My blue Volkswagen," Donald said.

"And that white blob is Rififi, in the back seat. See it? I told you Roy would remember her, I told you it isn't that easy to erase a dog from a child's memory, just like that. It's interesting that he has the times right—we did have that car when we had Rififi. Would you have remembered it yourself?"

"No. Maybe," Donald said.

He was strangely disappointed. He had thought his son could draw better than this. He stared at the painting and tried to imagine Roy bent over it, making those reckless jagged lines. But he had not seen Roy for nearly a year, and he could remember only a smiling, red-cheeked child, the child of the snapshot he carried everywhere with him in his wallet.

Sylvia picked up another painting from the immense, circular, glass-topped coffee table, which was comfortably cluttered with glossy magazines and new hard-cover books in bright dust jackets, and ceramic birds—peacocks, doves, swans. This painting was warped. Donald flinched at it, disturbed by the big moon in the sky, like a human head, streaked with water-color green. The moon was clumsily done. Evidently Roy had tried to erase the green and had painted over it with white, but it looked soiled and heavy. "I see—that's the same scene as the first one. But at night," Donald said quickly. He spoke before Sylvia could explain; he wanted her to know how close his imagination was to Roy's. And he resented a little her careful, methodical voice. She was being very polite. He was being very polite. "Yes, those are the mountains at night, and down there is the car again. He must have been very angry, painting both pictures. The road is so thick and black, the mountain peaks look so sharp. . . . What did he tell the doctor about this one?"

"That he made a mistake with the road. That it should have been lighter—he looked out the window here to check. It was meant to be the road outside this house."

"This house? But why the mountains, and why aren't there other houses around?"

Donald took the painting from her. He was disturbed by all the streaks, the heavy flat black road, the dirty moon. It seemed to him he could remember Roy drawing better when he was only three or four; now he was seven.

"I don't know," Sylvia said.

"What does the doctor say about that? That he draws us up

in the mountains, with no other houses around, that it takes place at night—were we ever up in the mountains with him at night? What sense does it make?"

"I don't know," Sylvia said.

"Jesus, why don't you ask!" he said, suddenly exasperated. "Don't you want Roy to get over this? You should ask as many questions as you can."

Sylvia responded immediately, as if she had been waiting for him to say this. "You aren't paying for this. You don't have to complain."

"I know I'm not paying for it. But I would be happy to pay for it—for part of it, anyway—as much as I can afford—" He was speaking angrily. He paused and forced himself to be calm. He was not going to let her upset him, not going to let her icy, civilized, superior politeness tease him into a rage. That was finished. "I did offer to pay a little," he said.

"I'm sorry, I shouldn't have brought that up," Sylvia said. "It's just that this is so terrible . . . so crazy. . . . I mean, the situation is crazy," she said, frightened at her own words. Donald understood perfectly her confusion and did not take advantage of her by looking up. He turned the painting in his hands, pretending to examine it more closely. Sylvia said, faltering, "Eliot has been wonderful about it, and you know he has two girls of his own . . . twelve and fourteen years old . . . he has to pay for their tuition to some fantastic school up the coast, where the bill for their modern dance lessons alone is *fifty dollars a week* . . . and his ex-wife is very bitter, very stubborn. But he's never complained about Dr. Belitt's fee. He's said that he can afford it, that's all. He never mentions you."

"That's very generous of him," Donald said ironically.

"Yes, it is generous."

But he was not going to let her tempt him into irony. As a child Donald had been clever and sarcastic, as a young man he had cultivated a withering ironic style, priding himself on his wit—and now, an adult, he had to consciously resist sarcasm. He disliked it in others and especially in himself. For several years he had taught basic courses in anthropology at the University of Southern California, and he had come to loathe the dry, cold, all-knowing sound of his own public voice, that devastating whine that had been his most effective teaching trick. His students had appreciated his wit, they had been a most flattering audience. But he had grown to hate his classroom personality. He could not bear it, the sterility of his lecturing and the adulation of his students, who would bring visitors to his class, ready to laugh sharply and daringly at his jokes.

"I appreciate his generosity," Donald said sincerely.

"It's too bad you can't meet him this time, Donald," Sylvia said earnestly. "But he thinks he should stay up in Vancouver until they finish this part of the film; you know, it's costing so many thousands of dollars a day, the whole thing has become so complicated, I can't even get it straight. He's very sorry not to be here. He does want to meet you sometime."

"Yes, sometime. That would be fine," Donald said. "What is that next picture? Is that Roy himself?"

She held it up. It was of a child with his back turned, a child with a long, thin neck and a head of black hair, crudely painted. The boy's clothes were all blue. He wore no shoes. The background had been left blank, so that the figure floated in air.

"He insists it isn't him, but a boy named William," Sylvia said. She spoke gently looking down at the painting as if she were looking at Roy himself. "The doctor asked if we knew anyone named William but I said I didn't think so, unless it was a boy at school or from our other neighborhood. But William is such a formal name for a child. . . . Of course it's Roy himself. He says the boy is aware of someone behind him who is going to hit him. He's going to be hit on the back of the head very hard. But he's afraid to turn around and look."

Donald leaned forward to examine the picture. He didn't take it from her.

"Yes. Well," he whispered.

The boy was painted in stiff, pained strokes, little choppy lines. Evidently Roy had spent some time on it. Except for the heavy black circle that was meant to be the boy's hair, the painting was fairly good. The shoulders and torso were in the right proportion; the legs were thin but not too long; the neck gave the impression of being very vulnerable, of seeming to listen. The boy's hands were at his sides, small fists. It was a disturbing picture because it suggested terror. He would have understood it, Donald thought, if he had seen it somewhere else, anywhere, and had not known it was by his own son.

"He must have done this at another session, on another day," Donald said slowly. "It looks quite different from the first two."

"Yes, that's right," Sylvia said. "He did this one at home. He spent hours on it."

"Did he show it to you?"

"No. But he didn't try to hide it."

"Did you ask him what he was painting?"

"No. I didn't want to make him self-conscious."

"So the boy is standing like this, listening . . . ? Waiting for someone to hit him?"

"For the woman to hit him with the rock," Sylvia said flatly. "For me to hit him with the rock."

She began to cry.

Donald looked away. The living room of this house was enormous—flooded with sunshine, festive and shouting with color, more ceramic birds at the other end of the room, a bust of a women who might have been Sylvia, though very stylized, done in black; on the walls thick paint-encrusted squares and rectangles, some of them edged with gleaming metallic strips. One wall of the room was glass and looked out onto the pool and a number of small palm trees.

Donald fumbled for cigarettes, extricated one, and then hesitated like someone in a movie—he remembered that his wife had stopped smoking a few years ago, before the divorce, and he wondered if he should smoke now, so selfishly, in front of her. She had been very agitated for weeks, unable to sleep, miserable. He sat with the cigarette between his fingers, embarrassed.

"Please smoke, it's all right," she said.

"It isn't necessary," he said.

"Eliot still smokes—"

"No." He mashed the cigarette back into the package.

She was still crying. She got to her feet and left the room, walking slowly, with the calm, poised gait he remembered from many years ago, though her long tanned arms and legs were something new, and the careful elegance of her head was unfamiliar. He had always admired her sanity, her control. He believed she was in control of herself at this moment but he thought he should follow her. Now that they were no longer married, he must behave politely and conventionally toward her, as he would toward any woman.

He glanced hurriedly through the last three paintings. One was of a number of streaks, blue and green and red, like lightning, an indecipherable painting. Another showed a stick-child sitting at a table, with a round face and a grin. The last was very messy, stained, the figure of a human being that was evidently female, since it was wearing a dress. Its face was blank and soiled, like the moon, except for a large black hole where the mouth should have been.

Donald shuddered and let the painting fall back onto the table.

3

Walking with Roy down the enormous sloping lawn, holding Roy's hand: it was a little awkward because he didn't remember having held the boy's hand very often back in the days when he was Roy's full-time father. Sylvia must have held it.

"Do you like all the flowers here? All the trees? This is a beautiful place, isn't it?" Donald asked.

Roy seemed to assent. Then he asked shyly, "Do you like it where you live now?"

"I don't live in any particular place. But I like all the places I stay in."

"Where are you now?"

"Right here," Donald said cheerfully.

But he felt his son's subtle, dignified rejection of this joke.

"I'm traveling back and forth from Belfast to a village near Dublin, called Howth," Donald said seriously. "My things are in Howth, in an old broken-down cottage right on the water. On the edge of a cliff. But I spend a lot of my time up in Belfast, taking notes for a study I want to do. Didn't your mother tell you about this?"

Roy did not reply.

"I'm sure she told you; didn't Mommy say I was flying back to visit? To see how you are?"

Again Roy said nothing. His gaze seemed to skim the tall palm trees at the border of the lawn, avoiding Donald. He was very quiet, cautious. His hand lay in his father's hand without emphasis.

"Mommy lent me the keys to her new car," Donald said. "This looks like a great car, do you like it? I'm glad she finally got a yellow convertible—she always wanted a yellow convertible— Do you like your mother's new car?"

Try to get him to talk, Sylvia had begged.

He was taking Roy out for a drive, to be alone with him. But he felt rather awkward, even a little intimidated, at the thought of being alone with this child of his. The Roy he remembered had been a little boy, easily cheered up, easily handled. This boy was no longer little, really, no longer childlike; he seemed stiff, prematurely self-conscious. Donald wondered if he should speak seriously and frankly to Roy, or whether he should continue to ask him light, casual questions. Roy was not exactly well, but he was not sick either. Certainly he looked fine: in fact, he looked healthier than Donald remembered. His fair, blond-brown hair was thick and wavy; his cheeks were tinged with red, like those of the Celtic children Donald saw so often now; he was a boy who looked normal, destined for sports and the friendship of other boys. But he was not normal.

Donald said, smiling, "Mommy explained to you, didn't she, that I was coming to visit you for a week? That I was a little worried about you?"

"No," Roy said tonelessly.

"What do you mean, no?"

"She isn't here."

"Who isn't here?"

"Mommy."

"Then who told you I was coming?—who just said good-by to us?"

Roy made a careless jerking gesture with his head, back toward the house. "*She* did."

"Who?"

"Her."

Donald stooped to take him by the shoulders. Not to shake him, not in exasperation, not pleading; he simply held Roy and looked him in the face. Eye to eye. Must make contact, sane contact. The basis of all communication. "Who told you?" he asked gently.

"The one up there."

He was patient. He really did not think Roy could keep this up much longer.

"Up there . . . ?"

"Up in the house."

"But who is that, up in the house? That is your mother, isn't it?"

"No. She isn't here."

"Your mother isn't here?"

"No."

"What happened to her?"

Roy shrugged his shoulders, as if this question had no answer.

Donald looked at him and saw his own eyes, his own skin, even a stubborn, set expression that he'd noticed in himself in occasional photographs. He resisted the impulse to shout into his son's face.

He decided to change the subject; he asked Roy where he would like to go. "To the ocean," Roy said automatically. He might have planned to give this answer all along. He might have been waiting to be asked. But Donald said, "Fine. Sounds fine," and they got in his ex-wife's car, which smelled expensive and creaked with newness. It was a Mercedes convertible and Donald wondered how much it had cost. *But he remembered the old Volkswagen,* Donald thought with satisfaction.

Donald drove around the circular driveway, past banks of lush, cream-colored roses and trumpet-shaped red flowers on long spindly green stalks, flowers he'd never really liked in the past, though he could appreciate their explosive, oversized beauty. He had never known their names. Southern California had not seemed so magnificent to him years ago. He was a little disoriented because of the cloudless sky, the windless day, the perfect, still sun: all this struck him as gigantically beautiful, overpowering. When he and Sylvia had been married, they had lived in an ordinary high-rise apartment building in central Los Angeles, far from the Hollywood Hills where his wife now lived. At first he had been sharply jealous of her new marriage, her surprising good luck, as much as he had heard from mutual friends. Then he had written to wish her well, remembering when they had always wished each other well, before the emotional complications.

Out on Mulholland Drive he asked Roy how he liked the hills. Roy said he liked the hills very much. All this while he was adjusting the safety belt, a harnesslike contraption. "The air is very fresh up here; that's a surprise," Donald said. Roy nodded, buckling the belt and pulling it tight across his lap and chest. Donald saw that the Drive was nearly built up now, that new houses crowded one another, all of them elaborate and expensive ranch houses. In the distance more hills had been bulldozed and subdivisions laid out. Houses had even been constructed over the edges of steep hills, propped up on what appeared to be stilts. So precarious, so dreamily absurb!—Donald felt a tinge of alarm, almost of panic, at the sight of those houses. He hoped Roy would not notice.

But Roy did not seem to notice anything, was hardly looking around; he fussed with the seat belt, frowning. Donald tried to hide the irritation he felt. He said, "That's a nice house your stepfather bought. I like it. If it were on the water, like the place I rent, it would be perfect. Do you use the swimming pool much?"

Roy must have decided that the belt was on properly, because he looked up. "No," he said vaguely.

"Why not?"

"He was teaching me how to swim, then he stopped."

"That's too bad, because it's very important to learn to swim. After you're grown up," Donald said, hearing the pomposity in his voice but unable to stop, "it's very difficult. You should learn how to swim now, Roy."

"They think I'm sick," Roy said tonelessly.

Donald drove along the narrow, unpaved road, wondering what he should say now. It was very important that he say the right thing. "But you're not sick . . . ?" he said softly.

Roy shrugged his shoulders.

"Roy, I was very worried about you when I heard what had happened. I was out of reach for three days, then when I heard about it. . . . The earthquake, and that vase or whatever it was that fell over . . . it was an urn, wasn't it, from Mexico? The one I brought back, with the condors and bulls painted on it? It must have been a terrible shock, to be struck by that thing. Without any warning, just struck by it and knocked unconscious. . . . Thank God it wasn't anything heavier."

Roy said nothing.

As they drove down out of the hills Donald glanced at his son, who seemed to be getting nervous. He licked his lips, then gnawed at his lower lip. His toes appeared to be squirming inside his canvas shoes. Finally Donald asked, "Is something wrong?"

"The seat belt," Roy muttered.

"Is it too tight?"

"Yours. S'posed to have it on. . . ."

Donald did not protest. He did something he would never have bothered to do in the past—braked to a stop at the side of the road and buckled the seat belt. It was a trivial enough thing to do for his son.

"How's that?" he said cheerfully.

"You're always s'posed to have them on," Roy muttered, embarrassed.

Donald headed west, toward the ocean, into the bright glaring sun. He had become accustomed to the misty, changeable skies of Ireland, and he thought perhaps it was easier to live in a less illuminated world. He no longer felt at home here. But Roy stared ahead, not flinching from the glowing light; in a way sightless, untouched. He was not even as tanned as Sylvia. Donald sensed that his son was waiting, patiently, waiting for Donald to begin arguing with him. But he would not argue. He would talk only about safe, pleasant matters. "Do you have any special friends where you live now?" he asked.

"A boy named Mike, and another boy named Ramie," Roy said. He spoke flatly, as if giving information he knew did not matter. "I like them both."

"Do you like the new school?"

Roy hesitated, as if trying to remember the new school. He had attended several in the last few years, Donald knew, because Sylvia had moved after the divorce and then again and then once again, and finally up to the Hills, to her present address. Donald had received notices from the post office telling of her changes of address. He had filed them all in chronological order.

"I like all the schools," Roy said without emphasis.

A careful, cautious child, Donald thought. It was like an interview.

"Do you like Dr. Belitt?" Donald asked.

Roy shifted inside the safety harness. He looked out the side window now, at a thick wall of trees, spidery limbs that passed in neat, silent plunges. There was a rich fragrance to the air, mingled with the odor of exhaust from the other cars. Donald glanced at his son's profile and thought it both stubborn and vulnerable. Like the beggar children of Dublin, those prematurely shrewd, perplexed, filthy faces: those pathetic children who sat on the sidewalks near the expensive hotels at night, waiting passively for coins to be dropped into their laps.

"Roy, why are you saying those things about your mother?" Donald asked suddenly.

Roy did not move. He did not look back at Donald. It was evident from his rigidity that he had been expecting this question all along.

"Your mother is alive. You know she's alive. She hasn't gone away anywhere—your mother is with you, as always, and you know it. Your mother did not throw anything at you. The urn fell by itself, there was an earthquake, you know very well what happened. Why are you saying those things about her?"

Roy did not answer. Donald wanted to shake him, to shout at him—but he forced himself to remain calm. He had not flown thousands of miles just to lose his temper. "Roy . . . ?" he whispered. He touched the boy's shoulder gently. Experimentally. How did you touch a child—should your fingers close tightly on him, or should they be light, unthreatening?

His son gave no resistance, as if he would have accepted any kind of caress or any blow.

"Your mother loves you very much and you've upset her with the things you say. I love you too, Roy, very much, though I can't get over here to see you often—and I'm very upset too, very worried. Can you talk to me, Roy? Can you talk about it? I know you're going to be well again. . . ."

"I'm not sick," Roy said faintly.

"No, not the way you were at first, when you were in the hospital, no," Donald said carefully. "You had a minor concussion and now you're over that. You got over it very well. But there is something else that's wrong, isn't there?"

Roy appeared to be thinking. He shifted his position nervously but did not reply.

"You see Dr. Belitt every day, don't you?—to help you with something that seems to be wrong?"

Roy did not answer, and Donald, trembling, released him and said nothing for the rest of the drive until they reached the ocean. He drove up along the highway for a while, looking for a place to turn onto the beach. This took all his concentration. He felt jumpy, frustrated; he kept missing turns. Finally he turned into a paved drive that led out to the beach and the sound of the waves comforted him: he felt he was presenting a powerful argument to his son just by bringing him here. He had always loved the ocean, the noise of the waves and the lovely silence inside that pounding, which had nothing human about it, nothing petty or confusing. . . . He parked the car in the crowded lot and said cheerfully, "Should we get out and walk a little?"

But Roy shook his head.

"No? Why not? It's a lovely day."

Roy said nothing.

"You're not afraid of the water, are you? We used to take you swimming when you were very little. . . . You used to laugh like crazy when the water tickled your toes. Do you remember? Do you remember how Mommy squealed, how we had to splash her?"

Roy nodded.

"You do remember? You remember how the three of us used to go swimming?"

"Yes," Roy said.

But he did not want to get out of the car. He stared out at the other people—most of them young mothers with small children —and sat motionless. Donald unbuckled his own seat belt. He wondered what to do. A young couple passed nearby, barefoot, the long-haired young man carrying an infant in his arms. Roy seemed to be watching them.

"You're living in a paradise, Roy," Donald said softly. "This part of the world, in spite of what people say, is really a paradise. . . . I know what I'm talking about because I've been everywhere, I've seen children starving, dying, in the mud . . . with people just walking around and paying no attention. . . . I've seen boys your age who will never be well again. . . . The city I visit now, the city I'm writing about, is really at war, and every night bombs explode, people are shot, children wake up screaming from bad dreams. . . . Did your mother tell you what I'm doing? Where I am?"

He realized that he had used the past tense, speaking of Roy's mother.

"She had pins on a map," Roy said.

"She did? What? Pins on a map?"

"She had maps up on the wall and she put pins in, to show where you were. That was at the other house."

Donald tried to keep the surprise out of his voice. "Before you moved to where you live now?"

"At the other house. The green pins showed where you used to be, like Mexico and Tokyo, and the white pin showed where you were right then . . . so we could keep track. . . . She said you would never go to a place where there wasn't a map for it. So I would always know where you were. She promised that."

"Then what happened?"

"She went away." Roy's voice was detached and conversational.

"No, Roy. What happened?"

"She went away. She isn't there."

"*She?* Your mother?"

"Yes."

"When did she go away? After the earthquake?"

"She screamed at me but I didn't see her. When I woke up I was in the hospital and she was gone."

Donald stared at him, baffled. "But didn't she come to see you in the hospital?"

"Somebody else came," Roy said without emphasis.

"Another woman?"

Roy nodded.

"But your mother is still here," Donald said. He was beginning to feel alarmed, as if this might not be a matter of conversation, of gentle, logical argument, the careful arranging of words. Outside the car children were running and squealing with laughter. The couple with the infant were down at the water's edge; Roy was still watching them. "You must know that. She's been with you all along—the same woman— You were having breakfast and there was a very small earthquake, and that thing fell forward and hit you, that Mexican urn—you were stunned, knocked unconscious—it must have been very frightening— I can understand that. Your mother ran into the kitchen when the earthquake began, and evidently she was screaming—she tried to get to you but the urn struck you on the back of the head— That was what happened. You understand, don't you? It wasn't a rock, it was a vase. Your mother didn't throw anything at you. Your mother loves you and has always loved you—"

"She went away," Roy said in his flat, unarguing, dead voice.

Donald rubbed his face. "Oh Jesus," he whispered to himself.

He lit a cigarette. Roy sat beside him quietly, his fingers hooked into the belt that cut tightly across his lap. He was watching the couple with the infant down at the shore. The young man with the long, straight hair was tossing the child into the air and catching it.

4

That night Donald and Sylvia washed their son, together, crowded into the small bathroom adjacent to his room, and put him to bed. It was a ritual they had performed many times in the past, but Donald had the peculiar idea that he himself had really not participated in it. Another father had helped another woman, the child's mother, with the child's pajamas, feeling himself a little in the way, but pleased to be helping. He could recall these people doing certain things, he could recall the child's mechanical raising of his arms over his head.

The child was older now, taller. Sturdier. His face had grown sturdier, set in that polite calm expression. The mother was older too, but surprisingly more vulnerable, even with her new fashionable hair and her manicured nails; she kept asking Roy trivial little questions, peering anxiously at him, smiling at him, as if she were an impostor anxious to play her role well. Roy was polite to her, never quite meeting her eye, obeying her with the mechanical meek irony of a child who is trapped and has decided not to fight. When he was in his pajamas, Sylvia squatted before him to kiss him good night, and he submitted politely. Then Donald bent over him to kiss him too. Roy looked at him and said, "Are you leaving tonight?"

"No, not so soon. Didn't I tell you I'd be staying for a few days?"

"Are you leaving in the morning?"

"No," Donald said, surprised. "I'm going to spend a few days with you."

Afterward they wandered out to the kitchen and Sylvia asked if he wanted coffee. Donald sat down gratefully at the table; he was too restless to be alone, and the kitchen seemed the most cheerful part of the house. Altogether it was a striking house, but rather impersonal and glaring, like a museum stocked with the latest art.

Sylvia's back was to him. She said casually, "That's where he was sitting."

Donald started. Then he looked around, behind him, at the open-backed shelves of dark green plastic that served as a screen from the other part of the kitchen. Each rectangular shape was of a different size from the others, routinely filled with objects— spice jars, a ceramic dove, a pot of cascading ivy with neat, polished leaves. Donald guessed that the tallest shelf must have con-

tained the Mexican urn. He could almost see it again: dull, mud-
colored, quite coarse and primitive, decorated with the shapes of
condors and bulls and horses. He had bought it for one dollar in
a village near the Yucatan on his first study-trip to Mexico in
1966.

"The urn was just one thing," Sylvia said. "Everything fell
over—all over the house—everything that could break did break—
I thought it was the end of the world. I thought the house would
collapse on us and we'd be buried beneath the rubble. Roy and
me." She smiled sadly at Donald, and he breathed in deeply and
then exhaled, repeating her smile, gently, to show her how he
sympathized.

"Jesus, it's crazy. The things that happen," he said.

They drank the coffee together and ate muffins Sylvia said
contained no artificial preservatives, bought at a health-food store
on Sunset Boulevard. Donald was warmed by the desire, which
he discovered gradually in himself, to make friends with this interesting woman.

She talked about Roy, frankly and without emotion. She was
Donald's age exactly, thirty-six, but she looked younger. He was
pleased with her California self, this slender, tanned near-beauty
who was something of a stranger to him. During the years of
their marriage Sylvia had been different to him, with him, in relationship with him; she had been somehow secondary to him
and his work—a minor personality in a way, though he had
never exactly assessed her like that. Perhaps because she had
never finished college and he had done graduate work in both
sociology and anthropology, perhaps because he was accustomed
to women colleagues at the university who were much more confident and articulate than his wife—for some reason he had never
considered her a personality in herself. She had been girlish, shy,
uncertain of herself, quick to notice sarcasm in his voice when
he hadn't meant to be sarcastic; near the end of their marriage
she had nagged him with a reckless plodding indifference about
the girls who admired him at the university. "They have nothing

to do but admire men like you because they don't know any better," he remembered her saying. How stupid her accusations had been, how tedious! He had never been able to convince her that he hadn't cared about being admired, not by anyone, not for his academic work. But if he had said that, he would also have rushed on to say that no one's admiration—no one's love—was really important to him any longer. And he had not been able to say those words.

Sylvia asked him about his work, sitting with him in this easy, confidential friendliness; she seemed genuinely interested in the book he was writing. Now that they were not connected by attorneys' letters and checks and the frightening hints and innuendos that came third hand from mutual friends, they were quite cordial, relaxed, like people in a train who know they will be leaving one another soon. Donald sensed her approval of him and he found it easy to approve of her, to like her. He kept thinking of the maps she had put up to show where he had traveled. But of course he would not mention this, because it might embarrass her.

"What you're doing sounds very interesting, but depressing," Sylvia said.

"Oh, yes, I could let it depress me, but actually writing about something is a way of transcending it," Donald said. "That isn't evident to the reader. It never was to me, but now I understand. . . . The writer puts everything in his writing, all the bewilderment and convolutions and despair, but he leaves out the vision of himself writing. That's invisible, that's what you don't get. So you have the wrong idea. . . . I'm going to bring together the Northern Ireland business with other things I've worked on, the survival mechanism, why some people survived in the Nazi concentration camps and others didn't," Donald said excitedly. "But right now I'm so deep in it I can't seem to get things clear. . . ."

"So you're settled in Howth for a while? Are all your books in one place now?"

"My books are all over hell," Donald said. "I have a few boxes with my publishers in London; they've been very nice—the place is like a warehouse and my junk doesn't disturb anything. Then a few things are with Ken Hanson—you know, in Rome—where he has a marvelous big flat. The things I have in Howth aren't really what I need most—I keep buying the same things all the time, a dictionary, pots and pans and cheap silverware, typewriters—"

"What happened to that little portable of yours?"

"That disintegrated. Before I left New York I bought an electric typewriter, but it didn't work in Europe—so I bought a cheap portable and then I couldn't get ribbons for it—so I gave up and bought another. So it goes," he said helplessly.

Sylvia smiled a slight, teasing smile. "But you like your life now. Obviously you're very happy with all that traveling. Aren't you? And you're getting famous. Friends of ours—I mean Eliot's and mine," she said gracefully, lowering her voice—"read your article in the *Atlantic*, about the children in Belfast. It was very powerful, heartbreaking, like fiction—I mean, it seemed almost to be written from the inside, like fiction. Did those children really tell you all those things?"

"Much more," Donald said. "It was maddening to select the episodes, to cut everything back. . . . I tried to make it dramatic, to use the most vivid examples." He heard something in his voice that puzzled him—he sounded like a man being interviewed, explaining his success in an effortless and modest way. But Sylvia seemed not to notice. She was listening closely. "Yes," he said, "I do like my life now. I love it. Travel can be exhausting, but I don't want to stop. A kind of momentum keeps you going, once you start. I haven't stayed in one place for more than four months, since . . . since— Since Los Angeles, with you."

"You shouldn't have gotten married," Sylvia said. But she had said that before, many times, years ago when they had shouted such accusations at each other; she seemed to hear the echo, and in order to erase it she said conversationally, without pausing,

"You are a type of man who shouldn't marry. It was just a temporary mistake. You didn't want a personal, private life with me —with anyone—I think you wanted to be impersonal, didn't you? To pare yourself down almost to nothing?"

"Yes, almost to nothing, yes," Donald said, nodding enthusiastically. "I couldn't stand owning all those things—even having a six-month lease on an apartment made me restless— Yes, I wanted to pare myself down so there wasn't all that personal, emotional confusion about me—I wanted to be—well, to be universal—to get down to a universal core—"

"Isn't that like suicide? Wanting to be nothing?" Sylvia asked casually.

"No. It's the alternative to suicide," Donald said.

He had spoken with the kind of blunt, almost academic certainty that had silenced his wife in the past. It silenced her now; she seemed startled, rebuffed.

But after a moment she said, suddenly, in another voice: "Donald, do you remember Betty Long? She killed herself, they think. She drove her car off the freeway one night. . . . Do you remember her?"

"Betty Long?" Donald searched his memory but couldn't locate a face. No face for Betty Long. Had she been a friend, a friend's wife? Out of respect for her death he said vaguely, "Yes, I remember her . . . that's terrible. . . . That's terrible news. . . . It's unusual for a woman to kill herself like that, you know. It almost never happens, violence, like that. . . ." He went on to tell Sylvia about his next-door neighbors at Howth. The woman, who was in her forties, had been married at one time to the novelist Richard Grauer, who had survived Dachau, wrote several books that were considered brilliant, and then gassed himself as if to complete the process begun in Dachau. Sylvia shook her head, not understanding or pretending not to understand. "That isn't as uncommon as it sounds," Donald said grimly. "Physical suicide, or psychic collapse—it's the tragedy of the survivor. People like us can't understand what it is to *sur-*

vive. There are thousands of Poles in English mental hospitals right now, to take just one example. They grow old, they don't adjust, they die there in the hospitals. . . . It's like the camps again, the same thing. The same closed system. I'm going to do a book on totalitarian systems," Donald said, tapping his fingers energetically, "the psychological mechanisms involved, and how the way to survive resembles the system itself. That is, the victim assimilates the system and becomes its representative, as if he were transparent, hollowed out. . . ." Then he remembered where he was. He had been speaking rather loudly. To change the subject he said, "Well, Sylvia, your life is quite different too. I don't know if I congratulated you properly on your marriage. You never dreamed you'd get this far up into the hills, out of the smog, did you?" he teased. "Stuck with me in the inner city—"

"Oh, it gets smoggy here too," Sylvia said, smiling. "And then . . . well, you know . . . there's no marriage like the first. It only happens once. It can't be repeated. . . . Well, about Roy. . . ."

"Yes," Donald said vaguely, "about Roy. . . ."

"I thought about him constantly for weeks, until I almost went mad," Sylvia said. "I could feel my head getting ready to explode. And then I hate to involve Eliot in all this misery—one rotten marriage was enough for him— You're the only person I can really talk to about Roy. But there isn't much to say."

"Should I meet Belitt?"

"Not unless you want to. I've told you everything. You don't have to hang around here if you have work to do. . . . The situation doesn't change. That's what is so terrifying, so maddening; after three weeks nothing has changed. . . . It isn't like a crisis at a hospital, where the patient either survives or dies. It just continues. He's very stubborn." Sylvia frowned. "No, that isn't the right word—I mean something else— He's very disturbed."

"Yes."

"Because he's killed his mother, maybe," she said bitterly.

"That isn't necessarily—"

"No, I didn't mean that either. I mean—"

"I wouldn't interpret it that way necessarily, not so bluntly," Donald said.

Sylvia nodded wearily. She pushed the coffee cup away from her. "Donald," she said, "I was looking through some old books of ours, yours and mine, and I came across that paperback of Kafka's diaries. . . . Do you remember it, with a white and yellow cover? I leafed through it and came across something you had underlined; it went like this, I memorized it: 'What an effort to keep alive! Erecting a monument does not require the expenditure of so much strength.' Do you remember that?"

"No," Donald said.

"Would you like to take the book with you? It's more yours than mine."

"No, you keep it. I think I've gone beyond Kafka, at my age," Donald said.

5

He slept in a handsome oak-paneled guest room, really a suite of rooms, above the garage; but his sleep was interrupted by jumps and starts and sudden flashes of clarity, the false clarity of dreams. He woke just before dawn, telling himself he must leave, must get back to Ireland.

Then he argued himself out of that: he had to control his restlessness. He had to control himself.

Waking again after eight, he felt a little better, though still uneasy, out of place. He hated being a guest, staying with anyone. He hated the violation of his privacy. He smoked several cigarettes, staring out at the cactus trees that had the neat, self-conscious appearance of sculpture. The swimming pool was just out of the range of his vision. In the light of morning—the same absolute, unblinking light—everything looked as perfect as it had looked the day before.

When he went down to breakfast there was a surprise for

him: Sylvia's husband, Eliot, had flown down from Vancouver after all. "I had the day free and here I am," he said, shaking Donald's hand energetically. He was tall, tanned, probably in his mid-fifties; Donald was disoriented at first, then pleased to meet him, very pleased. He was flattered that this man should fly down to meet him. "Is it Doctor—? No? I thought maybe you had a Ph.D. Look, Donald, this is an honor, really, I read that article of yours about the children and I was very moved—the Irish children—that one— Yes, I was very moved. Someone should do a movie on that subject. Very close in, very tight, the people in that part of the world telling their own stories. . . . I'm very happy to meet you at last. But I'm sorry it had to be on this particular occasion."

They all had breakfast together. The meal went well. Roy was cautious and formal with his mother, and maybe a little mocking, Donald thought; but maybe not. It was hard to tell. Afterward, when a Mexican cleaning woman showed up, Roy spoke to her in the same voice, saying "Good morning" like a small adult.

As the morning went on, Donald began to think of his work back in Howth, the cottage overlooking the Bay, the table cluttered with papers, the typewriter ready for him. He thought of the streets of Belfast, the excitement of driving up there again and going out with one of the army patrols. . . . It was difficult for him to follow the hearty conversation that Sylvia's husband led, and even Sylvia was altered now, in her new husband's presence, glancing at him constantly, obviously proud of him in a way she had never been proud of Donald.

Donald told himself he was an intruder here. Everyone was friendly to him, yet he did not belong. His own son was friendly —not like a son, but like a polite friend—and there didn't seem to be much for them to talk about. He did not dare ask Roy certain questions, not after the drive to the ocean. Not again. Not that again.

By mid-afternoon he had decided he must leave; Sylvia's husband tried to talk him into staying overnight, but he insisted. He had become quite restless. Eliot telephoned the airport for him, got him a reservation on the 5:30 flight to Kennedy Airport—very good luck!—and he spent the last hour on the back terrace with Sylvia and Roy and Eliot, enjoying the sunlight. From time to time he glanced surreptitiously at his watch. He was getting a little nervous, studying his son's face. It was stern, composed, perfectly rigid. It could even smile when other people laughed, sensing a joke. But what if that face collapsed? Donald had the sudden, absurd idea that his son would begin to cry as he had cried years ago, when either Donald or Sylvia had had to leave him.

Roy had gone through a phase—"through a phase," as Sylvia's mother expressed it—from about the age of eighteen months to the age of three years, when he would shriek and throw himself around violently. So terrible had these sessions been that Donald had had to rush out of the apartment, angry and trembling himself, convinced that his son was abnormal—until a pediatrician told him that it was not uncommon, really.

"*Children are capable of extraordinary rage," the doctor said.
"But then they get over it?" Donald had asked doubtfully.
"They get over it.*"

When the taxi arrived, Sylvia's husband insisted upon carrying out Donald's single battered suitcase, and everyone smiled and shook hands, good-by, good-by! Donald lifted Roy up for a last-minute embrace, kissed him roughly on the cheek, and felt tears spring into his eyes. "Next time I'll be able to stay longer," he said.

He got into the cab, waving. The new, handsome family assembled itself at the edge of the walk, waving at him. The father and the mother were attractive people, quite tanned and slender; the child was not so tan, but robust enough. He waved good-by to Donald like a child on television waving at the camera. His face was still composed as he called out, "Good-by, Daddy!"

So he hadn't cried, hadn't broken down. Donald was driven away, down out of the hills; he felt suddenly dizzy with freedom and relief, his eyes stinging, seared. Roy hadn't run after him. Nothing had happened. He rubbed at his stinging eyes, wondering why he felt so moved. But he had to think of the trip ahead: had to think of the plane, the confusion at the big, crowded airport, the rapid loss of time he would have to endure. He liked to travel, but it was tiring. It exhausted him. Once he was back in Howth, back where he could think seriously, he would think about this visit and what it meant. He would have plenty of time for thinking then.

By the River

Helen thought: "Am I in love again, some new kind of love? Is that why I'm here?"

She was sitting in the waiting room of the Yellow Bus Lines station; she knew the big old room with its dirty tile floor and its solitary telephone booth in the corner and its candy machine and cigarette machine and popcorn machine by heart. Everything was familiar, though she had been gone for five months, even the old woman with the dyed red hair who sold tickets and had been selling them there, behind that counter, for as long as Helen could remember. Years ago, before Helen's marriage, she and her girl friends would be driven into town by someone's father and after they tired of walking around town they would stroll over to the bus station to watch the buses unload. They were anxious to see who was getting off, but few of the passengers who got off stayed in Oriskany—they were just passing through, stopping for a rest and a drink, and their faces seemed to say that they didn't think much of the town. Nor did they seem to think much of the girls from the country who stood around in their colorful dresses and smiled shyly at strangers, not knowing any better: they were taught to be kind to people, to smile first, you never knew who it might be. So now Helen was back in Oriskany, but this time she had come in on a bus herself. Had ridden alone, all the way from the city of Derby, all alone, and was waiting for her father to pick her up so she could go back to her old life without any more fuss.

It was hot. Flies crawled languidly around; a woman with a small sickly-faced baby had to keep waving them away. The old woman selling tickets looked at Helen as if her eyes were drawn irresistibly that way, as if she knew every nasty rumor and wanted to let Helen know that she knew. Helen's forehead broke out in perspiration and she stood, abruptly, wanting to dislodge that old woman's stare. She went over to the candy machine but did not look at the candy bars; she looked at herself in the mirror. Her own reflection always made her feel better. Whatever went on inside her head—and right now she felt nervous about something—had nothing to do with the way she looked, her smooth gentle skin and the faint freckles on her forehead and nose and the cool, innocent green of her eyes; she was just a girl from the country and anyone in town would know that, even if they didn't know her personally, one of those easy, friendly girls who hummed to themselves and seemed always to be glancing up as if expecting something pleasant, some deliberate surprise. Her light brown hair curled back lazily toward her ears, cut short now because it was the style; in high school she had worn it long. She watched her eyes in the mirror. No alarm there, really. She would be back home in an hour or so. Not her husband's home, of course, but her parents' home. And her face in the mirror was the face she had always seen—twenty-two she was now, and to her that seemed very old, but she looked no different from the way she had looked on her wedding day five years ago.

But it was stupid to try to link together those two Helens, she thought. She went back to the row of seats and sat heavily. If the old woman was still watching, she did not care. A sailor in a soiled white uniform sat nearby, smoking, watching her but not with too much interest; he had other girls to recall. Helen opened her purse and looked inside at nothing and closed it again. The man she had been living with in the city for five months had told her it was stupid—no, he had not used that word; he said something fancy like "immature"—to confuse herself with the child she had been, married woman as she was now, and a mother, an adulterous married woman. . . . And the word *adulterous* made her lips turn up in a slow bemused smile, the first flash of incredulous pride one might feel when told at last the disease that is going to be fatal. For there were so many diseases and only one way out of the world, only one death and so many ways to get to it. They were like doors, Helen thought dreamily. You walked down a hallway like those in movies, in huge wealthy homes, crystal chandeliers and marble floors and . . . great sweeping lawns . . . and doors all along those hallways; if you picked the wrong door you had to go through it. She was dreamy, drowsy. When thought became too much for her—when he had pestered her so much about marrying him, divorcing her husband and marrying him, always him!—she had felt so sleepy she could not listen. If she was not interested in a word her mind wouldn't hear it but made it blurred and strange, like words half heard in dreams or through some thick substance. You didn't have to hear a word if you didn't want to.

So she had telephoned her father the night before and told him the 3:15 bus and now it was 3:30; where was he? Over the telephone he had sounded slow and solemn, it could have been a stranger's voice. Helen had never liked telephones because you could not see smiles or gestures and talking like that made her tired. Listening to her father, she had felt for the first time since she had run away and left them all behind—husband, baby girl, family, in-laws, the minister, the dreary sun-bleached look of the land—that she had perhaps died and only imagined she was running away. Nobody here trusted the city; it was too big. Helen had wanted to go there all her life, not being afraid of anything, and so she had gone, and was coming back; but it was an odd feeling, this dreamy ghostliness, as if she were really dead and coming back in a form that only looked like herself. . . . She was bored, thinking of this, and crossed her bare legs. The sailor crushed out a cigarette in the dirty tin ashtray and their eyes met. Helen felt a little smile tug at her lips. That was the trouble, she knew men too well. She knew their eyes and their gestures—like the sailor rubbing thoughtfully at his chin now, as if he hadn't shaved well enough but really liked to feel his own skin. She knew them too well and had never figured out why: her sister, four years older, wasn't like that. But to Helen the same man one hundred times or one hundred men, different men, seemed the same. It was wrong, of course, because she had been taught it and believed what she had been taught; but she could not understand the difference. The sailor watched her but she looked away, half closing her eyes. She had no time for him. Her father should be here now, he would be here in a few minutes, so there was no time; she would be home in an hour. When she thought of her father, the ugly bus station with its odor of tobacco and spilled soft drinks seemed to fade away—she remembered his voice the night before, how gentle and soft she had felt listening to that voice, giving in to the protection he represented. She had endured his rough hands, as a child, because she knew they protected her, and all her life they had protected her. There had always been trouble, sometimes the kind you laughed about later and sometimes not; that was one of the reasons she had married John, and before John there had been others—just boys who didn't count, who had no jobs and thought mainly about their cars. Once, when she was fifteen, she had called her father from a roadhouse sixty miles away; she and her best friend Annie had gotten mixed up with some men they had met at a picnic. That had been frightening, Helen thought, but now she could have handled them. She gave everyone too much, that was her trouble. Her father had said that. Even her mother. Lent money to girls at the telephone company where she'd worked; lent her girl friends clothes; would run outside when some man drove up and blew his horn, not bothering to get out and knock at the door the way he should. She liked to make other people happy, what was wrong with that? Was she too lazy to care? Her head had begun to ache.

Always her thoughts ran one way, fast and innocent, but her body did other things. It got warm, nervous, it could not relax. Was she afraid of what her father's face would tell her? She pushed that idea away, it was nonsense. If she had to think of something, let it be of that muddy spring day when her family had first moved to this part of the country, into an old farmhouse her father had bought at a "bargain." At that time the road out in front of the house had been no more than a single dirt lane . . . now it was wider, covered with blacktop that smelled ugly and made your eyes shimmer and water with confusion in the summer. Yes, that big old house. Nothing about it would have changed. She did not think of her own house, her husband's house, because it mixed her up too much right now. Maybe she would go back and maybe not. She did not think of him—if she wanted to go back she would, he would take her in. When she tried to think of what had brought her back, it was never her husband—so much younger, quicker, happier than the man she had just left—and not the little girl, either, but something to do with her family's house and that misty, warm day seventeen years ago when they had first moved in. So one morning when that man left for work her thoughts had turned back to home and she had sat at the breakfast table for an hour or so, not clearing off the dishes, looking at the coffee left in his cup as if it were a forlorn reminder of him—a man she was even then beginning to forget. She knew then that she did not belong there in the city. It wasn't that she had stopped loving this man—she never stopped loving anyone who needed her, and he had needed her more than anyone—it was something else, something she did not understand. Not her husband, not her baby, not even the look of the river way off down the hill, through the trees that got so solemn and intricate with their bare branches in winter. Those things she loved, she hadn't stopped loving them because she had had to love this new man more . . . but something else made her get up and run into the next room and look through the bureau drawers and the closet, as if looking for something. That evening, when he returned, she explained to him that she was going back. He was over forty, she wasn't sure how much, and it had always been his hesitant, apologetic manner that made her love him, the odor of failure about him that mixed with the odor of the drinking he could not stop, even though he had "cut down" now with her help. Why were so many men afraid, why did they think so much? He did something that had to do with keeping books, was that nervous work? He was an attractive man but that wasn't what Helen had seen in him. It was his staring at her when they had first met, and the way he had run his hand through his thinning hair, telling her in that gesture that he wanted her and wanted to be young enough to tell her so. That had been five months ago. The months all rushed to Helen's mind in the memory she had of his keen intelligent baffled eyes, and the tears she had had to see in them when she went out to call her father. . . .

Now, back in Oriskany, she would think of him no more.

A few minutes later her father came. Was that really him? she thought. Her heart beat furiously. If blood drained out of her face she would look mottled and sick, as if she had a rash . . . how she hated that! Though he had seen her at once, though the bus station was nearly empty, her father hesitated until she stood and ran to him. "Pa," she said, "I'm so glad to see you." It might have been years ago and he was just going to drive back

home now, finished with his business in town, and Helen fourteen or fifteen, waiting to go back with him.

"I'll get your suitcase," he said. The sailor was reading a magazine, no longer interested. Helen watched her father nervously.
What was wrong? He stooped, taking hold of the suitcase handle,
but he did not straighten fast enough. Just a heartbeat too slow.
Why was that? Helen took a tissue already stained with lipstick
and dabbed it on her forehead.

On the way home he drove oddly, as if the steering wheel,
heated by the sun, were too painful for him to hold. "No more
trouble with the car, huh?" Helen said.

"It's all right," he said. They were nearly out of town already.
Helen saw few people she knew. "Why are you looking around?"
her father said. His voice was pleasant and his eyes fastened seriously upon the road, as if he did not dare look elsewhere.

"Oh, just looking," Helen said. "How is Davey?"

Waiting for her father to answer—he always took his time—
Helen arranged her skirt nervously beneath her. Davey was her
sister's baby, could he be sick? She had forgotten to ask about
him the night before. "Nothing's wrong with Davey, is there,
Pa?" she said.

"No, nothing."

"I thought Ma might come, maybe," Helen said.

"No."

"Didn't she want to? Mad at me, huh?"

In the past her mother's dissatisfaction with her had always
ranged Helen and her father together; Helen could tell by a
glance of her father's when this was so. But he did not look away
from the road. They were passing the new high school, the consolidated high school Helen had attended for a year. No one had
known what "consolidated" meant or was interested in knowing.
Helen frowned at the dark brick and there came to her mind, out
of nowhere, the word *adulterous*, for it too had been a word she
had not understood for years. A word out of the Bible. It was like

a mosquito bothering her at night, or a stain on her dress—the
kind she would have to hide without seeming to, letting her hand
fall over it accidentally. For some reason the peculiar smell of the
old car, the rattling sunshades above the windshield, the same old
khaki blanket they used for a seat cover did not comfort her and
let her mind get drowsy, to push that word away.

She was not sleepy, but she said she was.

"Yes, honey. Why don't you lay back and try to sleep, then,"
her father said.

He glanced toward her. She felt relieved at once, made simple
and safe. She slid over and leaned her head against her father's
shoulder. "Bus ride was long, I hate bus rides," she said. "I used
to like them."

"You can sleep till we get home."

"Is Ma mad?"

"No."

His shoulder wasn't as comfortable as it should have been. But
she closed her eyes, trying to force sleep. She remembered that
April day they had come here—their moving to the house that
was new to them, a house of their own they would have to share
with no one else, but a house it turned out had things wrong with
it, secret things, that had made Helen's father furious. She could
not remember the city and the house they had lived in there, but
she had been old enough to sense the simplicity of the country
and the eagerness of her parents, and then the angry perplexity
that had followed. The family was big—six children then, before
Arthur died at ten—and half an hour after they had moved in
the house was crowded and shabby. And she remembered being
frightened at something and her father picking her up right in
the middle of moving, and not asking her why she cried—her
mother had always asked her that, as if there were a reason—but
rocked her and comforted her with his rough hands. And she
could remember how the house had looked so well: the balloon-
ing curtains in the windows, the first things her mother had put
up. The gusty spring air, already too warm, smelling of good

earth and the Eden River not too far behind them, and leaves, sunlight, wind; and the sagging porch piled with cartons and bundles and pieces of furniture from the old house. The grandparents—her mother's parents—had died in that old dark house in the city, and Helen did not remember them at all except as her father summoned them back, recalling with hatred his wife's father—some little confused argument they had had years ago that he should have won. That old man had died and the house had gone to the bank, somewhere mysterious, and her father had brought them all out here to the country. A new world, a new life. A farm. And four boys to help, and the promise of such good soil. . . .

Her father turned the wheel sharply. "Rabbit run acrost," he said. He had this strange air of apology for whatever he did, even if it was something gentle; he hated to kill animals, even weasels and hawks. Helen wanted to cover his right hand with hers, that thickened, dirt-creased hand that could never be made clean. But she said, stirring a little as if he had awakened her, "Then why didn't Ma want to come?"

They were taking a long, slow curve. Helen knew without looking up which curve this was, between two wheat fields that belonged to one of the old, old families, those prosperous men who drove broken-down pickup trucks and dressed no better than their own hired hands, but who had money, much money, not just in one bank but in many. "Yes, they're money people," Helen remembered her father saying, years ago, passing someone's pasture. Those ugly red cows meant nothing to Helen, but they meant something to her father. And so after her father had said that—they had been out for a drive after church—her mother got sharp and impatient and the ride was ruined. That was years ago. Helen's father had been a young man then, with a raw, waiting, untested look, with muscular arms and shoulders that needed only to be directed to their work. "They're money people," he had said, and that had ruined the ride, as if by magic. It had been as if the air itself had changed, the direction of the wind changing and easing to them from the river that was often stagnant in August and September, and not from the green land. With an effort Helen remembered that she had been thinking about her mother. Why did her mind push her into the past so often these days?—she only twenty-two (that was not old, not really) and going to begin a new life. Once she got home and took a bath and washed out the things in the suitcase, and got some rest, and took a walk down by the river as she had as a child, skipping stones across it, and sat around the round kitchen table with the old oilcloth cover to listen to their advice ("You got to grow up, now. You ain't fifteen any more"—that had been her mother, last time), then she would decide what to do. Make her decision about her husband and the baby and there would be nothing left to think about.

"Why didn't Ma come?"

"I didn't want her to," he said.

Helen swallowed, without meaning to. His shoulder was thin and hard against the side of her face. Were those same muscles still there, or had they become worn away like the soil that was sucked down into the river every year, stolen from them, so that the farm Helen's father had bought turned out to be a kind of joke on him? Or were they a different kind of muscle, hard and compressed like steel, drawn into themselves from years of resisting violence?

"How come?" Helen said.

He did not answer. She shut her eyes tight and distracting, eerie images came to her, stars exploding and shadowy figures like those in movies—she had gone to the movies all the time in the city, often taking in the first show at eleven in the morning not because she was lonely or had nothing to do but because she liked movies. Five-twenty and he would come up the stairs, grimacing a little with the strange inexplicable pain in his chest: and there Helen would be, back from downtown, dressed up and her hair shining and her face ripe and fresh as a child's, not because she was proud of the look in his eyes but because she knew sh could make that pain of his abate for a while. And so why had she left him, when he had needed her more than anyone? "Pa, is something wrong?" she said, as if the recollection of that other man's invisible pain were in some way connected with her father.

He reached down vaguely and touched her hand. She was surprised at this. The movie images vanished—those beautiful people she had wanted to believe in, as she had wanted to believe in God and the saints in their movie-world heaven—and she opened her eyes. The sun was bright. It had been too bright all summer. Helen's mind felt sharp and nervous, as if pricked by tiny needles, but when she tried to think of what they could be no explanation came to her. She would be home soon, she would be able to rest. Tomorrow she could get in touch with John. Things could begin where they had left off—John had always loved her so much, and he had always understood her, had known what she was like. "Ma isn't sick, is she?" Helen said suddenly. "No," said her father. He released her fingers to take hold of the steering wheel again. Another curve. Off to the side, if she bothered to look, the river had swung toward them—low at this time of year, covered in places with a fine brown-green layer of scum. She did not bother to look.

"We moved out here seventeen years ago," her father said. He cleared his throat; the gesture of a man unaccustomed to speech. "You don't remember that."

"Yes, I do," Helen said. "I remember that."

"You don't, you were just a baby."

"Pa, I remember it. I remember you carrying the big rug into the house, you and Eddie. And I started to cry and you picked me up. I was such a big baby, always crying. . . . And Ma came out and chased me inside so I wouldn't bother you."

"You don't remember that," her father said. He was driving jerkily, pressing down on the gas pedal and then letting it up, as if new thoughts continually struck him. What was wrong with him? Helen had an idea she didn't like: he was older now, he was going to become an old man.

If she had been afraid of the dark, upstairs in that big old
farmhouse in the room she shared with her sister, all she had had
to do was to think of him. He had a way of sitting at the supper
table that was so still, so silent, you knew nothing could budge
him. Nothing could frighten him. So, as a child, and even now
that she was grown up, it helped her to think of her father's face
—those pale surprised green eyes that could be simple or cun
ning, depending upon the light, and the lines working them
selves in deeper every year around his mouth, and the hard angle
of his jaw going back to the ear, burned by the sun and then
tanned by it, turned into leather, then going pale again in the
winter. The sun could not burn its color deep enough into that
skin that was almost as fair as Helen's. At Sunday school she and
the other children had been told to think of Christ when they
were afraid, but the Christ she saw on the little Bible bookmark
cards and calendars was no one to protect you. That was a man
who would be your cousin, maybe, some cousin you liked but
saw rarely, but He looked so given over to thinking and trusting
that He could not be of much help; not like her father. When he
and the boys came in from the fields with the sweat drenching
their clothes and their faces looking as if they were dissolving
with heat, you could still see the solid flesh beneath, the skeleton
that hung onto its muscles and would never get old, never die.
The boys—her brothers, all older—had liked her well enough,
Helen being the baby, and her sister had watched her most of the
time, and her mother had liked her too—or did her mother like
anyone, having been brought up by German-speaking parents
who had had no time to teach her love? But it had always been
her father she had run to. She had started knowing men by
knowing him. She could read things in his face that taught her
about the faces of other men, the slowness or quickness of their
thoughts, if they were beginning to be impatient, or were pleased
and didn't want to show it yet. Was it for this she had come
home?—And the thought surprised her so that she sat up, be
cause she did not understand. Was it for this she had com

home? "Pa," she said, "like I told you on the telephone, I don't know why I did it. I don't know why I went. That's all right, isn't it? I mean, I'm sorry for it, isn't that enough? Did you talk to John?"

"John? Why John?"

"What?"

"You haven't asked about him until now, so why now?"

"What do you mean? He's my husband, isn't he? Did you talk to him?"

"He came over to the house almost every night for two weeks. Three weeks," he said. Helen could not understand the queer chatty tone of his voice. "Then off and on, all the time. No, I didn't tell him you were coming."

"But why not?" Helen laughed nervously. "Don't you like him?"

"You know I like him. You know that. But if I told him he'd of gone down to get you, not me."

"Not if I said it was you I wanted. . . ."

"I didn't want him to know. Your mother doesn't know either."

"What? You mean you didn't tell her?" Helen looked at the side of his face. It was rigid and bloodless behind the tan, as if something inside were shrinking away and leaving just his voice. "You mean you didn't even tell Ma? She doesn't know I'm coming?"

"No."

The nervous prickling in her brain returned suddenly. Helen rubbed her forehead. "Pa," she said gently, "why didn't you tell anybody? You're ashamed of me, huh?"

He drove on slowly. They were following the bends of the river, that wide shallow meandering river the boys said wasn't worth fishing in any longer. One of its tributaries branched out suddenly—Mud Creek, it was called, all mud and bullfrogs and dragonflies and weeds—and they drove over it on a rickety wooden bridge that thumped beneath them. "Pa," Helen said carefully, "you said you weren't mad, on the phone. And I wrote you that letter explaining. I wanted to write some more, but you know . . . I don't write much, never even wrote to Annie when she moved away. I never forgot about you or anything, or Ma. . . . I thought about the baby, too, and John, but John could always take care of himself. He's smart. He really is. I was in the store with him one time and he was arguing with some salesmen and got the best of them; he never learned all that from his father. The whole family is smart, though, aren't they?"

"The Hendrikses? Sure. You don't get money without brains.'

"Yes, and they got money too, John never had to worry. In a house like his parents' house nothing gets lost or broken. You know? It isn't like it was at ours, when we were all kids. That's part of it—when John's father built us our house I was real pleased and real happy, but then something of them came in with it too. Everything is s'post to be clean and put in its place and after you have a baby you get so tired. . . . But his mother was always real nice to me. I don't complain about them. I like them all real well."

"Money people always act nice," her father said. "Why shouldn't they?"

"Oh, Pa!" Helen said, tapping at his arm. "What do you mean by that? You always been nicer than anybody I know, that's the truth. Real nice. A lot of them with those big farms, like John's father, and that tractor store they got—they complain a lot. They do. You just don't hear about it. And when that baby got polio over in the Rapids—that real big farm, you know what I mean?—the McGuires. How do you think they felt? They got trouble just like everybody else."

Then her father did a strange thing: here they were, seven or eight miles from home, no house near, and he stopped the car. "Want to rest for a minute," he said. Yet he kept staring out the windshield as if he were still driving.

"What's wrong?"

"Sun on the hood of the car. . . ."

Helen tugged at the collar of her dress, pulling it away from her damp neck. When had the heat ever bothered her father before? She remembered going out to the farthest field with water for him, before he had given up that part of the farm. And he would take the jug from her and lift it to his lips and it would seem to Helen, the sweet child Helen standing in the dusty corn, that the water flowed into her magnificent father and enlivened him as if it were secret blood of her own she had given him. And his chest would swell, his reddened arms eager with muscle emerging out from his rolled-up sleeves, and his eyes now wiped of sweat and exhaustion. . . . The vision pleased and confused her, for what had it to do with the man now beside her? She stared at him and saw that his nose was queerly white and that there were many tiny red veins about it, hardly more than pen lines; and his hair was thinning and jagged, growing back stiffly from his forehead as if he had brushed it back impatiently with his hand once too often. When Eddie, the oldest boy, moved away now and lost to them, had pushed their father hard in the chest and knocked him back against the supper table, that same amazed white look had come to his face, starting at his nose.

"I was thinking if, if we got home now, I could help Ma with supper," Helen said. She touched her father's arm as if to wake him. "It's real hot, she'd like some help."

"She doesn't know you're coming."

"But I . . . I could help anyway." She tried to smile, watching his face for a hint of something: many times in the past he had looked stern but could be made to break into a smile, finally, if she teased him long enough. "But didn't Ma hear you talk on the phone? Wasn't she there?"

"She was there."

"Well, but then. . . ."

"I told her you just talked. Never said nothing about coming home."

The heat had begun to make Helen dizzy. Her father opened the door on his side. "Let's get out for a minute, go down by the

river," he said. Helen slid across and got out. The ground felt uncertain beneath her feet. Her father was walking and saying
something and she had to run to catch up with him. He said:
"We moved out here seventeen years ago. There were six of you
then, but you don't remember. Then the boy died. And you don't
remember your mother's parents and their house, that goddamn
stinking house, and how I did all the work for him in his store.
You remember the store down front? The dirty sawdust floor and
the old women coming in for sausage, enough to make you want
to puke, and pigs' feet and brains out of cows or guts or what the
hell they were that people ate in that neighborhood. I could puke
for all my life and not get clean of it. You just got born then. And
we were dirt to your mother's people, just dirt. I was dirt. And
when they died somebody else got the house, it was all owned by
somebody else, and so we said how it was for the best and we'd
come out here and start all over. You don't remember it or know
nothing about us."

"What's wrong, Pa?" Helen said. She took his arm as they descended the weedy bank. "You talk so funny, did you get something to drink before you came to the bus station? You never said
these things before. I thought it wasn't just meat, but a grocery
store, like the one in. . . ."

"And we came out here," he said loudly, interrupting her, "and
bought that son of a bitch of a house with the roof half rotted
through and the well all shot to hell . . . and those bastards
never looked at us, never believed we were real people. The
Hendrikses too. They were like all of them. They looked through
me in town, do you know that? Like you look through a window.
They didn't see me. It was because hillbilly families were in that
house, came and went, pulled out in the middle of the night
owing everybody money; they all thought we were like that. I said
we were poor but we weren't hillbillies. I said, do I talk like a
hillbilly? We come from the city. But nobody gave a damn. You
could go up to them and shout in their faces and they wouldn'

hear you, not even when they started losing money themselves. I prayed to God during them bad times that they'd all lose what they had, every bastard one of them, that Swede with the fancy cattle most of all! I prayed to God to bring them down to me so they could see me, my children as good as theirs, and me a harder worker than any of them—if you work till you feel like dying you done the best you can do, whatever money you get. I'd of told them that. I wanted to come into their world even if I had to be on the bottom of it, just so long as they gave me a name. . . ."

"Pa, you been drinking," Helen said softly.

"I had it all fixed, what I'd tell them," he said. They were down by the river bank now. Fishermen had cleared a little area and stuck Y-shaped branches into the dried mud, to rest their poles on. Helen's father prodded one of the little sticks with his foot and then did something Helen had never seen anyone do in her life, not even boys—he brought his foot down on it and smashed it.

"You oughtn't of done that," Helen said. "Why'd you do that?"

"And I kept on and on; it was seventeen years. I never talked about it to anyone. Your mother and me never had much to say, you know that. She was like her father. You remember that first day? It was spring, nice and warm, and the wind came along when we were moving the stuff in and was so different from that smell in the city—my God! It was a whole new world here."

"I remember it," Helen said. She was staring out at the shallow muddy river. Across the way birds were sunning themselves stupidly on flat, white rocks covered with dried moss like veils.

"You don't remember nothing!" her father said angrily. "Nothing! You were the only one of them I loved, because you didn't remember. It was all for you. First I did it for me, myself, to show that bastard father of hers that was dead—then those other bastards, those big farms around us—but then for you, for you. You were the baby. I said to God that when you grew up it'd be you in one of them big houses with everything fixed and painted all the time, and new machinery, and driving around in a nice car, not this thing we got. I said I would do that for you or die."

"That's real nice, Pa," Helen said nervously, "but I never . . . I never knew nothing about it, or. . . . I was happy enough any way I was. I liked it at home, I got along with Ma better than anybody did. And I liked John too, I didn't marry him just because you told me to. I mean, you never pushed me around. I wanted to marry him all by myself, because he loved me. I was always happy, Pa. If John didn't have the store coming to him, and that land and all, I'd have married him anyway—You oughtn't to have worked all that hard for me."

In spite of the heat she felt suddenly chilled. On either side of them tall grass shrank back from the cleared, patted area, stiff and dried with August heat. These weeds gathered upon themselves in a brittle tumult back where the vines and foliage of trees began, the weeds dead and whitened and the vines a glossy, rich green, as if sucking life out of the water into which they drooped. All along the river bank trees and bushes leaned out and showed a yard or two of dead, whitish brown where the water line had once been. This river bent so often you could never see far along it. Only a mile or so. Then foliage began, confused and unmoving. What were they doing here, she and her father? A thought came to Helen and frightened her—she was not used to thinking —that they ought not to be here, that this was some other kind of slow, patient world where time didn't care at all for her or her girl's face or her generosity of love, but would push right past her and go on to touch the faces of other people.

"Pa, let's go home. Let's go home," she said.

Her father bent and put his hands into the river. He brought them dripping to his face. "That's dirty there, Pa," she said. A mad dry buzzing started up somewhere—hornets or wasps. Helen looked around but saw nothing.

"God listened and didn't say yes or no," her father said. He was squatting at the river and now looked back at her, his chin creasing. The back of his shirt was wet. "If I could read Him righ it was something like this—that I was caught in myself and them money people caught in themselves and God Himself caught in what He was and so couldn't be anything else. Then I never thought about God again."

"I think about God," Helen said. "I do. People should think about God, then they wouldn't have wars and things. . . ."

"No, I never bothered about God again," he said slowly. "If He was up there or not it never had nothing to do with me. A hailstorm that knocked down the wheat, or a drought—what the hell? Whose fault? It wasn't God's no more than mine so I let Him out of it. I knew I was in it all on my own. Then after a while it got better, year by year. We paid off the farm and the new machines. You were in school then, in town. And when we went into the church they said hello to us sometimes, because we outlasted them hillbillies by ten years. And now Mike ain't doing bad on his own place, got a nice car, and me and Bill get enough out of the farm so it ain't too bad, I mean it ain't too bad. But it wasn't money I wanted!"

He was staring at her. She saw something in his face that mixed with the buzzing of the hornets and fascinated her so that she could not move, could not even try to tease him into smiling too. "It wasn't never money I wanted," he said.

"Pa, why don't we go home?"

"I don't know what it was, exactly," he said, still squatting. His hands touched the ground idly. "I tried to think of it, last night when you called and all night long and driving in to town today. I tried to think of it."

"I guess I'm awful tired from that bus. I . . . I don't feel good," Helen said.

"Why did you leave with that man?"

"What? Oh," she said, touching the tip of one of the weeds, "I met him at John's cousin's place, where they got that real nice tavern and a dance hall. . . ."

"Why did you run away with him?"

"I don't know, I told you in the letter. I wrote it to you, Pa. He

acted so nice and liked me so, he still does, he loves me so much.
. . . And he was always so sad and tired, he made me think
of . . . you, Pa . . . but not really, because he's not strong like
you and couldn't ever do work like you. And if he loved me that
much I had to go with him."

"Then why did you come back?"

"Come back?" Helen tried to smile out across the water. Sluggish, ugly water, this river that disappointed everyone, so familiar
to her that she could not really get used to a house without a river
or a creek somewhere behind it, flowing along night and day:
perhaps that was what she had missed in the city?

"I came back because . . . because. . . ."

And she shredded the weed in her cold fingers, but no words
came to her. She watched the weed-fragments fall. No words
came to her, her mind had turned hollow and cold, she had come
too far down to this river bank but it was not a mistake any more
than the way the river kept moving was a mistake; it just happened.

Her father got slowly to his feet and she saw in his hand a
knife she had been seeing all her life. Her eyes seized upon it and
her mind tried to remember: where had she seen it last, whose
was it, her father's or her brother's? He came to her and touched
her shoulder as if waking her, and they looked at each other
Helen so terrified by now that she was no longer afraid but only
curious with the mute marblelike curiosity of a child, and her
father stern and silent until a rush of hatred transformed his face
into a mass of wrinkles, the skin mottled red and white. He did
not raise the knife but slammed it into her chest, up to the hilt, so
that his whitened fist struck her body and her blood exploded out
upon it.

Afterward, he washed the knife in the dirty water and put it
away. He squatted and looked out over the river, then his thigh
began to ache and he sat on the ground, a few feet from her
body. He sat there for hours as if waiting for some idea to com

to him. Then the water began to darken, very slowly, and the sky darkened a little while later—as if belonging to another, separate time—and he tried to turn his mind with an effort to the next thing he must do.

*E*xtraordinary Popular Delusions

Six o'clock on an overcast, unpromising day in late March: Pau
Cassity left for a drive of several hours, most of it along an inter
state expressway famous for its accidents. He was going to visi
his father.

On the seat beside him was the lunch his wife, Ann, had pre
pared for him—sandwiches of cheese and ham wrapped carefull
in cellophane, an apple, some cookies.

His car sagged and creaked; it was a constant, almost fon
worry to him. It seemed to him an extension of his own bod
creaking and rattling mysteriously. He thought about the lon
drive in this car, the hours ahead of him, and he thought abou
his home behind, the warm dark bedroom, the comfortable be
the sleepy, absent-minded embrace of his wife who loved hin

She had risen with him, a little baffled by the early hour, sleepy and confused, to make breakfast for him; she always made breakfast for him, fondly. He felt the strangeness of these two things —the barrenness of the expressway and the personal, unique, precious warmth of his own home, which belonged only to him.

Homes, houses—he worked for a large real-estate agency—his business was houses, listing them and selling them. The signs for Moore Realtors were all over the city, black and yellow signs, exclamations of change. Home owners, seeing them up the street, were frightened; they telephoned Moore Realtors to list their own homes, anxious to see what they were worth, not wanting to be left behind. The city of Detroit was changing, history was pushing everyone along with it, who could resist? . . . Paul had sold two houses in two days last week, both to blacks.

But he was embarrassed to think of his successful days; he was embarrassed thinking of money. His father had never had enough money.

This father of his had become mysterious. A widower this past year, he had aged suddenly, spitefully; he was seventy-three but looked much older. He had had the telephone taken out of his house so that Paul couldn't call him. If Paul wanted to talk to him, he had to call the next-door neighbors. He never answered letters; he lived alone in the old house, in a city some distance north of Detroit, and would not acknowledge Paul and his family. But today Paul would speak frankly with him, everything would be made clear: would he like to come live with them? Living alone, at his age, had become too much of a burden, surely, too much of a risk? . . .

Paul was thirty-seven now, a tall, stooping man with watery brown eyes, a quick smile, a firm handshake. The handshake was practiced. He found himself thinking often of his father, now that he himself was approaching middle age; most of his life he had not thought of his father; his father and whatever life he led had been alien to him, unclear. Now he found himself thinking that his sons needed a grandfather who was real to them, a real

presence. They needed a sense of continuity between the generations; they would be grateful to him, to Paul, for bringing their
grandfather back to Detroit. What was it they would be grateful
for, exactly? . . . A sense of family, of the generations? . . .
He did not quite understand, himself. But he felt it strongly, so
strongly that tears came into his eyes, the thought of his family,
his own specific family with himself at the center, a family he
had created.

Traffic had begun, surrounding him. He thought: *This stream
of traffic, this pressure, this power, will carry me all the way to my
father's house.*

His wife, Ann, had gone back to bed after he left. But she
could not sleep. She was alert, jerky, thinking of the hours on the
clock, existing on the clock, between six o'clock and eight o'clock:
the boys would be up at eight. Then the hurry of breakfast, the
boys' scuffling, their abrupt alliances and complaints and needs.
. . . And Paul in that old car, coming down with a cold. . . .
When she had first met him he'd been sick with a cold—they
had met in a college cafeteria, Paul at that time thin and eager to
smile, a tall, slightly hunched-over, eager boy with hair that always looked damp.

She put her fists against her eyes and lay still. She was not
thinking about the boy who had grown into her husband. She
was thinking about another man. His last name was Stanford: it
floated to her like pollen, light and deadly, that particular name.
She felt her body weakening.

At the same time she was waiting for the boys to get up. Two
boys, eleven and eight—they would knock each other against the
walls of their room and they would wrestle dangerously on the
stairs. Their lives meant nothing to them; they had no idea of
their bodies possessing lives. They were always running. But at
8:30 they would be gone. The house would be quiet and she
would lie in it, feeling the quiet, back in bed where she would be
safe. Her body was weak and strange to her, like a body in a
dream, roughly dreamt. She could not understand herself, lying

here, but she could see herself as if from the doorway of the room —a woman lying on top of the covers, thin, messy, looking exhausted before the day had begun, as if this day would be an extraordinary day and she feared getting up.

A week ago she had decided to kill herself. But she had not killed herself. She went about the house muttering aloud in a long, confused, angry conversation with Stanford, ". . . What you don't understand about me is. . . . Why don't you say anything? Do anything? . . . You're as much of a failure as *he* is. . . ." But Stanford was half a city away. She had not killed herself.

After all, killing herself meant giving up her body: that was her last tie with Stanford. Why should she kill herself?

Her spirit wandered downstairs, leaving her behind. There it saw the dishes in the sink from her husband's breakfast. Her husband must always have a real breakfast; his mother had trained him to eat. Thin and bony, his hands busy with a perpetual, inexplicable anxiety, he must always sit down calmly to a large breakfast, eating for minutes, carefully, patiently, all food important to him, signs of love. She had gotten up at 5:30 to make him breakfast. Fine. She had packed a lunch for him. In a while she would turn her mind to the question of what to make for dinner that night, for him and the boys. . . . Stanford, who taught school somewhere on the other side of town, picked up hamburgers and pizzas at corner carry-out restaurants, he drank instant coffee all day and all evening, he chewed gum because he had given up smoking. He never ate right because he had no time and because he hated to eat, having the wrong memories of home, a family. Ann and he had talked about their lives for hours, lying together in his room, reviewing the shadowy lives that were somehow their own lives, trying to make them harsh and dramatic. Ann had no family, really—her mother had kept her for a while and then she had lived with an aunt, then with her grandmother. It fell away from her, this early life, it was loose and insubstantial, unimportant. Now her mother was dead, but it was unimportant. Stanford had parents still living, in Florida. He knew little about them. Ann told him about her husband, who had loved his mother and father—his mother who fed him so well, pancakes and eggs and sausages for breakfast, his father who worked all the time, overtime, on Saturdays and during the two weeks of his annual vacation, working, making money, a member of the UAW and grim, relentless, steady, secretive about money, money, money . . . he even did a little work on the side, fixing up cars at the corner garage, he was good at mechanical things and well-liked by other men. . . .

"And so your father-in-law is going to live with you?" Stanford had asked.

"We think it's a good idea," Ann had said.

"*You* think it's a good idea?"

"He's old, he lives alone . . . he might have an accident, by himself. . . ."

He had laughed, hearing the hollowness of her voice. She did not reply. She felt her lover in that instant joined with all men—laughing, passing judgment, having no faces. In that way men passed judgment upon women. Stanford lay with his arm across his face, turned partly away from her.

Paul swerved to avoid an accident—a low-hanging dump truck that changed lanes suddenly.

His heart pounded in fear. Why didn't people think of what they were doing, why were they so careless of their lives?

His wife was afraid to drive in the city. *I'm not a good enough driver,* she kept saying. Often he had to take her in his arms and comfort her, rock her to sleep, silence her. She was a thin, nervous woman, with a startled, attractive face; she worried about the boys, thinking herself a bad mother. Her face was pale and beautiful at times, her eyes very light, surprised-looking. She had been an art education major at college, a girl of nineteen when they had met, very pretty with her freckled face and her long red hair, only a girl. He had loved her violently. He had talked her into marriage. Ann had quit school, relieved in a way, and he had finished after some years. . . . Now she worried about herself as a woman, as a mother, she worried about driving the boys around, she worried about the boys' health, about their grades, their friends. She worried that the other mothers slighted her or bullied her; she was so small beside them, overrun by their energy, their plans, their robust interest in their children's wars and revenges and triumphs.

The other evening the boys had fought off and on for hours, and Ann had burst into tears in the kitchen. Paul had gone in to comfort her.

"Why are you crying?"

"Because I don't love them. I don't know how."

"Of course you love them!"

"I love them but . . . I don't know how . . . I get tired. . . . I can't keep up with them, day after day . . . I don't know what will happen to me. . . ."

She wept wildly in his arms. It touched him to know how she needed him. He thought of himself in the kitchen of his house, with his wife, holding her. Minutes would pass. The boys, upstairs, would be whispering together, frightened . . . in a while he would call them in. Snap on the lights in the kitchen! Look at one another! And the fearful moment would pass, the boys would apologize, ready to cry themselves, Ann would forgive them, he would draw them all together, this precious and unique evening in their lives drawing them all together, irreparably, locked in bonds of love they would never outgrow.

Ann tasted panic against the roof of her mouth: *The boys are up, the day is starting.* . . .

She dressed hurriedly and went downstairs, bare-legged, her feet stuck into old slippers. Snap on the kitchen lights. Rinse the dishes in the sink, that sticky egg yolk . . . and set them aside. . . . The boys hurried in upon her. Bobby sneezed at once, into his hand; he had no tissue. "Go upstairs and get some! Why are you acting so stupid?" Ann said.

"Because he's a stupid dope," Stevie said.

Cereal, milk and sugar. The sugar was already spilled on the table, in tiny mounds. The boys ate with their elbows out, aggressively, a new trick.

"Hey, it looks like a great day out," Stevie said sarcastically.

She turned to look outside, hurt. It was as if the day had been a gift she were offering her son. . . .

They went to school. The house fell back into silence. Ann wandered out of the kitchen, a little nauseated by the bowls of soggy cereal, the loneliness of those discarded dishes. . . . The living room was divided from the dining room by an archway of polished dark wood. It looked like a stage setting: on that stage a confined, familiar domestic drama would take place. A woman would weep, a man would shout. Children would be alienated and then won back. The play would be completed. . . . And what would she make them for dinner tonight? All three of them liked hamburger dishes. Fine. She could make a "Mexican treat": hamburger and stewed tomatoes and corn and chili powder. But they had had that last week. Would they remember?

Her mind reeled backward. She turned away and went upstairs.

She took a shower. Her body was small, thin. She stared in the mirror at the lines of her ribs and shoulder bones, moving her arms, wondering at the prominence of her breastbones. Lines had begun on her neck, only beginning. Stanford, loving her, had loved this body and had said it was beautiful, but she did not believe him. Cautious, she had studied his face for small wrinkles of deception, of evil . . . but she had found none, nothing. Yet she did not trust him.

"You're wearing yourself out, ruining yourself," he would say. "You must be doing it on purpose."

Angry at him, she had defended her marriage, her husband, her boys. He didn't understand! What did he know of normal life, a man like him? a lonely man like him?

She washed her hair in the shower. Soap was important to her, the feel of soap. To wash her body and her hair, the outside of her body, to get everything smooth and clean. . . . Inside, her body was unwashable; it was secret and dark and coiled. With Stanford she had felt her body sink away from her, too powerful for her to control, grappling with him, with the man who clutched at her, forcing her to feel the surprise of love. . . . It was a surprise to her, a fearful thing. Afterward her head ached, her teeth ached, her heart ached with that love! A body drenched with sweat should have no memory beyond the sweat, shower it off. Soap. She washed her hair and loose hairs lay on her body. She loathed this. She thought, *These hairs will drive me mad if I don't get them off.* . . .

She dried her hair in a towel.

Once Stanford had come here, to this house. When he left she lay in bed, feeling how her body pressed upon the damp, rumpled sheets as if pressing upon a plain, a field open to the sky, unashamed. Her body was simple then, turned inside-out. Her skull was turned inside-out.

Then she had gone out shopping, she had grunted as she put the groceries in the car, too small a woman to handle such heavy things. How did it happen that she must go out shopping this afternoon, buy so many cans and packages, so many bags of frozen French fries, so many tubes of toothpaste? Her mind had reeled. She must think of the man she loved, she must think of the center of her life: Stanford, a lonely man, ironic and dissatisfied, with an unimagined future. He taught mathematics in a run-down high school, feeling himself superior to his colleagues, haughty and contemptuous, a failure having no future. She must think of him. The world rushed to him, he was the center of the world, she must clutch at him or she would go mad. . . . She had met him one evening at the branch library. He was a slight acquaintance of her husband's, from college. She had noticed him sitting at a table, watching her, almost recognizing her, a man with dark, shaggy hair, his manner both aggressive and withdrawn . . . he had gotten clumsily to his feet, he had whispered to her, "You're Paul Cassity's wife? . . ."

In those early weeks she had loved him playfully, lightly. She had looked into everyone's face with her own frank, honest face, thinking of what a liar she was, pleased with herself, thinking, *Now I am in love!*

Paul reached in his pocket for a tissue. His head ached, he had to blow his nose. He had a weakness for colds and sore throats. As a child he had almost died from an infected throat . . . he thought of his throat as delicate, vulnerable, the part of his body he must protect. If he had an accident the glass from the windshield might pierce his throat. But he must not have an accident: he must stay awake, alert. He must resist the hypnotic flow of the pavement, the dreary sunlight, the half-light. No sounds. No noises. He must resist the silence.

He must bring his father back to Detroit with him.

Nine-thirty, twenty to ten . . . the morning was opaque and dull, smoggy, not quite in focus. The three-lane expressway seemed enormous. The March sky was enormous. He might have been plowing through the density of time, driving so fast, so far, alone. . . . In the back seat, however, there were things to remind him of himself, his family: an old khaki blanket used as a seat cover, an umbrella with a broken handle, a miniature plastic football of Bobby's, broken. He had gotten this cold from Bobby, who had gotten it from Stevie. Stevie never stayed sick, he was a husky, noisy boy, already his mother's height. . . . Paul's fondest memory was of his older son's birth. That child, that baby . . . the fact of that baby had redeemed Paul, resurrected him: he had become a man then, a man who has given birth to another man. He had been an adult. Twenty-one years of age himself, he had realized the core of life, and he had wanted desperately to take this knowledge somehow to his own father, to say to him, *Now I understand! I understand all the things you've felt.* . . .

He was approaching the small industrial city where his father lived. Railroad yards, factories, piles of gravel . . . pools of oily water . . . block after block of small frame houses. . . . In a few minutes he would pass the high school he had gone to. His father lived in one of those little houses; he had lived there for forty years. Paul felt a sense of excitement rising in him. *In a few minutes he would be home. . . .*

Ann was brushing her hair. The hairbrush was old and not very clean. She was not thinking about Stanford and yet he was present to her, as if in the house somewhere, awaiting her.

Two days ago she had gone to Stanford's apartment, late in the afternoon. He had just returned from teaching; he looked tired, vulnerable. She felt something leap in her, seeing him like this. She had said to him: "I'm thirty-two years old. These are the choices I have—I can kill myself, I can cut my wrists and bleed to death in the bathtub at home, I can tell my husband I'm leaving him and I can leave him, I can live with you and marry you or not marry you, I can break everything off with you."

He had said nothing, waiting.

"I think I want to break everything off," she had said.

She had returned home. It seemed clear to her that nothing mattered to her, really, except Stanford; in the three months of their love this had become a certainty. She could think of nothing else for long. She made dinner for her husband and her boys, she bumped into the edges of things, she pressed the palm of her hand hesitantly against her breast, as if trying to recall something, baffled and ashamed, and still she made dinner, she made dinners, piercing the stubborn tops of cans with the rusty can opener, forcing the tops open, her fingers aching . . . she could not think of much else except him, what her body had felt like in his embrace. And yet it had hardly been her body, hardly this body that belonged to her husband and her children—another body, made nervous and lean by sensuality, tendons laid bare, limbs slick with perspiration, eyes burning in their sockets— Nothing mattered to her except this violent coming-alive of passion, and yet she had cut herself off from it. "I think I want to break everything off," she had heard herself say, in her small, hollow, woman's voice.

The next day she had heard Stevie and two of his friends out on the back porch, kicking off their boots. They had said shocking things, dirty, unimaginable, unforgivable things . . . what if Paul had heard? . . . voicing the words lightly, experimentally. It was all a joke. It was a joke. And then they crowded into the kitchen, fresh-faced, boys of about eleven years of age and nowhere near being men, only boys, not understanding what they were saying. . . . And yet she had heard the words echoing about them, the words they would say when, years later, they were men, and these words would have meaning to them; she flinched away from them. She was a woman confronted with filth. Why should she love that boy, that curly-haired boy said to be her son? The other two boys were strangers. The sons of strangers. She did not love them, she was not expected to love them, and why must she love the one who was her son?

The knowledge her body gave her was a single love: for that man in that apartment, that other man, his face and his arms and his legs, his private, personal body, the beauty of his body, which had nothing to do with these boys or with her husband.

She had dragged herself through the following day, which was always a difficult day for her husband—Sunday, with open houses for pieces of property he was handling, a house in particular that should be sold immediately for a high price. How hard that man worked, her husband! He talked lightly of his disappointments, of his competitors, those energetic, bustling, good-natured men and women, the women more aggressive than the men, widows with straining waists and straining smiles, smelling of talcum powder and fear—he talked, lightly, grimly, of money, with a small private smile for Ann to show her that he placed no real value on this, this busy struggle—and she listened, numb, her own face strained into a kind of wifely smile, while he spoke of new listings, sales, buyers, the hiking of federal interest rates, the new FHA map of the city of Detroit that extended the "high risk" areas, probable risks, failures, successes, bonuses, surprises. She listened, she nodded. Yet her mind kept reeling backward to that other man, to that room.

She tried to concentrate on Paul while he was home. She heard him blowing his nose in the bathroom, first one nostril and then the other, carefully, seriously; she thought of him when hanging up his clothes, brushing at the new stain on his trench coat—was it tar? how could it be tar?—she held him at night and thought of the early, unreal days and nights of their marriage, Paul still a student and Ann a secretary for a Florida "land-investment" business, their intimacy tender and hurried and embarrassed, giving her no pleasure but instead a sense of accomplishment, of duty accomplished—*Now I am a woman, a wife!* She thought of her boys. But they kept pulling away from her, even in her thoughts; they were too energetic. She thought with a kind of chilled, final disbelief that it was her fate to think all these things, routinely, and to drive her car unsteadily to the grocery store and back again to the three-bedroom colonial house in which they lived, her fate to enter that particular kitchen, prepare dinner, and listen with a jumpy, nervous sense of responsibility to her sons' arguing over the television set—"Oh, you're a stupid—" one of them would snarl, and she would strain to hear that word, what word was it?—oh, a harmless word. Harmless. She was responsible for their remaining harmless, innocent, and yet they were growing up into men, their maleness was already a threat about them, it could not be stopped. She thought with disbelief that she had given up those afternoons with her lover and those private thoughts he had given her: *Now I am in love . . . now I am changed completely. . . .*

She had been redeemed by adultery. Now she lived alone, in a house with three males whom she must feed and take care of. She contemplated the days she would live through, the rest of March, dragging herself through the month. Then April.

She must pick up her husband's trench coat at the cleaner's, today was Wednesday. He might need it tomorrow.

Paul parked in front of his father's house. The same old house —one-story, wooden, with a small front porch, peeling paint, a lawn ravaged by winter like all the lawns on the street. It was a crowded, ordinary street. Paul believed he still knew the neighbors—a retired policeman on one side, a retired factory worker on the other, a UAW man like his father. Or had Larsen died? Paul took his lunch bag with him and went to the side door of the house.

He peered through the window of the door and saw the old man—his father—right away. He was sitting at the kitchen table. It was too quick, too much of a surprise, seeing him like this! His father was sitting at the table, just sitting there. The kitchen was not lighted.

Paul rapped at the door, embarrassed.

His father's head jerked around. Paul said, "Pa? It's just me. It's Paul."

The old man sat motionless. Seconds passed. A frozen body, at a small table, in an unlighted kitchen—his body had that inert, dead look of animals that camouflage themselves by not moving, imagining themselves invisible. "Pa? It's Paul. Is something wrong? I drove over to. . . ."

He stared the few yards into his father's face, an old man's face. It crossed his mind that this particular old man was not his father, and what then? But the shabby house was familiar, the small, old-fashioned kitchen, the linoleum floor, the stained tile were familiar—

His father opened the door. An exchange of embarrassed greetings, a clumsy handshake. "I drove over for a few hours, just to talk," Paul said, speaking loudly as if identifying himself. He felt like a salesman. He held his lunch bag before him, as if to show his father that he had his own food, don't worry. . . . "I'm glad I found you at home like this. This is wonderful." His fathe was staring at him, yet without much interest. Paul was shocked at his father's face, which was withered, sour, spiteful; even his eyes looked unnaturally small. Once he had been a big, hearty, bullying man, a good man in his own way . . . now he spent his mornings in this darkened room, alone, his face taking on some of the ghastly light of the morning, a light that had no true clarity.

"Is something wrong? Aren't you well?" Paul asked, suddenly alarmed.

His father waved this question away as if it were too stupid to answer. He sat down again at the table, heavily. He sighed. "You drive all the way over here, eh? How come?"

"To see you. To see how you are. Were you just sitting out here, alone? I mean . . . what were you doing?"

His father glanced at him.

"Sitting thinking. Resting."

Paul sat across the table from his father. He felt his face go taut and bright, a salesman's face. "I must have had a hunch something was wrong, I felt certain I should come to see you this week. . . ." He imagined himself saying: *Now you will come home with me, now everything will come together again in a kind of circle. . . .*

Behind his father was a clutter of dishes, rags, a cardboard box. The kitchen smelled. Paul could smell his father's flesh—unwashed limbs, a stale, harsh odor, a familiar odor. Why did his father sit so quietly, so settled in this mess? Paul would have to run next door and ask Mrs. Larsen how long he had been like this, he would have to telephone the doctor at the clinic and demand to know how long his father had been in this state of depression, a man who has given up. . . .

"How're the kids, eh?" his father asked finally.

"They're fine."

His father nodded, as if cutting him off. Their eyes did not meet. Then, suddenly, his father stood and left the room. He went back to the bathroom, not bothering to close the door . . . that too was familiar, Paul remembered his mother stamping over to slam the door shut, muttering, "Pig!"

Paul looked in the living room—a mess of newspapers, beer bottles. The shades were pulled and were not straight.

When his father returned they sat again at the table. It seemed to be the center of the house; his father had always sat there. Paul cleared his throat as if beginning an important speech. He blew one nostril and then the other, slowly. His father, suddenly self-conscious, rubbed his hands across his face. His hands were spotted with small brown spots. The skin stretched from knuckle to knuckle, the veins grotesquely prominent; ponderous, aged hands. They still looked strong. Paul remembered those hands grasping at the front bumper of a car, trying to push a car out of a ditch somewhere in the country . . . the awful straining, pushing, the whine of his mother's voice, "You'll kill yourself! Stop it! You're crazy!" But still the strain, the pushing, the effort of that man's muscles. . . . Now he rubbed his face as if feeling it, identifying it.

Paul was well into his speech—". . . if you came, then . . . then we could all be together . . . This house might sell for eight thousand . . . wouldn't it be nice to have that much money? You could do anything you wanted with it, anything. . . . Do you still go fishing?"

His father shook his head. "Naw."

"Don't you go with Ed Hegley?"

He shook his head again.

"Stevie and Bobby would go wild if you came, it would be like Christmas all the time, you know . . . kids need their grand-parents, their grandfathers. . . ."

His father looked at Paul's lunch bag. "You bring your lunch? You want to eat?"

Ann put on stockings and good shoes, zipped up a dress, hurried and angry. Her heart fluttered. She must get out of this house. But the unmade bed disturbed her, it had been said of her by her mother-in-law and her own grandmother that she was a very neat girl, and though both old women were dead, and had been mistaken, she felt a nagging desire to be that neat girl, that neat Ann. . . . So she made the bed, tugging impatiently at the sheets. She was not herself, making the bed, but a woman imagining a man embracing her: lying heavily upon her, his closeness dense upon her.

She felt faint, she left the room.

The boys' room needed picking up. But she had no energy for it. It was bewildering to her, their energy, their lives . . . they were always squirming, always pulling the towel-rack screw out of the wall, knocking bits of plaster down, breaking glasses, cutting themselves, bumping into each other. She loved them and yet believed that they did not love her; did not even notice her. She had said to her lover, the first time she had come to his apartment with him: "I used to think that when I was married, or when I had a baby, or when I was thirty, then I would come to a stop . . . I will be a certain person, I thought, and the world will come to a stop. Why didn't it turn out that way? I'm so tired of all these years, these decades, and nothing comes to an end . . . and I don't know any answers. . . ."

"The same with me," he had said brightly, seizing her hand, "I sure as hell don't know any answers!"

She had no time to bother straightening out the boys' room. She went downstairs. The back room with the basket of ironing; the kitchen; the rinsed dishes. No time. She went outside, cautious. It was a cold, disappointing day. She had a vision of her husband in an accident, a hundred miles away, the car smashed in, everything lost . . . and then what would happen? Her lover could not move in here. He could not be a father to another man's boys. She tried to imagine Paul feeling pain, crying out in anguish, *a man crying out in anguish*, but her mind wandered to the scruffy front lawn; the same dreary front lawn; a deadliness, a stupor from winter, shared by all the lawns on this street. And what if her father-in-law came here to live, what then? What if he came to this house and to this street to live, what then?

Paul's father had always been one of those men who closed themselves off from women, imagining themselves superior, secretive about their private lives and about money, money, money! —for men provided money, money was sacred. Women did not dare to ask for money. They were insulted, abused, when they asked for it, even to buy food. He had always been one of those men who hung around other men, in taverns and at garages, fooling around in mechanics' pits, drinking, vomiting in the bathroom or out in the back yard, never bothering to close doors after himself. Ann hated these sour, knowing male faces, the closeness of their maleness, their secrecy. No woman could penetrate their lives. Stupidly, blindly, they were creatures united in a permanent conspiracy against women, and this conspiracy gave them a certain uncanny strength.

The first time Paul had brought her home, his father had been late returning from work; a rough-faced, handsome man in his early sixties, his body still muscular, his working clothes soiled. Paul had introduced him to Ann. He had said, "Yah," and turned aside to spit in the driveway . . . his face screwing up to spit, as if showing his contempt for her.

She walked slowly along the street. She imagined other women, mothers like herself, were watching her . . . house after house, window after window. . . . She walked past them, unhurried. Her face would show nothing, after all. She still looked young; her skin was lightly freckled, still smooth. It was still the face her lover had noticed in the library, a man staring at her, singling her out. She had turned, curiously, to see a man staring at her. Something had stirred in her body, already wanting him.

In his room she had wanted him, many times, and she had understood that nothing else mattered, really. This was a fact. The anguish of her body, its straining, its heartbreaking weakness, were all that mattered in life, in her own life or in anyone's life. Lying with this man was the only meaning to her life . . . her mind kept circling that fact, numbly.

No, nothing else mattered.

What could these women, spying on her, know of her truest life? They were deluded themselves—their bodies heavy and triumphant with motherhood, like horses fitted out to battle, corseted and aging, their faces bunched up into glowing, robust smiles—deluded, all deluded. Her husband was deluded, sitting at the kitchen table with her, his partner and his wife, going over the bills and the receipts and the canceled checks and the notations in the checkbook—*Now, honey, this entry is yours; let's see what went wrong*—so kindly, so loving, bullying her, believing that he was her husband when in reality she had nothing to do with him at all.

Her mind kept leaping back to Stanford, to their first conversation.

"Tell me about your life. Your teaching. I was going to . . . I had wanted to teach, myself . . ." she said breathlessly.

They were holding hands.

"Ordinary teaching, ordinary students," he said. He had curly hair, he must have thought of himself as handsome; a handsome failure. She leaned toward him, feeling a slow cold terror begin in herself, unable to stop it or to stop herself, to withdraw, to take her hand out of his. Fluttering moths in her chest, her eyelashes. What was going to happen between them? He spoke quickly, licking his lips. "Everyone but me wants to get out of the city, the suburban schools are swamped with applications. Even up north. All the rats want to get out, everyone is anxious to escape Detroit. . . ."

They laughed at this, nervously, not knowing why they laughed. They were in a small pizzeria not far from the library. The only other customers were noisy teen-aged boys, but they did not hear the boys, they were smiling at each other, cautious and dreamy and nervous all at once, wondering what would hap-

pen between them. Of course, it did not seem possible that anything could happen. Stanford talked quickly, as if embarrassed.
He liked teaching, yes. It paid badly but he could not imagine
any other job. "I want to help kids, really. I guess I do," he said.
He rubbed self-consciously at his face. "But when I'm with them,
actually with them, it all seems so . . . absurd. . . . They're
all going in different directions, a dozen directions . . . there's
one boy whose father is a nut, evidently, a real nut who goes after
the mother and kids from time to time, and this boy is brilliant
in math . . . really brilliant at the age of fifteen. . . . I encourage him, I spend time with him after school. Great. But what will
happen? He's failing two other subjects, he cuts school half the
time, he takes pills or dope or some crap and I think even his
teeth are rotting. . . . And a cute little girl who hung around all
the time, who was always asking for help after school in geome-
try. . . ."

He smiled at Ann, the smile almost a twitch he could not control, and Ann felt his very nervousness draw her to him. His
words, devoid of sense, were an intimate music she could not
resist.

". . . all winter I worked with her, she'd hang around giggling . . . she gave me some stuff at Valentine's Day. . . .
Well, this girl, Sue, she was found in the basement of our
school with a plastic thing over her head, a bag, she'd been inhal-
ing some crap . . . glue, or nail-polish remover . . . and she
passed out and suffocated, she was found dead right in the
school. . . ."

"What, found dead?"

"Found dead. A cute little blond girl, fifteen, found
dead. . . ."

They had stared at each other. The words, the story produced
by the words, had no special meaning; he had recited it in a
rapid, tense, soothing manner to draw her to him, to seduce her.
She felt with shock that he was seducing her, unconsciously,

with this story of a dead girl; a cute little girl, a student of his, who was now dead; he was seducing her with this story.

"You mean she . . . she was found dead? Like that?"

"Yes, dead."

The excitement grew between them as if, somewhere near them, in some invisible dimension adjacent to them, a dead fifteen-year-old girl lay, her head in a plastic bag, her face blue in death. Dead! A girl dead! Staring at Ann, Stanford had squeezed her hand, his own hand cool and damp.

"But that's terrible . . ." Ann had whispered.

Paul was saying, "The house is easily worth eight, maybe nine thousand. . . . I can list it myself, I can save you the commission. . . ."

They had been talking like this for some time. His father grunted Yah or Naw, as if pretending to be interested. Finally he stood. "Time to get the paper," he announced.

They walked together four or five blocks to a small shopping center where Paul's father bought a newspaper at a drugstore. Paul, feeling bewildered, a little hurt, wandered up and down the aisles of the store while his father talked with the druggist, a short, ratlike man with greasy dark hair and a high, quick laugh. The man was about fifty-five, sixty. What were they talking about? Paul joined his father again and they walked back home, the two of them side by side, having nothing to say.

His father glanced at the headlines of the newspaper.

Back at the house they both opened cans of beer. Paul glanced at his watch. It was almost time for him to leave and he had had no chance to say what he must say. . . . He took out a rumpled tissue and dabbed at his forehead, his eyes, and then blew his nose. He felt deeply, unaccountably sad, as if he had driven hundreds of miles across the state and back into time, at great cost to himself, to present a gift to his father that his father did not want. Nothing had happened, nothing had been said. They had not even argued. On the expressway, so much alone that perhaps he had become a little giddy, Paul had imagined saying to his father, *You know I have always loved you.* . . . Now his father shook the newspaper open and sat frowning at it, as if he suspected what the news would be and did not look forward to it.

"Eh, look at this, the trouble you guys have over there!" he said.

He pointed to a headline about racial disturbances in Detroit. A policeman had shot a black, bands of blacks had milled together angrily in the streets. . . .

Ann went into the drugstore. The saleswoman greeted her, she waved in return, she went to the telephone booth at the back of the store. Her heart was pounding. If she telephoned him now he might not be home, it was early; she might not have to talk with him. She dreaded hearing his voice. She sat with her forehead pressed against the wall of the booth—it was made of some strange corrugated material, probably plastic. Another self, deeper and more knowing, bitter, sensual, impatient, seemed to be shaping itself out of her bones and nerves, ready to shake itself free of her. She felt this self in her; she clenched her teeth, waiting. If she telephoned him . . . everything would begin again. . . .

Once, after an argument, she had walked out on him and had telephoned him a few days later. She had been terrified, hearing the telephone ring at the other end of the line, hoping it would not be answered. Then it had been answered. In a guarded voice he said, "Hello? . . ."

"Hello," she said softly.

A few seconds of silence.

"Where are you?" he said.

"In a telephone booth. In a store."

She could hear herself breathing.

"What . . . what are you doing? How have you been?" he asked.

She hesitated as if preparing to throw herself off a precipice; she imagined herself at the bottom, broken and complete. She said quickly, "I'm sorry, I love you . . . I can't help it. . . ."

And so, then, it had all begun again; she had been fated to be that woman, telephoning that man, weeping in a telephone booth.

She put a dime in the slot and dialed him. The telephone rang at that end while she sat very straight, listening, and after several rings she said to herself, "He isn't home from school yet." Relieved, she hung up. Her hands were trembling.

She went down the street to the dry cleaner's, to pick up her husband's trench coat. They had charged three dollars to clean it. *Goddamn him,* she thought. "Was it tar? What was it?" she asked the woman. "I don't know, we thought maybe it was tar," the woman said.

She hurried home so that she would be there when the boys returned from school. She thought it was important for her to be home; her own mother, unstable and alcoholic, a very sad woman, had rarely been home when Ann had returned from school; Ann had remembered that. She went into the kitchen and looked in the freezer: minute steaks, she would give them to Paul and the boys for dinner, and French fries with ketchup, their favorite dinner. Good. That was settled. Waiting for the boys, she began cleaning the kitchen, feeling oddly light, free . . . if the boys came home right away she would not be able to call Stanford, that would be decided. This particular day, a Wednesday, would have passed and she would not have telephoned him.

It was nearly dark when Paul turned up his street. He had been driving fast, anxious to get home. Accidents along the expressway—one of them involving five or six cars—had frightened him, spurred him on. He was afraid of those heaped-up images, those indecipherable twists of metal and glass. The pull of his father had lessened along with the miles and now, nearly home, the pull of his wife and sons was powerful . . . he thought fiercely of their home, their life together, and how he must explain it to his father before it was too late; he must make his father understand.

He parked the car in the garage. Everything was quiet here—his wife would be in the kitchen, his boys in the living room watching television. He had lived evenings like this before. There was no threat. Preparing dinner right now, his wife would be in the kitchen; he would eat; and then he would sleep.

The long day would complete itself.

S_talking_

The Invisible Adversary is fleeing across a field.

Gretchen, walking slowly, deliberately, watches with her keen unblinking eyes the figure of the Invisible Adversary some distance ahead. The Adversary has run boldly in front of all that traffic—on long spiky legs brisk as colts' legs—and jumped up onto a curb of new concrete, and now is running across a vacant field. The Adversary glances over his shoulder at Gretchen.

Bastard, Gretchen thinks.

Saturday afternoon. November. A cold gritty day. Gretchen is out stalking. She has hours for her game. Hours. She is dressed for the hunt, her solid legs crammed into old blue jeans, her big, square, strong feet jammed into white leather boots that cost her mother forty dollars not long ago, but are now scuffed and filthy with mud. Hopeless to get them clean again, Gretchen doesn't give a damn. She is wearing a dark green corduroy jacket that is worn out at the elbows and the rear, with a zipper that can be zipped swiftly up or down, attached to a fringed leather strip. On her head nothing, though it is windy today.

She has hours ahead.

Cars and trucks and buses from the city and enormous inter-state trucks hauling automobiles pass by on the highway; Gretchen waits until the way is nearly clear, then starts out. A single car is approaching. *Slow down, you bastard,* Gretchen thinks; and like magic he does.

Following the footprints of the Invisible Adversary. There is no sidewalk here yet, so she might as well cut right across the field. A gigantic sign announces the site of the new Pace & Fischbach Building, an office building of fifteen floors to be com-pleted the following year. The land around here is all dug up and muddy; she can see the Adversary's footsteps leading right past the gouged-up area . . . and there he is, smirking back at her, pretending panic.

I'll get you. Don't worry, Gretchen thinks carefully.

Because the Adversary is so light-footed and invisible, Gretchen doesn't make any effort to be that way. She plods along as she does at school, passing from classroom to classroom, unhur-ried and not even sullen, just unhurried. She knows she is very visible. She is thirteen years old and weighs one hundred and thirty-five pounds. She's only five feet three—stocky, muscular, squat in the torso and shoulders, with good strong legs and thighs. She could be good at gym, if she bothered; instead, she just stands around, her face empty, her arms crossed and her shoulders a little slumped. If forced, she takes part in the games of volleyball and basketball, but she runs heavily, without spirit, and sometimes bumps into other girls, hurting them. *Out of my way,* she thinks; at such times her face shows no expression.

And now? . . . The Adversary is peeking out at her from around the corner of a gas station. Something flickers in her brain. *I see you,* she thinks, with quiet excitement. The Adversary ducks back out of sight. Gretchen heads in his direction, plodding through a jumbled, bulldozed field of mud and thistles and debris that is mainly rocks and chunks of glass. The gas station is brand new and not yet opened for business. It is all white tile, white concrete, perfect plate-glass windows with whitewashed X's on them, a large driveway and eight gasoline pumps, all proudly erect and ready for business. But the gas station has not opened since Gretchen and her family moved here—about six months ago. Something must have gone wrong. Gretchen fixes her eyes on the corner where the Adversary was last seen. He can't escape.

One wall of the gas station's white tile has been smeared with something like tar. Dreamy, snakelike, thick twistings of black. Black tar. Several windows have been broken. Gretchen stands in the empty driveway, her hands jammed into her pockets. Traffic is moving slowly over here. A barricade has been set up that directs traffic out onto the shoulder of the highway, on a narrow, bumpy, muddy lane that loops out and back again onto the pavement. Cars move slowly, carefully. Their bottoms scrape against the road. The detour signs are great rectangular things, bright yellow with black zigzag lines. SLOW. DETOUR. In the two center lanes of the highway are bulldozers not being used today, and gigantic concrete pipes to be used for storm sewers. Eight pipes. They are really enormous; Gretchen's eyes crinkle with awe, just to see them.

She remembers the Adversary.

There he is—headed for the shopping plaza. *He won't get away in the crowds,* Gretchen promises herself. She follows. Now she is approaching an area that is more completed, though there are still no sidewalks and some of the buildings are brandnew and yet unoccupied, vacant. She jumps over a concrete ditch that is stained with rust-colored water and heads up a slight incline to the service drive of the Federal Savings Bank. The drive-in tellers' windows are all dark today, behind their green-tinted glass. The whole bank is dark, closed. Is this the bank her parents go to now? It takes Gretchen a minute to recognize it.

Now a steady line of traffic, a single lane, turns onto the service drive that leads to the shopping plaza. BUCKINGHAM MALL. 101 STORES. Gretchen notices a few kids her own age, boys or girls, trudging in jeans and jackets ahead of her, through the mud. They might be classmates of hers. Her attention is captured again by the Invisible Adversary, who has run all the way up to the Mall and is hanging around the entrance of the Cunningham Drug Store, teasing her.

You'll be sorry for that, you bastard, Gretchen thinks with a smile.

Automobiles pass her slowly. The parking lot for the Mall is enormous, many acres. A city of cars on a Saturday afternoon. Gretchen sees a car that might be her mother's, but she isn't sure. Cars are parked slanted here, in lanes marked LOT K, LANE 15; LOT K, LANE 16. The signs are spheres, bubbles, perched up on long slender poles. At night they are illuminated.

Ten or twelve older kids are hanging around the drugstore entrance. One of them is sitting on top of a mailbox, rocking it back and forth. Gretchen pushes past them—they are kidding around, trying to block people—and inside the store her eye darts rapidly up and down the aisles, looking for the Invisible Adversary.

Hiding here? Hiding?

She strolls along, cunning and patient. At the cosmetics counter a girl is showing an older woman some liquid make-up. She smears a small oval onto the back of the woman's hand, rubs it in gently. "That's Peach Pride," the girl says. She has shimmering blond hair and eyes that are penciled to show a permanent exclamatory interest. She does not notice Gretchen, who lets one hand drift idly over a display of marked-down lipsticks, each for only $1.59.

Gretchen slips the tube of lipstick into her pocket. Neatly. Nimbly. Ignoring the Invisible Adversary, who is shaking a finger at her, she drifts over to the newsstand, looks at the magazine covers without reading them, and edges over to another display. Packages in a cardboard barrel, out in the aisle. Big bargains. Gretchen doesn't even glance in the barrel to see what is being offered . . . she just slips one of the packages in her pocket. No trouble.

She leaves by the other door, the side exit. A small smile tugs at her mouth.

The Adversary is trotting ahead of her. The Mall is divided into geometric areas, each colored differently; the Adversary leaves the blue pavement and is now on the green. Gretchen follows. She notices the Adversary going into a Franklin Joseph store.

Gretchen enters the store, sniffs in the perfumy, overheated smell, sees nothing that interests her on the counters or at the dress racks, and so walks right to the back of the store, to the Ladies Room. No one inside. She takes the tube of lipstick out of her pocket, opens it, examines the lipstick. It has a tart, sweet smell. A very light pink: *Spring Blossom.* Gretchen goes to the mirror and smears the lipstick onto it, at first lightly, then coarsely; part of the lipstick breaks and falls into a hair-littered sink. Gretchen goes into one of the toilet stalls and tosses the tube into the toilet bowl. She takes handfuls of toilet paper and crumbles them into a ball and throws them into the toilet. Remembering the package from the drugstore, she takes it out of her pocket—just toothpaste. She throws it, cardboard package and all, into the toilet bowl, then, her mind glimmering with an idea, she goes to the apparatus that holds the towel—a single cloth towel on a roll—and tugs at it until it comes loose, then pulls it out hand over hand, patiently, until the entire towel is out. She scoops it up and carries it to the toilet. She pushes it in and flushes the toilet.

The stuff doesn't go down, so she tries again. This time it goes part-way down before it gets stuck.

Gretchen leaves the rest room and strolls unhurried through the store. The Adversary is waiting for her outside—peeking through the window—wagging a finger at her. *Don't you wag no finger at me*, she thinks, with a small tight smile. Outside, she follows him at a distance. Loud music is blaring around her head. It is rock music, piped out onto the colored squares and rectangles of the Mall, blown everywhere by the November wind, but Gretchen hardly hears it.

Some boys are fooling around in front of the record store. One of them bumps into Gretchen and they all laugh as she is pushed against a trash can. "Watch it, babe!" the boy sings out. Her leg hurts. Gretchen doesn't look at them but, with a cold, swift anger, her face averted, she knocks the trash can over onto the sidewalk. Junk falls out. The can rolls. Some women shoppers scurry to get out of the way and the boys laugh.

Gretchen walks away without looking back.

She wanders through Sampson Furniture, which has two entrances. In one door and out the other, as always; it is a ritual with her. Again she notices the sofa that is like the sofa in their family room at home—covered with black and white fur, real goatskin. All over the store there are sofas, chairs, tables, beds. A jumble of furnishings. People stroll around them, in and out of little displays, displays meant to be living rooms, dining rooms, bedrooms, family rooms. . . . It makes Gretchen's eyes squint to see so many displays: like seeing the inside of a hundred houses. She slows down, almost comes to a stop. Gazing at a living-room display on a raised platform. Only after a moment does she remember why she is here—whom she is following—and she turns to see the Adversary beckoning to her.

She follows him outside again. He goes into Dodi's Boutique and, with her head lowered so that her eyes seem to move to the bottom of her eyebrows, pressing up against her forehead, Gretchen follows him. *You'll regret this*, she thinks. Dodi's Boutique is decorated in silver and black. Metallic strips hang down from a dark ceiling, quivering. Salesgirls dressed in pants suits stand around with nothing to do except giggle with one another and nod their heads in time to the music amplified throughout the store. It is music from a local radio station. Gretchen wanders over to the dress rack, for the hell of it. Size 14. "The time is now 2:35," a radio announcer says cheerfully. "The weather is 32 degrees with a chance of showers and possible sleet tonight. You're listening to WCKK, Radio Wonderful. . . ." Gretchen selects several dresses and a salesgirl shows her to a dressing room.

"Need any help?" the girl asks. She has long swinging hair and a high-shouldered, indifferent, bright manner.

"No," Gretchen mutters.

Alone, Gretchen takes off her jacket. She is wearing a navy blue sweater. She zips one of the dresses open and it falls off the flimsy plastic hanger before she can catch it. She steps on it, smearing mud onto the white wool. *The hell with it.* She lets it lie there and holds up another dress, gazing at herself in the mirror.

She has untidy, curly hair that looks like a wig set loosely on her head. Light brown curls spill out everywhere, bouncy, a little frizzy, a cascade, a tumbling of curls. Her eyes are deep set, her eyebrows heavy and dark. She has a stern, staring look, like an adult man. Her nose is perfectly formed, neat and noble. Her upper lip is long, as if it were stretched to close with difficulty over the front teeth. She wears no make-up, her lips are perfectly colorless, pale, a little chapped, and they are usually held tight, pursed tightly shut. She has a firm, rounded chin. Her facial structure is strong, pensive, its features stern and symmetrical as a statue's, blank, neutral, withdrawn. Her face is attractive. But there is a blunt, neutral, sexless stillness to it, as if she were detached from it and somewhere else, uninterested.

She holds the dress up to her body, smooths it down over her breasts, staring.

After a moment she hangs the dress up again, and runs down the zipper so roughly that it breaks. The other dress she doesn't bother with. She leaves the dressing room, putting on her jacket.

At the front of the store the salesgirl glances at her . . . "—Didn't fit?—"

"No," says Gretchen.

She wanders around for a while, in and out of Carmichael's, the Mall's big famous store, where she catches sight of her mother on an escalator going up. Her mother doesn't notice her. She pauses by a display of "winter homes." Her family owns a home like this, in the Upper Peninsula, except theirs is larger. This one comes complete for only $5330: PACKAGE ERECTED ON YOUR LOT —YEAR-ROUND HOME FIBER GLASS INSULATION—BEAUTIFUL ROUGH-SAWN VERTICAL B. C. CEDAR SIDING WITH DEEP SIMULATED SHADOW LINES FOR A RUGGED EXTERIOR.

Only 3:15. For the hell of it, Gretchen goes into the Big Boy restaurant and orders a ground-round hamburger with French fries. Also a Coke. She sits at the crowded counter and eats slowly, her jaws grinding slowly, as she glances at her reflection in the mirror directly in front of her—her mop of hair moving almost imperceptibly with the grinding of her jaws—and occasionally she sees the Adversary waiting outside, coyly. *You'll get yours,* she thinks.

She leaves the Big Boy and wanders out into the parking lot, eating from a bag of potato chips. She wipes her greasy hands on her thighs. The afternoon has turned dark and cold. Shivering a little, she scans the maze of cars for the Adversary—yes, there he is—and starts after him. He runs ahead of her. He runs through the parking lot, waits teasingly at the edge of a field, and as she approaches he runs across the field, trotting along with a noisy crowd of four or five loose dogs that don't seem to notice him.

Gretchen follows him through that field, trudging in the mud, and through another muddy field, her eyes fixed on him. Now he is at the highway—hesitating there—now he is about to run across in front of traffic—now, now—now he darts out—

Now! He is struck by a car! His body knocked backward, spinning backward. Ah, now, *now how does it feel?* Gretchen asks.

He picks himself up. Gets to his feet. Is he bleeding? Yes, bleeding! He stumbles across the highway to the other side, where there is a sidewalk. Gretchen follows him as soon as the traffic lets up. He is staggering now, like a drunken man. *How does it feel? Do you like it now?*

The Adversary staggers along the sidewalk. He turns onto a side street, beneath an archway. *Piney Woods*. He is leading Gretchen into the Piney Woods subdivision. Here the homes are quite large, on artificial hills that show them to good advantage. Most of the homes are white colonials with attached garages. There are no sidewalks here, so the Adversary has to walk in the street, limping like an old man, and Gretchen follows him in the street, with her eyes fixed on him.

Are you happy now? Does it hurt? Does it?

She giggles at the way he walks. He looks like a drunken man. He glances back at her, white-faced, and turns up a flagstone walk . . . goes right up to a big white colonial house. . . .

Gretchen follows him inside. She inspects the simulated brick of the foyer: yes, there are blood spots. He is dripping blood. Entranced, she follows the splashes of blood into the hall, to the stairs . . . forgets her own boots, which are muddy . . . but she doesn't feel like going back to wipe her feet. The hell with it.

Nobody seems to be home. Her mother is probably still shopping, her father is out of town for the weekend. The house empty. Gretchen goes into the kitchen, opens the refrigerator, takes out a Coke, and wanders to the rear of the house, to the family room. It is two steps down from the rest of the house. She takes off her jacket and tosses it somewhere. Turns on the television set. Sits on the goatskin sofa and stares at the screen: a return of a Shotgun Steve show, which she has already seen.

If the Adversary comes crawling behind her, groaning in pain, weeping, she won't even bother to glance at him.

Scenes of Passion and Despair

Walking quickly. The path become mud. She walked in the weeds at the edge of the path—then, her good luck, some planks had been put down in the mud, for cattle to walk on. She walked on the planks.

A hill leading down to the river, bumpy and desolate. Ragged weeds, bushes, piles of debris. NO DUMPING ALLOWED. The Hudson River: she stared at the wild gray water and its shapelessness. Familiar sight. She'd been seeing it from this path, hurrying along this path, for weeks. *Weeks?* It was only the end of June and it seemed to her the summer had lasted years already. *How to survive the summer?*

The planks wobbled in the mud. Her legs straining to go faster, faster. Down on the river bank were old bedsprings and mattresses, broken chairs, washing machines. . . . If one of these planks slipped she might tumble down there herself.

Her hands up to her face, warding off the stinging branches. Almost running. Sometimes she slipped off the cow plank and into the mud, her shoes splattered, damp; she felt with disgust her wet toes inside the gauze of her stockings. Heart thudding impatiently. The eerie light of this June morning, still half an hour before dawn: would it turn into an ordinary day later on? Could this gray still air turn into ordinary air, riddled with sunlight and the songs of June birds? Up at so early an hour, alone on the river bank, alone hurrying along the path, she felt her cunning and yet could not keep down a rising sense of panic—was this visit going to be a mistake? Did he want her? Why this particular June morning, before dawn? Why this particular dress of hers, a blue and white flowered dress, cotton, with a dipping white collar with machine-made lace, why this, why its looseness as if she'd lost weight, why the light splattering of mud and dew across her thighs? And why did she take the cowpath, why not dare the road?

Now she cut up from the path, up through a meager clump of trees. Legs aching from the climb. The house came into view suddenly: an old farmhouse, fixed up a little, the chimney restored. A car in the driveway, mud puddles stretching out long, narrow, glimmering around it, the water crystalline at this hour and at this distance, as if it meant something. Rehearsing her words: *I had to come—I had to see you*—Panting. Brushing strands of hair out of her face. Tried to imagine the exact appearance of her face—her face was very important—her face—her face and his face, confronting each other again—

She ran to the front door, up on the rickety porch. Uncut grass. *A real farmhouse in the country. Near the Hudson.* She did not knock, but opened the door, which was unlocked—*You don't even have to lock your doors*—went inside. Heart pounding desperately. She called his name, ran to his bedroom at the back of the house—in the air the smell of his tobacco, the smell of food from last night—the slight staleness of a body in these close, cluttered rooms—he was waking up, his hair matted from sleep —staring at her in amazement—

She ran to him. *I had to see you*—He interrupted her, they embraced, a feverish embrace. The blank startled love in his face: she saw it and could not speak. *Had to see you*—

Wonder. His voice, his surprise. Hips jammed together, bodies cool and yet slippery as if with the predawn dew, the start of the birds singing outside, ordinary singing for June, the rocky tumult of the run along the path, the planks, the mud puddles, the banks of the river, her mind flitting back to the house she had run from, running out in her blue and white cotton dress, no scarf on her head, shivering, reckless, calculating the amount of time she had before her husband—who had left for the airport at 5:30—might get to New York, might telephone her to check on her loneliness—

So long, you bastard.

2

Hips jammed together in languid violence. A need. A demand. Do the leaves glisten outside in the lead-gray air? Are they strong enough to last all summer? Only June, the flesh of her face is not firm enough to last. Her lover's hands, chest, stomach, his face, his soft kindly mouth, sucking at her mouth, the force of him jerking the bed out inches from the wall, the heaving of covers— she sees how grimy the khaki-colored blanket has become—her lover's parts are firm enough to last all summer, to last forever, even if she wears out.

How many times had they loved like this, exactly?

Lost count.

He is saying something: ". . . is he like now?"

"What is he like? . . ."

"With this, with us . . . doesn't he know, doesn't he sense it . . . what is he like now with you? Can't he guess?"

"I don't know. I don't think about it."

"Does he drink a lot?"

"No more than before."

"Can he sleep?"

"No more than before. He's always had insomnia. . . ."

"Do you sleep beside him, then, can you fall asleep while he's awake? . . ."

Wants to know if that other man, my husband, still makes love to me.

"I don't know. I don't know him at all."

3

The cow planks sigh in the oozing mud, she runs holding her side, panting, her bowels feel like rocks this morning, poison, poisoned; she hates the man she is running from—eleven years invested in him—and she hates the man she is running toward, asleep in that room with the bedraggled wallpaper, and no telephone in his *authentic rented farmhouse on the Hudson River,* so he brags to his friends; she must run to him shivering, her face splotched from the slaps of branches, saliva gathering sourly in her mouth as if forcing her to spit—Can't stop running. Her heart pounds. Can't look down at the river because it is so brutal, a mass that would not support her weight if she suddenly slipped down the bank; imagine the shrieking, the lonely complexities of thought, the electric shocks of terror as she drowns, having a lot of time to reconsider her life—And then they would fish her body out of the river a hundred miles downstream. So long, my love.

The cow planks sigh and bounce. She runs up the hill to the farm he has rented, her flesh aches to be embraced, she scrambles up the hill in her muddy ruined shoes, panting, and she dreams suddenly of an ice pick—wide-awake, she dreams of an ice pick —remembers her mother with an ice pick twenty years ago, raising it to jam it down into a piece of ice—dreams of an ice pick raised in her two trembling hands and brought down hard into whose chest?—his chest?—but what about the wispy light-brown hairs of his chest, which she supposedly loves?

4

Hips grinding, jammed together. You might imagine music in the background, the grinding is so fierce. An ancient bed: brass bedstead. It came with the house. *A semifurnished old farmhouse with a restored chimney!* The one time her lover ventured into her own home, her husband's handsome white Cape Cod, he clowned around and peeked into drawers nervously, joking about hidden tape recorders and other ingenious spying devices he'd just read about in a national newsmagazine, and then, serious with a sudden manly frown, he told her he had to leave, he couldn't make love to her *there,* in her husband's bed, that magical marriage bed with the satin bedspread.

Why not?

A manly code, a masculine code she couldn't appreciate, maybe?

Now she lies with him in his own rented bed, an old farmhouse bed with a brass headboard, and she sees at the back of his skull a shadowy area like a fatal shadow in an x-ray. Secret from her. Their toes tickle one another. Twenty toes together at the foot of the bed, under the khaki cover! Such loving toes! But the shadow inside his head isn't loving; she fears it growing bigger, darker; she shuts her eyes hard to keep it from oozing into her own skull, because she has always tried to be optimistic about life.

5

Ducks on the river. Mallards. Male and female in pairs and in loose busy groups, Canadian geese bouncing on the waves, going one way in a large confederation of birds, then turning unaccountably and going the other way, back and forth across the choppy waves, back and forth, their calls strident and dismal as she runs, her brow furrowed with some strange stray memory of her mother and an ice pick—

He, the husband, took the Volkswagen to the airport and left her the Buick. *I'll call you from New York,* he said. Darkness at the back of his skull. If his drinking got too bad and he really got sick, she would abandon her lover and nurse him. If he killed himself she would abandon her lover and wear black. Years of mourning. Guilt. Sin. If he found out about her lover and ran over and killed him, shot him right in that bed, she would wear black, she would not give evidence against him, she would come haggard to court, a faithful wife once again.

The husband will not get sick, will not kill himself, will not kill the lover or even find out about him; he will only grow old.

She will not need to wear black or to be faithful. She will grow old.

The lover will not even grow old: he will explode into molecules as into a mythology.

6

I don't know him at all.

A stormy river, small cataclysms. Quakes, spouts, whirlpools a few yards deep. She doesn't dare to look at the water because her mind might suddenly go into a spin.

You take things too seriously before dawn.

Climbs up the path to his house, up the back way to his meager one-acre farm. Feet already wet from a lifetime of puddles that must be glimpsed far ahead of time in order to be avoided, and suddenly there is a blow against the back of her neck, she pitches forward, a man's feet stumble with her feet, she cries out at the sight of large muddy boots—The blow is so hard that her teeth seem shaken loose. She is thrown forward and would fall except he has caught hold of her.

Jerks her around to face him.

Small panicked screams. She hears someone screaming feebly —hears the sounds of toil, struggle—the man, whose face she can't see, trips her neatly with one ankle behind hers, she falls on her right side, on her hip and thigh and shoulder, already she is scrambling to get away—trying to slide sideways, backward in the mud—but the man has gripped her by the shoulders and lifts her and slams her back against the ground again, up, and then down again, as if trying to break her into pieces, and she sees a swirl of eyes, yellow-rimmed, the small hard dots of black at the center of each eye somehow familiar and eternal, even the dried mucus at the inside corner of each eye absolutely familiar, eternal—

A body jammed against hers. A bent knee, the strain of his thigh muscles communicated to her body, his wheezing, panting, his small cries overpowering hers, his grasping, nudging, glowering face, his leathery skin jammed against her skin; *I don't know him at all,* the bridge of his nose suddenly very important, lowered to her face again and again. Tufts of pale hair in his ears, swollen veins in his throat, his eager grunts, his groveling above her, the stale fury of his breath, his hands, his straining bent knees, the cold mud, the lead-gray patch of sky overhead; inch by inch she is being driven up the hill by his love for her, his thudding against her in a rapid series of blows that jar her entire body and seem to have loosened the teeth in her head—

7

Once by chance but not really by chance she had met her lover in the general store in town, where he had a post-office box to insure his anonymity (exaggerating the world's interest in him, he imagined a crowd of curious friends sailing up the Hudson to claim him). That rushed exchange of hellos, that eager snatching of eyes, smiles. The anxiety: *Am I still loved?* Adultery makes people nervous. She saw that he hadn't shaved and was disappointed. They whispered between shelves of soup cans and cereal boxes and jars of instant coffee, the brand names and their heraldic colors and designs so familiar that she felt uneasy, as if spied upon by old friends. Her husband was at the lumberyard to buy a few things and would only be a few minutes, she had no time to waste; backing away, she put out her hands prettily as if to ward off her eager lover, and he, unshaven, dressed in a red-and-black checked wool jacket, took a step toward her, grinning, *Why are you so skittish?* Between the towering shelves of fading, souring food he lunged at her with his face, kissed her lips, more of a joke than a true kiss, and she felt a drop of his saliva on her lips and, involuntarily, she licked it off, and the drop was swept along by the powerful tiny muscles of her tongue, to the back of her throat, and down in a sudden pulsation of secret muscles to her insides, where it entered her bloodstream before she had even laughed nervously and backed away, paid for her jar of Maxwell House instant coffee and a leaky carton of milk, hurried outside without glancing back, walked over to the lumberyard where her husband was standing in a brightly lit little office made of concrete blocks talking with a fat man in a red-and-black checked wool jacket; by now the drop of saliva was soaring along her bloodstream, minute and bright and stable as a tiny balloon, rushing through the veins to the right ventricle—*I don't know you at all*—and faster and faster into the pulmonary artery, and into the secret left side of the heart, where it inflated itself suddenly, proudly, and caused her heart to pound—

Did you get the things you wanted? her husband asked.

8

Late winter. Freezing air. A car parked on the river bank, by the edge of the big park—barbecue fireplaces with tiny soiled drifts of snow on their grills, you have to imagine people at the picnic tables, you have to imagine a transistor radio squealing, and the smell of burning charcoal; but you can still see the remains of Sunday comics blown into the bushes.

She turns, twists herself eagerly in his arms. His mouth rubs against hers damply, the lips seem soft but they are also hard, or maybe it is the hardness of his youthful teeth behind them. Desperation. Struggle. The toiling of their breaths. On the radio is WKBT's "Sunday Scene," a thumping tumult of voices and their echoes, yes, everything is wonderful—everything is desperate—he begins his frantic nudging, they are both eighteen, she discovers herself lying in the same position again, making the same writhing sharp twists with her body, as if fending him off and inviting him closer, she moves in time with the music, and then they are sitting up again and he is smoking a cigarette like someone in a movie. Small fixed uneasy smiles. They will marry, obviously.

9

Early spring. Freezing air. The heater in his car won't work right. *State Police find lovers dead in an embrace.* They kiss each other wetly, hotly, eagerly on the lips, they slide their bodies out of their clothes, snakelike, eager and urgent, the man's breath is like a hiss, the woman's breath is shallow and seems to go no farther than the back of her throat, he lifts her legs up onto the front seat again, onto the scratchy plastic seat cover; such a difficult trick; after all, they are a lot older than eighteen.

10

A woman in a long blue dress. Her stockings white cotton; her shoes handmade. The man in a waistcoat, holding her hand, slipping down the incline to the river bank. They turn to each other eagerly and embrace. So friendly! So helpful! They kneel in the grass, whispering words that can't be heard by the children who are hiding in the bushes. The lovers undress each other. The woman is shy and efficient, the man keeps laughing in small nervous embarrassed delighted spurts, and the children in the bushes have to stand up to see more clearly what is happening—

11

In his bed, before dawn, she notices the grimy blanket that she will think about with shame, hours later, and as he kneels above her she senses something fraudulent about him, no, yes, but it is too late; she grips his back and his legs though she is exhausted, and her constricted throat gives out small, gentle, fading, souring sounds of love, but she feels the toughness of his skin, like hide, and the leathery cracks of his skin, and down at his buttocks the cold little grainy pimples, like coarse sandpaper, and one hand darts in terror to his head as if she wanted to grip the hair and pull his head away from hers, and she feels his loosening hair— Ah, clumps of his thick brown hair come away in her hand! *I love you,* he is muttering, but she seems to recognize the pitch and rhythm of his voice, she has heard this before, in a movie perhaps, and now, as they kiss so urgently, she tries not to notice the way his facial structure sags, *dear God, the entire face can be moved from one side to the other, should she mention it?* And he didn't bother shaving again. He could have shaved before going to bed, guessing, hoping she might come this morning, before dawn. . . . The eyeballs can be pushed backward . . . and then they move slowly forward again, springing slowly forward, in slow motion, not the way you would expect eyeballs to spring forward. . . .

12

God, her body aches. There is an itchiness too, probably an infection. That tiny bubble in the blood, exploding into splashes of excited colorless water, probably infected. His swarming germs, seed. The stain on her clothes.

At home, upstairs in the white Cape Cod, she cleans herself of him outside and inside.

No, she is not cleaning herself of him, but preparing herself for him: a shower the night before, the glimpse of her flushed face in the steamy mirror, the sorrow of those little pinched lines about her breasts, the urgent, slightly protruding bone of her forehead, wanting to push ahead to the next morning and through the impending sleepless night beside her husband. She has caught insomnia from him during the eleven years of their marriage.

No, she is not preparing herself for anyone. She is simply standing in the bathroom staring at herself. The bathtub with the bluebells on the shower curtain. Put the shower curtain on the *outside* of the tub when you take a bath, on the *inside* when you take a shower, her mother has explained for the hundredth time. Why are you always in a daze? What are you daydreaming about, may I ask? No, not daydreaming. She is just staring in the mirror at her small hard breasts, at the disappointing pallor of her chest, at her stomach where the faint brown hairs seem to grow in a circle, in a pale circle around her belly button. She is four-teen years old. She is just staring in the mirror, reluctant to leave the bathroom; she is not preparing herself for anyone, she is just standing on the fluffy blue rug from Woolworth's, she is not thinking about anything at all, she is reluctant to think.

13

Eight years old, the man finds himself again at a kitchen table, he glances up in surprise to see that it is the kitchen of his parents' house, and he is reduced in size—no more than eight years old! It's a rainy day and from the sound of the house (his father in the cellar) it must be a Saturday. He's fooling around with his clay kit. He has made four snakes by rolling clay between his hands; now he twists the snakes into circles, heads mashed against tails, and makes a pot, but it doesn't look right—too small. The clock is whirring above the stove: a yellow-backed General Electric clock. He is alone in the kitchen. His father is sawing something in the cellar and his mother is probably out shopping. He mashes all the clay together again and makes a column, about six inches high, and he molds the column into a body. With a pencil he pricks holes for the eyes and fashions a smiling mouth, pinches a little nose out, on the chest he pinches out two breasts, makes them very large and pointed, and between the legs he pokes a hole. Sits staring at this for a few minutes. He is aware of his father in the cellar, aware of the clock whirring, the rain outside, and suddenly a raw, sick sensation begins in him, in his bowels, and he is transfixed with dread. . . . He picks up a tiny piece of clay and makes a small wormlike thing and tries to press it against the figure, between her legs. It falls off. Perspiring, he presses it into place again and manages to make it stick. It is a small grub-sized thing but it makes sense. He stares at it and his panic subsides, slowly. He feels slightly sick the rest of the day.

14

He crouches above her, she notices his narrowed, squinting eyes, the hard dark iris, the tension of his mouth, and he buries his face against her shoulder and throat as if to hide himself from her, oh, she loves him, oh, she is dying for him, no one but him. Their stomachs rub and twist hotly together and she feels herself gathered up in his arms, is surprised at how small her body is, how good it is to be small, gathered in a man's strong arms, and she thinks that the two of them might be lying anywhere, making love anywhere, the walls of this farmhouse might fall away to show them on a river bank, in the sunshine, or in a car, at the edge of a large state park with Dixie cups blowing hollowly about them as they love, and small white plastic spoons in the grass. . . .

Suddenly exhausted, her hands stop their caressing of his back as if a thought had occurred to them, she instructs herself to caress him again but her fingers seem to have lost interest, grown stiff as if with arthritis, *what is wrong?* At the back of her throat she feels a ticklish sensation as if she is going to cough, but instead of coughing she whispers *I love you,* involuntarily, and they are toiling upstream on the cold river, ducks and geese around them sadly, morosely; the lead-gray sky and the lead-gray water are enough to convince them that this act is utterly useless, but who can stop? On the grass a few feet away is her wide-brimmed straw hat, a hat for Sunday in the country, and he has not had time to take off his waistcoat, and his whiskers scratch her soft skin; but when he whispers *Am I hurting you?* she answers at once *No, no, you never hurt me.* Someone calls out to them. A mocking scream. A shout. They freeze together, wondering if they heard correctly—what was that? Someone is shouting.

It isn't in their imaginations, it isn't the cry of geese on the river, no, someone is really shouting at them—has her husband followed her here after all?—but no, it is a stranger who seems to know them. He stomps right over to them and they fall apart, dazed and embarrassed, they are so awkward together, being strangers themselves. The glaring lights make them squint. This stranger eyes them cynically. He squats, a more experienced lover, and arranges and rearranges arms, legs, the proper bending of the knee; with the palm of his practiced hand he urges the man's head down, down, just a few inches more, yes, hold it like that; he spreads the woman's hair in a fan around her head, a shimmering chestnut-brown fan, newly washed, and with his thumb he flecks something off her painted forehead—a drop of saliva, or a small leaf, or sweat from her lover's toiling face—yes, all right, hold this—now he backs away and the glare of the lights surrounds them again. Behind the lights is a crowd, in fact crowds of people, an audience, jostling one another and standing on tiptoe, elbowing one another aside, muttering and impatient. *Bring that camera in close! In close!* The itching raw reddened flesh between the woman's thighs, the moisture and the patch of hair, so forlorn with dampness, a monotonous detail; the camera itself slows with exhaustion and lingers too long upon this close-up, lacking the wit to draw back swiftly and dramatically. The woman with the hair fanned out around her head wonders if her make-up is smeared again, or if that slimy sensation is her skin coming loose. Someday, she knows, her skin must come loose and detach itself from her skull. So tired! She must not yawn. Must not. Must not even swallow her yawn because the tendons of her throat will move and her lover will notice and be hurt. Or angered. His whiskers rub against her face, her mouth and nose. She hates his whiskers. It is sickening how hair grows out of men's faces, constantly, pushing itself out. . . . There are tiny bits of hair on her lips. *Here is marriage. Permanent marriage,* she thinks. And he is whispering to her—*Am I hurting you?* and her pain fades as she realizes that she does love him and that though he hurts her, constantly and permanently, she must always whisper *no*, numb and smiling into his face, their bodies now comradely, soldierly in this grappling, their mouths hardened so that they are mainly teeth—the flesh seems to have rotted away—and she whispers *no, you're not hurting me, no, you have never hurt me.*

*P*lot

Given: the existence of X.
Given: the existence of myself.
Given: X's obsessive interest in me.
Given: the universe we share together, he and I, which has shrunk into an area about two miles square in the center of this city.

Hypothesized: X follows me continually, whenever I go out, for one of several reasons that are mutually exclusive. He is on a mission of reclamation, a private detective hired by my father; he is a police agent; he is an acquaintance in disguise or an acquaintance of someone I know/have known, who wants revenge for a real/unreal offense I have committed.

PLOT

There was once a young man of twenty-four, Nicholas Angoff, who woke one morning to discover that he was alone. Utter silence. A vacuum. His eyesight became sharper and he saw that he was in a room—a room with walls, peeling wallpaper, and a gash in the ceiling out of which wires hung. No lighting fixtures. The young man stood cautiously in the center of the room, measuring the distance between himself and the walls. There were also a window and a door. His arms moved to protect him—shielding the soft parts of his body. He did not have enough arms. There was a kind of fur over his face, especially over his eyeballs. A film, a fuzz. He stood in the center of the chilly room and began to think of the logical sequence of events that had brought him to this place in his life. . . .

No, before this I will have to get in certain information: a description of the young man, which will be approximately my own description except I'll give him black hair, long ratty black hair, instead of long ratty frizzy brown hair; black is more dramatic. When I've thought about it over the years, I've thought that I would prefer black hair. And perhaps I'll add an inch or so to his height, make him six feet two. Good. And what else? He is intelligent, like me, but sluggish and easily confused, like me, and not really very intelligent when you come down to it, like me, but ordinarily bright; accused sometimes of being a smart alec, but those days are past. . . . We're all too far gone now. I will have to work all this information in: how he/I popped too many brain cells, sensing immortality in the vigor of young manhood, etc. We both sleep ten/twelve/fifteen hours at a stretch, unless we are awake for three days straight.

He went to the window and looked out. The pressure had already begun at the base of his head, even before he saw the figure in the street below. . . .

Or is this too abrupt? I want only to write about him, that bastard who is starving me to death, whom I have never really seen face to face; but maybe I should hold Nicholas back from the window for a while?

He thought: *I will telephone my father.* . . .

But no, he wouldn't think of that. Not any more than I would. I will have to think of another way of getting the father in, getting him mentioned—his occupation, his money, his handsome graying urbane face, his distress, the "emotional divorce" from his wife/my mother, and all that.

He went to the window and stared down at the street below. Empty. Sidewalk, storefronts, a thin rib of litter blown up against the building across the way. The street was empty yet it had that bare, frozen look of a stage about to be entered. . . .

What, is that right? "A stage about to be entered. . . ." Do people *enter* stages? They walk on stages, they come in out of the wings and appear on stage, but they don't *enter* stages, what crap this all is! Erase everything.

Given: X, who is following N.
Given: the city, this building, this room, the toilet down the hall, the leaking faucet, the rubble in the foyer, the stench, the other people, their voices and thumping feet.
Given: the girl, Rebecca, the long lean legs in white slacks, soiled slacks; a sweater pulled down brutally over her thin hips—that awful fluorescent green, a sweater made of something called orlon—her hair straw-colored, long, limp. Has a habit of chewing on the ends of her hair. Her face is querulous, too sharp. But she

is a striking woman and carries herself, particularly her head, with that knowledge, that special knowledge women have—it would have carried into her old age, if she'd had an old age. Her eyes are large and shiny, brown eyes. Overlarge. Someone should have taken her moist hands in his, some kindly family doctor, and said: "Rebecca, you have beautiful big brown eyes. Have you ever had a basal metabolism test?" . . . So restless, Rebecca. She can't sit still for five minutes, she is always crossing and un-crossing her legs, twitching her toes, scratching between her toes with her jagged fingernails, throwing her head back so that her hair flips (a high-school girl's trick?) and stings my face, sighing loudly, angrily. "Why are you so restless, Rebecca?" I might say in exasperation. When the room got too much for us we went out, anywhere. Any weather. We didn't always notice the weather, to tell the truth. She always had a cold. If I had loved her, I would have taken her wet, cold feet between my hands and warmed them, just as a grandfatherly doctor (the kind now nearly extinct) should have taken her cold hands in his and warmed them, but nobody thought to do this for Rebecca, she was too impatient and too beautiful.

Given: the natural and normal biological attraction between Rebecca and me, somewhat dulled, hazed over by the circum-tances of our lives. Or rather: my attraction to Rebecca. I wonder if she could have loved any man, anyone at all. It had nothing to do with her body, which was a normal woman's body, or with her background (she had been married, had an ordinary squalid life; her parents were ordinary and resisted my penchant for mythologizing, as soon as I saw a snapshot of them), but with a peculiar boredom in her glands. Women have that boredom today. Never did I come across this phenomenon in the past, in history, browsing through old novels/biographies/journals in my former life as a student; it is something that has happened only this year. In the past, women wore twenty yards of cloth wrapped carefully around them, on the plump surfaces of their bodies, and carried themselves as if carrying an armful of eggs, but you could be certain of passion once all the cloth was unwound. Not now. Women like Rebecca (she was really a woman, not a girl—twenty-eight years old) come running across the street to you, a stranger, and gladly do they nuzzle their lips against your throat, eagerly do they wrap themselves around you, arms and legs, but then a hideous convulsive yawn begins deep in their throats. . . .

Given: the deteriorating nature of human relationships in America today. I don't pretend to understand it, though I am contributing to it. Just as I eluded my family, who love/loved me, so did Rebecca elude me, constantly. I wanted to kill her, it was awful. . . . But perhaps if she had ever kissed me full on the mouth, if she had stared at me with those large brown eyes, listening to me, perhaps I would have kicked her out. I can't say. I am a pendulum that swings between intense excitement (nervousness on the edge of terror: I don't even have to see that man, X, any longer before I break out into sweat, it's enough just to remember him) and an intense boredom, a desolation I can taste . . . yes, I can taste it, right now I can taste it . . . it is like sand, hard baked sand, sand that has been around for five thousand years, walked upon by barefoot people and dogs. Sometimes I get all the way downstairs to the foyer and then it comes upon me, the terror, the knowledge that X is waiting for me in the street, and so I run back up here, to this laughable sanctuary, walls that are probably collapsible or penetrable by his special spying devices anyway, and my heart is literally hammering with terror . . . my eyes jump into every corner and up to that wound in the ceiling, that gouged-out eye with the optical nerves hanging down, and I am paralyzed with. . . .

> Nicholas was sometimes paralyzed with himself. The thought of himself. The terror of himself. He carried his head around with him, so how could he get out of it? No way! Stuck. Stuck. Stuck.

. . . And at other times I drag myself up the stairs, I use that verb truly, intentionally, *drag*, I must drag my body up, I can feel the roots of my hair pulling wearily at my head, and my head pulling my neck, and the elastic cords in my neck tugging at my shoulders, my torso, *oh, come on! only a few more steps!* It is so boring, this stairway. This body. Heavy as a corpse, this body. I am tempted to give up. Surrender to gravity. Lie down on the dirty stairs, with head on one step, torso on another, stomach on another, legs and feet abandoned somewhere in the shadows below. Let the kids jump over me. Or maybe I should lie upside down, my head enriched by a rush of blood.

Nicholas lay upside down on the stairs, one day. Blood rushed into his head to rejuvenate the brain. Lying there, he imagined peacefully the wet gray-pink folds of his brain and could not believe that they were eroding, like ordinary ridges and hills made of earth. Similarly, he could not believe that his heart, which was always saying, *Hey you,* would come to a halt someday.

What a joke, if X came in here one day, barged right into this building, and found me like that! He is probably a very conventional man, a citizen. He must be, since he is so faithful, out here at his post. . . . If he saw me lying upside down it might frighten him so much that he would leave me alone. He might quit the assignment. Or, if he is out to get revenge on me, he might take pity on me and leave me alone. *That guy is crazy.* He might think that my trouble is contagious, that just gazing into my watery eyes would contaminate him. . . .

When I look out my window here, I see the building opposite this building, and that boarded-up store that was once a grocery store, with aged, tattered posters on it, I see the doorways opposite me and the windows opposite me, where people presumably live. Off to one side, at the periphery of my vision, I can see X. He is perfectly faithful. He is always there. Sometimes a rush of joy sweeps through me and I want to yell out the window to X and to traffic and pedestrians and people sleeping across the way that I am here, I am living, I love them, *I love them,* we are all human beings living together through this moment of history and we must, we must love one another—

> One day Nicholas approached three men on the street. They seemed to be turning from him. Their shoulders moved—three shoulders, three shoulders turning away. Heads turning. Away. He said: "I need some help." They said: "Move." He said: "What did you say? . . ." because the pressure on the back of his head made him a little deaf. They said: "Move on." The young man, Nicholas, began to cry. He thought wildly: Is someone crying? Who is crying? Why won't they talk to me when I love them and we are all here together, on this earth together, why won't they help me when I am in trouble, I am going crazy, I need money, I need a shot, why are they walking away, what is that noise—somebody crying? He said: "I know who you bastards are—I know your names and everything about you!" They were walking away. The sidewalk would fill up with other people. "You're afraid of me—I know your names and I could turn you in," he said. Maybe he did not say these words out loud. He was crying. His face smashed like a girl's, eyes crinkled and hot. Posters on a store window two feet in front of him: VOTE FOR FRANCIS T. JONES. He stood there for a while crying and a squad car passed by slowly, taking no notice of him, and what must have been an old man came by and paused, eying him, breathing hoarsely, but decided for some reason to walk on. When Nicholas came to he saw, in the doorway of a drugstore up the block, in the center of a loose, noisy crowd of blacks, *that man* calmly watching him.

Oh yes: *that man* is always watching me, in or out of a crowd of blacks. He has binoculars, a telescope, a mechanism to se through walls, a tape recorder, an instrument that measures my footsteps, my heartbeat, my thoughts. He is driving me crazy. He is Rebecca's ex-husband out to get me, or her ex-father, who was supposed to be a nut, so she hinted—or he is in the hire of my own father, who also hates me, or he belongs to the FBI and is waiting for me to lead him to someone important. . . . But what does he look like? My vision is off a little. That is the horror I live with now; I can never quite see the man's face. If I could see it I might understand something. I might see a human face there, human features—the two of us might turn out to be friends, we might shake hands, introduce ourselves, say hello, filled with a sudden spurt of generosity—

He loved her, he imagined her forever trapped in his arms, he lay with her for long damp sticky hours, he pressed his face everywhere against her flesh, yearning to suck out her soul. Her stubborn female soul. Where was it? Where could he suck at it? On her lovely arms there were many tiny pricks and red spots and sores and scabs and even a raised welt, which was infected and drained fluid if it was picked at. Nicholas closed his eyes against the body of his beloved Rebecca: rubbing his eyes, his eyelashes, against her. In honor of her body, her face, her beauty, her soul. It was not enough to say, "I love you," because other men had said that to her. Other men had said everything to her, using up all the words. She lay her hand on Nicholas's head as if in pity. She stretched back, her mouth open and yearning backward into a patch of cold clear winter sunlight from the window. . . . "Why do you want to leave me? Why do you want to get money on your own? I can give you money, I can take care of you," Nicholas begged. Her body was warm and slippery and though he was lying with her she seemed to be eluding him. *Better to kill her.*

But no: he loved her. That was why he pressed his tender eyes against her, rubbing the eyeballs against her flesh, offering his eyelashes to her—how much more gentle could a lover be, what is more gentle in a man than his eyelashes? She was sobbing. "Why do you want to leave? Is it the city? We could leave together," he said. She sobbed, she pushed his head away, she began to move her body on the bed, slowly, as if in a dance without music, and he stared at her until, after a while, she lay still and fell asleep.

That really happened, but I fell asleep too. Passion wore me out. We slept together, for many weeks, but in different parts of the globe. "Rebecca" and I. She dozed along the Pacific shore, the long length of her bobbing in warm waves, curved to the shoreline, her hair drifting, dreaming, her toes and fingers nibbled by tiny amorous fish. But I, being the male, was thrown in my stupor against the rocks along the Atlantic coast, my body bruised, a cracked rib here, a cracked rib there, a lacerated scalp, a head concussion, eyes pecked out by hungry sea gulls—We slept but the two waters of our sleep did not flow together.

He said to his father: "No, I won't talk to her. Why? She walks past my door so that I can hear her crying. Let her cry. I am not going to cry. I am not sick either. I am not going back to the clinic. If you call the docto I will throw myself out the front window. I will run naked across the golf course. No. Don't touch me. Nobody is going to touch me. You don't love me and yo don't love each other and I always had to see that pic ture of you, on the inside of my eyelids, when I wa in bed and you two were in bed, I had to see that pic ture of you, imagining you making love and fallin asleep, making love with your eyes closed, in the dar falling asleep before you were finished, because yo didn't love each other or me or anyone, and if you fe

asleep and slept all night in the same bed you were
not really in the same bed because you were not really
together. . . ."

Did I really say that to my father? Some of it. A few words.
When I said that about the golf course, he started coming toward
me, and when I said, "Don't touch me," he slapped me across the
face. I think that happened in December. The big tree was up in
the front hall. I went out of my mind with the frosting on that
tree, the glitter and the angels' hair and the smell of evergreen
needles; everything was so lovely, why did he have to slap me?
He and Sol Mintz own the Silk Touch, cosmetics for black
women, you see the billboards and the ads all over, beautiful
leggy black women wearing Silk Touch make-up on their flawless faces or their flawless bodies, every square inch of flesh as far
as I know, and Melvin T. Riddle, a handsome black man, a
member of the Black Capitalists Coalition, is president of the
company and often interviewed, his picture even in *Newsweek*,
very grateful to my father and Sol. My father also owns Caesar
Aluminum. He had to fly back from Munich fast to get me out of
jail. The two of us wept together for five hours. Off and on he
kept asking me, "Did they molest you in there?" and didn't believe me when I said I couldn't exactly remember. Oh, I don't
take my body so seriously, Father, it isn't that important or that
private, why not do a good deed for some bastard worse off than I
am? . . . But I told him I didn't think so. No. I didn't think
anyone had "molested" me. What I said wasn't enough, he got
disgusted. He stopped crying and started getting disgusted. The
next morning he was more disgusted. He wouldn't let my mother
in to see me. He kicked me out. In December, I think . . . then
he came down to get me, where I was staying with a friend, but it
lasted only a few days and then I left home again without saying
good-by. The end. It must have been embarrassing for him to
have a thirty-year-old freak of a son, always crying.

Yes, I really am thirty years old. A thirty-year-old son. There is something outlandish about that term, it is not as agreeable as a twenty-four-year-old son or, better yet, a nineteen-year-old son. Once I was these sons. I was once a fifteen-year-old son also, but that was so long ago it isn't worth remembering. One time I threw out all the snapshots of me. The hell with them. I burned Father's miles of film, the gawky grins and smirks. Hell. The hell with them. Now I am thirty years old, unlike my hero Nicholas, soon to be thirty-one, and I spend all of my life waiting for that man to come up here and knock on my door and claim me. All the rest is fiction: I am making up a plot to keep him away.

> Nicholas loved Dorothy but she kept falling asleep in his arms. She kept yearning backward, backward. He hated her, lying above her, "above" her body even though he was touching her along every inch of her flesh, because he could not make her stay awake. So he thought, suddenly, "I will make up a story to keep her awake."

Well, yes, her name is Dorothy; it was Dorothy. Not Rebecca. Blond hair, yes, but not very clean. It looked bitten off at its ends. A film to her fair skin that would roll a little beneath my curious thumb. It would roll out black: thin black rolls of dirt, like the black spines of shrimp when they haven't been carefully deveined.

> Dorothy touched her lovely flesh with the needle point. *Music, a cascade of notes!* But no music. Puring her lips, perspiring, she searched for a vein . . . but no vein. A bead of sweat darted down her nose unnoticed. She maneuvered the plunger again, shyly but—no blood! Not even a drop! She squinted to see if maybe there was a drop loosed, just a drop? . . . No try again. Try again. Don't tremble. Nicholas stood above her, encouraging her. *Don't tremble like that, Dorothy,* he whispered. The back of his head was

bloated and silly and he couldn't hear her reply. Only music, a cascade of notes, and his beloved dipping the needle in, timidly, not yet impatiently, "deveining" herself with infinite patience. . . .

This morning I woke to discover I was alone. What, alone? Where had they all gone? I saw that the room had walls, four walls, the wallpaper was peeling, exactly like the inside of my skull; why did this surprise me? A rumpled bed. That smell. That smell, friends, is *me*. In the ceiling there is a hole, a gash. No light fixtures, just torn wires. A gouged-out eye. There was something over my skin, prominent against the moist parts of my face, where my thoughts move especially fast—my mouth and eyes—it was like a second skin. Fur. Transparent fur. Is it before birth, am I still in a silken cocoon, in a female womb, a stranger's womb, waiting to be born? . . . I stood in the center of the room, my knees shaking slightly, trying to think of the logical sequence of events that had brought me to this place in my life.

The examined life is not worth living.

Every time I wake up I jump out of bed, terrified, and I spend some long minutes in the center of this room; thoughts whirl in my brain or what is left of my brain, the pressure builds up, I carefully prepare a shot for myself and take it, loving myself tenderly, being very good to myself, and the terror fades, the way people's faces fade if you don't see them daily. Joy propels me to the window and I want to shout down at everyone about life, love, happiness, I want to exhibit myself so that the sick and unhappy can take heart from me, a thirty-year-old creature of skin and bones and constant diarrhea who is nevertheless very happy. On fire with happiness! At such times I am not even certain who I am. Whose body this is. Am I myself, a boy of fifteen or a young man of nineteen or twenty-four or thirty, or already aged into a man of thirty-one, or am I someone else (an ex-friend of mine, a black man named Dill; or Dorothy herself, an ex-lover, now dead; or someone in the building across the street, behind those mysterious mourning windows), because my soul has exploded outward to take in all of the universe. Nothing is excluded. I know this fact: that something miraculous exists where I stand, some being, pinpricked and marveling, his skull open so that the very stars themselves (invisible during the ugly daytime) make little love pinches in his brain. But then—

> But then it faded. Stopped. Nicholas sat down heavily, slack-mouthed. Was it over so soon? Over? What was over? He couldn't remember. Was it Nicholas himself that was coming to an end? *Oh, my brain,* he thought in surprise, *it is being squeezed out of shape! Somebody's hand, the fleshy palm of his hand, is pressing against the base of my skull and making it numb.* He did not know if he was going crazy, or if "craziness" was coming his way and would sweep him up in it.

This is the record of someone going crazy, in case you are curious. I wish you could feel the itching that runs up and down my body, like those fancy bubble lights on Christmas trees, lights bubbling and blinking on and off. Nails, fingernails also itch. Itches. Scratching. Blood. I think it was a few days after Dorothy died that I ran out onto the street—bumped into a woman—kept on running. I went to a gas station near Cass to get a container of gasoline. The gas station is across the street from TransLove, Inc., stucco and streaked white paint, now boarded up. Kids with books brush by me, not seeing me, going to the university a few blocks away. A heavy container of gasoline. I like the smell of gasoline. I always have. In a White Tower diner I can see a row of people at the counter, sitting—it must be late afternoon and not morning, as I had thought for a while—I've been sleeping for a long while—and one of the men is *that man,* X himself. He sits with his overcoat on, his back to me. Sipping coffee. Eyes in the back of his head, watching me perpetually. He is driving me crazy. Should I rush inside the diner and scream at him, should try to kill him, should I wait outside and introduce myself and shake hands, should I run back to my room and slam the door behind me, sobbing? . . .

> Rebecca said in a voice like music: "I want to die." She put her hand on his bare back. She said gently: "I want to die." Her lips moved back from her gums, the gums of a young woman who has been strung out for two weeks, gray gums, gums streaked with a yellowish substance, and she whispered: "I want to die." Nicholas wanted to tell her that his love was enough to keep her living. He wanted to declaim certain truths that have existed throughout history. The truth of love: of why life is worth living, through love, of how the chemistry of love makes for better living, makes living livable. He wanted to recite a poem to her in which these statements were articulated. But his mind blanked out at the touch of her hand. Her words moved soundlessly inside his head. Words, syllables, sounds. A breath. He wanted to carve out on the back of her hand, into those cheap flimsy useless veins we all have there: I LOVE YOU. But the idea faded.

Anyway we were not alone, my friend Streeter was there with us. In fact he was watching us. He had just finished reading out loud something from the *Detroit News*—probably the Jane Lee Advice column—and now he was just watching us, a smile below the faint little smile of his mustache. He had to shave once in a while because he had a job. What effect would it have, I wonder, to inform readers that a love scene is not private, that a third party is present? I think it would destroy everything. I think it would offend people. I know it would offend me, if I were the reader . . . and it offends me now, to remember Streeter, that son of a bitch. He still owes me money. It might be Streeter who is following me, in disguise, or maybe he has convinced the police that I am important and that I should be followed, knowing it would drive me crazy? Because Streeter loved Dorothy too. He once said to her: "I hate your name. Why aren't you Rebecca? I will call you Rebecca." Streeter was always changing people's names and calling them whatever he wanted. He called me Buddy and Brick, I don't know why. He was always turning up when you thought he had left for good. He liked to impersonate people who wore uniforms on the job: policemen, deliverymen, soldiers, sailors, even chauffeurs. He bought a chauffeur's outfit and lived in it for a long time—two weeks straight—carrying himself with dignity everywhere, very vain. He tried to get a job as a real chauffeur, but didn't know how to advertise himself. He never did get a job as a chauffeur. So Streeter was in the room with us that day—

> She said: "Will you let me go? Because I want to die."
> He said: "Why do you want to die?" Her large, shiny, confused eyes. Her chemistry brewed to a storm, uncontainable. A raging thyroid. Raging liver. Heart. Lungs. She was burning out, burning away. She said: "If you love me, you'll let go of me." He said: "I can't let you go. . . ." He said: "You don't love me or you would want to live." He said: "All right, goddamn it, I will let you go. . . ."
> And so she died.

"And so she died."

> Dill ran in and started reading them a news story, in a terrible voice. Mrs. Mungo, the mother of Herb Mungo, a police informer and a traitor, a betrayer, a thief, an evil young man, Mrs. Mungo had been interviewed by a reporter. Dill had made the bomb himself with materials Nicholas had bought and the bomb had been sent to Herb Mungo's apartment, left outside in the hall, and a few days later Mrs. Mungo came to see where her son was (out of town on busi-

ness, maybe) and saw the package addressed to him. So she took it home with her. Mr. Mungo, a Greyhound bus driver, was not home at the time; but the five Mungo kids, Herb's younger brothers and sisters, were all there. What fun! A present! So they opened the package on the kitchen table, and . . . and the bomb did not go off. . . . Mrs. Mungo said to police: "I took a look at that thing and told Bobby to throw it out in the back yard, fast! I knew what it was right away from all the stuff on television. Now, can you imagine anybody sending a thing like that through the mail? People should know what might happen with a thing like that, and five children in a family. I don't know what the world is coming to. . . ."

Dill was very angry. He read the story over several times, shouting. Dill had wanted to be an actor, in his former life. Perhaps he had actually been an actor.

But none of this is a logical sequence of events. It does not add up to anything logical. If a human life, my own life, is to make sense it must add up to a certain unit, reducible to a certain statement: *He was a hero. He was a hero because he resisted suicide. He was a coward. He was a coward because he resisted suicide. He was somebody's thirty-year-old aging archaic son.* My brain is going, but before it goes completely I want to make very clear my dislike for you: my readers, who are reading through my life as fast as possible, skimming along, impatient with me and hoping for some final mess. You read, people like you, only to whistle through your teeth and think: *Jesus, there's somebody worse off than I am!* Why else read, why plow your way through somebody else's plots? A "plot" is not fiction, as you know, but very real; it is the record of someone's brain, a trail like a snail's trail, sticky and shameful. . . . But in creating a plot to explain my life, I am being forced to change things around. The essential story gets away from me. The main thing is that I am being followed and tortured to madness by someone, probably a stranger, probably a hired stranger, and I have to keep repeating this for fear I will forget it as my mind goes. Otherwise I will keep asking myself about certain events—people—memories—that are confusing. Did I love Rebecca/Dorothy, or is that a lie? I loved her when my chemistry ordered *Love!* but the rest of the time I think I forgot her. She certainly forgot me. We lay dreamily together in our two halves of the globe, but when I told her I loved her she fell asleep; when she told me, one day, of her ex-husband and what he had done to her, I shut my mind off and watched her lips move but I heard nothing. And I never really knew . . . I never really knew whether Dorothy and Streeter and Dill and some of the others liked me for myself or because I had money— an allowance my father finally gave me—because I was the only one down here who had money and who was generous. . . .

> After Rebecca's death, Nicholas himself declined.
> . . . After Rebecca's death, Nicholas himself thought increasingly of death, of an end, a conclusion, of the stairway outside his room where one might lie upside down forever. . . .
> After Rebecca's death he began to think of the marriage they might have made, the children they might have made, now that it was certain she could not return to him. . . .
> After Dorothy's death, in fact the next day, X appeared at the top of a stairway and looked down at Nicholas, claiming him. . . .

Dorothy did die. I keep thinking of her death, again and again. Her death. "Her" death. She never said most of those things—" want to die," etc. She never spoke gently, delicately, musically to me at all. I don't think she noticed me except to ask for money. Only a dry brushing of her lips against mine—she would never kiss me the right way, though I begged her—and the way she died was not suicide, it was not deliberate at all, but like this: th three of us had shared everything, Dorothy and Streeter and I, and we shared our best times as well as our worst times, and one night when we were all high together we seized one another's hands, everything raging in me, a delirious storm, everything joyful, and I could feel their friendly hearts racing like mine, our pulses racing, our eyeballs burning, and then . . . and then I had to sneeze suddenly. . . .

> A sneeze! Rebecca leaped back from them, terrified. Her body quaked. She could not take it—the noise was too much, too much of a surprise—her body raced in terror—too much stress, too much heartbeat. It exploded in her—the heart. Blood gushed out of mouth, nose, ears, eyes. Oh, exclamations of blood! Nicholas stared at her in disbelief. Blood poured out of her. Streeter began to run and Nicholas followed, out of the room and down the stairs and into the street. They were in the street before the corpse stopped its convulsions!

It was no dramatic moment. There is no drama when lovers part like that—no preparation, nothing. How do you prepare for your beloved's sudden death—the explosion of her heart? A muscular little fist that stretches out all its fingers suddenly in terror, in despair. . . . (This morning my own heart pounded in cold, brutal, militant palpitations for an hour and a half, frightened by a cat prowling around in the alley. Goddamn these stray cats!) If only I hadn't sneezed. . . . What do you do when your love dies so quickly, so strangely? You must write about it. Rewrite it. You can change both your names, exaggerate your love for her, exaggerate her beauty, try to figure out how this leads to your being followed now by her ex-husband, the boy from Midland, Michigan, who was so unkind to her.

> There was once a young man of twenty-four who, having been praised years before by an instructor at

Cornell, and given a B+ in freshman English, decided
he would write a story about himself. He decided that
it would begin in the past—some personal history, but
not too much, because obvious autobiographical information tires readers—and move quickly to the near-
present, the break with his family, the three months
camping out in the city of Detroit, the friendships with
certain people, the unhappy love affair with a girl he
would call Rebecca, the suicide of Rebecca (how?
slashed wrists? gas? an overdose of pills would be too
close to the truth), some description of the city, the
jumbled skyline, the traffic two blocks over on the
John Lodge Expressway, etc., the Narcotics Squad,
the Vice Squad, dirt and flu and a constant leaking
faucet, etc., some sentimental remarks about the human condition, being a son/having a father, etc. What
made him pause was the knowledge that if he wrote
something terrible he might have to fulfill it; might
have to make it come true. But what other possibility
of salvation would there be for him, except this writing
of the scenario of his own life, his predicament with
the deadly X, who is always waiting? No other way.
No. So he would write a story that would make sense
of X. By creating a coherent plot he would then explain to his own satisfaction why someone was obsessed with him. Or he would hint (and convince himself) that the man, X, was only imagined—a harmless
dot in front of the eyes, bouncing and wiggling like
crazy, only bothersome if it is taken seriously—and so
he would exorcise the man, the phantom, the perpetual
X on the edge of his consciousness. . . . But, having
written twenty-two pages he discovered that X could
not be explained away so easily. There was the X on
paper, and the X out in the street. Two X's. X out in
the street is never in the narrative, really, but only

mentioned—always out of eyesight, out of the range of human affection and pleas! The police, or a police agent, followed an acquaintance of Nicholas's once and indicated, somehow, that there was a relationship between them that resulted in the acquaintance being found dead one day. . . . The police knew how to put certain pressure on one's associates to kill: after all, nobody wants to be betrayed. But Nicholas is no threat to anyone and cannot betray anyone now. Therefore it makes no sense for anyone to follow him; therefore X is not really following him. . . .

If I go out to get something to eat he will see me. I can't go out. I could buy some more food from kids in the building, cookies and crackers and other junk, which they steal from their mothers' cupboards, but the kids haven't been around today; I could break into their mothers' cupboards and eliminate the kids entirely, but if I break into someone's apartment I am likely to be shot. How long can I stay holed up here? I can put my hands around myself, around my waist. A skeleton. A thirty-year-old skeleton. My long skinny thumbs touching, straining to touch like lovers, and the third finger of each hand touching firmly. It would be interesting to know how much I weigh. . . .

I will escape this self-pity by returning to my plot.

The end of the story: a logical sequence of events that results in the young hero cleaning up his life, walking out into the street, confronting X—who turns out to be, I suspect, a private detective hired by his father—and the two of them eye each other for a few suspenseful minutes, the young man shaky from going without food, and from taking too prodigious a variety of drugs, but still essentially healthy and intelligent and rational, an obviously civilized young man whom society would be eager to rehabilitate. And the dialogue will go something like this: "Your father is very worried about you, Nicholas. Don't you realize that?" Nicholas, his face serious and handsomely pale: "I'm be-

ginning to realize what I've done to him." "Shall we go now?" the
man will say. "Yes, I'm ready now," Nicholas will say. He and X
walk down the block together, side by side, walking together
down the block, together, the two of them, walking down the
block together, together. . . .

Tears spilled out of his eyes at the look of himself: his
hands, his two hands, could span his entire body.
Trembling. Weeping. He understood that his mind
was about to go and that he must not wind up in
Lafayette Clinic like the rest of them, gibbering and
drooling all over himself; he had enough dignity left,
so he moved one leg and then the other, left and right
and left again and right, lifting his knees with his
two hands, until he came to the Mobile station near
Cass and bought a can of gasoline. Was he being followed? He didn't look around. On Woodward he
hitched a ride north with someone who took pity on
him—no matter that he looks like hell and his hair is
frizzed out around his head in an explosion of kinky
brown curls and he weighs about one hundred and ten
pounds, still the can of gasoline suggests that he is an
automobile owner and therefore a good citizen—and
drove him all the way up to Six Mile. Good. Coming
home. He crossed over to Hamilton Road and went
along the deserted sidewalk of the private street to his
parents' home, past the Detroit Golf Club, too large
complex, and magnificent a home to describe, and
walked up the broad front flagstone walk, in the gauzy
pleasant lilac-scented air of a May evening, and around
to the garage, where a single car was parked, and in the
garage, sitting suddenly, coming to rest, sitting Indian
fashion with his ankles locked whitely about each other
he dumped the gasoline over himself and, before any
one could catch up with him, X or anyone at all, befor

anyone even knew he had come back, he set himself on fire. So many times had Nicholas returned to this home, this house, wandering homeward in his head!— like a ghost wandering, yearning back, backward, but never until this moment did he know why he would return. Yes, constantly was he going home, always going home in the confused plot of his life, and never until the last hour of his life did he understand what home meant—

The Children

This is not really a story about children, or even about a mar
riage, though a marriage is at its center. It is not even a stor
about a "husband" and a "wife," for the two never thought o
themselves in those terms. They were married in their mid
twenties; they had been doing chemical research, and the matc
was considered a sensible, attractive one. It had the flavor o
graduate student romances—a premature camaraderie about i
difficult to explain. Consider Ronald and Ginny: serious and i
telligent, a little nervous, uncertain of themselves, but very goo
people; in short, a sensible, attractive match. The story is abou
the girl, Ginny, revealed to her through children. All her life sl
had been fascinated and a little frightened of children, and of th

thought of having children of her own, as if she might somehow not be worthy of them.

When they married, her career passed from her and left her relieved. Beneath her fastidiousness was a peculiar laziness, a desire to be left alone and to watch others. She liked to read, idly. She liked to listen to Ronald's ideas, it was perhaps her notion of marriage—the young wife listening to her husband quietly, agreeing with him, not allowing her mind to jump ahead in an attempt to outguess him. That sort of thing was over now that she was married. So her career passed away from her and her husband concentrated on his work, with enough energy for both of them. He soon moved beyond her, and this too was a kind of relief for her; she was finished with that sort of thing, the competition and the uneasiness.

While he was still at the university they had their first child, a girl. It had been a difficult pregnancy and Ginny felt a firm, stubborn satisfaction in the baby who had caused her so much suffering. At that time they lived in a one-room apartment. She felt harassed and a little wild, with so much pressure upon her, so much work that had to be done—unlike her husband's work in the laboratory, which could wait. She thought of his life as infinitely easier than hers. She was anxious about the baby, always thinking about its future—what if it were retarded? What if she failed as a mother? For months after the birth she never really slept, lying in a daze of lukewarm sleep as if she were lying just below the surface of a body of water, waiting in suspense for something to happen. Many things happened but they were all minor. The "something" never happened.

Ronald said to her often, "You're an excellent mother. Where did you learn all these things?"

She blushed at this and could think of no reply. For they were not easy, open people, either of them. Ronald worked too hard, studied too much, stayed far too long in the laboratory. It was difficult to say whether he loved his work; he would never have said that himself. Instead, he seemed to be "in" his work all the time, never out of it. He thought about it all the time and it was colored by his mood, it never caused his mood. He had a reputation for being brilliant. He was twenty-seven when they married, a tall, thin, easily embarrassed young man with a wedge-shaped face and hair that was already thinning; he looked at once older and younger than twenty-seven.

Ginny was as tall as he, the kind of intelligent, shapeless girl one often sees late in the afternoon in university buildings—dark-rimmed glasses, a distracted, vaguely startled look, intelligence marring her forehead with tiny heartbreaking lines. She was twenty-five but looked older. She wore dark, quiet colors, and her feet were long and narrow and a source of embarrassment to her. After the marriage she let her hair grow. She had worn it cut short for years, she was tired of that style. It was as if she were discovering girlhood, which she had scrupulously bypassed; she let her hair grow long, she put away her chemistry books and read the new, important books on sociology and psychology that all their friends read, and in a while she was pregnant.

They were both guiltily proud of what they had accomplished. It had nothing to do with their parents' pride—that was an embarrassment. It was instead a kind of secret, astonished pride in the discovery of themselves, in the discovery of their bodies. Ginny felt that her baby girl was an extension of her own body, an innocent being linked mysteriously to her and through her to Ronald, binding them all together. It was a mystery that bewildered her. She sometimes sat for hours staring into the crib, alone with the baby in their apartment. But of course she never thought of herself as alone. At these times her mind seemed to pass out of her and she had no "ideas" at all. She was baffled by the mystery of life, her having accomplished—what? She had passed over the boundary into another life, the world of adults who have secrets, who cannot be mastered. Was she now an adult? What had happened to her?

They were very happy together.

But beneath their enchantment they were still serious and intelligent, very intelligent. Ronald finished his studies and was
offered a good job in a Midwestern city. And they accepted this,
too, eagerly, as a sign of their being adults—what did it matter if,
at the very center of their being, there was a kind of doubt, of
wonder? Ronald kept saying, pleased with himself and with
everything, "She's going to bring us good luck." The "she" was
Rachel; she was one year old when they moved.

They lived in an apartment for some time, and Ronald began
his career. Ginny, left to herself and the baby, scuffed around in
bedroom slippers, began to gain weight, took to standing at the
window with the baby, in a kind of wistful happy daze. It was
difficult for her to understand that she was an adult, that she was
married and had a baby. Rachel seemed to her a delicate, exqui-
site creature—really an amazing creature. There were times
when Ginny felt inert and ugly beside her own child, though of
course this was nonsense. She liked to read stories to the child.
Rachel, naturally, was advanced for her age. They believed she
could distinguish between different types of music, preferring
baroque. . . . It was one of their fables, but they took it seriously.

New acquaintances in this city congratulated them on their
child. "It's such a relief to see a really pretty baby, not to have
to lie about it," one girl told them. They were very pleased
to hear this. Ronald was a fine person but he was not handsome, not at all; there was something gently perplexed about
him, as if a thought were working its way to the surface of
his mind, upsetting him. And Ginny, with her thin, severe
face, her rather lifeless hair . . . no, she had never been pretty,
exactly. So it pleased them to have a child other people considered pretty.

They lived in that apartment for two years, and then Ronald
was taken on by another company. He had an excellent salary
now for a man of thirty. So they bought a house some distance
out of the city, in a new subdivision called Fox Hollow.

"Because of the children," Ginny was going to say, when their acquaintances asked why they had moved so far out. The "children"—she was pregnant again and quite satisfied. She was proud of Rachel and of her husband and of the new house, and of her new pregnancy. Most of all, perhaps, she was proud of her satisfaction, for she was the kind of woman one might have thought terrified of childbirth: that long, lean, offended body, that overscrupulous gaze. . . . But if she was terrified, she never allowed herself to think about it. She thought instead of how normal she was, of how she had crossed over into the world of adulthood and taken up greedily all its symbols, without hesitation. The house was another symbol. It was a colonial, rather boxlike, "economical," located on an unpaved road called Glen Lane.

They moved into the house in spring, and already the neighboring lots were being leveled. New houses were going up everywhere. All day long they heard the screech of trees being cut down, which upset Ronald but which Ginny accepted with a kind of ferocity as another sign of her being in the real world—not hiding in an apartment, afraid to grow up. She thought with scorn of their friends, childless and city bred, who had not really considered this move to the suburbs wise. "But the suburbs? *The suburbs?*" they said. Ginny thought of them with scorn, pitying them.

One morning on her walk back from the mailboxes she was absurdly pleased by this event: a young woman in a yellow sunsuit, whom she had often heard scolding her two boys, crossed the street to say hello to her. Ginny stopped and the two of them talked, with the rapid, gushing relief of young mothers who have located each other. "Just what do you think about that mud? Isn't that a *crime?*" the girl said. She had an animated, enthusiastic face, a faint odor of milk about her, and front teeth flecked with curious white spots. Her sunsuit was rather soiled. "My husband has an hour's drive and he's pretty crabby on bad days—what about yours?"

"It takes him an hour too," Ginny said.

"I think they should pave these streets," said the girl. She spoke with the sort of delicious, rushed anger Ginny had often heard in the young mothers who met out on the sidewalk. One of her boys was tugging at her wrist, but she brushed him away without seeming to notice him. She smiled at Ginny and showed her big frank teeth, speckled with tiny cords of white. "Hey, my name is Louise! Louise Shuter!" she said, as if she had just thought of this.

"My name is Ginny. . . ."

It was absurd to be pleased about this. Ginny seemed to move away from herself and watch in amazement the two young mothers chatting over their children's heads, animated and oddly pleased with themselves, as if intoxicated. What intoxicated them? They were sisters, they recognized each other. They were alike. It was good to complain like this, with such proud, self-righteous anger—about the mailboxes all in a group down at the road, and the mud puddle around them, and the unpaved lanes (Spruce Way, Willow Pass), and their husbands' long drives into the city. "But of course this is the only place to live, with children," Ginny's new friend said. The patch of freckles on her cheeks and nose seemed to darken with the wisdom of this remark.

Their children made friends. One of Louise's boys was Rachel's age, exactly. The other boy was five. "Oh, they're lots of trouble, they're regular pests. Aren't you pests?" Louise cried happily at her boys.

The next day, Ginny met Louise and another girl, in a green sunsuit. They chatted. They chatted for two hours. Ginny once again seemed to hear them from a distance, marveling at herself, at the way in which she agreed with these women and seemed a sister to them; it was all so strange! And when one of them said, "You know that was just a rumor about a nigger moving in?" Ginny not only showed no surprise but felt none. Some change worked upon her in the presence of these women.

She told Ronald that she had made some friends. "And Rachel has too. It's good for her to have someone to play with." Ronald thought this was good, but he did not ask much about Ginny's friends. Ginny resented this. Heavy and warm, she spent hours sitting out back on their "patio"—a nine-foot square slab of concrete, unshaded—watching Rachel play with her little friends, sipping coffee with Louise and the other girl. Sometimes she watched the children alone, happy to take care of the other mothers' children. She was anxious to see how Rachel talked to other children—she wanted to see if the girl was more popular than she herself had been as a child. She hoped desperately that this would be so. So she stayed home and watched them, slow, happy, lazy, her dark-rimmed glasses sliding slowly down her perspiring nose.

The children were so delicate—two girls and two boys—they played in the sandbox, they played with dolls and toy automobiles and shovels, they were marvelous creatures and Ginny felt that the other mothers did not know enough to appreciate them. Swollen with her second pregnancy, she felt overcome by the mystery of birth, in a kind of trance with the very promise of physical suffering. The other women were too simple to understand this.

One day Ginny looked out her patio window to check on the children, and she saw an older boy with them. He was a stranger, about seven. He had thin, bony shoulders and a small head, and his clothes were filthy. She saw him squat down in the midst of the smaller children and distend his mouth in a peculiar way, so that his tongue appeared between his teeth like an animal slyly peeking out. Ginny went to the door, trembling. "What do you want?" she said. The boy's head jerked up and he got to his feet, not frightened but cunning. He ran around the side of the house. "Who was that?" Ginny said.

One of Louise's boys said, "That's Goober"—or "Gomber"—a strange name Ginny could not make out. "Does he live around here?" she asked. The children seemed not to know or to understand.

But the boy returned that afternoon. Ginny actually saw him coming, through the living-room window. She was frightened by the urgent, foolish shape of his head—it reminded her of an ant's head, set forward and slightly crooked on his neck—and by his filthy clothes, as if these were symbols she somehow recognized but did not want to admit. He ran around the house and, before she could get out there, he had trampled on the smaller children's toys. With a high inhuman shriek he ran around the other side of the house again. The children began to cry, terrified. Rachel cried convulsively, gasping for breath, and Ginny was filled with a terrible anguish. She knelt to embrace the child. "It's all right, darling. It's all right," she whispered. Sobs shook Rachel's body and Ginny was overcome by a sense of the child's vulnerability; it was a terrible thing for her to understand.

That week, Ronald had a fence installed around the house. "It was about time, really. Most of the other houses have fences," he said, trying to make little of the incident. He was rather upset by Ginny's strange, fierce stare. She kept saying, "That little bastard, if that little bastard comes back here . . ." and he heard in her voice a sound he'd never heard in it before.

It was a relief to him when the new baby was born. That birth was more trouble, even, than the first, and when Ginny returned it was as if she were coming to a new house, to a new family. She seemed more intense, concentrated upon herself more, very serious about her motherhood. She had a queenly air about her even when she was dressed in her old, sloppy clothes. What made her happy was the other mothers' attention turned upon her—they were so generous, so helpful! When she was recovered enough to go out she began to go to their houses for coffee, taking Rachel and the baby along. They all spent hours together, every day. These young mothers were not sloppy but they had no "pretensions," as they put it, and Ginny agreed. "There was one girl here was real pretentious, she had napkins and silver stuff—Christ! We all came in our shorts and she was dressed up, what a phony. They finally moved out," Louise said in her rush of chatty, amazed anger. Ginny felt very comfortable with them, like a new person. She seemed indeed to be a new person. She could almost feel her face grow slack, the very muscles in her body sagging with comfort. They all talked about such easy, simple things— they were going to vote Republican—they were all putting a little extra on their mortgage when they could afford it, "that really cuts down on the interest"—they were interested in recipes, complaints about in-laws, their husbands' jobs. One day Thelma, who was a very short, plump girl with bleached hair, pointed out the front window and cried: "That's that Gower, look at him! I thought he was put away!"

They crowded around to look, and it was the boy who had run through Ginny's yard a few weeks before. Ginny asked about him. She was told that he was a devil, wouldn't mind anyone, "mentally nuts if you ask me," and he was small for his age—he was almost ten. Ginny felt a stab of fear. "But can't his parents do anything about him—for him?" she asked.

"Oh, they're nuts too," Thelma said in disgust.

"Not nuts *exactly*," Katie Farmalow said.

"Nuts is nuts, don't tell me," Thelma said. "That kid is going to kill somebody someday, and it hadn't better be my kid."

Ginny looked at her. "Are you serious about that?"

"Sure I'm serious."

"But—why would he do that?"

"Because he's nuts."

As time went on she noticed the other children, the small children, speaking of someone named Bambah. They played noisily out back of her house, and she sometimes hid behind the patio door to listen to them. Now that Rachel was older she was less quiet. She was in excellent health. One day Ginny said, coming outside with the baby, "Who's this Bambah you're talking about?"

A little boy snickered. Rachel had to answer, since this woman was her mother. "Oh, nobody," she said.

"Is it a friend of yours?"

"Nobody, I guess."

"Somebody you made up? Did you make him up?"

"Nobody."

And another time, seeing a dead squirrel in the street as she drove home, she heard Rachel beside her blurt out with a kind of shocked, astonished delight: "Bambah!"

"But what do you mean by that, honey?" Ginny asked.

"Oh, nothing."

"Who is Bambah? What's that?"

"Nothing."

So the children had a language of their own, and Ginny could not understand it.

She spent most of her time with the baby, of course. She fed him, and put him to bed, and while he napped she waited for him to wake again; and when he did not wake for several hours she woke him herself, a little impatiently. He was her best baby, her darling. She lifted him from the crib that had been Rachel's and carried him down into the kitchen and set him into the highchair. It was warm still and Rachel was playing outside, next door. When she paused she could hear the sound of the children playing, and Rachel's clear high laughter. It pleased her to think that Rachel could assert herself, as a child, while Ginny could not remember having had a self to assert until her marriage. It was strange, how that child had come from her and Ronald, and had a life now of her own, a nature that was totally her own.

Ginny liked to lift the baby in and out of the highchair, in and out of the crib. There was something about his warm squirming weight that pleased her. He was able to smile at his mother, knowing who she was. It was time to eat. She opened a jar of baby food, pressing it against her hip as she twisted the cap, and she noticed that on her bathrobe was a red stain from an earlier jar of baby food—beets. She fed the baby. Outside an automobile passed, older children on bicycles rode shouting by, but inside the house everything was under control. It was hers. It was comfortable and safe here, with the baby who could not yet speak, and she felt an odd disappointment when the feeding time was over. So close to this baby, as if she and the baby were somehow one person, she thought with a remote bewilderment about her other child and about her husband, as if uncertain of their relationship to her.

Rachel was a healthy girl with fair, curly hair, who liked to dart about like a delighted little animal. In fact, she looked always as if she were about to jump up and dash away and hide. She was so pretty! She sang little songs at the top of her voice, nonsense words and chants, she rocked from one side to the other so that the room shook, she was able to wrestle her father off balance at times. She had too much energy, Ginny complained happily to the other mothers. She was so healthy, growing so well, she liked to eat and there was certainly no problem about getting food down her—but there was one problem, which she did not mention.

If she wasn't watched closely she would tease her baby brother. Ginny noticed her tickling him one day, much too roughly, and as a final parting gesture she jabbed her fingers into his stomach—that startled Ginny, who was not quite sure of what she had seen. This was important, a very important thing, so Ginny came to Rachel and said carefully, "Rachel? Why did you do that?" Rachel said she was sorry.

But still, she did it if she wasn't watched. It was a strange thing. Ginny never became angry but instead knelt down to look into Rachel's small flushed face. "Honey, you don't want to hurt Baby Brother, do you? He isn't big and strong like you."

Rachel looked guiltily at the floor.

"He's just a baby, so you should take care of him, shouldn't you?"

Rachel shook her head, yes.

And while there was no problem exactly about her eating,

there was another problem at the supper table. Rachel jiggled the table while Ginny fed the baby, anything to get attention away from the baby and onto herself. She pounded with her little fists and laughed feverishly, especially when the baby drooled or spat out food. "Lookit the pig! Little piggy!" she cried. When they calmed her they felt how hot her skin was, really hot to the touch. She sometimes distorted her face and rolled her eyes crazily, to make them laugh; this was a trick she had picked up from that boy Gower. Ginny was a little alarmed to see the real violence, the intense, crazy violence Rachel showed, just in screwing up her face like that and rolling her eyes. It was as if she were trying to break her face into pieces, or trying to break by some confused magic the face of the baby who was gaping at her.

This sign of an outside force, some demented force of disorder and brutality, frightened Ginny. She remembered the small children playing and the boy Gower trampling their toys, ruining the peace of that summer afternoon with no fear, no regret, hardly any effort. . . . Everything was so very vulnerable, so very easily ruined. And she had no idea what she could do about it.

But the time just before bed was the nicest time: they had special little games involving pieces of furniture, a game invented by Rachel and Ronald. At these times Rachel showed a delicate, feverish joy of life that Ginny loved, and there was no sign of any outside world; nothing but their own world. When Rachel ran from one piece of furniture to another, in a hectic game, Ginny watched the little girl closely and thought that she did love her. She loved her very much. And yet her mind detached itself from the cramped living room, moving spaciously into the distance. She seemed at such times to be awaiting a certain understanding of herself. What were these children, after all, but a part of herself? And yet the understanding did not come. Surely some vision lay at the very center of her life? . . . She summoned up intelligently the differences that lay between her and the woman she had become, this rather slovenly mother with nondescript hair and a fretful, maternal frown, a husband who never quite looked at her and did not need to look at her. Yes, there was a difference. It seemed to her that everyone else moved without defenses and without disguise, while she was never quite herself, always harassed or taken off guard.

Rachel lay on her back one night and shrieked with laughter, kicking the floor with her heels. Ginny said, "Rachel, be quiet!" because the baby was upstairs, sleeping. Rachel paid no attention; she simply did not hear her. "The baby is trying to sleep," Ginny said helplessly.

"I don't like him," Rachel said.

"What, you what?" Ronald cried in mock surprise, not seeing or not caring to see that Rachel was serious, and he scooped her up in his arms and swung her toward the ceiling. . . .

It was in such ways that she was taken off guard; she was never really herself. What would her real self have said to that flushed, spiteful child?

At another time Rachel said, close to tears because of some mishap: "You're a bad mommy and I hate you."

"Well, that's too bad."

"You're a bad mommy."

"You're a bad little girl."

"No, I'm not," Rachel said loudly. She was sucking her thumb because she knew Ginny disliked this. "But you are too a bad mommy."

"Who says so, you?"

Ginny was trying to keep her anger and nervousness down, wiping the counter in her kitchen.

"Reeny's mother says so. She says so."

Reeny's mother was Thelma. "Reeny's mother does not say so," Ginny said.

"She does too. Says you're a bad mother."

Ginny made a derisive snorting noise and did not reply. But Rachel's use of the word "mother" was strange, for it was a word Rachel did not ordinarily use. Ginny kept on wiping the counter, busy. She felt so weak, so strangely vulnerable herself, that it occurred to her suddenly that a life of this kind was no good, not worth living. How could she endure being always open to hurt? Like the children themselves, she was open to any sudden attack, any spurt of senseless aggression, and she could not defend herself. . . .

But in the next instant Rachel no longer "hated" her; she loved her mommy, yes, it was all forgotten. And it was truly forgotten. Ginny read her a story, Rachel clambered up onto her lap, the whole strange incident passed away.

Ginny thought of her life in two parts: she had been a girl, and now she was a woman. Her identity, when it did not detach itself from her, was confused with the two children, meshed in with their two quite different personalities. She liked to spend time with them, alone with them. She really did like the rainy days when Rachel had to stay inside, despite Rachel's fretfulness, and she felt a violent dislike for the mothers who suggested that all the children get together in someone's house. "They get in my hair, these two," Louise complained, "couldn't we herd them all together somewhere?" This was over the telephone and so Ginny could keep Rachel from hearing. The little girl always tugged at her skirt when she talked on the phone, as if certain that the message was really for her and Ginny was keeping it from her. But Ginny said, "Not today, Louise. It's a good idea, though." So she stayed with them, close to the baby as if guarding him, and her life was certainly united with theirs. And yet there had been another life, before these children. She could not quite remember it. Had she ever been a child herself? For some reason it frightened her to think so.

Because there was so much danger in that world: consider the Farmalow boy. With a toy rake he had scratched the face of Thelma's littlest girl, in a scuffle over someone's tricycle. It had happened suddenly, though Thelma had been nearby, and who could have prevented it? Everyone said, "What if it had been her eye? . . ." And the Farmalow boy was forbidden to play with their children, and nothing Katie Farmalow could do would change their minds. "He's as bad as Gower," Louise said angrily.

Gower was still with them, too. Ginny met his mother one day in the supermarket, by accident. They met in the baby food aisle and could hardly have avoided each other, though the other woman was slouched over her shopping cart as if she needed it to support her. She was peering at the labels with a scrupulous, exaggerated concern, knowing that Ginny had seen her. Though they had never been introduced, they knew each other, everyone knew one another. "Hello," said Ginny. "Hello," said the woman. Ginny understood bitterly that while she and her husband had bought a house well within their income, everyone else in Fox Hollow had mortgaged and borrowed themselves to the limit, to buy houses they could not really afford. That was the kind of people Ginny and Ronald were neighbors with.

The woman was in her mid-thirties. She had a seedy, slightly criminal, apologetic look, not just because of her clothes—pink pedal pushers and a too-sheer blouse—but because of her face and body themselves. Her eyes protruded slightly, as if forced out of her skull by some profound mysterious pressure inside. Her lips did not quite close. Her body was thin and alert, her shoulders terribly slouched.

She and Ginny passed each other politely. But then, in order to avoid another encounter, both skipped the next aisle and started down the cereal aisle, Ginny at one end and the woman at the other. So of course they could not back out again.

This time they stopped to chat, it was the only thing to do. The woman was chewing gum. A little girl appeared alongside her, whining, "Mummy, Mummy," but did not expect to be noticed. The girl had come out of nowhere. As they talked this little girl gaped up at Ginny, and Ginny felt a cold sensation of revulsion. She forced herself to pay attention to the woman's chatter: "I saw your little girl and she's real cute, wish this one had hair like that. . . . So I said, I know he's bad but I can't help it. How can I help it? Little Gower was always like that, he always had so much energy. I know he's bad," she said, turning the palm of one hand up in a frank gesture. "The principal said he'd have to stay home, but I said don't we pay taxes? Anyway, how can I help it, I said—how can *I* help it?"

"I don't know," Ginny said uneasily.

"I mean, what can *I* do about it? Kill him?" The woman was leaning over her shopping cart again, staring earnestly into Ginny's face. Ginny could smell the fresh, fruity odor of her gum. The woman's eyes were yellowish and unclear, the irises looked enlarged. "He's just got a mind of his own," she said.

Ginny said slowly, "I heard he pushed a little boy out into the road. That could be dangerous."

"Oh, I know, I know," the woman said at once, "I know that. And he did something in someone's house—I don't know them. He did something nasty in there, right on the rug. Everybody tells me. But what can I do about it? He always had a mind of his own, right in the crib."

On television that evening there was a news photograph of a man injured in a gunfight with police, and Rachel blurted out: "Bambah!" Ronald said, "What was that?" but Rachel wouldn't tell. She chortled secretively, quite pleased.

"Oh, she won't tell. She never tells," Ginny said, making light of it. "It's just something she made up."

"It is not," Rachel said.

"What is it then, honey?" said Ronald.

It irritated Ginny to see how Rachel preferred her father, but she never let this irritation show. Rachel said in a high, lilting voice, "That's what he's gonna do."

"Who?"

"Bwa-wah," she said. It was baby talk of some kind.

"Who is that?" said Ronald.

"Bow-wab."

Ginny, across the room from them, said suddenly: "Gower?" Rachel laughed. She shook her head and would not answer.

"Are you talking about Gower? What about him?" Ginny said.

Rachel giggled but would not answer.

"Is that the boy who's always in trouble?" Ronald said.

Ginny and Rachel ignored him, he was so foolish, so far from their own world! "Did Gower do something bad?" Ginny said.

"I don't know."

"What did he do?"

"I don't know."

"Did he kill something?"

Silence. Rachel stared at a spot on the floor, her cheeks flushed.

"Did he kill an animal, or what?"

Ronald interrupted uneasily, saying, "Ginny, really—"

"This is none of your business, Ronald," Ginny said.

"It certainly is my business. You're frightening her."

"I'm not frightening her!" Ginny cried. She wanted to laugh, he was so stupid. Imagine looking at that flushed, pleased face and thinking the child was afraid! "Rachel, tell me what it means. Did Gower kill something? Is he going to kill something —what is it?"

"I don't know."

"Rachel, you'd better tell me."

"No, it's a secrud."

"What do you mean, a secret?"

"We can't—we're not s'post to—" She fell silent and the corners of her damp little mouth turned up, as if by themselves. "It's a secrud."

"Rachel, come over here."

"No. I don't like you."

"Rachel—"

"I don't like you. You're a bad mommy."

And so Ginny had to let her go, could not push it any further. The blood pulsed violently in her body. She felt as if she were in the presence of a terrible danger, almost a kind of corruption. It was as if the boy, Gower, were lurking in the room with them.

That night Ronald tried to console her but she said slowly,

"You don't understand. You don't know what it means." And Rachel, the next morning, flew about the house impatiently because it was drizzling, as if she could not bear to stay cooped up with her mother and baby brother: she was such a healthy, busy child! Ginny wondered why it was so hard for her, now, to love her daughter. Why couldn't she love her? Rachel must have guessed. She came over to where mother and infant sat on the sofa, and rocked from side to side in imitation of something, and rolled her eyes wildly in her head, and made a high, earsplitting noise. "Don't scare Baby Brother now," Ginny said. In immediate response to this, Rachel's fist jerked out and she struck the baby on the chest.

It was a hard, sharp blow, and the baby gasped at once and began to bellow.

"What did you do? What did you do?" Ginny cried.

She was shaking, she could not control herself. She banished Rachel upstairs, to bed. Muttering, she held the baby in her arms and tried to calm him, to restore that sleepy blank contentment; the room was now pierced with the baby's screams. Her brain throbbed with this sound and with a rage she could hardly understand. The word *Bambah, Bambah* kept running through her mind.

When the weather cleared that afternoon she let Rachel out. The child was sleepy with having cried so long, her eyes reddened, her playsuit soiled. She stared up at Ginny shyly. Ginny moved in a kind of trance, hardly seeing her. "Go outside and play. Go outside now," Ginny said. Rachel waited, waiting to be told to play in the back yard, or next door, or waiting to be scolded again; but Ginny said nothing. She was holding the baby, on her way to the bedroom. She seemed hardly to notice Rachel.

When the baby slept that afternoon Ginny slept with him. Rachel had gone and they were alone, she had pulled the crib up beside the bed. She slept heavily. She had a confusing dream, a nightmare, about a pack of wild dogs breaking loose upon her and her children . . . barking, yipping, the wild dogs rushed upon them and tore Rachel from her arms, and were about to seize the baby when Ginny woke, terrified. The dream had been so real that she could not get the terror out of her for some minutes.

But the baby slept peacefully in his crib. Outside, a dog was barking. It had a forlorn furious bark. Ginny got up and at once her head ached; it was as if the dream she had had was somehow still present in her brain. The dream pained her. She felt overwhelmed with a terrible burden, a kind of guilt. Another dog joined in and the two yipped, whined, barked sharply at each other. . . . Ginny went downstairs to make dinner. She opened cans and dumped their contents into a casserole dish, wearing her bathrobe, groggy and apprehensive. She heard a siren in the distance. The noise meant nothing to her, where once it would have signaled danger—for Rachel was still outside—but there were so many noises in the neighborhood, too many noises. No one could hear them all. Dogs, chain saws, automobiles, children. . . . She realized groggily that Rachel had not come back yet, and in a minute she would go to the door and call. Her head ached under the pressure of that mysterious dream.

It was about 5:30 when Rachel returned, by herself. She was very dirty. She crept in around the screen door and said, "Mommy?" Ginny looked at her. "Mommy, it's nice out now," the little girl said. She had a sweet, clear voice. Her eyes were very blue and her hair light, almost blond. Ginny stared at her and had the same feeling, sudden and unmistakable, that she had felt about the little girl in the supermarket. She stared. "It isn't wet out now, it's nice," Rachel said, rubbing her hands together to get the mud off, awkward and fetching. Ginny understood that the child had secrets, terrible secrets. The children had a language of their own and secrets of their own. Once they had played near her, with no secrets, but now they ran like wild creatures down the block and through everyone's front lawns, screeching and stopping for nothing.

"You wanted to hurt your brother," Ginny said suddenly.

"What, Mommy?"

She stared down at Rachel, half-turned from the stove. The sun in the west was dazzling in this part of the house. It was somehow mixed up with her vision of Rachel, of the terrible secrets the girl had and of the hurt she had wanted to do to her brother. A nerve moved frantically in Ginny's brain and she reached out for Rachel, who instinctively leaped back. But Ginny grabbed her and began spanking her. She woke up, now, to this spanking; she had not really been awake before. Rachel cried at once, exaggerating her surprise and pain. How she cried! It was terrible to hear her cry, and maddening, because it was so exaggerated. Ginny pulled down the little girl's panties to spank her harder. Rachel pushed at her mother. Ginny, grunting, bending over her, wrestled with the strong, furious little body, and, to keep it still, began striking her anywhere—on her back, her chest, her shoulders. The girl's body was so delicate. She could feel her bones beneath her skin, fine delicate bones that were an outrage to Ginny, so perfect were they, so finely structured to last that lifetime, a lifetime that had taken itself out of Ginny and would run and run away from her and never come back, stinking with the mud of great distances and beyond all the range of Ginny's voice. "A bad girl, you're a bad girl!" she cried. Rachel screeched; the sound was shrill and crazy, an animal's sound. She was like a crazed little animal twisting and jerking in her mother's embrace.

"A bad girl! A bad girl!"

Ginny reached around blindly, into the dazzling sunshine, and took something from the counter—a big metal spoon with a wooden handle. She beat the child with this, she could swing it with great strength and rapidity, every instant waking to what she was doing, shaking off the lethargy of sleep; the very feel of the handle encouraged her, sending strange waves of strength up into her arm. She screamed, "A bad girl! A bad girl!" Then time must have jumped, or perhaps did not jump at all, and her husband was in the kitchen trying to stop her. He was a terrified man with glasses, still holding a newspaper. He snatched the bloody spoon from her and with a groan of hatred she pushed him away, both hands against his chest. She cried impatiently, as if speaking to a child, "Oh, *you* don't know! What do *you* know about it? What the hell do *you* know?"

Happy Onion

I

There he is, Ly Cooper himself, on stage at the Megadome, his heated face turned up into the lights that overlap one another, white radiant darting lights, circles moving agitatedly back and forth over Ly's thumping body and over the bodies of the other members of the Happy Onion, who are in top form tonight: Plum Newly, who is singing, bawling out the words to a song Maryliz knows the way she knows her own soul, and Bixby, who plays electric guitar along with Ly, and H.J., wired up high tonight, playing drums. The Happy Onion! The audience can hardly keep still, and Maryliz sits among them, in the tenth row, singing under her breath in short nervous pants, wishing good luck for Ly.

How she loves Ly Cooper!

He is wearing his white buckskin outfit, and the fringes are fluttering like mad with the frenzy of his music. His violet silk shirt glistens and ripples in the nervous, reeling spotlights as Ly bangs at the guitar, his torso bouncing along with Plum's hoarse bawling voice. His large, squarish feet in high black leather boots do a kind of perpetual dance; it is hard to imagine Ly Cooper standing still. His feet move more rapidly now that the Happy Onion is winding up their spot on the concert bill with the song that made them famous, the song that is their trademark—

> *peeling the onion*
> *petals that pry away and weep*
> *peeling the onion*
> *crying us all to sleep—*

Plum Newly shakes ragged black hair as he sings this sad, happy song, while Ly, his blond mop light and fluffy and just washed that morning, gazes out into the audience and grins his wide, transfixed, gentle grin, like a boy just waking from sleep, not knowing yet where he is. Maryliz stares at him, wondering if he can see her. No. Yes, maybe. Yes, he is looking for her in this mob of kids. But she prefers to watch him like this, to stare at him when he can't see back. She is in love with Ly Cooper. *In love with Ly Cooper.* All around her girls strain forward, already clapping, shaking their heads in time with the rocky bouncing mocking tune of the "Happy Onion," all of them in love with Ly Cooper or with his face and his broad, strong shoulders, his hands so hard and so skillful on that battered guitar, in love with Ly or maybe with Plum, who is wearing sunglasses tonight, Plum grinning with his mouthful of new capped teeth that hurt him like hell, or they are in love with H.J., though he is short, almost midget-sized, or Bixby, who is heavyset and sullen as a child's teddy bear banged around too often, inert with a bitter stubbornness. . . .

The audience claps and cheers and screams for another round. All right, another round. Another "Happy Onion" with verses that expand and contract and dissolve into the air. Plum bows and does a hopped-up little dance, looks over his shoulder at Ly and the others, and they go back to the beginning again. Maryliz sits with her arms folded, not cheering. She is concerned about Ly: his grin has become stuck. It is too wide. His cheeks appear bunched up, paralyzed, stuck.

She wonders if he is taking something. Pills. It must be pills. He goes around in only a pair of trousers and a denim vest some-times, showing his arms, so he can't be jabbing himself in the arms. No, it must be pills. His handsome, strained face looks glossy, not like a face coated with ordinary perspiration: this looks like a film of grease. Maryliz wonders. She does not want to become alarmed. No. But she notices that his eyes are oddly bright and enlarged. His blue eyes. Blue flecked with brown, with gray. Hazy blue eyes. A blue you could stare into without ever coming to any end, any conclusion. . . .

> *peeling the onion we're all used up*
> *peeling the onion back to the bone*
> *no bone*
> *no one home*
> *no fears*
> *onion all used up and no fears*

The words are all a put-on but Maryliz finds it difficult to smile tonight. Plum is singing too loud. H.J. looks too frantic. And Ly seems to be pushing himself up and forward, making himself jerk along with the music, while his face stays intact and strange. Maryliz is sitting by herself in the tenth row, dressed in dead white bleached buckskin, like Ly, the skirt cut very short, almost to her buttocks, and the fringes cut and worried into shreds that tickle her thighs and make her want to sneeze. Her heavy "In-dian" earrings, made of silver, bounce and jingle and drag at her ear lobes. She is sitting alone because she is angry at Ly and at Jonathan, the manager of the Happy Onion. She wants to sit alone. She sees with scorn that everyone in the audience, all the girls, love Ly, or they love the Happy Onion itself, the noise of the Happy Onion, the jumpy bouncing mock-sad songs that Plum sings (the lipstick pencil's outline is too purplish on his lips!), the rhythm banged out by H.J. on the drums, by Ly and Bixby on their walloping guitars—

> *peeling the onion with no regret*
> *once you get home there's nothing left*

The sound is turned up so high, amplified so sharply from all corners of the drafty old Megadome, that Maryliz can hardly hear it. She's in it, sitting in it, and the vibrations keep her eyes frizzed with those bright, sparkly tears she can't help when she hears the group singing. The strange thing is, Maryliz thinks, that when the group sings a song you think it will never come to an end, it's so long and energetic and confident. But it does come to an end. That is a surprise: the way it always comes to an end. Every concert comes to an end.

Now Plum bows low and his ragged black hair sweeps the floor and he has to snatch at his sunglasses to keep them from flying off. Maryliz can almost hear him grunt with the effort of that athletic bow—she feels the strain of his white satin jumpsuit, which is tighter than it was a few months ago when the group began their tour. H.J. jumps up from his drums and squeezes his pudgy little hands between his knees. Bixby manages a sullen dark grin of relief. Strange how his eyes are smudged—Maryliz will have to scold him about his make-up again. Only Ly looks good, really handsome now that his face is back to normal. Pure and smooth and blond, his face, an angel's face, a manly tough angel you might wake to see in your bedroom some night. His clean hair gleams like that fake fluffy hair on Christmas tree angels, so light you wonder why it doesn't float up around his face like hair floating up from the head of a drowned man.

Maryliz washed that hair for him this morning.

A tumult of farewells. Backing away from the microphone, lurching forward again, teasing the girls in the crowd. Plum is fooling around with Bixby's guitar. Ly snatches the microphone and cries out, "I want my girl! I want my girl Maryliz! I want a little lovin'! You, Maryliz, you come up here and stand with me!"

Maryliz shrinks with alarm—what! He is calling her name! calling *her name* up on that stage!

"You, Maryliz Tone, I see you Maryliz Tone, you come up here and take a bow with the Happy Onion!"

One moment Maryliz is sitting, stunned, her arms still folded against her rib cage, and the next moment she springs to her feet, as if this were all planned (which it wasn't), a tall light-boned girl with flaxen hair that tumbles down to her waist, past her waist to her hips—so long she can sit primly on it if she wishes—Maryliz Tone, dressed in a white buckskin skirt with a five-inch brown leather belt, a violet shirt of the flimsiest see-through material tucked into the belt—she gets to her feet and climbs over the rows of knees into the aisle while everyone gapes at her.

"Oh you Ly Cooper! Goddam show-off bitch!" she laughs, waving at him, hurrying down to the stage with her birdlike little walk, so that her hair bounces down around her thighs and everyone stares at her, craning their necks. So many little girls staring at her, *at her,* so many boys, she can't help but forgive Ly and blow kisses at him, she loves him so. "Ly Cooper is a goddamn fool, a show-off freak," Maryliz giggles. Ly has come to the edge of the stage to help her, he slides his hands under her arms and swings her over onto the stage. The audience is cheering. Plum bawls into the microphone, "Wanna announce the engagement of Ly Cooper and Maryliz Tone—the engagement of Ly Cooper and Maryliz Tone—"

Flush-faced, Maryliz smiles out into the audience, catches her breath, and draws herself up to her height of five feet nine inches. She is suddenly very calm and clear about herself: she is the girl engaged to Ly Cooper. Ly stands with his arm around her shoulders, a good six inches taller than Maryliz, and nuzzles his mouth into her ear. "Maryliz, you are my closest dearest friend," he whispers.

After they finish bowing and fooling around and hurry out back and over to the hotel, and manage to get up to the hotel suite, Maryliz has a spare moment to kiss Ly on the lips. She discovers that his lips are dry and feverish. Plum cries, "Jesus, am I hot!" and his face is indeed orange. He runs to open some windows. TV cameras are already in the room, cameramen, stray visitors, flowers in big plastic containers set on the floor, and H.J. has already turned on the color TV set, sound and all. Maryliz whispers to Ly, "It's too late for an interview! You all are tired!" Ly squeezes her hand but says nothing. Jonathan hurries in the room, rubbing his hands, is approached by a man who must be the TV interviewer, but takes time to call out to Maryliz: "Sweetheart, you made the show tonight! Beautiful!"

Maryliz knows this isn't true, because the Happy Onion was really flying tonight and needed no assistance from anyone, but she throws Jonathan a kiss anyway. Jonathan is herding people around. He is a razor-faced young man of twenty-nine, with bristling black sideburns and a cowboy getup, a flabby waist: a Roanoke lawyer who has the boys under contract.

"H.J., you sit here. Bixby here. Maryliz and Ly, c'm' over here. *I'm* not in the picture—nope—you, Plum, what've you got in your goddamn mouth?"

The interviewer, a short balding young man, has already begun his show: "Plum Newly, you tell us, please, how the Happy Onion got started. . . ."

Plum adjusts his sunglasses and squints happily into the television camera. "Just a buncha kids working out together, you know, in our daddies' basements and at school 'n' all that . . . got real crazy about music. . . ."

"How did you, you know, get your first break? . . ."

"Well, there was Ly's dad, who's so well-known back in Roanoke, on account of he's a great guy, and mayor of the town, and he started these amateur contests for kids to have something to do on Friday nights, you know, and the Happy Onion sort of came on pretty strong, and pretty soon we got ourselves under contract 'n' everything," Plum laughs.

"Well, you know, your group has really taken off, your special sound means a lot to a lot of kids. . . . What are your plans for the future, Plum?"

"Yes, we look to the future 'n' not to the past, all of us," Plum says emphatically. "After Lexington here we're flying to Jackson, Kentucky, for a one-night, then we got a place on a big twelve-band rock concert at Murfreesboro College, then it's up to Cicero for another one-night—"

Out of camera range, Jonathan loses his temper suddenly and says, "Plum, you speak up more clearly now, you hear? Don't need to mumble like that."

"Wasn't mumbling," Plum says sullenly.

"What've you got in your mouth, boy? What're you chewing on?"

Plum spits something out—it looks like a rubber band.

Everyone laughs.

Maryliz pats her hair and feels for the curly little tendrils by her ears that make her baby-doll face look so fragile. She happens to notice Ly making a face as if he just thought of something.

"Honey?" she whispers. "Something wrong?"

"These clown-around bastards get me down," he says. "Let's leave."

"But Ly—"

He pulls her gently away, around behind the cameras, and Jonathan shakes a finger at him. "Hey, you two! Don't you sneak out on us!" But Ly just laughs. Going out the door he and Maryliz nearly collide with a waiter who is pushing a cart, and behind him comes a man with a hat on his head, looking baffled and irritated. He is probably from a newspaper. "I'm Mort Dansky," he says to Ly, as if this name meant something, and Ly solemnly shakes hands with him. Ly flops his hair forward and then backward, out of his eyes, a gesture friendly as a puppy's.

"Ly Cooper, and this is my girl Maryliz," Ly says politely.

The man shakes hands with him and Liz, staring at her.

"I am honored to meet you," Liz says in a little-girl whisper, feeling how fringed her eyes are—her false eyelashes like tiny whisk brooms, maybe a little overdone when someone stares right into her face, but the hell with it. She knows she looks good.

"You two get engaged tonight?"

"Oh ho, we been engaged a long time," Ly says.

"Childhood sweethearts, eh?"

"High-school sweethearts is more like it," Ly corrects him politely.

Behind them the other interview is getting louder. H.J. has been asked a question, and he soars into answering it as only H.J. can, primed and ready to fly (he's been gobbling something for the last five minutes—which is against doctor's orders, but you can't control H.J. after a good concert). His voice is like music, very high and tinny, like a musical mouse, a small squeaky delighted voice that could belong to a five-year-old rather than a four-feet-ten farm boy with an I.Q. of 149, "All you people out there watching, you get this: the Happy Onion is a unique phenomenon in the United States 'cause we are bringing the gospel of happiness to the nation by storm. Yes. We're always happy and you can count on that. We make up all our own songs, nothing second hand for *us*, and you know our trademark is happy sounds that are much needed in this old rattling United States of 1971. Right? No subjects are so serious and even fatal that they can't raise a smile on the faces of America," H.J. cries, out of breath.

"Ladies 'n' gentlemen, that is H.J. Farmer," the interviewer cries, "and did you ever witness such optimism? The Happy Onion is ushering in, according to *Time* magazine, which listed the boys in a story last month, a whole new era of right-thinking positive-thinking music for us to rejoice upon—"

Ly and Maryliz escape from the suite and over to their own room 309. Ly flops onto the bed without taking off his boots. He has a fearless face, Ly, and usually a good hearty appetite, but Maryliz wonders if this six-month tour of the kiddy circuit isn't getting him down.

"Ly, you look so peaked," she says. "Ly, I love you."

"Love you, honey," he says.

"I can't think why I was mad at you."

"No more can't I."

"It's just all this fooling around, and Jonathan's big mouth. . . ."

His eyes are half closed, she can see only a bluish gaze, a film between his lashes. He has blond lashes, almost as thick as her own. Is he going to fall asleep at 11:30 at night? So early? He looks pale, even shaky, though he is lying flat on his back. Maryliz tries to tickle him but he doesn't respond. Years ago she tickled him, on their first dates back in Roanoke—in fact, on their very first date, when she wouldn't let him kiss her, she was so tomboyish and skittish at the time. But he pushes her hands away now and manages only a distracted laugh.

"Time for me to call home, Ly?" Maryliz asks. She sits on the edge of the bed, looks down at him. "I can't think why I was so mad at you. . . ."

"No more can't I," Ly says. It is a refrain that's an old joke—a line from a hillbilly song the group once worked up, then abandoned. Ly must know that this line annoys Maryliz.

"Should I call my parents, Ly, and tell them? About the engagement?"

Ly hesitates.

"This engagement is the real thing?" she asks.

"Okay. Yes."

"Will it be a public wedding?"

"Okay."

"How soon, Ly? Ly, are you feeling bad?"

"Soon as you want it, honey."

"Can I tell my parents a June wedding?"

"What month is it now?"

"I don't know—April?"

Ly counts something on his fingers but comes to no conclusion. He opens his eyes and looks at her. "Don't you get your daddy any madder at me when you call, Maryliz. Please."

"Why would he be all that mad, now we're engaged?" Maryliz giggles.

Ly closes his eyes again. He must be tired. His handsome purple shirt is stained with perspiration under the arms. Maryliz unbuttons the first button, and the little pearly bulb comes off in her fingers. She'll have to sew it on, she thinks lovingly. Ly hasn't noticed it came off.

"A June wedding, Ly? And me in a real wedding dress? A white wedding dress with lace and veils and flowers?"

"Oh yes," Ly sighs.

"Bridesmaids and ushers and the whole church decorated just for me—for us?" Maryliz asks.

"Oh yes."

"And my daddy can reserve the whole lodge for us—the honeymoon suite most of all—and have a sit-down dinner for everybody—and champagne and orchids for our wedding night—okay?"

"Absolutely okay."

Maryliz's father, Mr. David Sprigg Tone, owns a good part of Roanoke—apartment buildings, office buildings, and the Tone Travel Agency—and in 1969 he acquired the franchise for the local Welcome Traveler Motor Lodge out on U.S. 304, with five hundred guest rooms, a heated indoor pool, a cocktail lounge (Lincolnshire Pub), a restaurant, a coffee shop, and facilities for banquets, conferences, and wedding parties, which Maryliz has had at the back of her mind ever since she dropped out of high school to travel around with Ly Cooper.

Maryliz tears off her left earring and tosses it on the bed and prepares to dial home. But she catches sight of Ly's face and something cold touches her heart.

"Ly, you are sick tonight, aren't you?"

"Don't worry, honey."

"Did you take something, Ly? Shoot yourself up with something?"

"Not me, honey."

"Ly, you can confess to me, honey, I won't bitch at you again —did you maybe shoot something when I wasn't looking? Did you?"

"No."

"You started getting bad during the concert, didn't you?"

Ly hesitates. He is so handsome, so striking! On his last birthday, only a week ago, he was twenty years old. With the Happy Onion he grew to his present full height, very American, golden, dressed sometimes in his buckskin outfit and sometimes in his satin bell-bottom jeans, sometimes in this violet silk shirt, or a bright gold shirt with a vest of curly black Chilean lamb—sometimes he and the Happy Onion are number ten on a crowded bill, under such groups as the Jefferson Airplane or the Snatched From Famine, and sometimes in smaller towns they are number one, and once they played number five on a bill in St. Louis with Janis Joplin at the top. All this usually shows in his face, but tonight he is not himself.

"You didn't answer me, Ly," Maryliz cries.

Ly raises himself on one elbow. "On second thought I want to ask a favor of you."

"Yes?"

"Instead of calling your people, how'd you like to call mine? My father?"

"Your father?"

"I think it's time."

"What does that mean?" Maryliz asks, staring.

Ly's father, Dr. Cooper, is a widower, a physician who works three days out of the week, an ob. man with an enormous healthy practice, gone into local politics with wonderful success. He is sandy-haired, jovial, with a build like a pregnant woman, all bouncy and good-natured, like many physicians with his specialty something of an actor, a happy actor. Ly has imitated his daddy on stage, Maryliz thinks, but nobody had better tell him that. Maryliz adores Dr. Cooper, and in fact Dr. Cooper delivered *her* seventeen years ago; a nine-pound baby girl, said to be beautiful already, but with big feet! During this long tour Maryliz has always put in a good word for Dr. Cooper, asking Ly to please call home just to say hello, but Ly has always been too busy.

"You actually want to talk to your daddy? Yourself? Right now?"

"No, you talk to him. Tell him about the wedding and about us coming home."

"Oh, are we coming home?"

Maryliz is playing with the telephone dial. Click, click, click . . . it is like time passing, the clicking of the dial. Ly is propped up on one elbow. He is smiling strangely at her. *I am going to remember this moment all my life,* Maryliz thinks, and it strikes her, dizzyingly, that this thought belongs to one of the Happy Onion songs, composed by Plum and Ly himself. She can see in Ly's muscular, kindly face the face of soft plump Dr. Cooper, the aging of Ly that will begin around the eyes and mouth from too much smiling into bright lights. Dr. Cooper is often on stage back in Roanoke, speaking to the high-school assembly on Friday mornings or before the Kiwanis and the J.C.'s and the Ladies' Hospital Guild, urging donations of any body parts people can spare: he himself seems anxious to give away his eyes, his kidneys, even his heart.

"Are you awful sick? . . ." Maryliz whispers.

"There's been something wrong with me for a while. I guess I'm sick."

"How sick? How?"

2

At the Roanoke airport, as the airplane taxied to a stop, Maryliz and Ly could see a small crowd waiting for them. "There wasn't supposed to be anyone told about this," Ly said. Maryliz squeezed his hand. "Goddamn my daddy," he said, wiping at his eyes.

As they climbed out of the airplane Maryliz was surprised to see the high-school band there, playing a welcome song in the form of a march, and a banner in the high-school colors, fluttering in the windy airport breeze: WELCOME LY & MARYLIZ! It was a nice surprise to see her own name there—she'd been a cheerleader her freshman and sophomore years, then got kicked off the squad because she'd missed too many practices. She and Ly waved to the crowd. Maryliz almost stumbled on the steps in her ticklish confusion.

A kind of procession was arranged, with Dr. Cooper's long white Cadillac going first—"It's lucky my father is also the mayor," Ly grumbled—and then the Tones's automobile, then the rest. Maryliz rode up front with Ly. She felt as if her body were being tickled at a dozen places, she felt as if she were about to sneeze, her nose ticklish and strange. She knew that the two of them were a sight—they were both wearing peach-colored gaucho pants bought in Bermuda that March, and flimsy black see-through shirts, and high black leather boots, and amber beads, and their hair—which was very pale blond—fluttered in the wind. After an embarrassed embrace, Maryliz's parents couldn't think of much to say to her; then her mother said meekly, "We're so happy about the engagement, Liz, and you look beautiful except—except for that blouse, but is that what they're all wearing now?"

Maryliz laughed and told her yes and kissed her again. But she had to ride with Ly, she had to be with him. When they drove out through the airport's parking lot, through the narrow lanes, people were throwing artificial roses at the white Cadillac—or were they real roses?—and Maryliz held onto Ly's hand, hard, and thought clearly, sternly, that she was exactly where she belonged, in the entire universe: sitting alongside Ly Cooper, dressed like Ly Cooper, holding his cool, perspiring hand in the midst of all this excitement and clamor, making the universe balanced, correct. Yes, it was her place here beside him; it was her duty to be beside him.

"When did this trouble begin, Ly?" Dr. Cooper asked.

"Oh I don't know, I didn't pay attention all the time," Ly said.

"If you had difficulty with bowel movements you should have told me. Should have told someone," Dr. Cooper said.

Ly squirmed and sighed miserably.

"How long you been bleeding down there? . . ." Dr. Cooper asked.

"Off and on I had pain, I sort of felt pain," Ly said vaguely, as if he were talking about someone else, "but I didn't bother with it. . . . We were always on the move, you know, one hotel then another, and anyway I was high a lot of the time, you know, and I didn't want to come down . . . the pain was so far below me . . . Also, you know, I am a happy kid without the wish to depress others."

Maryliz glanced at him, surprised by the mockery in his voice. But he did not meet her eye.

Ly checked into the hospital for tests the next morning, and Maryliz was there at 8 A.M. sharp, in a white pants suit, with several strands of pearls around her neck. The nurses stared at her in amazement. She waited around all morning in a visitors' lounge, leafing through magazines, then Dr. Cooper had lunch with her in the grimy little cafeteria in the basement, then she waited out the afternoon again, alone. She began to feel downhearted and a little nervous. Her outfit was soiled from this place and her skin felt prickly because she usually patted astringent on it every few hours—she had slightly oily skin and was terrified of pimples—and she couldn't do that here at the hospital.

"Ly Cooper, you better get well . . ." she whispered aloud.

The first day's tests were over at five. Ly was wheeled into a private room, and Maryliz and Dr. Cooper visited with him for a while. But he seemed very tired. In his white hospital gown he looked like someone Maryliz should feel sorry for. "Honey, what I would really like to do is sleep now," Ly said gently.

"Sleep so early in the day? . . ." Maryliz asked, startled.

She returned the next morning, early, but couldn't see Ly. She waited around all day. Dr. Cooper dropped in to say hello to her, but he was busy with a woman in labor in a far wing of the hospital, so Maryliz was alone most of the time. She began to chip at her fingernail polish. She called home to reassure her mother that she was well, yes, but she didn't know how Ly was. Not yet. The tests weren't completed yet.

What was going to happen to Ly?

On the morning of the operation—something about his stomach, maybe an ulcer—Maryliz was at the hospital before it was even open for visitors. She wore a white dress so that she could fit in with the nurses, whom she admired—they were so plain and efficient and good. She loaded her hair up on her head and tied an Indian headband around it, and wore no make-up except on her eyes. She wandered chastely through the hospital, thinking of Ly, wondering about him, wondering if he was going to be well soon, in time for a June wedding. It was already the end of April.

But after the operation she couldn't see him right away. She lingered in the visitors' lounge, waiting for Dr. Cooper to come get her. Her mother showed up and tried to talk her into coming home. But she said, "Mamma, I have to be here. Ly might ask for me and then what?"

Ly wasn't wheeled back to his room but put into a part of the hospital called I.C.U. Maryliz had never heard of this before. She began to get frightened. She and her mother asked the woman at the front desk what I.C.U. meant and the woman explained, kindly, that this was the Intensive Care Unit and patients there were given special treatment—nurses on duty all the time.

"Then it's for very sick people? Very sick people?" Maryliz cried.

"Maryliz, it's just a place where they get good treatment. Maybe it's because Ly is Dr. Cooper's son . . . he would naturally get special treatment . . ." Maryliz's mother said faintly.

Maryliz got rid of her mother and tried to find Dr. Cooper. She wandered around the obstetrics ward but couldn't locate him. She was breathing hard, picking nervously at her nails; the heavy knot of hair at the back of her head had begun to loosen. What if Ly was really sick, badly sick? What if he couldn't get well in time for a June wedding? What if he died?

The next morning Ly was back in his private room. Dr. Cooper took Maryliz up to see him, and at the door of the room he held her hands and gazed into her face, with a look that was gentle and pitying and yet somehow, in Maryliz's imagination, not original. "Don't be upset when you see him," Dr. Cooper said. "He's been through a terrible ordeal. . . ."

Maryliz walked into the room as if walking into a dream, her eyes fastened right on Ly, unblinkingly: there he lay beneath the covers, with a tube attached to his arm, the inside of his arm, and another tube attached to his nose. But he was awake. She could see that he was trying to smile at her.

Something cold brushed against her heart. She felt her lips go pale and chaste, felt the blood rush out of them. Her eyes brimmed with tears that were frizzy, like carbonated water. But she went right to Ly's bedside and never let on anything, and sat there and took hold of one of his hands and began kissing it. "You're going to be well, all well. You're going to be well," she whispered.

Ly made a sound to indicate that he heard her.

She stayed an hour, then a staff physician and two nurses came in, and Dr. Cooper walked Maryliz out to the lounge. She didn't ask him what was wrong. He began telling her, in a confused rambling way, as if he were reporting a story that was not convincing, that she wouldn't believe. Her mind was dead to him. She listened to him, allowed him to comfort her, and yet she did not really hear what he said.

She visited with Ly as much as she was allowed. Sometimes he lay in a stupor, not quite asleep and not quite awake, drugged, and Maryliz sat at his bedside staring at him. She remembered Ly jumping out of bed, out of another bed, and kissing her up and down—that had been in a hotel room in Jacksonville, Florida. Months ago. The memory made her head wobble, it was so vivid and yet so finished. When Ly's eyelids fluttered and she saw that he was looking at her, recognizing her, she felt her face break into an instantaneous smile. "Ly? . . . Ly? . . . Are you waking up?" she whispered.

One day Ly woke quite bluntly. He was still a handsome boy but a decade had passed in his face. He said, "Don't cry, Maryliz, what the hell. I don't mind. And don't jiggle the bed, please. . . ."

She began to cry harder, not because he was dying but because of the tone of his voice.

"I said I don't mind. This is a snap. Maryliz, be a good girl and get out of this dump. This place is not for you. You don't fit in here."

She lost count of the days: she dragged herself up to his room on the fifth floor, she dragged herself out to the ladies room, which was the only place she could safely weep—her eye make-up streaked and she looked like a drowned owl. She ran out to fetch nurses when Ly seemed to need them. She went down to the cafeteria for coffee and green salad—she couldn't eat anything else—and sometimes Dr. Cooper dropped by to talk with her. His manner had become vague and apologetic. He seemed embarrassed because of his son. According to him, Ly's "trouble" was everywhere in him—another operation would do no good—he had cancer of the colon, his liver was damaged—Maryliz sat and listened to this, her mind turning off, going absolutely blank. She wanted to jump up and run back to Ly's bedside. She would be his nurse. His only nurse. She loved him and belonged with him, out of all the places in the universe she belonged with *him*.

Back upstairs she kissed his hands feverishly. Ly mumbled her name. She smelled a strange sharp odor about him.

The smell of cancer?

When he was awake enough to speak, he told her to go home. "I don't mind any of this," he assured her. But Maryliz brought her chair closer to him. Closer to him. She stared at his yellowing, wasted face and thought that there was no home for her apart from him, no place she should be. "It's my duty to be with you," she said.

The universe would be unbalanced, if she left him.

Yes, unbalanced. Rocking to one side. Tilting, crazily awry, like one healthy eye easing out of line from the other. As she paced the hospital corridor she almost felt her vision go out of focus. Almost go cross-eyed. She was so *tired*. Recorded music was piped into the hospital elevators—always the same music, the same pallid rhumbas, and aged love songs without any words —and after a while she began to hear this music in her head. It drove out her own humming, her murmuring of song lyrics: the Happy Onion's jumpy bouncy rhythms were being displaced.

One day while Ly slept, heavily drugged, she sat and watched him and remembered how they had scrambled around in bed together, so many times, tickling each other . . . though Maryliz had declared that tickling was against the rules. . . . Something doubtful passed through her mind: was this really Ly Cooper?

She took out her Cover Girl compact and examined herself. She was still Maryliz Tone. Yes, she was certain of that.

Ly was moved back into the Intensive Care Unit, where he died two days later. Maryliz happened to be in the hospital at the time, listening to the Muzak around her head. She was sipping a cup of cold coffee. Dr. Cooper, his own face eroded and yellowish, broke the news to her. "And if only, if only there weren't the side effects," he said, "if only his eyes were healthy, we could give his eyes to the eye bank. Think of that, Maryliz, we could give his eyes to some poor blind person! I wish to God we could have done that, Maryliz. . . ."

Maryliz lowered her coffee cup in amazement. "But why can't we?"

"The corneas are ruined. Hemorrhages."

Maryliz was wearing her hair in braids, like a twelve-year-old. Her dress was plain and white, her stockings were pale, transparent, like a nurse's stockings. She weighed only ninety-eight pounds now, and she was in danger of fainting except for this news about Ly: so awful it woke her up permanently.

"Then he is really dead?" she asked.

"Maryliz, he died forty-five minutes ago."

"I mean, is he really dead? I mean . . . *dead?*" she asked in bewilderment.

3

The pathologist had a name she could not remember, though Dr. Cooper had introduced her carefully to him. The attendant's name was Ted—she had no trouble remembering that. Ted was a big, husky boy in his twenties, with an acne-ravaged face and shy eyes. The pathologist was probably in his thirties; the lower half of his face looked darkened, as if he had not bothered to shave that morning. He stared at Maryliz, up and down, not boldly, just in surprise, as if he had never seen anyone like her or heard a request like hers.

"We were going to be married next month," she said softly.

She wore a black cotton dress with a peasant collar and sleeves, and her handsome black boots, and black stockings; tight around her forehead she had tied a headband of small black and white beads. Her hair was fixed into an enormous stiff bun and covered with a hair net of her mother's. Though she had tried to fix herself up before leaving home, her eyes and nose were red-rimmed.

They brought her into the pathology lab. Maryliz was careful to breathe very lightly, shallowly, so that she wouldn't faint from the odor of chemicals and disinfectant. The pathologist said something to her but she didn't seem to hear him. She was staring at Ly. There he was—Ly Cooper himself, on a table that seemed to be made of porcelain, his face turned up into the powerful but oddly dull white lights of the laboratory, diffuse white radiant lights that were absolutely still, static, fixed in the ceiling and shining without imagination down upon Ly's body. The table was massive, thick, ugly. It rose from the floor in one piece. Everything was white porcelain or tile.

The table had a shallow depression in it which tilted, like a small river, down to a drain hole like the drain in a bathtub. Ly lay flat on the table, on top of the depression. Maryliz saw that they had done something to him already, but her eyes didn't quite take it in. She wanted to say hello to him. She had the idea he might sit up and say hello back.

"You didn't hurt him? . . ." she asked.

The pathologist did not look at her. The orderly glanced at her, startled. But she was watching Ly all the while. She thought that he looked more interesting now than he had during the last week. His features were sharper, more taut, as if the skin had begun to shrink around them. His lips were slightly parted: he might have been about to smile, maybe his mocking smile. She loved that smile. Pale, white, he seemed fashioned of some doughlike material that had stiffened, against its own nature. . . . She stared at him, fascinated. She wanted to stroke his face to make it relax. It looked stuck, locked into that expression. That was really not Ly Cooper's natural expression. His hair was not so fine now, or so clean; they had not washed it for him for some time. But how handsome he was, still, with his manly nose and his slightly stubbled jaw, that had rubbed the softest parts of her body so often, rubbing them raw! . . . and how silently he lay there, after the bustle of his life, after all the jokes and the guitar workouts and the songs!

"Why, this is hard to believe," Maryliz said.

No safe space around anyone in a hospital, Maryliz had noticed: the orderly went right up to the table, though he was a stranger to Ly, and drew the thin white sheet away. The pathologist handed him an instrument. Maryliz's brain throbbed. Ly was very thin, almost emaciated—maybe she hadn't made him eat right? she hadn't taken care of him right? The orderly, his face scarlet, manipulated a large instrument against Ly's breast, as if it were a giant can opener, and while Maryliz stared he brought it down from the neck to the stomach and back up again, sawing, his elbow jerking. Something opened up. Maryliz took a step forward: why, Ly's chest had been opened up!

The pathologist, his face grim and angry, took over now and began to extract from Ly's body certain things, organs, one right after another, his fingers in pink rubber gloves moving skillfully, never hesitating. The way he groped around and snipped and brought out these organs made Maryliz feel dizzy. Some sacs were brought out—filmy and bloody—and a tough-looking muscle that might have been a heart, and now a coil of intestines, and other things that Maryliz could not recognize except to know they belonged to Ly. She stood there, blinking. There was a fuzzy antiseptic odor in this room that made her want to sneeze.

For some reason she had a strange thought: she wondered what her parents would have given her and Ly for a wedding present.

The pathologist instructed the orderly to watch, in a voice too low for Maryliz to really hear, and he began cutting the scalp. One hard firm slash. Then he took hold of Ly's hair and drew it forward, gently, so that the scalp was brought forward, drawn inside out. The top of Ly's scalp now lay lightly against his face and hid it!

The pathologist began sawing at the skull in back. Ted, his face turned away from Maryliz, stooped to watch. When the skull was sawed—nearly in two—the pathologist reached in for the brain.

"They said his system collapsed," Maryliz said politely, feeling she ought to break this tension. "That's hard to understand."

The pathologist bent over his work as if he hadn't heard.

"And nobody wanted his eyes, then, or his kidneys or heart or anything?" she asked. She felt a film of moisture on her upper lip.

The brain was now placed alongside the other organs on a low ceramic table. Maryliz stared at Ly's body, at his hidden face, and made a sudden frantic, pitying gesture—the orderly guessed her wishes and smoothed Ly's scalp back over the hole in the skull so that his face appeared again. That was better. It was easy to adjust the scalp. His eyes were still open, partly open. The lips were still frozen in that half smile. Maryliz remembered him on stage that last night, in Lexington, every part of his body quick with life, jerking with life, and she knew that she loved him. Yes, she still loved him and she was not even sorry he had died: they had already had so much love together.

She was married to him, really. To that face. That body and its parts. She would marry someone, a man, but when she lay with him it would be Ly's face she summoned up, always: she had to memorize that face in order to make love to it.

One, two, several seconds passed. . . . Maryliz stared at Ly, at his face, feeling the emphatic, certain beat of her heart. The universe seemed perfectly balanced. There was no danger.

But after these moments she realized that the pathologist and his orderly were embarrassed. So she must leave. "Thank you for allowing me in," she said, and she put out one hand to shake hands—the pathologist quickly drew off his gloves—and looked him straight in the eye, to show that she wasn't going to faint or become hysterical. Then she shook hands with Ted, who gaped at her.

Outside in the corridor a few nurses stood around, and when she appeared they fell silent. They were staring at her. She saw their eyes dip to take in her leather boots. Farther along the corridor two hulking male attendants stood by a water fountain, also staring at her. She ignored them and walked to the closest exit, so that she could get to the parking lot without going up through the lobby and all that, where more people might be standing around to gape at her. She walked in her rapid birdlike way, Ly's bride in black, his beautiful permanent darling.

Normal Love

Downtown

   I park my car in a high-rise garage, three floors up. Everything is silent. The garage is gray, the color of concrete blocks and metal. Many cars are parked here, in silence, but no one is around. A small tension rises in me, an alarm. Is there anyone around? Anyone? Our city is not a large city, there is no danger. There might be danger late at night for a woman alone. Now it is a winter afternoon, a weekday, overcast, too cold for anyone to make trouble. . . . I lock the car door, I put the keys in my purse, I walk quickly to the elevator and press the button for Down.

   The elevator is slow. Is it out of order? Why is there no one around? A sudden noise behind me . . . behind me a man is walking this way, putting something in his pocket. Car keys, probably. His footsteps make brisk noises on the concrete. The air is cold. My heart begins to pound absurdly, I know there is no danger and yet my muscles stiffen as if in expectation of danger, the very shape of my skeleton tensing as if to receive a blow. . . . The man waits with me for the elevator. I don't look at him. He doesn't look at me. He is wearing a fairly good overcoat, he is no danger to me. There is no danger in this city; the very coldness of the air on this December day makes everything abrupt and undramatic, there is no tension, nothing. The elevator comes. The door opens. I step inside, the man steps quickly inside, for a moment I feel a sense of panic, as if inside me a door is opening suddenly upon nothing, upon blackness. The elevator takes us down. The man says nothing, makes no movement, does not take his hands out of his pockets as if . . . as if to take them out would be a sign, and he dare not make a sign. I wait with my heart hammering. I wait. The elevator stops, the door opens, a woman and some children are waiting to get inside, I step out quickly and escape. . . .

I spend the afternoon shopping. I am not followed.

My husband

sits alone downstairs after we have all gone to bed. This is a sacred time for him, I think. Secrets rise in him at this time. If I come to the landing to say, "It's after two o'clock," he will stare up at me, startled. He sits on the sofa with an ashtray beside him. He is smoking and thinking. He is sitting there in a kind of troubled peace, a man of forty, six feet two and lean, unmuscular, a city man with dark hair thinning on top, the tension and bewilderment of the city in the lines of his face. His face is lined, yes. Why is his face lined? He has not the power of true amazement any longer, yet his face, in the light of two o'clock in the morning, in the fuzzy beige light from our lamp, shows a bewilderment that should be stronger. He is thinking, dreaming, a terrible sadness fills him, he is sitting there alone and will glance up at me, startled, if I come to the landing. The newspaper is out back, folded to be thrown out tomorrow, the newspaper with the story about the missing girl.

My children

are eager to get out of the doors of the house and eager to get back through them again. They jerk one way, scrambling for freedom. Then they are hurrying back. They are hungry. The boys have long unpredictable legs. They are always knocking against tables. They spill milk, drop plates, their nostrils have been raw with colds for weeks. They like hot dogs and hamburgers. The meat comes processed in strange shapes they never notice—tied neatly with a tiny knot of intestine, pink, or ground to an intricate maze of wormlike red tissue. It is all tissue. The boys like this meat very much. One of my daughters is melancholy and selfish, remote and spiteful, thirteen years old . . . the corners of her eyes narrow at things I can't imagine. She is always thinking. She looks like her father, with the same pinched calculating face; a smile can transform such a face. The other girl is only nine, a good-natured child, she loves us all and can't understand why her father is drifting from us, at the age of forty, a mysterious stubborn drifting we can't understand.

My neighborhood supermarket

has a tinsel Christmas tree inside. A fluffy angel blows horn at its very top. The tree is pretty but difficult to look at, the metallic branches catch light and reflect it painfully. A radio playing "Jingle Bells" but the rhythm is very fast, speeded up . . . Which day of the week is this? I do most of my shopping on Tuesday. But sometimes on Wednesday we have already run out of something, or I forgot to buy something, and I go back the store. By the time Thursday comes I need something more, usually milk, and on Friday I have my hair done and the hairdresser is just down the block so it's no trouble to drop in again the store is very pleasant. Christmas carols are being played now. But the sounds are filmy and vague, in the distance, as if the angels singing such songs are distracted, glancing over their shoulders at something. During the week the supermarket is not very crowded. Sometimes I come back again on Saturday and it's crowded then, but more girls are stationed at the check-out counters, so I suppose everything works out. I suppose they have it all figured out.

It is necessary for me to look carefully at everything. Most things are familiar—these cans and packages—but still I look carefully, to see if there is any change, to see if there are special things that I want. I have to buy a lot of groceries. Two shopping carts are necessary sometimes, so one of the boys comes along. As long as he doesn't knock anything over, he's helpful. I should be proud of him, a son of my own, but I don't have time to be proud of him. His nose is running, he wipes it on the side of his hand . . on his sleeve. . . . "Take this," I tell him and give him a Kleenex. He accepts it. He wipes his nose as if his nose had become suddenly delicate.

But I prefer to shop alone. I take my time with everything. I take my time buying meat, inspecting the shapes of meat. The radio is now playing "Let It Snow." Far beyond my hearing are the cries of amazed animals stunned by hammer blows, their hoofs skidding in the dirt, their shoulders and heads wrenching to get free of the horns that imprison them—men have hold of these horns! They are herded into trucks. Their flanks and sides are carried frozen out of trucks, big refrigerated trucks so long they can hardly make the turns of our old-fashioned little intersections.

Our house

is on a street that is partly good, partly bad. There are boarding houses at the corner. This is a college town, quiet and unexciting, a nice place to live; only in the last several years has the crime rate begun to rise, but nothing has happened to us. Students living in those boarding houses sometimes make trouble, but inside the houses only; they have never bothered us. The street has potholes. I drive automatically around them now, not even seeing them.

The university's president lives a few blocks away, in a large, old home.

Mornings in our house are quiet. All my children go to school now. The telephone rings suddenly and my mouth goes dry; I hurry to answer the phone, I am anxious, wondering . . . could it be a wrong number? Or is it a friend? Is it someone inviting us out? There is so much cruel power in that person calling me, in his anonymity! But the telephone must ring also when I am not home and then, then I am the one who is in power, then the caller (probably another wife, like myself) must stand listening sadly to the ringing of a telephone in an empty house, denied a few minutes' conversation. All my children go to school now. They walk to school. When the telephone rings in the empty house I go blank with anxiety, with hope. The noise rings through me. When no one calls I do housework, laundry or vacuuming, making all the beds, straightening things out; then I go out shopping. I work around my house thinking to myself about the mystery of a house, the lives dreamed out in it. My children are eager to get away in the morning and eager to come back in the afternoon. I catch myself up quickly, dreaming of them, their bouncing impatient limbs somehow inside me, damaging me . . . Do they want to damage me, my flesh? No. Does my husband want to damage me? No. The house, which I wanted so badly eight years ago, is very silent in the morning. I walk through the rooms, buttoning my car coat, getting ready to go out and shop . . . I am thinking with part of my mind about what must buy today, clothes for one of the kids, a shower curtain to replace the ripped one, some of those new dark stockings, maybe a new pair of shoes. . . . I like to shop, I go shopping every day. I cannot locate myself precisely in this house, so I go out. I have bought everything for the rooms myself, choosing the pieces of furniture carefully, worrying over them, studying magazines like *House Beautiful.* Our sofa is dark brown, our rug is light beige

The coffee table is a long modern oval, of dark walnut. The room used to seem striking to me, even beautiful, but now it looks a little worn and cheap, I don't know why. I picked out all this furniture and my husband and I argued over its cost but isn't it the furniture of a strange family, something another woman has chosen? My husband shows no sign of himself here. He puts everything of his away, as his own father did. Nothing remains of him downstairs, he is a professor at the university and most of his books are at school, his real life is somewhere else, not here. He is invisible here, in this house.

I look out the front window. Across the street is a house like this one, of dark red brick, two stories high with a big attic where, as in our house, two boys have their room. These houses were built in the forties. I look out the window. It seems to me that something moves against the window of that house—another woman, looking out? Is she looking across the street at me?

The purse

came into our lives by accident. My husband took the car to have the brakes fixed and on his way home, walking back home, he cut across a vacant lot. I have seen him out walking, alone, and the strength of his walk has always impressed me—a man with somewhere to get to, a stubbornness that women need in men. But he is not really like that. He was wearing his trench coat, a soiled tan coat, his hands were stuck in his pockets, he was walking fast and with his head bowed as usual (thinking of what? of his students? of the bill for the car?), his eyes drifting along the ground . . . and something caught his eye, the corner of his eye. It happened that way.

He saw a woman's purse. It had been thrown into the frozen grass, a few yards from the path, a black patent-leather purse. He paused. He leaned over and picked it up. . . .

Around him in the field was frozen milkweed.

"I found this," he said to me, coming in the back door. He looked worried, slightly embarrassed, as if I would blame him for

something. Inside the purse was a wallet of some brown cheap
plastic material, and inside the wallet some snapshots, a few dollar bills, some change, an identification card. Crumpled tissue
stained with pink lipstick, and a comb, and a tube of lipstick, a
few loose pennies . . . keys on a chain with a small fake rabbit's
foot. . . .

Linda Slater, 1463 St. Clair. In case of emergency notify Mr.
and Mrs. Frank Slater, 1463 St. Clair.

At the dentist's   at the hairdresser's   at the supermarket

Betty has three cavities this time. She won't brush her teeth.
I check her toothbrush at night: sometimes it is wet, but what
does that mean? All my children tell lies.

The dental assistant is about nineteen years old, with her hair
in a big frothy mess, bleached. I glance through my checkbook
ahead of time and see that I have forgotten already today to record one check . . . what was that check? A small storm rises in
me, irritation and alarm. My husband never makes mistakes with
the checkbook or with money or figures of any kind, he does
them in his head, he never makes mistakes. He doesn't make
much money as a professor but he never makes mistakes adding
up that money or subtracting it.

Outside in the waiting room while I wait for Betty I notice last
night's newspaper still here. From across the room I can see the
headline on the left-hand side of the page: GIRL MISSING. Last
night we read that story. Linda Slater, 20, was reported missing
and her whereabouts not known. Her purse was found in a vacant lot late Monday afternoon by Dr. Norman York, Professor
of History at the University. He telephoned her parents. He
brought the purse over to them. My eye darted at his name again
and again—his name is my name, that is my name in the newspaper, about a man who found a girl's purse. The girl is now
missing. She is five feet three inches tall, weighs one hundred ten
pounds, dark brown hair, blue eyes, I can't remember. . . .

I leaf through a magazine and look at the photographs of food

Christmas is coming. We will all make Christmas cookies, the children and I. I will plan meals, a week of meals for Christmas week, I will make up things ahead of time and freeze them . . . and on Christmas day we will have a ham, I think, instead of a turkey. . . . The table settings in the magazine are very beautiful, decorated with holly and pine boughs.

Finally I pick up the newspaper and look at her picture again—Linda Slater, 20, dark hair and firm, staring, curious eyes, a very short upper lip. A posed photograph. It probably exaggerates her beauty.

Friday, the hairdresser's. Glenda does my hair. She is a big cheerful girl. She washes my hair enthusiastically, scrubbing my scalp. One time her fingers slipped and one of them, or a knuckle, went into my eye. The soap stung but I didn't make any fuss, I don't mind pain, I usually laugh it off in embarrassment.

Glenda pins my hair up in big rollers. There are four chairs before the big mirror, two others occupied, women having their hair pinned up. This place is not very clean, but it is reasonable. The air is chatty and warm. All the girls are friendly. Glenda has a big, robust air about her, I can smell the gum she is chewing. Her diamond ring looks much too big to be real; I know her husband is a factory worker.

"Hey, you ever seen a thalidomide baby?" Glenda asks the girl who is working next to her.

"What kind?"

"Thalidomide, you know—that sleeping pill they had."

"Oh yeah. No. Where is there one?"

"He's not a baby now, he's pretty grown-up."

"Where?"

"My mother-in-law's street, across the street from her."

The woman whose hair is being done next to me twists her head around. I see her here often, she has a bleached-out, staring face, a redhead with pale freckles. She is about my age, forty. "There's a thalidomide girl lives down the street from us," she said.

"How old?"

"Twelve."

"This boy, this one I was telling you about, is real nasty. He's maybe six feet tall, he goes to high school already and is a real brat. His mother spoiled him."

"The girl has little arms, real short arms, little flippers."

"*He's* got flippers. He wears some wool things, like mittens, up around them in the winter. He can use them flippers like they were arms."

"Is he smart?"

"He's a smart aleck."

"The girl is pretty smart, I guess. But she's a show-off too; I seen her once in a store downtown acting up. Her and two other girls. They're about in seventh grade, these girls, and flirting with some guy. This girl's got real short little flippers, just like baby arms, and she was touching some salesguy's chin with one of them. It was a shoe store."

"She was what?"

"She was kidding around, flirting—that guy's face was so red it wasn't even funny."

"Flirting, she was flirting?"

"Yeah, with those little arms of hers. They say she's real smart but she's nasty."

"*He's* nasty. Down at school the girls are just crazy for him and they call him up all the time, because he's cute, and they don't seem to care about the flippers or anything. But around the house his mother has to do everything for him . . . he can't even go to the bathroom by himself, he thinks he's so smart but he has to have help. They asked him if he would like some artificial arms but he wouldn't. He said no. They tried to get him to take them but he wouldn't. He gets all this attention because of them short arms. . . ."

At the supermarket I go back to the dairy products and get a carton of milk, lifting it up to see if it's leaking underneath. It seems all right. I buy some cottage cheese. I didn't bother with grocery cart but it occurs to me that I need other things, so my arms get full, it's awkward carrying everything. I carry the items pressed up against my chest. At the check-out counter I notice some watery milk on my coat.

The texture of wet snow
is stubborn, won't melt. It has turned gray and wet. I was not always forty years old. I remember looking out the front window of my parents' house in Indiana, watching the rain. I had long blond hair, I always dressed well, I was waiting for something to happen to me, and it happened. Once I went for a walk, alone, when I was visiting my grandmother in West Bend. I went for a walk into a little park. I looked at the roses because they had gone to all that trouble to plant roses; I stopped and looked at a sundial . . . but the sun was not shining, I couldn't see what time it was.

When I get home Susan says, "Betty is sort of sick."

Betty is throwing up in the bathroom upstairs. While I am with her the telephone rings, one of the children answers it. I wait but no one calls me; it must be for one of the children.

Dinner
always takes place at six. Everyone is ready to eat. My husband has been home since five, has had a drink, has looked through the paper. His name no longer appears in those stories about Linda Slater. I want to ask him about it, how does he feel, what is he thinking? . . . but his silence baffles me. I resent this silence in him, though it has always been in him, since we met twenty years ago.

He comes into the kitchen when Susan gets him. Susan hangs onto him, teasing. She loves him and her love is a torment to all of us and to herself, making her forehead rise in childish angry frowns. "Daddy you're not listening!" she often says, throwing herself around as if trying to damage herself; or she gets up from the table with dignity and walks away, and Norman calls her back, and she says *no,* and he makes a sudden movement to push his chair back and get her and, pretending to be frightened, perhaps a little frightened, she does come back. . . .

We sit. Tonight we are having creamed chicken with carrots and peas. It is a familiar dish, they like it, they are hungry. Now we are beginning dinner at last, sitting around the big kitchen table, all of us eased into our places as if at the start of a boat race . . . floating with difficulty on the element of our lives, which is love. Is it love? We are here, around this particular table, because two people loved each other and got married. On that day I stared at the sundial I was positive no one would marry me . . . but I needn't have worried, like most women. It happened.

Sometimes I lean over the bathroom sink, alone, feeling nauseated, clutching my head and thinking *What is going to happen?* Am I going to throw up? But I never throw up. I can't bring it up out of me, whatever is inside. Even when I was pregnant I had a strong stomach. The nausea passes and my head is filled suddenly with activity, the pictures of things I must use—the colored sponges I use in the kitchen, one for dishes exclusively and the other for wiping counters and the table, the sheets and pillow cases I must fold, fold, again and again, the beds I must make the small rugs I must straighten, the cans I must open with the can opener, rinse, and put under the sink in the garbage can. My head is filled suddenly with a love for these things. I must go downstairs and open cupboards and the refrigerator to seek out certain packages and cans and jars, the containers of love. Every day I must do this. I must go down into the kitchen and prepare meals for my family, with love, careful of the delicate shapes of love. Plates, forks, spoons, knives, paper napkins, glasses . . . these achieve a secret meaning, placed on the table. Will one of the boys knock his milk glass over? No matter. Mop it up. Norman will mop it up, he takes care of emergencies, a tradition

Everyone sits. A Friday-night dinner. Do they understand this bouquet of love I have set out for them? What, precisely, do they see? If the carrots were missing from the main dish and there were only peas in it, along with pepper and salt and a few other spices, would this make any difference? I should have put pimiento in the cream sauce, but what was left in the jar had spoiled. In the salad I have put two kinds of lettuce, tomatoes, radishes, cucumber slices, bits of celery and green pepper. If I had left out the green pepper would they notice? Do they notice that it is there? I have made biscuits from a mix. They all put the biscuits on their plates and the chicken and sauce over them, except for Susan, who can't stand soggy things; if the biscuits were missing? . . . Bobby drops his fork onto the floor. No matter, wipe it off. The dinner has begun. The race is on, no going back. My husband is saying something. Stern, or smiling? He smiles. Good. My husband is saying something to me about this evening. "What time are they coming?" He always asks that question when we have someone over for the evening; they are always invited for 8:30. "Eight-thirty," I tell him. My husband is an intelligent man and his intelligence is kindly, gentle; over the years he has perfected small attentions while his imagination drifts from me.

What can I say to him?

Around the table everyone is chattering, jiggling, reaching out, eating noisily. The boys bump elbows accidentally on purpose. Susan says, "Oh you're a little pig!" Jamie says, "Mind your own business!" Susan says, "Shut up!" Jamie says, "You shut up!" Susan says, "*You* shut up!" Around the table everyone is eating . . they are jockeying for position, anxious to finish dinner and get away. Susan will finish first. She has left all the peas on her plate, carefully picked out. Is this to anger me, or do the peas really sicken her?

After they are finished I gather up the plates, the forks, the spoons, the knives, the smudged glasses . . . the cream sauce is

hardening, I hate to get it on my fingers, its coldness appalls me
. . . the table is wet, someone has spilled sauce on it, but no
matter; we have a table nothing can hurt. Nothing can hurt it.
I gather everything up, taking away that night's pattern on the
table, and put it on the kitchen counter, a mess, setting it down
and feeling suddenly very strange. . . .

Friends
          come in, smile at us, take off their coats. Norm makes
drinks. Scotch and water. We sit. Arnold and Brenda look a little
tired? No, Brenda looks good. She is wearing those new stockings
that have a wet look to them, and her shoes look new too. People
sometimes mistake Brenda for me, and me for Brenda, though
my hair is lighter than hers and I am taller than she is. I don't
mind being mistaken for someone else. We are both faculty
wives. Our husbands talk together, we talk together. I look over
at Norman to see if he is still so distracted, but I can't tell. He
avoids people's eyes, an old habit of his. Around eleven I go out
into the kitchen and Brenda comes with me, carrying her drink. I
take slices of cheese and meat out of the refrigerator, which I
have prepared earlier and wrapped in cellophane. I put some
bread in a little wicker basket with a cloth napkin in it. I set out
some pickles and olives. Brenda leans her stomach against the
counter, looking into her drink. "I'm sorry Arnold is acting so
funny tonight," she says. She has creases in her neck that show
when she looks down, her chin creasing into her throat. "He
started drinking when he got home from school. He thinks
they're easing him out. . . ."
          We talk about Brenda's exercise sessions at the YWCA, the
hour of routines she and ten other housewives go through. They
wear leotards. They meet every Wednesday morning. We talk
about the wife of another professor, an older woman who never
goes out any longer, is never seen at school or in town. She had
had an operation this summer. "You'd think it would be enough
to get it removed successfully and to survive," Brenda says. He

face is screwed up into a look of sympathy and bewilderment. "I mean, a woman can wear all kinds of things now, nobody could tell. . . . How could anybody tell?"

Nobody could tell.

Norm and I sleep heavily at night, in the two halves of our bed. Vividly I can remember the past years, those months when I was pregnant. But I can't remember how it came to be that I was pregnant. I can remember being in my earlier twenties, a new wife, sitting in an erotic daze somewhere . . . on a train? . . . my loins dazzled with the memory of our love, the unbearable dazzling of what my young husband had done to me, again and again, but the girl on the train seems to be in a movie, on film, being taken away from me and not me at all . . . she stares dreamily out the window, in a trance, enchanted. I am not that girl.

I could never remember why I was pregnant, precisely. It had seemed important, it had seemed sacred, that I remember the precise day, the precise night . . . but I never could. I didn't have time. Everything fell away. I had a small baby, I was going to have another; I had two babies and I was going to have another; we had to pack, I was pregnant and afraid of a miscarriage, we couldn't afford to pay movers, we spent all day packing dishes and books . . . we drove across the country to a school where Norm taught for one year, then we drove back across the country to another school where he taught for five years, thinking he had found his place, then he decided that that school wasn't good enough for him and so we came to this school, nine years ago, or perhaps ten years ago, a school that seems to me precisely like the other two we were at.

"We heard on the radio coming over that part of a woman's torso was found on the shore, down river," Brenda says, making a face. "Some kids found it. Wouldn't that be awful to have one of our own kids find something like that? They were playing down by the river. . . ."

So she is dead.

Saturday

I take Betty to the doctor. Asian flu. That means they will all get it, all the children. Susan goes for her piano lessons. The car heater is broken, I must tell Norman, I am afraid to tell Norman . . . we can't afford to pay for it. I have started to buy Christmas presents. My head is dazzled suddenly with the thought of presents, Christmas presents, it makes me a little dizzy to think of them . . . I am dazzled as if by a sudden streaming of light, lovely light! Days of buying presents stretch out before me. And then Christmas week. Some presents I will mail all the way back to Indiana; it is important to keep up these traditions. Even my old uncles, they appreciate being remembered. Every one appreciates being remembered. It is terrible not to be remembered.

. . . A roast, roast beef. Wild rice. Gravy. Rolls from the bakery, hard rolls and soft rolls . . . salad . . . carrots? Not carrots. Cauliflower with cheddar-cheese sauce. Spiced apples. Tonight I will put spiced apples out in a white dish, on a white platter, spiced apples looking like lovely dark red wheels. . . .

The supermarket is crowded. Everyone is in a hurry, but it is a pleasant hurry. Music from somewhere. The floor seems to be rocking beneath me with this music, like the floor of a boat, but it is a pleasant sensation. I float along the aisles. The cans on the shelves stretch up over my head, so many different sizes and colors—I put cans in the cart, I put in boxes, packages, bottles, put in heads of lettuce—the lettuce isn't very good today and costs 39¢—and then on to the dairy counter—four cartons of milk—I check the bottoms of the cartons to see if they are leaking—bottles of orange juice with a special groove for a human hand to fit into! On another counter are bathroom things. Pills, shampoo, soap, deodorants . . . the pills remind me of an advertisement on television for cold tablets. The capsules detonate gradually over a period of twelve hours, I think. They release themselves in tiny fragments into the bloodstream. I think of the cells of my body with the seeds of my future inside them, unreadable. They have the seeds of cancer inside them, death itself, the particular way in which I will wear out and die, everything contained secretly in them and ready to go off at a certain time. But that time is a secret.

At the drugstore there is a pile of newspapers and one of the headlines is GIRL'S BODY FOUND IN RIVER. The picture of that girl appears again, a beautiful girl, staring out at the camera with her perky upper lip, lipsticked and pretty, very sure of herself. Parts of a body were found along the river and in the river, a woman's torso, a head. The face mutilated. And so her face is no longer that face, the one in the paper? . . . I stare down at her and I feel panic inside me, in the back of my head, behind my knees. What is this threat to me? Am I going to break down? Am I going to scream? A yellowish cell threatens to burst inside me; like sperm, it is yellow and living.

A man

in the corner of a woman's eye paralyzes the entire eye. A woman wants to rake her body with her nails, streaming blood, she wants to gash her face so that no man need look at it, she wants to be finished and safe. But why does my heart pound so? We are not at war. Yes, we are at war somewhere, soldiers somewhere "at war," but we ourselves are not at war and should therefore be at peace. Why am I not at peace, being forty years old?

This man has a weak face, he looks very young. The photograph is blurred. Why, he is only a boy, his eyes are a boy's eyes . . . but there is no youth in him, only finality. He has come to the end of something. Identified by a motel proprietor, last seen with Linda Slater on Saturday evening; the two of them came to a certain motel out on the highway and there, in a room, they argued, and then they left. . . . What did they argue about? Why will it never be known precisely what they argued about on that night?

Imagine the strength behind a knife that could sever a head

from a body, so beautiful a head! Imagine the torrents of blood
that would gush from the throat! There must have been confusion at the end, madness, not love or hate. Things are speeded up
as they approach the end of something. The boy must have been
hurried, making mistakes, whimpering to himself, everything
speeded up and dazzling and crazy beyond his imagination. . . .
At one o'clock neither of them, the girl or the boy, knew what
would happen at two o'clock. Perhaps they knew that something
would happen, some strange thing, but perhaps they had sensed
such events earlier in their lives, falsely, when nothing did happen. This time it happened.

My husband

lets the newspaper fall from him. A stunned, vacuous sorrow shows in his face; I watch him from the darkened dining
room. From another room the television noise continues, someone is laughing, a great crowd of people laughing over a machine
I don't have time for my husband's sorrow. I see the dreaminess
in him, the stunned clarity of some final perception—I would
like to shout in his face, "Why are you surprised? She had to die
like everyone else!" But I say nothing. He came home late from
school today, looking a little sick. If he gets the flu along with
Betty I will have to take care of him as if he were a child, worse
than a child, and a stab of pleasure comes to me . . . but no, no
it's more trouble than anything else, he has been sick many times
like a child, worse than a child; I can't feel pleasure. I am in a
hurry, I can't feel anything. Time is snatched from me in handfuls. The people who laugh over the television set, in the other
room, are laughing in a terrible unison, like tiny people with tiny
lungs, laughing at me. I stand here watching a man I have been
married to for many years and I can never possess him, my husband. I have lived with him for twenty years but I can never
possess him. I can never be that girl's age. My head and torso are
connected. He will never look at me as he has looked at her, at
her photograph.

I have to run out to the store before six. The metallic Christmas tree looks the same, the angel looks the same, I don't bother with a cart but hurry back to the dairy counter. A few housewives are there, in a hurry like me. Three children are fooling around but it is not possible to tell whose they are. I pick up a carton of eggs, Grade A eggs I forgot to buy earlier, and a few other things; I hurry back to the check-out counter.

The parking lot is nearly empty at this time of day. Rough ice on the pavement, a white and blue container marked "Salvation Army Pick-Up," a kid's jalopy idling noisily at the curb with some high-school kids in it, frozen weeds and trash between the parking lot and the sidewalk. . . . I hurry to my car.

I am not followed.

Stray Children

On his way to meet some friends for lunch, Charles Benedic[t] noticed someone keeping pace with him, across the street. Th[e] sidewalks were crowded with shoppers at this time of day, bu[t] the street was narrow, so that he had no trouble seeing this figure this person, darting in and out of clots of pedestrians, glancin[g] across at Charles as if to make sure he hadn't gotten away.

A boy, dressed strangely in off-white trousers, an off-whit[e] cowboy hat. He was rather short, almost dwarfish. He had t[o] walk fast to keep up with Charles, who was a tall, energetic ma[n] always in a hurry.

At a light Charles crossed the street quickly. The boy had n[o] chance to turn aside. As he approached the curb Charles saw tha[t] the person was not a boy but a girl—a girl dressed like a boy, [i] soiled clothing, with an ungainly, wide silver buckle on her belt. Her trousers were baggy. They were boy's trousers. Her shirt was pale blue, washed-out. She stared at Charles from beneath the rim of the felt hat while around her women shoppers dressed for downtown passed in their women's shoes, their heels making smart rapping sounds on the sidewalk.

Charles and the girl stared at each other.

He was challenged and irritated but he did not show it; his face relaxed into the look he used in public when he was conscious of being watched. He was a semipublic figure, a city planner in a city newly conscious of itself, always organizing itself into committees to plan the future, assess the future, control the future—a large, desperate city that probably had no future; but Charles believed in planning for all the decades that the calendar scheduled, whether they appeared or not. He hesitated now, ready to smile at the girl. Was she someone he should know? The runaway daughter of one of his friends? Two women, dressed in suits, glanced curiously at the girl and at Charles.

"Mr. Benedict?" the girl said.

"Yes?"

As soon as she spoke he realized she was no one he could know. Her voice was stale and flat. Her accent suggested the country, distant farmland, distance. Her face was small and plain, but rather fierce with concentration. An insane girl, Charles thought. A sick girl. Though she was a stranger to him there was something ominously familiar about her. She had pale, red-blond eyebrows, arched slightly, and her eyes were large and protruding. She might have been eighteen years old. She was too tall to be thought of as a woman, and yet her body was not a child's body.

"You are a very tall man . . . I didn't think you'd be this tall," she said slowly. Her words were unprepared, vague. Charles wondered if she were taking drugs.

"Yes? What did you? . . ."

"I read about you. You're planning houses and things for poor people, and parks. . . ." She toed the sidewalk with one foot, her ankle bare, showing up very white. Charles watched the ankle bone move inside her skin. The bone was clumsily, nervously large. There was a small scab on her skin that moved back and forth over this bone as she poked at the sidewalk with her foot. Her nervousness seemed to make her bolder, as if urging her forward. "I need money myself, I'm poor, I'm not from this city but I'm poor. . . . I need money right now. Today."

"I'm sorry. . . ."

He drew himself up. He was a pleasant, predictable, intelligent man, he had put many years into making himself what he was, and he never spoke too quickly. Even with his children—he had four boys—he never spoke without testing the words to himself, assessing their value. Once said, certain words could never be unsaid.

"Why are you sorry?" said the girl. "Because you don't recognize me?"

It was time to get away. He turned aside.

"Don't you recognize me?" the girl cried.

She followed alongside him, she stepped in front of him. Pain rose in his chest, suddenly—what if the girl were crazy or doped up? He saw how the nostrils of her small childish nose were ridged with white, the white of anger. Her teeth were uneven. When she bared them she had a furtive, rodentlike look, but without any grace or cunning. She stood in front of him, blocking his way, not like a child, but heavily, like a dwarf, ungainly even for her height of about five feet.

"I'm afraid I don't know you," Charles said gently.

He was accustomed to being addressed on the street and in lower corridors of the City-County Building. His name was often called out by strangers who might turn out to be polite, respectable women from his own neighborhood, or fumbling, angry men, mysterious old men of the type who spent their days sitting on downtown park benches, staring vacantly at shoppers. Rarely was he stopped by men like himself, unless they were acquaintances of his. But by young people—never. By someone like this girl—never.

"We have something in common," she said.

Her plain little face was about to screw itself up into a wink, but it remained empty, expressionless, as if its muscles had failed. Only her teeth seemed to move, baring themselves in a grin. Her eyes were rimmed with pale red lashes. Charles felt sorry for her, a girl so plain, with so thin and unattractive a body. Why was she smiling like that? Why was her face so empty?

"You think I'm crazy, eh? Just looking for a handout?"

He waved her aside, still smiling. Better to retreat smiling. And yet he did not exactly turn his back on her, fearing that small, fierce, empty face. He took a few steps, still facing her, then turned slightly aside and hurried into a crowd of pedestrians. He walked fast, with his large, anxious strides, wondering who that girl was. She was no one. She was not even a girl, a woman.

He spent two hours at lunch. His friends were pleasant, like himself, eager to agree with one another. They were all very intelligent but, like Charles, they knew enough to understate their intelligence; they were all successful men in their forties. As Charles had advanced in his profession he had moved from an office in one part of the city to one in another part, and then he had moved again, and again, ending up now at the very tip of downtown, in the City-County Building, and along the way he had met new people continually, men like himself becoming successful and semipublic and public, relinquishing his old friends and taking on the challenge of new friends, though none of these people were really "friends." They were important acquaintances.

He had no close friends. Men of his age and of his position did not have close friends; that belonged to simpler lives.

When he returned to his office his receptionist said, "There was a young woman to see you. She said you were going to put her on your staff."

He tried not to show his surprise. "What's her name?"

The receptionist gave him a slip of paper. *Elizabeth June Smith*.

"She was dressed strangely, in slacks . . . I think she had a cowboy hat on. . . ."

"I don't know her, I'm afraid," Charles said.

He went into his office and forgot about the girl. On the wall in front of him was a greatly magnified photograph of the city. He sat staring at it, dreaming of a beautiful city imposed upon this one, a magical city. Completed. Perfect. Out the window he could see part of this city, but it was hazy with smog and uninteresting.

A dull rising of disgust in him, in his body.

He came home late, after 7:30. His wife said apologetically, "The boys were hungry and ate earlier. I'm sorry."

"That's all right. Of course," Charles said.

The youngest boy, Terry, showed Charles a drawing. He chattered in his high, surprised, tireless voice—a boy of four, very blond, very vulnerable. Charles loved his sons very much and he could not quite believe in them; he could not believe they were his sons, that he had given them their lives.

Frances made him a drink and he went into his study with it. He was always pleased at this room—it was always the same, untouched. At the window he looked out into the back yard where two of his boys were playing with another boy. The grass was very green. The marks of the power mower showed in it, unnatural and sharp. It pleased him that the lawn-maintenance men had been there that day and that everything was ordinary, normal.

He had made his own life and he had made the lives of his sons; that seemed to him extraordinary.

Frances served him dinner and talked to him about what she had done that day. He was careful to listen to her, always. She was light and quick and blond, his wife, though their life together had become a little out of focus, not exactly in control. He had married her sixteen years ago, a girl his own age. Both their families had been poor, though hers were city people and his lived on what remained of a farm, outside a small town in the western part of the state. When they had met, their lives were similar; Frances even resembled him physically, a tall, big-boned girl with a liking for athletics. They had made a startling, attractive couple, very blond and open, a healthy, ordinary couple. . . . Then Charles had discovered, around his thirty-fifth year, that he was not an ordinary man after all.

Now his life was one of movement. Frances remained at home, a fixed point, still blond and loving and generous, a good woman, but now a little out of focus to him, like an older sister.

He loved her very much, as he loved his sons, knowing he must protect them.

After dinner he worked at his desk. He made telephone calls. Yet something kept distracting him from his work, a sense of disorder, of vague alarm. He was trying to remember something but he could not. His oldest son, Bruce, came to the doorway of his study, and Charles sensed at once that he wanted something; he was accustomed to people wanting something from him, he understood their mannerisms and clear, sincere smiles. Bruce was fourteen and was never home, but tonight he was home, chattering toward his father's mild, smiling face: "There's this kid who bugs me at school, and wouldn't you know it he's black. . . . I try to be real nice to him. . . . Today in history some kid didn't know what Hiroshima was, and we all knew that. . . ." This boy was Charles's favorite son, but in the last several years he had become mysterious to Charles, distant and edgy, as if fighting to be free of him. Yet now he was trading upon his instinct that he was his father's favorite; he had a joking, conspiratorial air about him, hiding behind that air.

"Did you want to talk to me about something?" Charles said.
Bruce lowered his eyes.

"Something weird . . . I didn't want to tell Mother. . . ."

"What is it?" Charles asked quickly.

"A person came to see me at school today, last period. Almost
time for baseball practice." Bruce made a face as if to reassure his
father: this wasn't bad news, this was nothing to worry about. "It
was a girl. . . ."

"A girl? Your age?"

"No, not my age. Older. She was twenty, maybe."

Charles stared at him, surprised. He had not thought the girl
that old.

"I couldn't figure out if she wanted a job with you, or what
. . . she was from Medina, she said it was your hometown
. . . how would she know that? I couldn't figure out what she
wanted. . . . She kept looking at me. She was very strange. She
said she was hungry. The principal was in the other room sort of
listening and he told her to leave. . . ."

"But what did she want?"

Bruce passed his hand over his eyes, a gesture he must have
learned from Charles. It was a melancholy, adult gesture.

"She was out at the house here, I guess. Anyway, she said so
She knew what things were like here, she must have been look
ing in the window. . . ."

"What?"

"She was very nervous and sort of grinning at me. That's when
Mr. Bedford came in. She was talking fast, she didn't make
sense . . . she said she had a right to live here, just like me, that
we would have to let her live with us . . . that you had a lot of
money and wanted to give it to poor people, but she was poor and
you owed it to her. . . ."

"I owed it to her?"

"Something like that. Oh, she was crazy . . . she kept grin
ning at me and moving her chair toward me. . . . She was
dressed like a real nut. . . ."

Charles felt his heart begin to pound. He stared at his son and wondered what his son's silence meant. . . . Bruce had stopped speaking, his words had faded and he was left standing there, awkwardly, staring directly at his father.

"What else? What else did she say?"

"That's all," Bruce said.

His face was mysterious to Charles—an intelligent, tanned, healthy face, the face of his oldest son. Yet Charles could not quite believe in it.

"She didn't say anything else?"

"No."

He did not believe this either.

She was waiting for him the next morning, sitting in the corridor outside his office. She was sitting on the floor with her knees drawn up to her chest.

Dressed in the same soiled white slacks, with her hat set upon her knees, she had the look of having waited for hours. Without her hat she looked even younger. Her hair was a dark, heavy red, cut very short about her face; the color of her hair was suddenly very familiar to Charles.

He brought her into his office and closed the door, trembling.

"Do you know who I am now?" she said. "Look at me!"

She walked pertly about the big office, assured of his attention. There was a coiled, childish, unhealthy energy in her. At the narrow window, which ran from the floor to the ceiling, she stood with her hands on her hips, critically, contemplating the city.

"I know all about you," she said, looking over her shoulder at him, speaking softly. "Ma kept stories about you. She got the paper of this city on purpose and all those years I never knew why. . . . The reason I know the truth now is that she died. A friend of hers told me, she told me everything. I know everything. Ma died a few weeks ago." Her plain face was illuminated with excitement and now she was almost pretty, looking over her shoulder at Charles. "Aren't you going to ask me how she died? Huh?"

Charles tried not to look away. "How did she die?"

"Accident. Car. She was drunk."

She swiveled away from the window, suddenly brisk and robust. She rubbed her hands together. "Well, Mr. Benedict, I got all the things with me, in a locker in the bus station, locked up safe. It's proof enough." Her voice was nasal and twangy, the accent of Charles's hometown. She kept smiling jerkily, showing her teeth. "I got the birth certificate. I got some pictures, real old ones. I got a bunch of letters and stuff, and some cutouts from the newspaper . . . they ain't proof exactly but they're good enough for you and me and anybody else that was interested. . . ."

"How old are you?" Charles said suddenly.

"Twenty-six."

"Ah!"

His hands dropped at his sides. *Twenty-six.*

"The name on the birth certificate is Elizabeth June Smith, but my friends call me Smith. Smith," she said brightly, coming right up to Charles. "Well, are you sorry she's dead? Why don't you say something?"

Charles felt panic spreading in him.

"Lori Hebb?" he said.

"Sure Lori Hebb! You should know her name!"

The girl patted his arm familiarly, laughing.

"I haven't seen her for a long time . . ." Charles said.

"Oh, sure, twenty-six years . . . sure . . . but anyway you know her, you know me. How do you like it, meeting your daughter like this? . . ." And she lifted her small face to him suddenly gentle. Her voice had become gentle.

"I didn't know about this," Charles said slowly. "Any of this. . . ."

"Well, now you know."

He put his hands to his face, feeling sick. She stood close in from

of him. He was afraid of fainting, of being sick to his stomach
. . . the girl chattered about a Greyhound bus, something about
"making contact," about buying some doughnuts. . . . Her chattering had a drunken gaiety about it. "I was out at your house
yesterday! Jesus, you must have money! What is your wife like,
huh? Some lady from around here?"

"I . . . I don't know what to. . . ."

"Did you ever tell her about me?"

"I didn't know about you. I still don't . . . I'm still
not. . . ."

"My name is Elizabeth June Smith," the girl said angrily, "and
you better not forget it! And you better not hand me any crap!
Don't look at me like that, I can talk as loud as I want to! This
goddamn fancy office doesn't cut any ice with *me*. All my life I
been pushed around by people, told to shut up. *She* used to leave
me off with Grandma, *she* ran around all the time—thought she
was something hot, not like me, she always said I was ugly and
she was ashamed—Now she's dead. Now I'm here. I only got a
few dollars left, I didn't eat anything but doughnuts for a long
time. . . ."

Charles stared at her, alarmed. He thought suddenly *She is not
even female, my daughter*. . . .

"Say that you love me. You love me," she said.

He could not speak. Her face was pale with anger. Many years
ago, when he was sixteen, he had gone out with a girl named
Lori Hebb. Now Lori's bright amused look shone out at him, from
his stranger's face.

"I . . . I don't know what. . . ."

"You don't want a daughter, maybe?" She grinned. "I talked to
your boy and *he's* your favorite, I bet. But you got a daughter
now. Here I am. This friend of Ma's told me everything. I know
everything. Ma found out she was pregnant and ditched you, and
got hold of this other guy she was going out with that she liked
better than you. So he married her. The dope. She thought she
was hot stuff and went after him and he married her! She

thought she was real pretty. I wouldn't want to look like her. I
want to look exactly, absolutely, the way I do. I don't want to look
like anybody else, her or *you*."

Charles seized at a fact: this girl was his daughter. Yes. She
was his daughter.

"She was always running around," the girl said angrily. "A lo
of good her face did her! That guy, Howie Bart, he was suppose
to be my father and he thought he was, he went in the Army an
when he got out he left her—I don't know why—then she wen
to work—I was just a little kid. She got a divorce and marrie
another guy, his name was Ernest Haas—you know him?"

"No. No, I don't know him. I didn't know him," Charle
stammered. "Did he—did all this happen back home? Medina?

"Right you are, Medina. Don't you ever go back?"

"My family is all dead."

"Hell, everybody is dead," the girl said cheerfully. "It gives u
more elbow room, don't it?"

"And your mother is dead? In an automobile accident?"

"She plowed into a tree. Like to knocked her goddamn head of
She was so stupid, mister, I mean so very stupid . . . not lik
us. . . ." She peered up into Charles's face with a flirtatiou
smile. "She got stuck in that dump of a town all her life, not lil
us. We got out. You and me are smart. . . ."

Charles stared at her. He thought of Lori Hebb, that girl, th
one he had been crazy about and who had cut him off, droppe
him in two weeks. At that time he hadn't been the Charles Ben
dict he was now, and he hadn't even been a boy liable to gro
into this Charles Benedict. He had been too tall, too thin, sh
miserable with loneliness, unable to talk in the jargon of his cla
mates, ignored by them . . . he had tried to imitate what
thought of as their glamour, but he hadn't known how, had
known anything. And Lori had come along to befriend hi
certain of herself and her place in that high-school world, willi
to risk friendship with him. Or perhaps she had done it to ma
him love her, or perhaps she had done it as a joke. She had bee

cheerful, simple girl, very cute. Cuteness. Nail polish, white wool socks, the cracking of gum . . . fragrant gum. . . . He remembered the single time he had made love to her, in a junked car at the edge of her father's orchard. One time. She had drawn him to her, gaily, and she had thrust him away again, just as gaily, indifferently, as if nothing had happened between them. Charles had not understood. He had thought his life must end, he must die. But his life as a sixteen-year-old had continued and he had gone on to graduate from high school and to win a scholarship to the state university, while Lori had dropped out to marry a boy a few years older than herself.

That was all.

These facts returned to him, disgusting him. He could not have said what disgusted him most, the sequence of events in which he had figured as a kind of child-father, the discarded father of a baby, or the culmination of these events, this person who stood eying him in his office in Detroit.

"A smart man like you don't want any trouble. Right?" the girl said.

"I'm perfectly willing to help you . . . to. . . ."

"You better be! I need money right now."

"I'll give you anything you want. . . ."

"I'm hungry. Right now."

He took out his billfold, fumbling, and counted several large bills into her hand. The girl was breathing quickly. She stared at the bills, looking from one to the other. "Well, I thank you. This is kind of you."

"I'll give you a check before you leave. You must . . . you must be very hungry. . . . You haven't eaten for a long time?"

She blushed, as if pleased by his sudden concern. She seemed almost womanly. "I can buy something. No worry."

"You will . . . you will take care of yourself?"

"Oh, sure." She put her hat on her head, suddenly, for a joke. She was now quite embarrassed. Charles could see clearly that she was no child, no young girl—there were lines on her face

and neck, edged faintly with dirt. A filthy child, his daughter.
Aged twenty-six.

"What will you do?" Charles asked. He was suffused by heat
and had an overwhelming urge to sit down, but he remained
standing.

"I will live. My own life."

"Where will you go?"

"Nowhere. This place is fine right here."

He was sweating painfully. "Right here?"

"Sure. This is the big city. It took me all my life to get here."

"You wouldn't rather go somewhere else—to Chicago?"

"No thanks," she said lightly. "I want to be near you, don't I?
Here I just met my father, my real father, and I don't want to lose
him. Could be I'll come out to visit you some Sunday. . . ."

"Don't do that!"

"Why not? Are you ashamed of me?"

"You know better . . . you know. . . . Look, please,"
Charles said, "I don't feel very well . . . this has been a terrible
shock to me. . . ."

"Don't you want a daughter?"

He closed his eyes in pain.

"Don't you want to get to know me? Huh?"

"Of course. . . ."

"You're lying. Like hell!" the girl said gaily.

"I don't mean to insult you. Please believe me," Charles stammered.

She pulled the hat down farther on her head, clownishly. She
turned to leave. "Don't let it throw you. I like to kid. Look. Let's
get this straight. I got my own life to live, actually, and I got plans
of my own. I can make contacts on my own. All I need is a place
to stay, some money. . . . I don't ask for much, not me. No
Smith. So you can relax."

He tried to smile. Her words were so precious to him!

"I want you to call me Smith. That's my name."

"Smith," he said faintly.

"We might even make up a contract between us. Get us a lawyer," she said jauntily, turning to go. "Like you guys here in Detroit, huh?"

For the next few days he kept waiting for her to call. When the telephone rang at home his heart leaped. But nothing happened. The routine of his life continued, his professional busyness, constant motion. The days became a week, two weeks. Men flew in from New York to see him; he himself flew to New York. He flew to Los Angeles for a convention. While he was away he thought constantly of his daughter, and of his wife and sons . . . he thought of his quiet, immaculate study at home and of his office downtown, of the great photographs and maps and sketches he worked with, trying to turn such plans into reality. But everything seemed to him weightless and transparent. He did not own anything, not really. He could not transform anything into anything else.

And he thought of Lori Hebb. Away in another city, having dinner in a dark, expensive restaurant, he nodded intelligently at the remarks of his hosts and thought of Lori Hebb, that lively little girl, hardly five feet tall, with her knowing smirks and her rapid talk, her charming wisecracks—a vulgar little girl, he knew now, but dazzling to him then. The carelessness of her legs, her arms—the constant motion of her jaws, chewing gum, always chewing gum!—the life of her body, so childishly energetic, and of her round, smooth, high-colored face, and of her orange-red hair, worn long and curled up cutely at the ends! She had betrayed him, Lori. Now, twenty-seven years later, he felt almost physical anguish at the thought: she had lied to him, betrayed him. That cheap little girl had betrayed Charles Benedict. She had lived her life without a thought for him, giving birth to his baby, his own baby; she had grown up in that town, grown nearly middle-aged, and evidently she had drunk, and now she was dead.

The mother of his daughter.

No matter where he was, even at the long, bitter, complex

committee meetings with the Mayor and his aides, he experienced convulsive, violent shudders at the thought of her. The
fact of her. Like all facts, like statistics and measurements and
dates, the fact of Lori could not be altered. So long as their
daughter lived, all the events that had brought her into being
would live, coiled secretly inside her as if in her genes. . . .

He kept waiting for her to call. She would need money soon. His
wife talked to him about her day at home, about telephone calls
she had taken for him, about their sons' problems . . . about
their sons' schools, for the public schools in this city were falling
apart . . . or she spoke to him, shyly, of the distance she felt
between them, the loneliness she felt . . . was it her fault?
What should she do?

"There's no distance between us. What do you mean?" he
would say, ashamed.

He embraced his wife often, as if to hide his face from her. He
embraced the smaller boys often, sensing their vulnerability.
When he came home every night he looked anxiously into his
wife's face, dreading a certain look, the look of terrible
news. . . .

The girl called him finally, at his office.

"Big shots like you have lunch all the time. Take me out to
lunch!" she said. She was very cheerful. "This is Smith speaking, your friend Smith, your *you-know-what!* I been eating real
well and having me a good time. This city is great. I made some
friends in the place where I am . . . you want to see where I
live? Come on down!"

Reassured by her merriment, he drove to the address she gave
him. It was in the near east side, in a slummy neighborhood.
This surprised him, since with the money he had given her she
could have lived somewhere else. This neighborhood was bor-
dered on its northern edge by the university, and in it, along with
the very poor, lived young people of a certain type—they looked
very poor themselves, costumed as poor, disheveled and unhealthy. His daughter's building was newly painted, a bright shril

green, and on the front stoop sat five or six young people, dressed badly, with long stringy hair and pale faces, their eyes jumpy and amused in their faces, curious at Charles.

His daughter's apartment was on the second floor. The door was open.

"Come in! Welcome! How do you like all this?" she cried.

He was aware of a confused clutter, the odor of incense or perfume, the girl's gay gesticulating hands. She wore the same outfit, exactly—even the same wide-buckled belt—and he could see that, beneath the faded blue shirt, her bare chest was very thin, very flat. She tried to get him to sit in a chair, fussing over him. She stood before him, chattering, catching the heel of one foot in her hand as if exhibiting herself, tempting him.

"Excuse me, I'm a little high. People are in and out of here, I'm very popular . . . but I don't tell anybody my secret. . . . Jesus, there's a black girl named Jeannie who hangs around here . . . wait'll you see her . . . she's six foot eight, a real big strong gal. . . . Jesus," the girl said, giggling, "she could break a man's back in two any time she wants. She. . . ."

Charles felt repulsed by her. But he remained listening, listening patiently while she chattered. The room was a mess, a clutter of junk—a shade at the window had flown up to the very top and had stuck there.

His daughter preened before him. "I got lots of friends here. We have a ball. People are really nice when you give them a chance, you know? I need a little money. I need a regular bank account. How are your kids—your son? He's cute. This isn't like back home, here I got friends who like me. Can I have a little money, please, and I won't bother you again for a long time?"

He took out his billfold. But the door to the apartment was still open.

"Oh, good! Good! Oh, I need this!" she cried.

He hesitated, then counted out fifteen hundred dollars for her. He had stopped at the bank on his way down and so was prepared for this. But he was not prepared for her drunken, fawning mut-

ter, the way she took the bills from him as if caressing him
through them. "Jesus, sweet Jesus," she murmured, "oh, how I
need this. . . ."

She ran to her bed and tried to stuff the bills inside a pillow.

"Don't do that! Don't leave it here!" Charles said, startled.
"Someone will steal it."

"Not my friends. Not here. This is a different life from yours,
Mr. Benedict," she said, her face glowing.

"You might get killed for that money. . . ."

She laughed and waved him away.

"Let me take it. I'll give it to you later," he said.

"Out for lunch. Let's go to lunch so I can show you off," she
said, as if forgetting the money. "Wait till I find some shoes . . .
oh, the hell with shoes. . . ."

They went out. She hung onto his arm, chattering. Barefoot,
she was even shorter than he remembered. There was an odor of
something sweet and vile about her, and Charles felt a sense of
loathing for her, for her energy, her bright nervous chatter, her
very being. She chattered about people, a string of names . . .
about her landlord . . . about her special friends, who were so
good to her. . . . "Jesus, you should talk with some of these
kids! They know what's going on! They could take over everything right now, any day, except they don't give a damn. It's all
so much shit to them, the city and the country, the whole goddamn United States, and I see their point of view, believe
me. . . ."

They went into a small pizzeria. The girl pushed her bright
hair back from her temples, talking wildly. Charles stared at her.
This was his daughter, speaking to him. His daughter. He could
see Lori's face, her old face, in this girl's face . . . he could imagine something of his own in it, buried.

How were such things possible?

He shook himself awake. He felt as if he were falling into a
dream. The girl ordered a pizza and a Coke. Charles had coffee.
She talked constantly, excited, bobbing up and down to wave out

the front window to someone in the street. Her face was flushed. Charles thought he could see something scurry across her forehead and disappear into her thick, dirty hair. . . .

She pushed the pizza from her. "Jesus. I might puke."

"What's wrong?"

"Hang on. Just hang on."

She closed her eyes and comically scratched at the edge of the table. But beads of sweat had formed on her face. In the restaurant a few other customers sat, glancing toward Charles and the girl. A fan turned noisily.

"Are you all right?" Charles asked.

"Oh. Jesus." She pressed her forehead against the edge of the table. He looked down at the thick mat of red hair, helpless. Was she crazy? Was she sick? She kept talking, muttering. "You're my father. It's a big deal for me, haha. I got plans for the future but I'm sort of shaky, I can't sleep at night without taking some heavy stuff . . . I want to go back home. . . . My mother is dead, I went to the funeral . . . at the funeral I saw her face, her hair . . . her hair is just like mine . . . I loved her, but it was good she smashed up the car . . . the car was broken down and I got the insurance. . . . I want a car of my own now! I want a place to stay all my own!"

Charles took her hand. It was very cold.

"But you do have a place of your own. You do," he said gently. *Better for her if she were dead*, he thought.

"There's noise here at night, sirens and things. . . . I can't sleep here. . . ."

She raised her head with an effort. The cords of her neck stiffened. Charles could see that the pupils of her eyes were queer, distorted.

"Oh Jesus," she said, as if waking painfully, "what time is it? I been sleeping all day . . . I can't wake up. . . . I got to sleep it off." She frowned; her forehead creased. She shook her head with a snap, waking. "Look, you. Relax. Forget it, the crap I been telling you. I talk too much. I'm just a hick."

"Are you all right? Are you well?"

She stood, bumping the table. She brushed her hair back angrily from her face.

"I'm late to meet somebody, a friend. You better give me that money now, I'm late. I forgot." She put out her hand to him, wiggling the fingers. She spoke rather loudly. "I told them all I could pay my own way all the way, and I don't need any screwing around. I'm not like that bitch back home. I'm my own person and nobody else. You better give me that money!"

He got to his feet, stunned.

"But—"

"I need it. Now. Don't you hand me any crap," she said.

He tried to walk her out of the restaurant so he could give it to her outside, but she wouldn't move. She stood with her hand outstretched. And so he gave it to her finally, fifteen bills counted out one by one, and she wadded them together and stuck them in her pants pocket.

She left.

When he got outside she had disappeared. She had merged with the slow, languid crowds of the neighborhood, whites and blacks, people with nowhere to go and unhurried, drifting. He stood on the sidewalk looking from side to side. His daughter? . . . This neighborhood reminded him suddenly of the Depression. It was as if time had hurtled itself backward, back into the thirties, into the ugly, empty years of that part of his life and of the life of the nation, when homeless, drifting people like his daughter had gravitated together, filthy, hopeful and yet without futures, looking for jobs. One city after another: looking for jobs. And on to the next city, looking for jobs. . . . Except these people, these young people, were not looking for jobs. They were not looking for anything.

He walked through them, past them. He was slow, dazed. Stunned by the look of this world, the smell of it. All around him were human shapes that were not quite human. A human avalanche that had begun to flow, slowly at first, gathering up momentum, building up pressure. . . . Perhaps there were thousands of them, like his daughter? Like the shabby, long-haired boys he passed? Perhaps there were millions of them, in a human avalanche, about to flow over him and destroy him? . . . A boy of about twenty appeared before Charles, carrying a knapsack. His back was oddly bent. He put out his hand to Charles, begging, but Charles turned aside. The boy said, "Shit on you," but he spoke without malice; he spoke lightly.

In the distance, the near distance, were the million-dollar buildings of downtown Detroit. Some of them were masterpieces of contemporary architecture.

Charles wondered if he were losing his mind.

He did not hear from his daughter for some time. Yet he thought of her constantly, remarking upon the brilliance of her hair, her energy. He imagined conversations with her. He would say, *You have changed my life, my future . . . I think I love you . . . I know you are my daughter. . . .*

Late one Saturday night, when they returned from a dinner party, Frances said suddenly to him: "Was it someone there tonight? At the party?"

He stared at her, unable to make sense of her words.

"Was it someone tonight, the woman you're in love with? Tell me. Please. I want to know everything."

She began to cry helplessly.

"What? . . . There is no woman, what are you saying? What woman? What do you mean?" Charles cried.

But Frances continued, she kept after him, she paced around their bedroom—she spoke in a raspy, frightened whisper, not wanting to wake the boys. He could feel the hysteria in her, hating it, her tears and her voice, her anguished face. She was so old! She had aged so quickly, so much faster than he! "If you want a divorce, tell me. Tell me. I want to know the truth—I want to know where that money is going, what you want from me, what

your life is—your secrets—who is she, what does she want? Is
she married too? Do you laugh at me with her? What do you
want? What is going to happen?"

He clutched at his head, feeling that he would go insane. A
woman hysterical, crying into his face. Whispering at him!
Words of terror, convulsive movements of her arms, the flabbiness
of her white upper arms as if tempting him to violence. . . .
Someone must die, someone must be lost! She cried out softly,
as if goading him, "What do you want? What do you want?"

He began to talk. After an hour he had convinced her, perhaps.
She fell asleep, worn out from crying, a little drunk, and he lay
awake thinking freely of his daughter.

In the morning he said to Frances, calmly, "You must never
talk to me like that again. Never."

She nodded, frightened.

He began to go for walks in his daughter's neighborhood, driving up during his lunchtime. He began to be familiar with the
broken-down stores, the alleys, the front steps where black children sat sunning themselves. He walked up to the university and
across its modern, vulgar, gleaming concrete campus, where young
people in rags dawdled and other young people, dressed normally, hurried with books into the glare of sunshine and concrete. Too much glass here, blank walls, scrubby lawns. He kept
shading his eyes from the glare, waiting for her, watching.

He watched for a girl with red hair. A girl not quite a girl.

Several times he went to her apartment and knocked on the
door. No answer. Once a radio was blaring inside, but still no
answer, nothing.

He dreamed of his daughter: a girl with orange-red hair.

At last she telephoned him. Her voice sounded faint. "I need
you. I'm in trouble," she said.

When he got there she was in bed. It was late one afternoon in
August, after five o'clock, hot and muggy and yet she lay in bed,
under some covers. She was shivering. She said to him, "Why
did you take so long? Did you call the police? I keep hearing

sirens. I won't get in any ambulance, I'll put my feet on the door here, on both sides of it, I won't let them take me out . . . they can split me in two, end to end, but they won't get me through that goddamn door. . . ."

"I didn't call anyone. You'll be all right," Charles said.

Her face was drawn and ugly. The room stank. She lay flat on her mattress, without a pillow, on a rumpled sheet that was twisted under her.

"What's wrong?" Charles said.

"Nothing. I need some money, that's all. I need it fast."

"But shouldn't I call a doctor?"

"No. No doctor."

"But you're . . . you're not well. . . ."

She said loudly, rising up on one elbow, "You stick your nose in my business and you'll be sorry! Okay, sure, you're my father and it's a big deal, but it ain't going any farther than that . . . I have my own plans . . . I am going to see the west coast of this country . . . I am clearing out of this puking city . . . I need some money. I lost the rent money. I had to give Jeannie a hundred dollars. I lost your telephone number and couldn't find a telephone book. . . ." She began to weep angrily. She pounded the covers with her small, bony fists. "You, I don't need you! I don't love you! You never call me by my name, you never call me anything! Never kiss me! I don't love you! I'm clearing out and I want some money and you better give it to me unless you want trouble. . . . I'm going to California and if I ever come back to this dump it will be so they can kiss my ass around here, the bastards here, there are some . . . some bastards here . . . they are asking to be turned in, they are begging for it, believe me," she said, her voice rising to a scream, "if they think they can cheat me! Me! Push me around! They ain't going to push me around! I told them I could turn them in in a minute, I got a father that is like this—" she raised two fingers, pressed together "—like this with the Mayor himself and the Police Commissioner and I can turn them all in, those freaky sons of bitches!"

"Who did you say those things to? Who are these people?"

"Give me that money and get out of here!" she cried.

"But—"

"I said give it to me! I'm dying! I can't take it like this! You want me to die, you dirty son of a bitch, you want me to pass out—I can tell—I can see it in your evil, evil eyes—If I pass out you'll stuff all these covers in my mouth and suffocate me; oh, don't lie, I know you, you'll climb on top of me and stuff everything in my mouth and suffocate me and set the place on fire—I know you—I saw your picture in the paper—"

She was sitting up, thrashing her arms around. Her small lifeless breasts swung angrily.

"Give me the money! Give me the money!"

His heart pounded violently. She was not a girl, not female. She was a living presence but nothing more, nothing more than angry, writhing flesh, somehow sired by him. His daughter. Could he really suffocate her? . . . Could he climb on top of that angry little body, holding her tight with his knees, and stuff that filthy blanket down her mouth? . . . her angry hole of a mouth?

He put his hand to his chest. He could feel his heart thumping wildly.

He took out his wallet. "Here, your allowance!" he whispered. "For you! Buy yourself anything! Live your life and do what you want. See California. See everything," he said, whispering quickly, as if fearful someone might overhear. "Everything is in front of you . . . you're very young . . . everything is waiting for you, promised to you . . . don't be afraid. . . ."

Seeing the money, she seemed to wake, snapping her head back and then forward. She leaned forward to snatch up the bills. "Oh, Jesus, you saved my life . . . you saved my life . . ." she said.

He watched her snatching up the money, bill by bill. Her breasts swung forward without life, very flat, white. Her breastbone was prominent.

"You saved my life. . . ." She wiped at her face, at her nose.

"Jesus Christ but this is good, this is just in time. . . . Now you can leave."

But he was afraid to leave. Wasn't there something more to say? He must explain something to her: *You have changed my life . . . I love you. . . .*

"Now you can leave," she said sharply.

"Don't . . . don't be afraid . . ." Charles said

She squinted at him. "Why the hell should I be afraid?" she said.

He stumbled outside.

Out in the street a patrol car was passing slowly. The air vibrated with heat. He walked toward his car and saw three young people—boys or girls, he couldn't tell—leaning against a building, staring peacefully, sleepily across the street. He followed their gaze but saw nothing—an abandoned grocery store. The young people were elderly in their passivity, their faces hollow, hungry, wise, the faces of cunning animals, but without strength. He felt a rush of pity for them and for his daughter, these young people who were already old, who were dying and must die, because the city had no place for them. Its future must obliterate theirs.

"Some change, mister?" the boy said.

He thrust his hand out at Charles. Charles emptied his pockets at once—a quarter, two quarters, a half dollar, some dimes. He placed the coins one by one in the boy's grimy, trembling, unsurprised hand, until he had nothing left to give.

Wednesday's Child

Around the high handsome roof of the house birds flew in the first hours of daylight, calling out, so that their small shadows fell against the bedroom curtains harmless as flowers thrown by anonymous admirers. Squirrels ran along the gutters. At some distance the horns of river freighters sounded, melancholy and exciting. Today he was not going to work; today he woke slowly, with a sense of luxury, aware of these sounds and their lovely softness, thinking that sound itself seemed a kind of touch.

His wife lay sleeping beside him. She was a dark-haired woman of thirty-five, attractive, exhausted even in sleep, wounded by small impatient lines in her forehead; he did not quite believe in those lines. He always expected them to be gone. Even in sleep his wife seemed to him thoughtful, thinking, sensitive to his feeling of luxury—so she lay perfectly still, not waking. She would not join him in it.

Several shadows fell against the curtains—the weightless shadows of birds. He watched. Everything was still. This house, thirty years old, had stood firm and wonderfully solid among its more contemporary neighbors, a high brick colonial home with white shutters, quite perfect. It was not his idea of a final home. It was his idea of a home for himself and his wife and daughter in this decade, just as this famous suburb was his idea of a way of preparing for a distant, delightful, aristocratic life in another part of the country. He was an architect and worked for an excellent firm. Only thirty-seven, he was successful in the eyes of his parents and even in the eyes of his friends, who were themselves scampering like squirrels with their tiny shrewd toenails pulling them, pulling them up, always up, their cheeks rosy with the exhilaration of success. He was one of them. He was not his parents' son any longer; his father had been a high-school teacher, a good, deferential, exploited man.

So he woke on Wednesday morning, very early. The day would be a long one. His wife was evidently not going to wake, but lay frowning and severe in sleep, as if giving up to him the burden of this day. Already he could hear his daughter. Coming out of her room . . . in the hall . . . now on her way downstairs. He listened closely. He could hear, or could imagine, her pulling the piano bench away from the piano, down in the living room. Yes, she must be there. The bench was white—a white grand piano, very beautiful—and she sat at it, seriously, frowning like her mother, staring down at the keys. White and black keys. Even the cracks arrested her attention. He lay in bed on the second floor of his house, imagining his daughter almost directly below him, sitting at the piano. He heard the first note. His face went rigid.

He got dressed quickly. He put on a tie his mother had given him, a very conservative tie, dark green. His secret was a dark, serious, grimly green soul—he liked to hide it behind smiles, en-

thusiasm for football, hearty compliments to his wife. . . . She
had turned over in bed, she was still asleep or pretending to sleep.
The other day she had told him she would not remain herself
much longer. "I can't live like this much longer," she had said. It
was not a threat or a warning, only a curious, exploratory remark.
They had come in late from a dinner party, from a marvelous
evening, and she had told him suddenly that she was failing, giving up, being conquered, defeated . . . all she had accomplished as a mother was failure. Failure.

Why should she wake up to see him off?

Downstairs he saw with a slight shock Brenda at the piano,
seated just as he had imagined her. She was running her fingers
gently over the keyboard. The sound was gentle, soft. It would
not shatter any crystal; there was no power behind it. Down at
the far end of the living room the wide French windows were
seared with light, the filmy curtains glowing. He appreciated
that; he appreciated beauty. The living room had been decorated
in white and gold. His daughter's face was pale, not quite white,
and her legs pale, limp, motionless. She had put her little white
socks on perfectly. She wore a yellow dress, perfectly ironed by
the laundry that did her father's shirts so meticulously, and her
hair was a fine, dull gold, very neat. Everything matched. He
appreciated that.

She was playing the "Moonlight Sonata" with a numb, feverish, heavy rhythm, leaning too hard on the more emphatic passages, too breathy and rushed with the delicate ones. She played
like a sixteen-year-old girl who had taken lessons dutifully for
years, mediocre and competent, with a firm failure of imagination underlying every note. Brenda was only six and had never
had any music lessons, did not even listen in any evident way to
music, and yet she could play for hours with this mysterious sub-
competence—why? He stood staring at her. She was oblivious to
him. Why, if his daughter must be insane, why not brilliantly
insane? Why not a genius?

Instead, she was extraordinary but not astonishing. She might be written up in someone's textbook someday, but the case history would not be important; there wasn't enough to her. "Good morning, honey," he said. He came to her and put his arms gently around her. She stopped playing the piano but did not seem to notice him. Instead, as if paralyzed by a thought that had nothing to do with him, she sat rigid, intense, staring at her fingers on the keyboard.

"You're all ready, are you? Scrubbed and clean and ready for the trip?"

She did not appear to have heard him. She did hear him, of course, every word, and some words hardly audible—they had discovered that when she was hardly a year old, her uncanny animal-like omnipotence. She heard what was breathed into his ear by his wife, up in their secret bed, she heard the secret date of her next appointment with the Dreaded Doctor, she knew instinctively when an innocent drive would take her to the dentist, she knew everything. . . . Today, Wednesday, was not a fearful day. She was not afraid of school. She gave no indication of liking it, or of anticipating it, but she was not afraid and she would not go limp, forcing them to carry her out to the car.

"I'll have some coffee, then we'll leave. Mommy's staying home today and I'm taking you. I thought we'd have a nice drive to school, then come back through the park. . . . I took the whole day off today. I hope the sun stays out."

He was aware of the paragraphs of his speech. Talking to his silent, frowning daughter, a child of six with an ageless look, he understood how silence mocks words; her blocks of silence, like terrible monstrous blocks of stone, fell heavily on either side of his words. What he said was never quite accurate. He was speaking to a child when, perhaps, he should have been speaking to an adult. Brenda's intelligence had never been measured. She might be ten years old, or eighteen, or two. It was a mystery, an abyss. As soon as he entered the kitchen he heard her begin to play where she had left off, the "Moonlight Sonata" in that sun-filled living room. . . .

He made instant coffee. His hands had begun to tremble. The harmonic green and brown of the kitchen did not soothe him, he could not sit down. When he came home from the office each day he always came out to the kitchen to talk to his wife, and he talked energetically about his work. His wife always appeared to listen with sympathy. His paragraphs of words, tossed against her appreciative silence, were attempts to keep her quiet; he realized that now. She made dinner and listened to him, flattering him with her complete attention. He hinted of trouble at work, maybe a union threatening to strike, or the federal government again raising mortgage interest rates . . . tricks to keep his wife from talking about Brenda. He realized that now.

When he returned to the living room Brenda slid dutifully off the bench. She never resisted physically; her body was not really her own. She was quite small for her age, with knobby white knees. He loved her knees. Her hair was thin and straight, cut off to show her delicate ears. Her face was a pretty face, though too thin, unnaturally pale; her eyes were a light green. Seeing her was always a shock; you expected to see a dull, squat child, a kind of dwarf. Not at all. Everyone, especially the two sets of grandparents, remarked on her beauty. "She's so pretty! It will all work itself out!" both grandmothers said constantly. They were anxious to share in her mythical progress and contributed toward the tuition charged by the private, expensive school she went to, though Arthur resented this. He made enough money to send his own child to school. But the grandparents wanted to get as close as possible, nudging their beautiful prodigy into life, breathing the mysterious breath of normal life into her. Why, why was she not normal, when it was so obviously easier to be normal than to be Brenda? Perfectly stupid children were normal, ugly children were normal, and this golden-haired little lady, with her perfect face and ears and limbs, was somehow not . . . not "normal." It was an abyss, the fact of her.

Drawing slightly away from him, with a woman's coolnesss, she put on her own coat. He knelt to check her, to see if the buttons were lined up correctly. Of course. It had been years since she'd buttoned them wrong. "All set? Great! We're on our way!" Arthur said heartily. She did not look at him. She never met his eye, that was part of her strangeness—she would not look anyone in the eye, as if some secret shame or hatred forced her away, like the invisible force of like magnets.

And so . . . they were on their way. No backing out. His wife had driven Brenda to school ever since Brenda had begun, and today he was driving her, a generous act. Minutes flew by. It was a surprise how quickly time had passed, getting him up out of bed and on his way, drawing him to the ride. The minutes had passed as if flying toward an execution. . . . He had tried to think of this day as a gift, a day off from work, but it had been nothing but pretense. He was afraid of the long trip and afraid of his daughter.

Between his wife and himself was the fact of their daughter. They had created her together, somehow they had brought her into the world. It was a mystery that jarred the soul; better not to think of it. His wife had accused him more than once of blaming her for the child. "You hate me unconsciously. You can't control it," she had said. Her wisdom was sour and impregnable. "You hate failure," she said. Didn't he hate, in his cheerful secretive way, his own father because his own father was something of a failure? "Jesus Christ, what are you saying?" he had shouted. He denied everything.

The school was experimental and chancy, very expensive. Was it really quite professional? The several doctors they'd taken Brenda to were not enthusiastic; they expressed their opinion of the school with a neutral shrug of the shoulders. Why not try? And so, desperate, they had driven fifty miles to talk with the director, a long-nosed, urgent female with grimy fingernails and great excitement, and she had agreed to take Brenda on. "But we make no promises. Everything is exploratory," she had said. "Nothing is given a form, no theories are allowed to be hardened into dogma, no theories are rejected without trial, no emotions are stifled. . . ." Why not try? After several months Brenda showed no signs of improvement, and no signs of degeneration. If she showed any "signs" at all, they were private and indecipherable. But Wednesday had become the center of the week. He and his wife looked to Wednesday, that magic day, as a kind of Sabbath; on that day he drove to work with a sense of anticipation, and his wife drove Brenda fifty miles to school and fifty miles back again, hoping. This was the usual procedure. Then, when he came home, he would always ask, "How do you think it went today?" and she would always reply, "The director is still hopeful . . . I think it's going well . . . yes, I think it's going well."

In the car Brenda seated herself as far from him as possible. No use to urge her to move over. She was not stubborn, not exactly. It was rather as if no one inhabited her body, as if her spirit had abandoned it. "A great day for a ride!" he said. He chatted with her, or toward her. His voice sounded nervous. He disliked silence because of its emptiness, the possibility of anything happening inside it—no warning, no form to it. He was amorous of forms, solid forms. He distrusted shapelessness. In his daydreams he had always wanted to force action into a shape, to freeze explosions into art, into the forms in which beauty is made bearable. He lived in one of those forms. The style of his living was one of them. Why not? The work he did was professional in every way, geared to a market, imagination within certain limiting forms. He was not a genius, he would not revolutionize architecture. Like his daughter, he was extraordinary but not astonishing.

Brenda took a piece of spaghetti out of her coat pocket. It was uncooked, broken in half. She began to chew on it. Except for random, unlikely things—fish sticks, bits of cardboard, cucumber, grapes with seeds—she ate nothing but uncooked spaghetti. She bit pieces off slowly, solemnly, chewing them with precision. Her green eyes were very serious. Every day she stuffed her pockets with pieces of spaghetti, broken in pieces. Bits of spaghetti were all over the house. His wife vacuumed every day, with great patience. It wasn't that Brenda seemed to like spaghetti, or that she had any concept of "liking" food at all. Perhaps she could not taste it. But she would not eat anything else. Arthur had long ago stopped snatching it away from her. He had stopped pleading with her. For what had seemed a decade she had sat at the table with them, listless and stony-eyed, refusing to eat. She did not quite *refuse*—nothing so emphatic. But she would not eat. She had no obvious conception of "eating." What she did was nibble slowly at pieces of spaghetti, all day long, or chew cardboard and shape it into little balls, or suck at grapes and very carefully extract the seeds. She walked around the house or out in the back yard as if in a trance, slow, precise, unhurried, spiritless. Demurely she turned aside when someone approached her. She went dead. The only life she showed was her piano playing, which was monotonous and predictable, the same pieces over and over again for months. . . . Her silence was immense as a mountain neither Arthur nor his wife could climb. And when the silence came to an end—when Brenda cried, which was infrequent—they heard to their horror the sobs of a six-year-old child, breathy and helpless. But how to help her? She could not be embraced, even by a distraught parent. A bump on the head, a bleeding scratch, would not soften her. The jolly mindlessness of Christmas would not give any grandparent the right to hug her. No nonsense. No touching. When his wife took Brenda for her monthly checkup, at which time the doctor gave her vitamin shots, she always asked the doctor how Brenda was "doing"; and the doctor always said, with a special serious smile to show how sorry he was about all this, "She's surprisingly healthy, considering her diet. You should be thankful."

It was a long drive. Arthur began to think longingly of his office—an older associate of his whom he admired and imitated, the naïveté of a secretary he could almost have loved, in another dimension. Elevators, high buildings. Occasional long lunches. He thought of his office, of his working space. He liked to work. He liked problems. They came to him in the shape of lines with three dimensions. It was remarkable how they were then transferred into shapes that were solid, into buildings. He was working on a shopping plaza. A shopping "mall." With love he dreamed of the proper shapes of banks, the proper shapes of supermarkets, of hardware stores—seductive as music! Their lines had to be gentle, seductive, attractive as the face of his secretary, who was only twenty-three. He wanted to love them. Certainly he had enough love in him . . . love for his work, for his wife, his secretary, his parents, his friends, his daughter. . . . Why did he feel so exhausted though it was early morning?

He entered the expressway in silence. Brenda was awake but silent. It was worse than being truly alone, for a swerving of the car would knock her around; if he slammed on the brakes she would fly forward and crack her skull. A limp weight. No true shape to her, because she was so empty. What was she thinking? He glanced sideways at her, smiling in case she noticed him. He and his wife believed that their daughter was thinking constantly. Her silence was not peaceful. It seemed to them nervous, jumpy, alert, but alert to invisible shapes. Something unseen would move in the corner of her eye and she would shiver, almost imperceptibly. What did she see? What did she think? Idiot children who giggle and squirm happily in their mothers' embraces make more sense, being only defective of intelligence. It would be possible to love them.

"Look at the cows!" he said, pointing. "Do you see the cows?"

No response. No cows.

"Look at the big truck up ahead . . . all those new cars on it. . . ." He felt the need to talk. He wanted to keep a sense of terror at some distance; her silence, her terrifying silence! He stared at the carrier with its double row of shining cars, cars of all colors, very handsome. He was preparing to pass the truck. What if, at the crucial moment, the truck wobbled and the cars came loose? They seemed precariously fastened to the carrier. He imagined metal shearing through metal, slicing off the top of his skull. The steering wheel would cut him in two. And his daughter would be crushed in an instant, pressed into her essential silence. The end.

"Like to hear some music, Brenda?" He turned on the radio. Strange, how he felt the need to talk to her in spurts, as if offering her a choice of remarks. Like his wife, he somehow thought that a magic moment would arrive and Brenda would wake up, a fairy princess awakened by the right incantation. . . . If only she would let them kiss her, perhaps the perfect kiss would awaken her. But she did not hear the words, did not hear the love and yearning behind them, would not suffer the kiss, nothing. She did not need them. She was a delicate weight in the corner of his eye, not a threat, not really a burden because she wanted nothing—unlike other children, she wanted nothing. And so there was nothing to give her.

She ate uncooked spaghetti for the rest of the drive.

The school was housed in a one-story building, previously a small-parts shop. On the walk he noticed a bit of drool about Brenda's mouth—should he wipe it off? He wanted to wipe it off, not because he was anxious for her to look neat for school but because he was her father and had the right to touch her.

"Do you have a handkerchief, honey?"

This was too mild. She sensed his weakness. She wiped her own mouth with her hand, blankly and efficiently. A college-age girl with a suntanned face took Brenda from him, all popeyed charm and enthusiasm. He watched Brenda walk away. It pained him to see how easily she left him, how unconnected they were. There was nothing between them. She did not glance back, did not notice that he was remaining behind. Nothing.

He drove around for a while, feeling sorry for himself, then stopped to have some coffee. Then he walked around the university, browsing in bookstores, wondering if he could remain sane —he had several hours to get through. What did his wife do on these holy Wednesdays? At noon he went to a good restaurant for lunch. Two cocktails first, then a steak sandwich. Women shoppers surrounded him. He admired their leisure, their rings, their gloves; women who had the air of being successes. They seemed happy. Once at a party he had noticed his wife in deep conversation with a stranger, and something in his wife's strained, rapt face had frightened him. When he asked her about it later she had said, "With him I felt anonymous, I could have begun everything again. He doesn't know about me. About Brenda." Like those bizarre unshaped pieces of sculpture that are placed around new buildings to suggest their important ties with the future, he and his wife had lost their ability to maintain a permanent shape; they were always being distorted. Too many false smiles, false enthusiasm and fear covered over. . . . The very passage of days had tugged at their faces and bodies, aging them. They were no longer able to touch each other and to recognize a human form. But he had seen her touch that man's arm, unconsciously, wanting from him the gift of a sane perspective, an anonymous freedom, that Arthur could no longer give her.

He wandered into another bookstore. In a mirror he caught sight of himself and was surprised, though pleasantly—so much worry and yet he was a fairly young man, still handsome, with light hair and light, friendly eyes, a good face. The necktie looked good. He wandered along the aisles, looking at textbooks. These manuals for beginning lives, for starting out fresh. . . . Engineering texts, medical texts. French dictionaries. A crunching sound at the back of the store put him in mind of his daughter eating. Spaghetti being bitten, snapped, crunched, chewed . . . an eternity of spaghetti. . . . He wandered to another part of the store and picked up a paperback book, *Forbidden Classics*. An Egyptian woman, heavily made up, beckoned to him from the cover. He picked up another book, *Bizarre Customs of the World*; on this cover a child beckoned to him, dressed in an outlandish outfit of feathers and furs. . . . He leafed through the book, paused at a few pages, then let the book fall. Garbage! He was insulted. A sense of disorder threatened. Better for him to leave.

He strolled through the campus but its buildings had no interest for him. They were dead, they were tombs. The sidewalks were newer, wide, functional. The university's landscaping was impressive. Students sat on the grass, reading. A girl caught his attention—she wore soiled white slacks, sat with her legs apart, her head flung back so that the sun might shine flatly onto her face. Her long brown hair hung down behind her. She was immobile, alone. Distracted, he nearly collided with someone. He stared at the girl and wondered why she frowned so, why her face was lined though she could not have been more than twenty —what strange intensity was in her?

He walked in another direction. There were too many young girls, all in a hurry. Their faces were impatient. Their hair swung around their eyes impatiently, irritably. His blood seemed to return to his heart alert and jumpy, as if infected by their intensity, by the mystery of their secret selves. He felt panic. A metallic taste rose to his mouth, as if staining his mouth. He felt that something was coming loose in him, something dangerous.

What did his wife do on these long hateful days?

He went to the periodical room of the university's undergraduate library. He leafed through magazines. World affairs; nothing of interest. Domestic affairs: no, nothing. What about medicine, what new miracles? What about architecture? He could not concentrate. He tried to daydream about his work, his problems, about the proper shapes of banks and stores. . . . Nothing. He thought of his salary, his impressive salary, and tried to feel satisfaction; but nothing. His brain was dazzled as if with sparks. Suddenly he saw the girl on the grass, in a blaze of light, her white slacks glowing. An anonymous girl. Beginning again with an anonymous girl. The girl shivered in his brain, wanting more from the sun than the sun could give her.

He wanted to leave the library and find her, but he did not move. He remained with the magazines on his lap. He waited. After a while, when he thought it was safe, he went to a campus bar and had a drink. Two drinks. Around him were music, noise;

young people who were not youthful. People jostled his chair all the time, as if seeking him out, contemptuous of his age. A slight fever had begun in his veins. Around him the boys and girls hung over one another, arguing, stabbing the air with their fingers, scraping their chairs angrily on the floor. "I am not defensive!" a girl cried. Now and then a girl passed by him who was striking as a poster—lovely face, lovely eyes. Why didn't she glance at Arthur? It was as if she sensed the failure of his genes, the quiet catastrophe of his chromosomes. He heard beneath the noise in the bar a terrible silence, violent as the withheld violence of great boulders.

When he picked Brenda up he felt a sense of levity rising in him, as if he had survived an ordeal. "How was it today, honey? What is that you've got—a paper flower?" He took it from her buttonhole, the buttonhole indifferent as her face. Yes, a paper flower. A red rose. "It's great. Did you make it yourself, honey?" He put it in his own buttonhole, as if his daughter had made it for him. She did not glance up. In the car she sat as far from him as possible, while he chattered wildly, feeling his grin slip out of control. Around him boulders precarious on mountainsides were beginning their long fall, soundlessly.

"We'll stop in the park for a few minutes. You should get out in the sun." He tried to sound festive. Parks meant fun; children knew that. The park was large, mostly trees, with a few swings and tennis courts. It was nearly empty. He walked alongside her on one of the paths, not touching her, the two of them together but wonderfully independent. "Look at the birds. Blue jays," he said. He wanted to take her hand but feared her rejection. Only by force could anyone take her hand. She took a stick of spaghetti out of her pocket and bit into it, munching slowly and solemnly. "Look at the squirrels, aren't they cute? There's a chipmunk," he said. He felt that he was in charge of all these animals and that he must point them out to his daughter, as if he had to inform her of their names. What terror, not to know the names of animals, of objects, of the world! What if his daughter woke someday to a world of total blankness, terror? He was responsible for her. He had created her.

"Stay nearby, honey. Stay on the path," he said. He was suddenly exhausted; he sat on a bench. Brenda walked along the path in her precise, spiritless baby steps, munching spaghetti. She seemed not to have noticed that he was sitting, weary. He put his hands to his head and heard the notes of the "Moonlight Sonata." Brenda walked on slowly, not looking around. She could walk like this for hours in the back yard of their house, circling the yard in a certain space of time. A safe child, predictable. She might have been walking on a ledge, high above a street. She might have been stepping through poisonous foam on a shore. . . . The shadows of leaves moved about her and on her, silently. Birds flew overhead. She saw nothing. Arthur thought suddenly of his father sitting on the steps of the back porch of their old house, his head in his hands, weeping. Why had his father wept?

It seemed suddenly important for him to know why his father had wept, and why Brenda so rarely wept.

And then something happened—afterward Arthur was never able to remember it clearly. Brenda was on the path not far from him, no one was in sight, the park was ordinary and unsurprising, and yet out of nowhere a man appeared, running. He was middle-aged. In spite of the mild September day he wore an overcoat that flapped around his knees; his face was very red; his hair was gray and spiky; he ran bent over, stooped as if about to snatch up something from the ground. Arthur was watching Brenda and then, in the next instant, this outlandish running figure appeared, colliding with her, knocking her down. The man began to scream. He seized Brenda's arm and shook her, screaming down into her face in a high, waspish, womanish voice, screaming words Arthur could not make out. "What are you doing— what are you doing?" Arthur cried. He ran to Brenda and the man jumped back. His mouth worked. He was crouching, foolishly alert, his face very red—he began to back up slowly, cunningly. Arthur picked Brenda up. "Are you all right? Are you hurt?" He stared into her face and saw the same face, unchanged. He wondered if he was going out of his mind. Now, as if released, the man in the overcoat turned and began walking quickly away. He was headed back into the woods. "You'd better get out of here before I call the police!" Arthur yelled. His voice was shrill. He was terribly agitated, he could not control the sickening fear in his body.

The man was nearly gone. He was escaping. Arthur's heart pounded, he looked down at Brenda and back up, at the woods, and suddenly decided to run after the man. "You, hey wait! You'd better wait!" he yelled. He left Brenda behind and ran after the man. "Come back here, you dirty bastard, dirty filthy pervert bastard!" The man crashed into something. He stumbled in a thicket. Arthur caught up with him and could hear his panicked breathing. The back of the man's neck was dirty and reddened, blushing fiercely. He turned away from the thicket and tried to run in another direction, but his knees seemed broken. He was sobbing. Panicked, defeated, stumbling, he turned suddenly toward Arthur as if to push past him—Arthur swung his fist around and struck the man on the side of the neck. One hard blow. The man cried out sharply, nearly fell. Arthur struck him again. "Dirty bastard! Filth!" Arthur cried. His third blow knocked the man down, and then he found himself standing over him, kicking him—his heel into the jawbone, into the nose, crunching the nose, splattering blood onto the grass, onto his shoe. He could actually feel the nose break! Something gave way, he felt even the vibrations of the man's screams, his stifled screams. Arthur bent over him, pounding with his fists. *I'll kill you, I'll tear you into pieces!* The man rolled over wildly onto his stomach, hiding his face in his hands. Arthur kicked viciously at his back. He kicked the back of his head. "I'm going to call the police —throw you in jail—you can rot—you dirty pervert, dirty bastard—" Arthur kicked at the body until he could not recall what he was doing; the paper rose fell out of his buttonhole and onto the man's back, and onto the ground. "You'd better get the hell out of here because I'm going to call the police. You'd better not be here when I come back," he said, backing away.

And he had forgotten . . . about Brenda. . . . What was wrong with him? He ran back to her and there she was, safe. Only her leg was a little dirty. A small scratch, small dots of blood. Nothing serious! Greatly relieved, panting with relief, Arthur bent to dab at her knee with a Kleenex. She stepped away. "There, there, it's just a tiny scratch . . ." he said. He was very hot, sweating. He could feel sweat everywhere on his body. Hardly able to bear the pounding of his heart, he made another attempt to blot the blood, but Brenda side-stepped him. He looked sharply up at her and saw her look away from him. Just in that instant she had been looking at him . . . and then she looked away, at once. Their eyes had almost met.

He took her back to the car. They were safe, nothing had happened. Safe. No one had seen. His clothes were rumpled, his breathing hoarse, but still they were safe. He was alarmed at the pounding of his heart. Excitement still rose in him in waves, overwhelming his heart. . . . Wait, he should wait for a few minutes. Sit quietly. The two of them sat in the front seat of the car, in silence. Arthur wiped his face. He looked over at his daughter and saw that her coat was perfectly buttoned, her hair was not even mussed, her face was once again composed and secret. His panting alarmed him. Did she notice? Of course she noticed, she noticed everything, understood everything, and yet would never inform on him; what gratitude he felt for her silence!

After a few minutes he felt well enough to drive. He was a little nauseous with excitement. A little lightheaded. He turned on the radio, heard static and loud music, then turned it off again, not knowing what he was doing. He headed for the expressway and saw with burning eyes the signs pointing toward home; everything had been composed in a perfect design, no one could get lost. It was impossible to get lost in this country.

Beside him, in the far corner of the seat, his daughter took out a small piece of spaghetti and began to chew on it. They were safe. He glanced at her now and then as if to check her— had that man really collided with her? Knocked her down and shaken her, screamed into her face? Or had he imagined it all— no man, no smashed nose, no blood? There was blood on his shoes. Good. He drove home at a leisurely pace, being in no hurry. Brenda said nothing.

Loving
Losing } a *M*an
Loving

In her heart she was already frightened; she was frightened that the sight of him would draw her out of herself.

A picture taken by a newspaper photographer had once shown Ruth not herself, hysterical and yanked out of herself, hardly recognizable. She had been in a picket line protesting the war. A group of antipicketers from an organization called Breakthrough had tried to disrupt the line, charging upon them, shouting. A man had snatched her sign from her and snapped it in two over his knee. And, in a frenzy of anger and loathing, she had screamed into his face, trying to get the broken sign back—at that moment the photographer had taken her picture. The caption, devised for the local pro-war newspaper, had said "Passive

Protester" or something like that, some dim sarcasm she had tried
to forget. But the shame of it remained with her, for she had had
to see that the young woman of the photograph was not really a
woman but only a force, a voice, hysterical, strangled, ugly, a
purity of violence run out of control. She hated to be broken
down, broken in two, like that. She hated to be drawn out of
herself into a kind of whirlwind.

The hospital was moderately crowded. Someday she would
have an adventure here, she thought. She was on her way to visit
her lover, who was in the hospital for ten days, for testing, sub-
jected to painful and humiliating tests . . . at this moment he
waited for her upstairs, in his semiprivate room, lying awake. She
felt a sense of excitement and dread, knowing that she must go to
the elevator, must take it up to the fifth floor, must go to his room
and confront him. Her visits were timed according to his command. He had said: "You come every day at two; the rest of them
will keep that clear." And it was true: "the rest of them" were his
many friends and acquaintances, who visited him before two but
never after, anxious to visit him, to show their affection now that
he was sick. The mystery of his sickness made him more desir-
able. They met one another out in the corridor and exchanged
glances and said, "What do you think it is? Cancer? Some kind of
paralysis?"

Harry in a hospital bed . . . Harry's blood drained into little
bottles . . . Harry's spine tapped . . . Harry's eyeballs examined by a two-ton machine . . . Harry's good humor too loud
in that narrow room . . . Harry groping through pain for a
hand to shake. His eyelids tended to flutter.

"Come at two. At two every day," he had told her.

And so every day she must see him, at two. Beginning at noon
she would draw her arms down around her knees and sit in a
chill, crystallike misery, rocking back and forth, watching the
clock. She loved him and yet she was terrified of him. Sometimes
her love for him was inside her, embedded in her, and sometimes

it was outside her, a thing of terror, threatening to draw her out into it.

. . . The faces of the nurses shone with mysterious health. Windows were open for the afternoon sun; the hospital was old, antique, but touched lightly with spring; the floors were waxed and smelled of antiseptic, a washroom door swung open behind a nurse and gave Ruth a vision of rough gray-green walls, institution walls, a bare light bulb stuck in the ceiling . . . She had come to know everything about her route in the hospital, as if she had been taking it for more than only six days.

About Harry: she loved him but could not believe in him. It did not seem real, his loving her, and his sickness also did not seem real. A man who jokes so often cannot really get sick. But if Harry was not immortal, then no one was immortal? . . . Sleeping alone now, she had strange, ugly dreams, hallucinations that were not quite dreams. She imagined Harry as a locomotive, speeding along a track into the night. Harry was a locomotive, or had been, but the tracks had drawn themselves out into blankness, darkness, running out of ties, no energy left, her imagination failed her, and the little locomotive had to come to a stop.

In the elevator she was bumped by a woman with a corsage on her coat.

Her eyes began to water. Someone got off, someone got on. Nurses with tiny green things, plastic things, stuck in their buttonholes. What did it mean? Ruth pressed herself against the rear of the elevator, not wanting anyone to look at her. That might be bad luck. The elevator was crowded this afternoon. The hospital itself was crowded, a large, old, inner-city hospital, famous for its excellent emergency ward, which was in frantic use every night of the week and especially Saturday night. The city was Detroit. It did not mean much to her, existing outside of her—Detroit, a place she had come to three years ago, not quite on purpose. Harry did not belong in Detroit, had been born far away. All of their friends were from somewhere else, no one seemed to be born here. Ruth remembered the place of her birth when she was forced to write it down, on those countless forms to be made out for countless bureaus, filed and forgotten.

She came in upon him quietly, though she saw that he was awake. The other bed was empty; the old man who had been in it was shipped away, to a convalescent home nearby. Harry lay in bed staring at the window, his hands up to his mouth. Seeing her, turning his head, he drew his hands away from his mouth at once.

There is some error in all this, Ruth thought.

Everything was gray-green. The inside of a skull had been flashed out upon the walls: gray-green. Hope was the cruelest thing of all, a woman had said on the elevator, the first time Ruth had come to visit. "Hope is the cruelest thing of all," the dumpy little woman had said to another woman with her, and Ruth had been frightened, unable to look at her, profoundly moved. Why did ordinary people, who were supposed to think ordinary thoughts, sometimes say such things? It frightened her; it opened everything. Her love for Harry had always been based on hope— the hope that they would be married—and now her expectations of his own future were based on hope, his getting well, his returning to her. He had a wife and a child somewhere out by the Pacific Ocean, in a marvelous landscape, blue skies and healthy white sand. He had been married for fifteen years, so he said. But the years had slipped from him, nothing had stayed, and when she met him in Detroit he spoke casually and frankly of his wife, as if she existed in another dimension and had nothing to do with Ruth or with himself.

They greeted each other. She bent over him, clutched at him, she kissed his mouth. "My darling? . . ." she said. His mouth seemed dry; why was that? Harry saw the tears welling in her eyes and laughed abruptly, to head her off. "Please sit down. You look so tired," he said.

She sat on a chair, there were magazines on the chair she half noticed, she felt very confused. As always, she stared at his face to see . . . to see if there were signs of hope. One day he would tell her what the diagnosis was. And then the hope would rise up in her chest like a trick flower.

"How are you?"

"The same."

"Did they do anything this morning?"

"More of the blood. Don't ask."

His dark blond hair was thinning. He had a strong, hawkish face, the bones lately become more prominent, vaguely threatening. About his knobby forehead and eyes a strange power seemed to gather itself, especially when he spoke, the pressure of his words gathering power inside his head. His eyes were dark, even the whites darkened, as if subtly bruised. He was not a handsome man; she thought him ugly, even a little repulsive; it excited her to think of his ugliness and to know that she possessed it, in him. What was ugly in him drew her to it, the power in him drew her to it: he was not an ordinary man. He had distinguished himself as a writer and a journalist, a man seemingly infatuated with writing, with the violence in America. He had written a number of magazine articles, and a book about the Watts riot that had been nominated for a Pulitzer Prize, and now, lately, he had joined the Detroit staff of a famous newspaper. Seeing so much of America, having traveled so much, had inspired in him a look of permanent irony.

"Tell me, please tell me everything that has happened . . ." she whispered.

"The infection is gone for good, evidently. I now eat with my mouth."

For two days he had been nearly unconscious, with a stomach infection that had made the rounds of the hospital. The nurses were cheerful and unworried about it. It happened all the time. Harry, already weakened, had been severely hit by the infection and had had to be fed intravenously.

She talked to him. He replied. She thought anxiously *What will I say next?* She wanted only to talk of love, but this would irritate him. Sometimes she talked of marriage, a game she played, *If we were married* . . . and he seemed to enjoy that game, in a way aerated by it, given youth. He was over forty. What would it mean to him to be married to this girl of twenty-four, this girl who was truly blond, a well-mannered and devoted young woman who cared about everything in his life, had sympathy for the father he had long forgotten—his father was in a mental institution somewhere in California—and was impatient to give up everything in her life for him, only for him? . . . He had been married twice and neither marriage had worked out. He attributed this to the failure of two women, she attributed it to their ordinariness. In the game of *if we were married* she made herself over constantly into a woman equal to his energy, ready to bound ahead of him, with an imagination that never gave out.

. . . To crawl in bed beside him, like a sister, sick with love as he was sick with a mystery. . . .

He asked about Martin. About Tony. The conversation kept going: he had a writer's nosiness, even for worthless news. He liked gossip. She answered all his questions, eager to please. She felt herself softened in his vision; she loved herself, being loved by this man.

"By the way, it's pretty bad," he said abruptly.

She did not quite hear. He had interrupted her story of Martin's car accident on the expressway; after a confused moment she continued again, faithful to Martin's anecdote. *He waited an hour for someone to pick him up . . . he kept thinking his skull was fractured, but it wasn't . . . he kept having shivering fits, waiting.* Harry seemed to find this story very interesting. He did not interrupt her again.

When the story came to an end he smiled at her, as if proud of her. He stroked her face. "My darling, my little girl . . ." he said gently. She got to her feet and leaned over him, trying to be gentle herself; she pressed her face against his chest. The hospital blanket was made of very thin wool She could feel this man's heart thumping in his rib cage; it terrified her, the dryness of that rib cage and the dryness of that heart.

"Oh, I love you so much . . ." she whispered.

What was there to do except clutch each other, in fear? But he would not show her his fear; he drew back from her, smiling stiffly.

"Hand me that copy of the *Nation*," he said.

"Is there anything interesting in it?" she said.

He opened it to a review of several books. He handed it to her. She tried to read it, her eyes watering over the delicate type, nodding, pretending to understand. She wanted to throw the magazine away and weep in his arms. *There is some error in this room.* . . . "Gregory has come a long way since I knew him in Los Angeles," Harry said. He shifted his long body restlessly, as if this other man, this "Gregory," disturbed him. Ruth could not make out if the reviewer was Gregory or if the author of the book reviewed was Gregory.

"I meant to tell you . . ." she said.

"Finish it. Did you read that last paragraph?"

Chastised, she skipped to the last paragraph. *The forms of neurotic energy are various and ingenious.* . . .

"What do you think?"

"It's very interesting."

"Gregory has come a long way . . . that bastard. . . ."

But Harry was smiling.

She put the magazine down. They stared at each other, in silence. She felt, bizarrely, her body warming for him, as if sunning itself in his gaze. Didn't her body understand that this man was sick? She dug at the tender skin around her fingernail. It was a mystery, a terrible confusion. She thought of his body and her own body, of the simplicity of love, and of this strange, new complexity. Her mind could not handle this complexity. She wanted to cry out at him, as if in an argument: "No! No! You are following the wrong script, you are giving yourself up to the wrong fate!"

But she said instead, "When you see Second Avenue again you'll be amazed. They've torn it all up in a week!"

He indicated that she should come to him. He stroked her face slowly, lovingly, as if he were blind. When Harry touched her she felt her beauty turned inward, secretive and warm. She was like something hard melting in water, in warm water, eager to return to its essential softness. Closed, her eyes were filled with a strange sharp light that blinded her.

"Do you still love me? . . ." she whispered.

"What a thing to say!"

His presence made her faint with a sharp, sweet dizziness, not just the dizziness of desire but one of expectation, hope, a complex future. She had read and reread his books, his articles. How could a man so brilliant not have a future? He was a great, powerful locomotive, she was someone clinging to its sides, trying to hang on, in danger of being crushed. They had met at someone's house. The men had been arguing. Ruth, upset by something that had happened earlier that day, had begun to cry. Everyone in the room was in opposition to the government's foreign policy, everyone wanted the war ended; but, united in their hatred of the President, they were not united in anything else, they could not agree on a hall to rent for a pacifist's "teach-in," they could not agree on a time (Friday night? Sunday night?), they could not agree on whom to invite, whom to snub, the right attitude to have toward the police, whom they really did need for protection. They could not agree on anything. They hated one another. And Ruth, crying, had felt the failure of their lives, mixed up with the larger failure of the nation, everything dwindling to a stupid end. . . .

Harry had taken hold of her hands to comfort her. He had introduced himself, though she already knew who he was.

Now she kissed his hands. The richness of this gesture overwhelmed her; it was the correct thing to do. But his hands were so clean, so pale. She kissed the fingers, the very clean finger-nails. Harry should not have been so clean. The arms of h sweaters, particularly his white sweater, were always dirty. Now, in the hospital, he had suddenly become clean. She was suspicious of his cleanliness.

"It isn't curable. They don't know how to stop it," he said.

She was bent over him. Again she did not quite hear him. Outside in the corridor someone was talking; something was pushed by—a wheelchair, a cart? She did not look up. She was spellbound in this moment, her lover's fingers against her face, his words resounding in her and yet not coming to any meaning, not dangerous. She touched his thighs through the blanket, gently. She thought of their love, how they had made love, and the pleasure of his love lay hard and unforgetting in her, permanent.

"What is it like outside, honey?" he said.

"It's nice."

"Today is St. Patrick's Day."

"Oh. . . ."

"What can I do for you, dear?" he said. Though his voice was gentle, there was something impatient behind it. She was still for a moment, thinking of the deadliness of their intimacy and the fact of their entangled lives, which could not be undone. She did not want their lives undone. She did not want him to stop stroking her face, though her mind jumped nervously ahead to the moment, to the precise moment, when he would stop.

"I mean, what do you want me to do? Is there anything?" he said.

"What do you mean?"

"Is there anything I can arrange for you?"

Still she did not understand him. She smiled anxiously, feeling the strain in her face, not wanting him to say more.

"Is there anything I should bring you tomorrow?" she said.

He stared at her. "What? No. Nothing special." A darkness began to pass over his face. He stared at her and beyond her, not if recognizing her or assessing her, but determining her existence, her reality. In their several months of love he had never

done this before; she had been his beloved, in love with him,
listening to him constantly. Now his hands groped against her
face and his fingers encircled her jaw as if surprised at the firm-
ness of her bones.

"Don't—please—" she said suddenly.

"What?"

"You're frightening me."

She wanted to forbid him that staring, that examination. He
bones, her very blood resisted it violently, this calm surprise a
her existence, her healthy existence apart from him. Since sh
had fallen in love with him all the old unruliness of her life hac
been abandoned, tears came easily to her now, she was loved b
a man worthy of any woman's love and this fact was the totality
of her existence. . . . Everything was subtle in her. Withou
him, before him, she had not been afraid to go out for grocerie
after dark, to the dirty supermarket near her place, she hac
walked hard and fast in her slacks, smoking a cigarette out on th
street. Now that he had valued her so highly, mythologizing he
into a woman of beauty, she had not that old courage; it woul
destroy her to be made herself once again, only herself. Sh
dreaded her existence apart from his own.

"I'm so unhappy. I can't sleep any more," she said.

He nodded sadly.

"I can't stand it, being alone. When will they let you out o
here?"

As if her weakness disappointed him, he could not answer. H
seemed overcome with sorrow.

"Why are you looking at me like that? Who has been here
see you?" she cried. She was angry. There was a war outsic
them, fought by their country; there was a war inside ther
Peace was unavailable. She wanted to tug at him, bitterly, for
ing him to acknowledge her dependence upon him, the fact
their love. Hadn't she flowed into him so many times in the
lives?—so many nights with him, a miracle to her, her bo
made into a miracle by him? But he was dressed now in a hos

tal outfit, thin white material, worn thin from many launderings. Men now dead had worn that same outfit. He had written books, he had typed out pages of yellow scrap paper, plotting his personal life, fixing his past. Now he seemed oblivious to it, drawn out of himself and out of her, free.

"Have you ever been sick yourself?" Harry said.

"How do you mean?"

"Seriously sick?"

"No."

It was a sign of her desperate innocence, this answer.

"It's only when you know you'll have to come back, when you'll have to make up for the wasted time, that it's bad," he said. He spoke to her gently and confidentially, as if from another world. "As soon as you know it's over, then you're in another element, another dimension, there really isn't any worry. I can assure you of that. Please don't confuse me with other people."

"What—what do you mean?"

"I'm beyond it. I don't hope for anything; it's over."

She wondered if he were insane.

"I read these things with interest, yes, but not with a personal interest," he said. "The magazines there, the letters . . . they're private in themselves. They don't disturb me." He indicated the magazines on the window sill and the chair, and some letters on the bedside table. Ruth stared at these letters. Was his wife writing to him? A sense of perfect, completed hatred rose in her, shaking her free of sorrow, hatred for a woman she had never met. She imagined Harry making love to this woman, Harry's habits and odd little grunts of amusement familiar and routine to another woman, whom she had never met.

"When I wake up in the morning I open one eye. My left eye sees things lighter than my right eye . . . more light is let in the lens of the eye. But I don't calculate which eye to use. If it's my left eye then I won't be hurt that morning; if it's my right eye the day is already dim and will get worse. . . ."

This was new to her, a surprise to her; he was becoming super-

stitious. He was like a stone wall, something she must press
against but which would not exert pressure back upon her, no
knowing her. He said, "Nothing can come in the mail that car
disturb me. All those envelopes come without letters in them
empty envelopes. . . ."

Off and on during the last several years, he had told her, he
had received empty envelopes. An enemy? . . . A friend play
ing a trick? . . .

"Did you get another of those letters? Here?" she asked.

"No. Those have stopped."

"When did they stop?"

"I don't know . . . when did they? A few months ago? Jus
after we met?"

The mask of his face troubled itself, to recall that time. It wa
clear that he was seeking out the facts of a past not his own; i
was local history, someone else's history. It was someone else'
autobiography.

He had been planning to write his autobiography: *Fragment*
of a Life.

At the time, hearing himself mention this book, she had fla
tered herself into thinking that she, Ruth, would be the la
chapter in it. With her face flushed and precious, her body eage
absolute, young, she had been equal to any dream of his: wh
not? Men flew back and forth across the country, they flew
Europe and Asia and returned, but their dreams ran back to
woman, a woman's arms, and came to rest there. She had thoug
herself equal to him.

"And you never found out who sent those envelopes," she sai

"No."

"It was so strange. . . ."

"Yes," he said vaguely, without conviction. It was not strang
to him now; he had forgotten it. Or, perhaps, everything h
become strange and therefore the letters, the empty envelope
had no power to alarm him.

"Ruth, do you want me to marry you?"

"Yes," she said at once.

He nodded. He seemed to be releasing her, giving her leave. But she did not move. She said, "Yes, if we were married . . . if. . . ."

But she felt with shock the emptiness of his being; he had gone vacant before her eyes. His emptiness was like the emptiness of those strange envelopes. She could not inhabit it.

"You make me afraid . . ." she whispered.

In the beginning he had had dizzy spells. Rapid, shallow breath. His eyes had bothered him, a numbness in his hands had bothered him, nothing that seemed serious. No pain. He had been able to force himself into movement when his legs ached, when his head was heavy as a weight, and his old, furious appetite had begun to diminish, at first pleasing and then alarming him. When they had met he had been slightly overweight, with a layer of fat around his waist; now his ribs were prominent, horrible to her touch. Flesh had dwindled, as if freeing him. She wanted always to touch him, test him, to see if the flesh had returned.

"I've never been lonely in my life and I'm not lonely now. I'm not afraid," he said.

She nodded.

"I have a wife and a boy, I should be thinking of them, but I can't fix my mind upon them . . . people come together, do things together, then they say good-by. What do people have to do with each other anyway?"

She shook her head. She didn't know.

Someone knocked on the door. It was a man named Federico, a friend of Harry's. He took a step forward, then hesitated. "May I come in? . . ."

"Of course, come in," said Harry.

"Or should I come back in a little while?"

"Please come in."

"I . . . I saw Tony downtown . . . he told me about you, about the hospital. . . . I hadn't heard anything about it. . . ."

"I've been in since last Tuesday. The tests are almost over."

Federico stared from Harry to Ruth and back again. He was a slight, nervous young man, dark-haired, intense, solemn. Ruth believed he was a photographer. She had been meeting him for years, being introduced to him again and again, impatient with his nervous, gentle laugh, and his humility. The men she knew were not humble. Once, he had told her at a party about an experience of his boyhood—two policemen had beaten him up, trying to make him confess to some strange crime, the rape of a child or the molesting of a child. But he had not confessed. Speaking of this, his eyes had taken on a glazed, stubborn look. It was clear that he had relived the beating, but from the outside, a photographer interested in details, stunned by an impersonal terror.

"How are you, Ruth? How are you?" he said. He spoke too loudly, almost crying out, so intense and eager was he to please.

He took her hand. He shook it. He turned to stare at Harry, not knowing what to say.

"How do you feel? Is it—what is it? Do they know yet?" he said.

Harry shook his head.

"I shouldn't be asking," Federico said, obviously relieved. "It's not my business. . . . But this room isn't bad! Is it expensive, have you been all alone in here?"

"They'll be bringing someone in here today."

Federico looked at the other bed, the turned-back mattress. He gnawed at his lip; Ruth knew he was thinking *Someone has died in this room, with Harry.*

"I had a premonition someone would come to visit me who looked like you," Harry said suddenly.

He did not seem to be joking.

"Someone—like me?" Federico grinned.

"Your height. With a colored shirt. But not your face, I couldn't quite make out the face. . . ."

There was an embarrassed silence. Federico did not look

Ruth. She was thinking of an aged aunt of hers, senile and quarrelsome, who had become very superstitious near the end. . . . Federico sat on the edge of the window sill, awkwardly. He talked. His chatter was amiable and fluid, something to fill up time. He seemed breathless. Ruth had the idea that this visit was very difficult for him, something he had been putting off for days; now it had become a duty. It was strange, how he avoided looking at Ruth, how he concentrated upon Harry . . . he talked quickly, breathlessly, about matters of no importance. His trench coat was open. He wore a shirt of heavy cotton, dull gold that lit up his face with a reluctant joy. His trousers were dark green. He wore scuffed gray suede shoes. The suede looked gentle, the softest, most delicate kind of suede. Ruth could not remember what Harry's shoes had been like.

The two men talked. Ruth felt her heart pumping slowly and wearily inside her. Day after day the flabby fat around her lover's body had worn off . . . day after miraculous day, freeing him. . . It had been a madness to rejoice in that freeing.

She would not give it up, her love for him.

While they talked she began to cry, helplessly. She pressed her hands against her eyes. What did she want except to press herself against Harry, her face against his, her body against his? What else did she want? His body still enveloped him, it was still Harry. . . .

"You—you can't—"

But she could not finish. She wept angrily.

"She's very tired. She can't sleep at night," Harry said. Federico hovered near her, as if afraid of her. She felt his hand on her shoulder and she jerked away.

"Don't touch me!"

"Ruth," Harry said, disapproving.

She jumped to her feet and turned to the window. She wept, her back to them. The bodies in this gray-green room were waiting to see what she would do; there was a heavy, dull shame in them,

the shame of men for the terror of women. She loathed this terror
but could not subdue it. Again Federico approached her, again
she leaned away.

"Ruth? . . ." he said.

"I don't want to leave. Not yet."

"Would you like me to take you home?"

"Not yet!"

"Honey, please," Harry said. "We'll talk about this tomorrow.
Come see me tomorrow."

He sounded very tired.

"I can't leave yet. . . ."

"Yes, please. It's best for you."

She turned. She nodded. Passing his bed, she stared at him
with a weary, satisfied subordination. It was good to obey him
even in this. But still she stared at him, anxious to locate the life
in him. He must remember himself and her, in all the moments
of their love; those moments still existed. Nothing was lost. She
stared at him as if to force him to acknowledge her. He nodded
sadly. Federico led her out of the room.

Out in the corridor she tried to turn back.

"There's something I should tell him. . . ."

"Ruth, please. You'll see him tomorrow."

"But. . . ."

"Nothing will happen to him before tomorrow."

She walked in a crowded daze. People loomed up near her,
they sank away. Her hand went out against the wall. She stead-
ied herself.

"You look sick. You look as if you haven't slept in days," Federico said. His feet were silent in the corridor. He led her to the
elevator as if he knew the way better than she. "Have you been
sleeping? Have you been eating?"

"Yes."

She wanted to return to Harry's room; something had not been
settled between them.

"I love him. I can't stand it," she said.

She rubbed her front teeth hard with her forefinger, wiping off the film of panic.

"I don't want to go away. What if he dies? I can't remember what . . . what he said, exactly. . . . I have to talk to him again. . . ."

"Tomorrow."

She was in the elevator with him, this stranger. She could not stop trembling. The elevator took them down, they fell helplessly, in a kind of daze. She felt that the motion of the elevator might hypnotize her, lose her to herself. Everything sank downward, mockingly.

Leaving the elevator, she stumbled and Federico took her arm. "You are such a strange girl, a silly girl . . ." he said.

Out in the sunlight she tested her eyes. She could still see.

Federico walked beside her, down the steps. His hands were in his pockets, as if to show that he did not worry about her falling. His shoes were silent, his feet silent. On the sidewalk they paused. They did not look at each other.

"Once you were beaten up . . ." she said slowly.

"You remember? That? I was drunk to tell you that!"

He made a gentle, surprised grunting noise, a sound of surprised good humor. Yet there was alarm in it, as if he had been found out.

They did not move away from each other. Ruth's eyes ached but she had stopped crying; she kept testing her eyes, testing the daylight. At her side Federico stood with his hands in his pockets. He was only an inch or so taller than she. Harry had been much taller. Federico was slight, with a humble, cunning look to his legs and feet. Harry had been abrupt. He had slammed doors, jerked open drawers, he had always been looking for things and had always been angry at not finding them. . . . Ruth looked shyly at Federico.

"I guess we've met a number of times," she said.

He shrugged his shoulders, grinning. "But you don't remember my name, eh?"

"Federico Soldati."

He laughed. It was a pleasant surprise to him, her remembering.

"But Harry isn't badly sick. Don't cry. Don't worry about him," he said seriously. "What good can you do, like that? He needs you."

"I don't think so," she said.

"What? Of course he needs you, up there like that. Just to think of you would help him."

"Yes. . . ."

But she stared uncomprehendingly at Federico.

"He needs your love, you know that. He needs you. . . ."

She nodded. Slowly, lethargically, she turned from him. She had to cross the street. Her car was in a parking lot on the other side.

She stepped off the curb. Federico grabbed her and pulled her back.

"Watch out! Are you crazy?" he shouted.

His shouting terrified her, she hated it. Yet she had stepped back with him, giving in as soon as he touched her. A city bus passed near. The black driver stared at her with hatred.

"You want to get killed? What good will you do him then?"

She stood on the curb and tried to get her mind clear. Federico was breathing angrily through his teeth.

"How did you come here?" he said.

"Car."

"I'll drive you back, all right?"

"All right."

"You don't mind me driving your car?"

"No."

He walked with her across the street. At the car he hesitated.

"Is this your car?"

"Harry's."

She handed him the keys. One of the keys was for the car, another for the apartment.

Behind her, somewhere, she heard her lover crying, the mask of his face cracking at last, breaking into fine painful cracks: *But me, you must love me, even if I can no longer love you. . . . How else will I be immortal?*

If he died, if his body died, she would no longer love him. The time of their love would have come to an end. She would be free then, living beyond him.

Federico took her hand. He raised it to his face.

"You love him so much, it's beautiful to see you, let me love you . . . let me?" He was coaxing, humble, and yet cunning; she felt herself drawn to him, but without intimacy. There was something affectionate and immediate between them, yet it was not an intimacy . . . yet perhaps it would turn into that, she had no way of knowing. Her love was immortal. It passed through her, it grew in her, the gift of Harry's body. In her, so deeply embedded, in that most secret part of her body, it might now radiate out through her veins and bones and into Federico's body, transforming him.

"What do you want to do? Which way should I drive?" he said.

"I don't care," she said.

*D*id You Ever Slip on Red Blood?

Did you? she asked him repeatedly, angrily. *Di‹ you ever? I mean did you ever slip on red bloo‹ yourself, do you know what it's like?*

She wept and brushed her hair back from her face, her eye‹ shut so that he could stare at her, starkly, closely, so that she hi‹ nothing from him. Her nudeness made her radiant in the dim coarse light of a winter afternoon. He felt how her nudeness wa‹ in her face, behind her eyes, in the pressure of her angry eyelic‹ against her eyes. Everything about her was hard, smooth, star‹ without deception.

"Nobody knows what we know," he said.

She said nothing. Her eyes were still closed.

The sheet had fallen away from her and she was shadowy i‹ the dim light of this room he had rented for them. It did not loc‹

out onto the sky but across a terrible precipice to another building. The blinds were always closed; there was nothing to see. Here he had to see her with his hands, groping anxiously at her body with his hands. He could not believe in her except when they were together like this. She slipped from his mind, slipped out of focus. When they were together in this room she was brought up close to him, as if centered in the telescopic sight of a rifle.

They met like this for the first time in December. That was six weeks after the day they first had seen each other, at La Guardia Airport, and about nine months after the trial had ended out in Milwaukee—a trial Marian knew little about, involving four young men in their twenties indicted for conspiracy to advocate resistance to induction into the United States Army. Of the four young men only one was well known: the folk singer Jacob Appleman, who was sentenced to three years in jail. Two others were given similar sentences. The youngest of the defendants, Robert Severin, who was twenty-three at the time of the trial and also at the time of his death, had been acquitted. No one knew why.

Why was Severin acquitted? people asked. *Why Severin and no one else?*

Quick, weasellike, nervous, with something melancholic in his expression and in the thin mustache he had refused to shave off for the trial; with a habit of raising his hand to his mouth when he spoke, as if he distrusted his own words or was ashamed of them. "I'm not going to shave it off. I'm not going to misrepresent myself. I don't lie," he told his lawyer. He wouldn't remove the mustache and he wouldn't dress properly and he wouldn't meet anyone's eye, a lifelong habit of his, not even the eyes of his codefendants or of his lawyer, whom his father had retained for him. Severin was short, slender, dark, with a boyish frame and a shallow chest. As he sat, he twisted his body in small, uncoordinated movements, without seeming to know what he was doing. During the trial he had squirmed in his seat, his heart accelerating at strange times—especially during long dull periods in which nothing seemed to be happening. Severin feared that something was really happening at these times, but that no one knew. No one could guess. His heart had gradually increased its beat until it was pounding like mad during one forty-five-minute period when an FBI agent, a stranger, talked about the size and colors and the texture of the paper and the type of print involved in a pamphlet written by the defendants and passed out to several thousand young men in Milwaukee at an antiwar meeting. Minutes and minutes passed as words were pronounced carefully by that man, that stranger, a courteous and handsome American in his thirties who spoke without any hatred or emphasis. . . Listening to these simple, incredible words, Severin was afraid he would begin to scream.

But he never screamed so that anyone could hear.

The trial ended on the morning of March 6, after the jury returned its verdict. Severin walked out. He did not say good-by to his lawyer, or to his parents, who had spent the four weeks of the trial at a hotel in Milwaukee, or to the other defendants. He disappeared. He willed himself into disappearing. In his head for many days there had been a vision of himself disappearing, a fading image on a screen, a slow fade-out at the conclusion of a movie.

His mind flashed its thoughts like pictures on a screen, and one of the thoughts was Robert Severin. Always alone. Walking somewhere quickly, alone. Since his boyhood he had imagined himself as a character in a film, a figure pacing across a screen, blown up, enlarged, exaggerated. He could be gigantic sometimes. He knew this even if other people did not. At the age of fifteen he had reached his full growth: five feet seven inches. As if to show that he did not mind being this short, he often stood with his weight balanced on one leg, the other leg bent in differently. He did not walk with his shoulders back, he did not "observe" good posture. This was one of the things that annoyed his lawyer. "It might be better not to slouch in court," his lawyer said gently. His name was Morton Fisher and he was from New York, not Wisconsin, like the other attorneys; but still Severin did not trust him. He was a lawyer Severin's father had insisted upon. At first Severin had been eager to talk to Fisher, to explain his life, but it turned out that Fisher was not really interested in his life. "We have to concentrate on what is relevant to your case," Fisher kept saying. Finally Severin understood, with a shock, that this man did not like him. He was hurt. And then he was bewildered, for why shouldn't this man like him? Why shouldn't everyone like him? He wanted only to do good and to help others to do good. In the end, Severin hardly spoke to Fisher. He sat with his shoulders slumped, in a green-gray tweed suit with a vest, which he had bought especially for this trial. It was much too large for him, ill-cut, a parody of a suit. He had told the salesman in the discount department store that he wanted a baggy, old man's suit, "a joke of a suit," a proper outfit in which he might be tried by his government, which was displeased with him.

"Do you think that's funny, that suit?" his father asked him.

"Everything is funny," Severin said.

"Is that what you believe?"

"No. I believe that nothing is funny," Severin said in the same tone. "But we have to make certain pretenses."

Why was Severin acquitted and no one else? He could hear everyone ask this question. Making his way up the aisle of the courtroom, out where people stood around in the corridor, ducking when someone seemed to be swinging at him—it turned out to be a student waving a placard—his face darkening, heating; yet he had never screamed. Not out loud. He was free, freed. Time to disappear. *Robert Severin disappearing into the sky.*

When he shut his eyes he could see quite precisely a dark shape drawing into itself, withering, retreating into something

that glowed fiercely, like the sun. Then it disappeared. That was
peace, that disappearing, that nullity. He wouldn't even have to
argue or explain himself. He would have no need for words.

It wasn't until several weeks later that the three others received their sentences; Severin read about it in a newspaper. By
then he was in Montreal, where he knew no one. He stared at
the photograph of Appleman—Appleman with his bushy hair
and glum, sardonic expression and his career "just beginning to
catch on," as people said—and Severin heard the voice in his
head cry, *I don't know why Severin was acquitted, I don't know
why Severin was acquitted, I don't know.* With these words he
might have wanted to dissociate himself from Severin.

An incantation: *I don't know why.*

A litany: *I don't know why.*

And he did not know why. He did not understand. His brain
replayed for him those hours of the trial, the testimony of FBI
agents and the testimony of witnesses and the level, reasoned arguing of the defense lawyers, all of whom had the dark-rimmed
glowing eyes of men drowning for a good cause, and the occasional snorts and interruptions of the judge, whose terrible eye
Severin had never quite seen. He knew that he was guilty, ye
he had been found not guilty. He was as guilty as the others
they were as innocent as he. Yet it had not turned out that way

He had tried to explain some of this to Marian Vernon, wh
had seemed to understand. "There was no difference betwee
any of us," he told her. His voice had rattled, accelerating. H
had not talked for many weeks and now he could not stop. Sh
had nodded, yes, yes, she understood or seemed to understan
staring in prim panic into his face, their faces level, like broth
and sister. "That was how I figured out they had me marked f
something special," he told her angrily. "That's why I have
get out of the country. I don't have much time left. I'm going
explode if I don't get out." *Yes, yes,* she had said dumbly, b
she had not really understood. Weeks and months after his dea
she went around saying she didn't understand, she didn't und

stand what he had wanted, why he had done it, why, why had it happened? "Jesus, if I could relive that hour," she said. She and Oberon talked about it all the time, talking about "it" as they embraced, closing their eyes upon a fast shocked image of Robert Severin's face. He was a stranger and yet they were close to him, intimate, knowing. He was always with them. His enlarged face followed them everywhere and excited them almost beyond endurance.

Sometimes she hated Oberon; her love shriveled into something bitter and white-hot and she hated him, she snapped at him, *You don't know what it's like to remember such a thing— did you ever slip on red blood yourself? You don't know what I know!*

And he would take her in his arms to quiet her.

Marian never had time for newspapers, never watched television, picked up important news and catastrophes from other people. Of course she had known nothing about the Milwaukee trial; the name Jacob Appleman was familiar to her, but she had never heard any of his records. She was a young woman of twenty-two, a stewardess with Pan American Airways. She had graduated with a Bachelor of Arts degree from the University of Oklahoma, which qualified her for teaching in the elementary schools of that state, but she had never really planned on teaching. The company of children, other teachers, the confinement of a room and a single building—these things frightened her. She wanted to live.

Her hair was a dark, wavy red, worn to her shoulders. Her face was lightly freckled, very healthy; her posture reflected health and enthusiasm; she had always been a happy child, a happy girl, arguing philosophically to herself that life was a wonderful adventure and that it should be faced with a constant smile. To a magazine reporter who had interviewed her in November she had confided, "That was how I got through that hour without cracking. I told myself that life is a wonderful adventure. I told myself that there is always a good, unexpected side to things, another arrangement we don't know about immediately."

"And did that turn out to be true?" the reporter asked.

She paused. She lowered her eyes, thinking of Oberon. She said finally, "I can't tell you about that."

Oberon had known about the trial, which was always referred to as the "Appleman Case," though three other men had been indicted. Oberon, who was interested in folk music, had followed Appleman's career since his first record, in 1965, and he had been very disappointed at Appleman's political activities—the organization of a series of antiwar demonstrations in Chicago and Milwaukee. In his imagination he had even written Jacob Appleman a letter of warning. "My name is David Oberon and I am a stranger to you, yet believe me when I say that I wish you well. Why are you trying to destroy yourself? Why are you trying to corrupt hundreds of young Americans? Our country is engaged in a certain action in Southeast Asia and it is everyone's duty to support his country. . . ." But he did not dare type the letter. This was in the fall of 1969; Appleman had not been arrested yet, but Oberon knew the government was preparing a case against him. His letter might be confiscated. Even if he sen it anonymously, it might be confiscated and traced back to him

Oberon had followed the case through the newspapers. He knew the names and a little of the facts concerning the othe defendants, so the name Robert Severin was immediately famil iar to him. Severin had been the only person acquitted and peo ple had wondered about that. Oberon himself had not wondered believing the jury had wanted to free someone, just to declare t the FBI and the Department of Justice that they could free defendant who had probably been guilty of committing a crim against the United States government. It was a harmless act. H had heard, anyway, that Severin, the youngest of the four, ha been indicted so that he could be acquitted—the governmen had had no interest in him, really.

He explained this to Marian, who was rosy, sunny, cheerf

by nature, a young American woman with a personality simple as slides shown on a screen, one after another, and yet whose nature changed even as Oberon spoke to her, as if he were teasing her with his words about Severin, his superior knowledge of Severin, drawing her out of herself in a maddening way. "I don't know what you're doing to me," she laughed. "You're making me drunk. I feel drunk. Don't stop talking."

"What else do you want to know?" he asked her.

She hesitated. "What it was like."

"What it was like . . . ?"

"You know. What it felt like. To you. When it happened."

He had fallen helplessly in love with her.

He was fourteen years older than Marian Vernon, a tall, well-built man with brown hair, an amiable anonymous face, with something courteous and predictable in his smile. He was much taller than Robert Severin. If he had had the occasion to stand beside him, he would have towered over him—poor Severin, with his girlish weasellike body, his narrow shoulders! If he had had the occasion to fight with him, he could have picked him up and thrown him down, knocking him senseless. Very deftly and courteously he could have pinned Severin's shoulders to the ground, holding him there safely until he could be arrested.

Oberon sometimes thought of that. He thought, while he lay with Marian, of holding Severin's squirming body down against the pavement. Once he told her about it. "Like this, and like this . . like this . . . I would have held him down . . ." he whispered. They had lain together face to face, solemn, grieving, and then one of them had begun to laugh. Another time he hadn't told her what he was thinking of, but he sensed that she too was thinking of Severin, always of Severin. "I love you, I love *you*," he had sobbed, as if arguing.

Seen up close like this, Marian was a stark, beautiful woman. Drained of superficial energy, the friendly charity of her kind of woman, which Oberon had always detested, she was hollow,

hungry, almost unmanageable. Her love for him obviously frightened her. It was so violent, so intense, he almost sympathized
with her dread of it. *What must a woman feel, to be convulsed
like that, to suffer like that,* he thought. No one knew Marian
Vernon except him. When she appeared in that Pan American
Airways uniform—when she smiled her mechanical little smile
—it was a joke, a horror! Only Oberon knew her.

She brushed her hair back from her damp face, impatiently.
A strand of her hair stung his eye. He tried to listen to what she
was saying: something about his wife. "What does she know? I
saw her that evening. Her. She doesn't know. What do ordinary
people know?"

"She can sense something. . . ."

"No. She can't. She would have to have been there, where I
was. In my place. And she wasn't there, no one else was there
except me. . . . You don't love her. Why do you stay with
her?"

They stared at each other. He was perspiring, agitated, always
he must stare at her in order to locate himself—his love for this
woman, whom he hardly knew, whom he did not really like.
There was something coarse about her boldness with him, her
near-hysteria. She was younger than his wife, more beautiful
than his wife, and he was sick with love for her and yet he did
not want to think about divorce, remarriage, the routine intensity of married life.

"Do you love her?" Marian asked.

"No. It's another emotion."

"Another emotion, yes. It's ordinary. I don't want to hear about
it. Ordinary people, ordinary ugly people . . . I don't want to
hear about them."

As soon as he left her she began to slip out of focus. She began to fade back into that neat smiling little stewardess with the
uniform, the short skirt, and tight-fitting, buttoned little jacket
with the hat perched cockily on her head. It frightened him, that
he might lose her. That he might forget her. And yet he could

not locate in his memory of her the passion he always felt in her presence. A kind of energy dominated them, gave them life; it did not belong to either of them.

Sometimes he went to stare at himself in a mirror, at home or anywhere, in a public rest room, but he saw only his public, unpersonal face, which was like a uniform. It was like Marian's uniform. That face took him anywhere, flown in by helicopter to the airport, with his .308 Norma Magnum rifle. *What did it feel like?* Marian asked him, the first night they were together. *Did it have a kick? I felt the kick myself. I felt it. I felt you.* There was something anonymous and symmetrical about Oberon's face. As a younger man he had been annoyed when people were always coming up to him and calling him by the names of strangers—now it no longer bothered him. He could have grown a mustache, like Severin. But he never did. He thought of himself as belonging to a crowd, a crowd of American men as they might be imagined, or collected for a special photograph: not a real crowd of unruly and ugly people, but an ideal crowd of "average" American men, fairly good-looking, of a certain height, in good health. Therefore he was six feet two inches tall, with short, wavy brown hair, a face that was almost handsome, with a strong clean nose and chin. His brown eyes looked ordinary and unalarming, but they were, in fact, extraordinary. His vision was perfect. He had always been proud of his eyesight. Eyes like muscles, tensing, erect, precise, fixing themselves on that stranger's face, adjusting themselves to the face, getting to know it closely, intimately. . . . The face had been framed by jumbled, spiky hair; it had been partly hidden by sunglasses; its skin was an eerie olive, pale and waxen and yet greasy, sagging with fatigue. The mustache had aged it.

Severin had bought the sunglasses in a drugstore north of Portland, Maine. It had rained all day and yet the sky glowed; it reminded him of the sky in Milwaukee, that soulless glowering that had pressed upon him for so many months. Swollen gray sky and lake, remote, bulbous, inescapable. . . . He wanted to break through to a place where the sun shone. He bought the sun-glasses for $1.98 and they looked like aviators' glasses, with large lenses and wire frames. They were made of some synthetic ma-terial, not glass, a kind of plastic that did not break easily or even crack; they were thrown a dozen yards from his body, and yet they did not break.

Now for the approach: how to approach New York? He had family there, parents. He feared his father and his father's face. It wasn't enough, loving them and then not loving them; somehow they were mixed up with his childhood and the na-tion itself. Awake, unable to sleep, he began having little split-second dreams out on the highway—going crazy, eh, Severin?— and one of his visions was his father stretched out flat, the face stretched out like a big welcome mat, the bumpy hilly terrain of the United States, all someone's face. That could be. Wasn't there a movie about someone crawling across the faces at Mt. Rushmore? Or had Severin imagined that movie? Or was he an insect himself, crawling across the face of his father, not able to put the various parts of the face together into a whole?

His night dreams did not work. Did not function properly. That was because he couldn't sleep any more at night—why bother getting a motel room if he couldn't use the bed?—but even when he had been sleeping normally his dreams had not worked. How do dreams *work*? What is there *function*? "My dreams all dissolve and disappear," he told his lawyer, Mr. Fisher. He had no one else to talk to; by then he had quarreled with Appleman and the others, and their attorneys had quarreled with one another; it was no good. The government had already won. A story in *Look* magazine implied that Appleman was a saint but Severin knew better than that, everyone knew better than that, it was just journalistic crap and yet you couldn't make you way through it: what would turn out to be true, what would turn out to be lies? "Jesus, I can't get myself straight; when I try t think about something it all dissolves. Even my dreams. . .

My dreams just disappear," he tried to explain to Fisher, who had pretended to be interested. "I don't dream like other people, only pieces of dreams like jigsaw puzzles. . . ."

After the verdict, Severin had walked away without saying good-by.

Not just his dreams but his bowels didn't work. Panic. Pain. Pain like fire. Sitting anxiously in the courtroom, fidgeting in his seat, he heard little of the testimony and fixed his gaze upon sterile, empty space, trying not to show the pain he felt. Small rocks seemed to be passing through his intestines. Yet he had never screamed out loud. . . . *And now Severin will eradicate himself,* he thought as he walked out of the courtroom and out of the courthouse. *Severin walking fast, a comic figure. Almost running.* During those four winter weeks his weight had dropped from 145 to 128. His skin had grown so sensitive that he could not bear to be touched, and he could feel people breathing on him, he could feel the subtle but very abrasive touch of breath, air, against his skin. Appleman had a habit of gripping his arm, his elbow, as if to make sure Severin wouldn't get away. He hated Appleman's closeness, hated the feel of his breath. If he could get a table between them, good. He couldn't make sense of Appleman's nervous strategies, and after a while he stopped listening.

Anyway they were all guilty. That was one thing they had agreed upon.

So he sat through the weeks of the trial, sensing how words flowed about him, submerging him, threatening to suffocate him, and yet never quite touching him. How they talked, these adults . . always talking, talking. . . . His lawyer wouldn't let him testify. None of the defendants was going to testify. All right, then, time would pass and nothing would matter, it was really completed; they were guilty and their punishment was beginning now, right now. That was why his bowels were turning to gas, poisonous rotting gas. That was why he couldn't sleep. In court, already a prisoner at the front of the courtroom, he stared at a certain space in the room, not a person or an object but a space, an invisible point in the air, and tried to hypnotize himself into calmness, silence, into nothing. Otherwise he might explode.

Grappling with the stewardess, the redhead, he had felt the danger of his body colliding with hers: a danger for her, not for himself.

"Don't make me kill you," he begged her.

She was his height, as full in the body as he, her face bleached out beneath her make-up.

As soon as the plane left the runway he stood, stood out in the aisle, and took the rolled-up towel out of his coat. She came toward him, a woman perfectly balanced as in a dream, while around her faces turned and chins creased and outside the windows the jumbled landscape of small houses fell backward and down, in silence. "Don't make me explode us all," he begged.

He had found the flare on a highway outside Montreal; he had laughed to see it so innocently left behind—it looked like a stick of dynamite! Walking in the perpetual drizzle, he had picked it up and hidden it in his jacket; you never knew when you might need dynamite, also you never knew when you might need a knife. He had bought a knife in a sporting goods store in a small town somewhere. He couldn't remember where, but probably someone had been watching him and knew. In grade school and high school he had never played with knives—you didn't "play with" knives in his family—but other boys had had knives and Severin had envied them. Now he had his own knife. And a flare that looked like dynamite. Maybe it *was* dynamite. It had a fuse that could be lit. The fuse was damp, but perhaps it could still be lit.

Outside Boston he took a motel room for a night, but he couldn't sleep. A waste of six dollars. He found a newspaper and looked up the weather report: always raining. From Montreal down to New York: rain. He couldn't remember where he was exactly, but it was always raining, a cold steady drizzle, and yet the sky was light. The weather seemed to him very important. He had stopped thinking about everything in his past, and now he thought about the weather instead. There was a weather map of the United States and also a very helpful list of temperatures in cities around the world. He looked through the list several times and discovered that Algiers was missing. Why was it missing? The FBI had reasons for everything.

In Montreal he had been spied on; he knew the feeling and didn't question it. But he had not cared. He walked in the street, up and down the hilly streets, openly. It was a foreign country—Canada—and he was free here. In fact, he was free anywhere. Even in Milwaukee. He sent himself back to Milwaukee, that raw, freezing, ugly city, to the courtroom, to see if Robert Severin was still sitting there; yes, there he was, the size of a boy, pretending to listen while words flooded his head. Yes, he was guilty. Didn't he love his parents? Did he want to destroy his mother? Oh yes. No. Did he want to destroy himself? The first step was dropping out of law school—his father had pointed that out to him. The first step toward self-destruction. And this Appleman, who was Appleman? "Who is this Appleman, that you should follow him blindly?" his father demanded. The irony was that Appleman envied Severin and the others because they had gone to college while he, Appleman, so wealthy and so nervous, had barely manged to graduate from high school; but Severin didn't bother to tell his father that. Was he guilty of certain lies? Of avoiding certain statements? Guilty of a small unmanly body? The young man he had shared an apartment with near Columbia, a twenty-eight-year-old veteran of the Vietnam war and, like Severin, a law student, had flown out to Milwaukee to testify for him. *Very serious, very moral . . . a completely moral person. . . . We had little in common and we weren't friends, no, but I admired Bob for his honesty. . . .* Yet, when the courteous businesslike prosecutor had cross-examined him, he had faltered and said, *Yes, Bob is absolutely honest and he would never commit any crime, I mean any dishonest crime. . . .* Any dishonest crime! Severin himself had to laugh; by then he'd sat through one hundred hours of this crap and he knew what was what. Any dishonest

crime! *It's a strange distinction for a young man entering the law,*
the prosecutor had said gently, with a smile, as if a little embarrassed for the witness, *the division of crimes into honest and dis-*
honest crimes. . . .

Severin had stopped listening.

The jury spent ten hours discussing the case, and when they
came back Severin stood for them, in honor of them, "at attention," in a parody of a young man in a green-gray tweed suit
standing at attention in a courtroom, his face composed for a
smirk and his bowels churning with flame and lava. Bastards!
Bland faces and frank honest souls!

Mr. Foreman, how say you? Is Jacob Appleman, the defendant
at the bar, guilty or not guilty?

Guilty.

Is John Harvey, the defendant at the bar, guilty or not guilty?

Guilty.

Is Russell Kurzon, the defendant at the bar, guilty or not
guilty?

Guilty.

Is Robert Severin, the defendant at the bar, guilty or not
guilty?

Not guilty.

Not guilty.

So he sent himself out of there, on a Greyhound bus up to
Montreal. He was free. He had money. His father was always
giving him money, for good nourishing food and for good hotel
rooms. He tried to sleep on the bus but his skull seemed too
large for his brain. His brain slipped wetly around inside the
bone case, an unpleasant sensation. Were his thoughts dissolving, turning to poisonous intestinal vapors? They kept slipping
slithering, out of his grasp. He had to rely upon flashes of dream
in the daylight; that was where he got his best hunches. He telephoned home just once, collect, from a telephone booth that
looked over and up to McGill University, buildings and ground
and university students so normal and handsome that he wanted

to cry: his nose ran with envy and he could barely pay attention to his conversation with his father. . . . "Bob? Bob? Is that you, Bob? Are you all right, Bob?" his father had shouted across the distance. It was terrible to hear his voice. Severin changed his mind, he didn't want a father again, why hadn't he remembered what it was like? He hung up.

Anyway, the telephone was probably wiretapped.

"It is not necessary for the accused to have done anything," someone was explaining to the jury. It was the judge himself. He was the most adult of all the adults. "In a case like this, the prosecution has only to prove that they *agreed* to do something. The case rests entirely on intent and you must find the defendants guilty or not guilty according to their intent. . . ."

He intended now to blow up the country. He intended to fly up into the sun, to clean himself in the sun, to escape the rain of the East Coast. Why did it rain so often? And on clear days his head ached; he muttered in disgust, *Severin, you're going crazy.* Why else walk around with a fake stick of dynamite in your pocket, a kid's jackknife with three blades in your pocket? Oh it was a joke, like the green suit. People took him too seriously. Adults took him too seriously. Out in Milwaukee—maybe in the whole Midwest or the whole country—people thought the White House might be blown up just because Severin or someone with a mustache like his did not throw his shoulders back and blew his nose at the wrong time into a soiled Kleenex. The sunglasses helped his burning eyes but really they were part of the joke. You couldn't disguise yourself, of course. The FBI had cameras that x-rayed you antiseptically as you walked in the street. You couldn't hide from them; therefore, you joked with them in a mild and cavalier way.

"You don't joke with these people," Fisher had told him angrily, as if speaking to a child. "What do you think this is? A game?"

It turned out that all the defendants, when served with their indictments, had tried to joke nervously with the men who

brought them. Tried to establish a quick jocular rapport with the
low-level FBI men who questioned them, as if that would help.
Wouldn't it help? A quick jocular alliance against the hierarchy,
the Rulers. Wouldn't it help?

"No, you don't talk. You don't cooperate. You don't try to win
their good favor. They are out to get you whether you can believe
it or not. The government is out to get you. . . . Do you think
that's a joke?"

It was so hard to believe, so hard to believe, that anyone
wanted to hurt them, even the government that had dared to
arrest them. The government turned out to be men who looked
like Severin's father and his lawyer: that is, good citizens, well
dressed and polite. Of course, they hated the government and had
accused the government of being fascistic, in their speeches, even
in their televised speeches, but somehow it was hard to believe
that these men, the FBI agents and their attorneys and the prosecutor, really wanted to hurt them. . . . Like most Americans
Severin believed he could make anyone like him if he tried. He
had never been popular, in high school or college, but he had
always cherished the belief that he could be popular if he worked
at it.

The stewardess had smiled at him, her lipsticked lips baring
her teeth in a slow numbed grimace, the two of them staring at
each other levelly, the same height. He had felt like a brother
to her. She was one of those pretty, sisterly girls so popular in
high school, grinning hello to everyone in the halls, absolutely
confident and shadowless. "I don't want to kill you," he had
whispered. "Take me up front. Let me explain myself to the
pilot. Let me explain and you can see how clear everything
will be."

"Yes, I'll take you. Don't be upset," she said.

"I'm not upset. I'm not going to hurt you, or anyone, unless
I have to. I'm very calm," Severin said.

Severin gripped her close. The pilot had a title: Captain. He was a man who resembled one of the other defense lawyers. Severin saw at once that this man was intelligent and would play no tricks on him: were the lives of fifty passengers worth any risk? No. It was logical. You read about it in the newspapers all the time. Yet something in the back of Severin's head told him, *What a joke this is, now, what a laugh! Are you really on this plane? Or still back in Montreal, dreaming a daylight dream?* "My destination is Algeria," Severin stated. "I am defecting. I am demanding diplomatic immunity."

But on the turnpike leaving Boston, he had walked slowly along for several hours before someone stopped. It was an FBI agent in an ordinary car. He joked with the man knowingly, delicately. That was the charm of it: you walked a kind of fence with them, teasing them. This man claimed to be a publisher's representative. Severin laughed and said, "Which publishers? Name one."

The man did give a familiar name. "I'm in the college department. Textbooks. Are you a college student?"

"Ha ha," Severin said. "Are you offering me a scholarship if I turn over all the evidence? I wouldn't mind going back to law school."

"I don't understand," the man said slowly.

"No, never mind. It's just a joke. I'm on my way out of the country, I'm just going to say good-by to my family."

"Where does your family live?"

Severin glanced at the man, sizing him up. A big man, like all of them. If it came to a fight, he'd have to use his elbows and feet to paralyze the bastard. He wouldn't want to use the knife; then it would be murder. Still, it would probably not come to a fight. They rarely touched you. Why should they?

"New York," Severin said. He felt helpless, telling the truth like this; but when they already knew the truth you had no choice but to say it.

He put on his sunglasses carefully, hooking them behind his ears. The earpieces were made of wire and quite pliable. When Marian Vernon looked into his face for the first time—welcoming him frankly on board the plane—she did not see him. She did not remember seeing him. But after the take-off, when he stumbled to his feet and opened his oversized coat, she looked at him again and this time she saw him.

Out of his baggy green suit coat he drew a white towel, rolled up, and he unrolled it to show her a stick of dynamite. Mutely he raised it to her, his eyebrows arching. They walked together to the front of the plane. She felt his breath on the back of her neck, so close.

"I don't like violence. I don't like blood. I don't like knives and this is the first knife I ever bought," he told her earnestly. She glanced back to see that he had a knife in his hand. She went cold. *I went cold. The dynamite I couldn't believe in, it was so . . . so extreme. . . . But the knife was just the right size. . . . But he was very polite, very nice to me. . . . No. I wasn't afraid. I went cold, I was numb and like a robot, but I wasn't afraid. I would have been afraid to do what Mr. Oberon did. . . . that really took courage . . .*

"You don't resent the FBI risking your life, then?" they asked her.

"Oh, no. No. I don't consider it that, that they risked my life. I mean, it was their job. It was Mr. Oberon's job. He was given orders. It was all done very carefully. I had faith in them. I prayed and I had faith in them. I wasn't afraid."

"How close did he stay to you?"

"Oh, very close. He held me from behind, my arm. His fingers were very tight around my arm, my upper arm, and he kept asking me if he was hurting me; he was very polite and didn' talk loud, he was sort of short, no taller than I was, and all along I could feel the knife in my back, like a fingernail, a man's finger nail. . . . He wanted to go to Algeria, he said. Something abou the sun. He was tired of rain. The Captain told him, of course this plane was headed for Cleveland and it wasn't a transatlantic plane and if he wanted that he would have to wait. . . ."

"And did he believe that?"

"Oh, yes, he believed that at once. He was very polite and apologetic about hurting me."

Why are you working with planes? Severin asked her. *This is no job for a woman. Planes explode in the sky all the time, disintegrate in the sky.* . . . She seemed to be listening to him intently. She nodded. He could see a droplet of perspiration on her forehead. She was a pretty young woman, like a sister, so pretty, so eager to please him, docile and not argumentative, as he had feared she might be. . . . *The sky is for men, it's dangerous. After this you should stay on the ground. Are you listening?*

Oh yes I'm listening, yes I'm listening. . . .

The other passengers had filed out. Severin stood with her just inside the door, at the top of the ramp, squinting out into the drizzle. Someone was speaking to him through a loudspeaker. But the loudspeaker did not work very well. "Where is that plane? That big plane? I'm waiting for it," he yelled out into the rain. He held the stewardess back against him, an embrace and yet not an embrace; it was an impersonal embrace. Minutes passed. He had the idea that an hour had passed and could not be retrieved. He saw a large jetliner being moved toward him, far away in the rain, and then he wondered if he had seen correctly. Would they give him a pilot and a crew? All that expense, just for him?

"You might like Algeria yourself," he told the girl. "There, you could stay on the ground and forget about all this crap, this fooling around. You could stay there with me."

"You won't hurt me?"

"I don't want to hurt you."

"When will you let me go?"

"In Algeria."

They were calling to him: the plane is ready, the crew is ready. He saw the plane but it was some distance away.

"Closer, bring it closer! Don't you hear me?" he yelled.

The little knife, with one blade stuck out, pressed against the girl's back. Against the uniform. His face was hot from being so close to her hair. He breathed in and out, against the back of her neck. Her ear. He said, "I don't want to hurt you or kill you, I'm not in favor of violence or blood. . . . Tell them to bring that plane closer."

She cupped her hands to her mouth and tried to call to them, but she could not speak. He heard a sob from her. *I thought I would break down then, and that he would kill me, just slide the knife in me because he was disgusted.* . . . She sobbed, her shoulders shook; he relented and said, "All right, forget it, let's go. Let's go."

Stiffly he walked her down the ramp. She nearly slipped and he held her steady, his fingers tightening around her arm. She cried out with the surprise of it, the pain. He knew that people were watching him, from inside the hangars and from behind the steel fences; perhaps a camera crew was filming this. He imagined himself on film, on a television screen. An image of Robert Severin walking across a screen jerkily, streaks of rain on the camera lens. It would be so realistic. He could see his own figure, holding the stewardess tight against the front of him, walking her down the ramp carefully, stiffly, Robert Severin in his dirty, baggy suit wearing his aviator's sunglasses as if he were prepared for the sun of Algeria, his hair bunched and spiky from not having been washed for a month. *Robert Severin centered on a screen. Robert Severin centered in a telescopic sight.*

At the bottom of the ramp the girl slipped and stumbled two steps down, to the pavement. She turned as if to apologize to him and at that moment there was a shot. Severin jerked backward against the steps, away from her. Then another shot. His face exploded: she was looking up into his face when it exploded. It was as if something had been thrown against his face, an object stuffed with blood, and now the blood had burst out and was pouring from him. Did she hear him scream? Any sound at all? She caught the fullness of his weight as he fell, his body gone heavy, the blood gushing from him and onto her. She fell, she tried to get to her feet, screaming, but she slipped in his blood, she slipped to her knees and then pushed herself up, frantic to get away, to get away. . . .

I thought I was shot myself. I thought we were both shot.
Does this alter your plans?—your plans for a career?
Oh no. No.
You'll have something to tell your grandchildren, won't you?
Oh yes.
What do you think of the FBI man who did the shooting?

She studied the photographs in that evening's newspaper: a picture of herself, two microphones extended toward her, her face looking good enough, even her hair good enough; and a picture of the man at the steel wall, aiming his rifle. She stared. He had such dark hair, he held the gun so firmly, so certainly. . . . Other men stood below him, watching. They seemed such ordinary men. They watched him and he leaned over the wall, his back to them, aiming the rifle and peering through the scope, staring at her and Severin through the scope. . . . And yet neither she nor Severin had known about the rifle! She marveled at this, tracing with her forefinger her own face and then the outline of the FBI man's body and the rifle, aimed out of the picture, at that face of hers. Past her face. Over her shoulder and into Severin's face.

It was so confusing, so hard to think about. . . .

Powerfully, she felt the blow again: Severin slammed back from her, against the steps of the ramp. She had slipped on the wet steps. And then the shot, then the second shot. How she loved him! "Tell me what you felt," she said.

"I had the idea that the two of you could see me. Right back through the scope," he said.

"Did you? Did it seem as though I was watching you? What did I look like?"

"Very beautiful," he said.

"Was I beautiful? Was I? Even in the rain, even after that hour with him? Was I beautiful to you?"

"Yes, you were beautiful. . . . For fifteen minutes I was watching you, you and him. You. I had never seen a face like yours. . . ."

"Were you afraid?"

"No. I took my time. I knew how it would turn out. I had only to wait for the right moment in order to make it turn out that way. As soon as they flew me in, as soon as I got propped up on that wall, he was a dead man. But it took a while to kill him."

"Did you ever kill anyone before?"

"Never an American."

With his deer rifle he had shot the young man with the sunglasses, the first shot catching him squarely in the chest, the second shot squarely in the face. Excellent shots. For ten, fifteen minutes he had watched through the sight, hardly breathing, waiting patiently. He had been given his orders. Ah, that girl! That white, gasping face of hers!

The boy had bounced back. Blood had sprung out of his face like an exclamation.

One day Oberon sought her out, rang the doorbell to her apartment. He introduced himself. He heard her breathing inside the door, a few inches away. Silence. "You know who I am," he said. He was very excited; there was even an odor about him of intense excitement. The girl stood inside her door, which was latched with a safety lock, a chain, and he brought his smiling face to the crack in the door so that he could look at her. She was staring up at him.

"You know why I'm here," he said.

The Metamorphosis

Matthew woke suddenly from a daydream that was not his.

He shook himself awake, startled. He dislodged the dream from himself, out of his head. No one had noticed; the place was gleaming and empty, only the three new automobiles out on the floor, brilliant and massive and unseeing, all curves and sleek precise lines; no one else was around. Peter, one of the younger salesmen, was just coming through the door at the far end of the showroom, looking nervous, perplexed. . . .

Matthew hoped that Peter would not stop at his cubicle to talk with him.

He had stirred himself from a dream that was not his. It could not have belonged to him. He had never had such a dream before, he would not acknowledge it. Not his. He never daydreamed, he never let his thoughts wander. The dream had been someone else's, not his own. The tag end of a stranger's dream. . . . It was possible; you could be infected by the fears of strangers.

He looked through the calendar on his desk; he must make himself concentrate on something real. What was the date? His birthday was approaching—he would be forty-six in two weeks. He felt much younger. He looked much younger, a man of broad, vigorous shoulders, thighs thick and still muscular, like the trunks of small trees. That hard grainy muscularity. He was proud of his body and of his face—he had an intelligent, kindly face, marred only by the deep lines made by smiles. Years of smiling. His hair was brown, streaked with red; there was something exclamatory in the way he frequently raised his eyebrows.

He had been selling cars for twenty years here at Overmeyer Ford.

. . . On the gleaming fake-brick floor, a man of obvious energy. Excellent clothes, shoes, his hair kept carefully trimmed. He knew everything. He could answer any question about any car manufactured by Ford. He could answer the questions of the most methodical, suspicious customer. Everyone knew him, Matthew Brown; he had sold thousands of cars, old customers kept coming back to him, making appointments specifically with him . . . he knew everyone's name, he shook hands easily and yet without presumption; there was a sacred space around all men, a few feet of air, and he knew enough not to blunder into it. Though he was almost forty-six he could judge by the look in women's eyes his own youthful appearance, that blond, broad, generous Irish face, the good looks he had had for decades without especially prizing them. He was proud of his work, not of himself. Proud of his family. Not himself; his family. He was devoted to his wife and five children.

He did not think about the strange dream he had had, sitting here awake. He was a man who did not believe in dreams.

Yes, it said here on his calendar that someone was supposed to

have come to see him at three o'clock. He would wait. No reason
for uneasiness. Customers were often late. This month had been
a slow month . . . interest rates had risen again . . . there
were rumors of another dealer going bankrupt . . . but it did no
good to think of any of these things. He would sit in his cubicle
and wait quietly. He wondered if Peter had lost his customer—
that woman with the bone-white hair, bleached and sullen, who
had talked so loudly. It might be a good idea to stop by Peter's
cubicle on the way out, say something kind to him, it was the
least he could do. He felt sorry for Peter, who had not made any
sales yet this month. . . . Waiting, he looked idly at the tiny
crack on his desk top. It seemed that his daydream had sprung
somehow out of that crack. It was an irritant, the crack. Faint and
thin and curving as a hair. He often tried to brush it away while
talking with customers. His voice could move on, rapidly, knowing the answers to all questions, heading off questions before
they were asked, gauging by the customers' faces how well he
was doing. He usually did well. Very well. He could work swiftly
with numbers, adding up long columns, subtracting, figuring out
discounts, a routine performance of his that impressed customers.
If the trade-in is $1200, then. . . . Minus this. Minus. Plus.

Months in a long wavering column, adding up to decades.
Father came home early, about four-thirty, on that day. . . .
"Do you want some coffee, Matt? I'm going over now," Gardie
said. She wore a navy blue dress, trim as a uniform. Gardie. Hil-
degarde. He must have said yes because in a few minutes she
appeared again with coffee for him. He accepted the paper cup,
touched. Women had always liked him, had always been concerned about him. She leaned against the partition, her dress
stark and neutral against the frosted glass. Five or six years now
of Gardie's cheerful sagging face. Cheerful conversation, the
words slightly sagging as the years passed. A troubled marriage—
Matthew knew only a little, didn't want to know more. In spite
of his tall, broad, leggy personality he didn't want to know much
about people, resisted their hints of private, personal, grieved

lives, didn't want to get snagged by them. He carried himself cautiously through crowds.

He had five children of his own and thought about them constantly.

One of us saw his car coming up the boulevard, the big black Lincoln he drove in 1970. That was Ronnie, delivering papers. Then Len saw the car parked in front of the garage. Why wasn't it inside the garage the way Father always wanted it? He didn't want oil stains on the concrete . . . he had poured the concrete himself for the new driveway. But now the car was parked outside and might drip oil onto the concrete.

He drank the coffee slowly, grateful for its warmth. A bad habit, all this coffee. It was almost four o'clock. Someone named Mr. Yates had called Gardie yesterday to make this appointment with Matthew, but he had never heard of the man before; no Mr. Yates in his file of old customers. Should he have known him?

He would not think of Yates. Customers often came late, or showed up the next day. He would not think of the daydream that had disturbed him. Instead, he concentrated on the crack in his desk. The top was plastic, an unclean light yellow. Almost white. The crack was a stream, a river . . . a faint lifeline he must follow . . . a stubborn little artery. The daydream had come from this line, somehow. It had not been about automobiles. The automobiles, those magnificent new models, were right out there on the floor, a few yards away from him, and he had only to glance up to see how massive and patient they were. He did not dream about them. Never about them. He did not dream about selling cars, about breaking his own record, made three years ago. Not about his wife Florence. Not about his sons, his daughters. . . . This strange dream had been about sleep. A dream about sleep. There had been a body, a kind of mummy lying very still beneath heavy covers. Sheets pulled up to the chin. A faceless face. Formless bulges, ridges. A mystery. The figure had appeared in his mind's eye and had held itself there for some minutes, frightening him.

But it was not his dream. It must have belonged to someone else.

One of us, Vicky, heard Mother's voice upstairs. "Matt? What do you mean? Why is the door locked?" Vicky backed away from that sound in her mother's voice. She felt a sharp terrified thrill in the pit of her stomach; why was Father home, up in the bedroom, at four-thirty on a Tuesday afternoon?

She noticed a crack on the living-room ceiling. Had she ever seen that crack before?

Someone was infecting him with bad dreams, Matthew thought. He could hear Peter talking on the telephone—making a show of sounding efficient, talking too fast. Peter should know that customers did not trust salesmen who talked too fast. Peter was several years younger than Matthew, but he had stomach troubles, he probably had bad dreams. His commissions dissolved; too anxious to knock down prices. But Matthew had never talked with Peter about these tactics. Better not to talk. In the long run. . . . In the long run, he thought vaguely, the best salesman does best.

A rattle of voices. Mother washing dishes as if nothing was wrong, Vicky drying. Tommy fooling around. "Is Daddy sick? Why is the door locked?" Mother using the pink sponge, which was worn out. It looked eroded. Tommy pulled his lips away from his gums, making a face. He was five years old. Vicky stood with her back to him, her shoulders thin and tense. She kept listening for Father's footsteps upstairs. First the creaking of the bedsprings, then the heavy footsteps. Mother set dishes in the drying rack, her fingers slippery with soap. "Why didn't Daddy have supper with us? Is he sick?" Tommy whined.

He followed the crack with his eyes, then with his forefinger. Strange. It was a small river leading him up, back . . . up into what, back into what? The dream had come out of that small river. But he did not want to remember it. He did not want to see that figure in bed, hardly a human figure, lying so stiffly in bed, aged and silent. Where the hell was this Mr. Yates?

The telephone rang.

Gardie answered it and he knew before she buzzed him that it would be for him. He picked up the receiver: "This is Matthew Brown." He began talking at once. No trouble. Quoting prices: the advertisement in the Sunday paper. Yes. Subtract two hundred dollars. Three years to pay. His words rattled on with a false, bright energy of their own, while he stared at the little crack on his desk top. He had a sensation of falling and only the telephone conversation kept him upright.

He hung up. Gardie hurried over.

"That guy who just called," she said in a whisper, "he was Peter's customer a few years ago . . . oh, when was it? . . . caused all that trouble, do you remember? Something about the turn lights not working right. . . ."

He remembered exactly, every detail. No, he did not remember.

In the middle of their conversation—such a normal, conspiratorial conversation, of the kind they had every day!—he got to his feet. Not well. Sick. Must go home. Gardie's face immediately crinkling and maternal. "I have to go home. I'm not well," he said suddenly.

"Not well?" she said, shocked.

"Not well? You're not well?" Mother was saying outside the bedroom door. "Why can't you answer me?" Vicky next to her. Another one of us—Sally—was by the bathroom door, pretending to be swinging on it. Wanting attention. She had hold of the doorknob and stood with her knees on either side of the door, trying clumsily to swing on it. If Mother noticed, she would be scolded. Why were Mother and Vicky standing there like that, so strange, by the bedroom door? Mother and Vicky: the same height. Vicky was thirteen then. Her hair was cut very short, almost as short as a boy's. A deeper brown than Father's. She had Father's nose, wide at the bridge, making her eyes look clear and wise because they were spaced far apart. Vicky's wise monkeyish look. Mother, with her hair in a tangle, rapped on the door to her

own bedroom. A strange, formal gesture. "Why is the door locked? Why is the door locked?" she cried.

He left the agency and drove home. His car responded at once —the powerful motor made hardly any sound. So much strength, yet nearly silent. These machines were miraculous. No one could invent them if their secret were lost. The car leaped forward, hurtled itself forward. . . . Carrying him home. Safe. Back up that winding little river, safely back to something, into something, into darkness. His heart beat calmly in his chest. When he got home he would go upstairs at once and into the bedroom and lock the door. Better to lie down and rest. A short nap before dinner. He hoped that his wife would not be in the house.

Turning onto Claremont Boulevard he felt that he was losing strength, that it was somehow flowing out of his legs and into the engine of his car. Must get home, to bed. A sense of despair in his stomach—the very pit of his stomach—everything was settling down darkly, heavily. He must get home. Get to bed. He was dangerous, out here on the street, driving this large vehicle. Its mass hurtled itself across the pavement without much warning sound, a terrible danger to other people in spite of its beauty. What if he crashed into someone?—he did not even own this car—his legs had grown very weak—what if he crashed this car into one driven by an old customer of his, a car he himself had sold?

Other cars on the boulevard appeared to be winking and grimacing at him. Happy grillwork in front of the cars. The slope of the bumper: a happy look. Chrome, tinted windshield, whitewall tires that seemed to be winking, gesturing. . . .

His house was at the far end of the block. Two colonials had been built at the same time, identical except that one had dark orange brick and the other had pale buff brick. The dark orange brick home was his. His lawn had a clump of three birch trees, not doing well, and his neighbor's lawn had a single red-leafed tree, not doing well. Though he was nearly home, he felt very weak.

Maybe he should park in front of the house, not risk turning up the drive. His wrists and knees were especially weak. But he turned up the driveway and parked just in front of the garage, not daring to drive in because he feared brushing the side of the doorway. He turned off the ignition. Left the keys inside. Went into the house, through the back hall, upstairs, before anyone saw him. Florence called out, "Matt? . . ."

He closed the bedroom door behind him and locked it.

"What is happening to me?" he thought.

We sat around the kitchen table while Mother and Vicky were upstairs. The air was all jumbled. What was happening? Tommy was sniveling. Ronnie sat with his elbows on the table and his hands pressed against his forehead, imitating Father: the way Father sometimes sat at the table, by himself, in the evening. "What are they talking about up there? Where is Daddy?" Sally kept saying.

His hands were shaking. He tore off his suit coat and threw it onto a chair. Must get these hot, heavy clothes off. They were suffocating him. Unbuttoned his shirt, took off his necktie. Everything was damp. Smelled. There was a sour, panicked smell about him. Must get his clothes off. Must get naked. Already Florence was hurrying up the stairs. "Matt? Is that you? Is something wrong?"

Already it was beginning.

He slid in bed, trembling. Pulled the covers up to his chin. Every part of his body trembled. Lying flat, he could feel the panic spread everywhere inside him, like a pool of mercury. That sharp acrid taste. But he would force himself to think calmly, logically. He would relax, take a nap. A nap would restore his strength. Yes, a nap before supper, and then he would be feeling as good as ever . . . if only Florence would let him alone. . . . But she was right outside the door now, calling out in that surprised, slightly annoyed voice she used on the children. "Are you in there? Is the door locked? What on earth is wrong?"

He got a grip on his teeth, his jaws locked firmly together.

Good. He would relax every part of his body and sleep. It would do no good to reply to his wife because he would only be lying down here for a few minutes. The sensation of panic would pass. It was a foreign sensation, not his own. He did not recognize it. . . . What was that noise? A telephone ringing. Someone was running—one of the children—there was always someone running in this house. The boys wrestled one another, elbowed one another on the stairs and at meals. He closed his eyes and saw his oldest son's face. He loved Len more than any of the other children because he was the first child. Never another child, another miraculous birth, like that. But Vicky, sweet and waifish, he loved Vicky very much, he must explain to her that he loved her. . . .

Florence was saying: "Matt, it's Gardie. She wants to know if you're all right. Matt? Matt? Did you get sick at work?"

He must have slept. He saw now that the room was darker. It was not a very large room, but he had always liked it. Florence complained that the walls and ceiling should be painted. Everything was very still. The curtains caught his eye, pale green fishnet curtains. Dime-store curtains. His wife had always been clever at sewing, fixing up cheap things, searching for bargains. The curtains and the bureau and the rocking chair were very familiar, in the proper scale. He thought that perhaps he himself was out of proportion. He felt smaller. His legs seemed shorter. The covers on his chest formed a shallow ridge and he could not look past it. His mouth tasted sour from the spread of panic. What was that smell in the air? He had carried it up here with him, to bed—the odor of gasoline, exhaust fumes, the close smooth stench of oil. The rainbow stench of oil. He peered along his chest but could not see to the foot of the bed. His gaze skimmed the bottom of his eyebrows and came away tangled and befuddled. The fishnet material of the curtains was confused with the tangle of his eyebrows and the bumpy ridge of his chest.

Len with the screwdriver. Mother's angry tears. "Why doesn't he answer us?" Something harsh and soiled about her face. When

we used to see her out on the street, shopping, the oldest of us
would flinch a little from the sight of our mother—her breeziness,
the rapid skittish walk of hers—as if she were free, a woman
and not a mother, just a person out on her own—and we would
call out to her, to bring her to a halt. The oldest of us—Len and
Vicky and Ronnie—were embarrassed because she was so pretty.
But that day she wasn't a pretty woman, not a woman at all but
something frightened, smelling of fear. "He won't answer me!
He must be sick!" Mother kept saying.

Len stood with his cheek pressed against the locked door. Silence inside. "Father, this is Len. Father? I'm going to take the
lock off the door. . . . Father? Can you hear me?"

In bed he was thinking seriously about getting up. Like com-
mandments, certain phrases were going through his head: *front*
wheel drive, liquid suspension but no springs or shock absorbers,
a fully synchronized transmission, a luxurious all-vinyl interior,
nylon carpeting wall-to-wall, eight cylinders. . . . These words
were like summonses from another world. They were like shouts
from a cliff down to him as he lay here so peacefully in bed,
preparing his strength. . . . What was that about a lock on a
door? What did that mean?

Someone was rapping on wood and he thought of Mr. Yates,
the customer who had never shown up. Maybe he was knocking
now on a door, trying to get to see Matthew. Well, let him knock.
Matthew had survived many disappointments and now he felt
himself stronger, almost independent of his customers; he would
not even glance up to see who was knocking. So many disappointments! But they belonged to the past, to another Matthew,
and he felt that he had grown beyond them.

"No, don't open it! He doesn't want us to open it!" Vicky cried
suddenly. The screwdriver fell to the floor—she knocked it out
of Len's hand.

The problem: he had to think through his plans for the evening. He had to think through all the moves he would make.
"Getting up"—a generalized expression that took in a complex

an almost hopelessly complex, sequence of particularized movements, some of them muscular and some of them entirely cere-
bral. Just thinking about this made him exhausted. It was nearly
more than the human brain could assimilate. And, behind all
this, behind the demand placed upon him by the command "Get
up," was the mysterious rapping, the jumble of voices, which
seemed to be shouting individual and uncoordinated command-
ments to him. The need for "getting up" was one he could recognize clearly, privately, as originating inside himself, but these
other voices with their curious demands—they were obviously
the voices of other people, actual existing human beings who
could not even agree with one another.

. . . The world was busy and it wanted nothing so much as to
drag him out into it, sweep him along the river where he would
be lost, in all that shouting, that busyness. . . . What a kindness, if someone should think of bringing him a cup of coffee!
But no one thought of it and he was too tired to get it himself.

Instead, the voices of arguing people.

*Mother hurrying downstairs. She embraced Tommy and Sally,
who were crying. "Daddy is sick, just a bad cold. Yes. He said so.
I'm going to call the doctor." Ronnie backed away from her,
bumped into a table. His face stern, rigid, small droplets of perspiration on his forehead. He wore a T-shirt and soiled khaki
pants and sneakers. Looking down at himself, he saw that he
was dressed like a kid and he was ashamed.*

*Mother was wearing old slacks and a white blouse we thought
was too sheer—you could see straps at her shoulders—we hated
that.*

*She called the doctor and Ronnie ran out to the back fence,
where everything was weedy. He pressed against the fence.*

In the corner of the room, his wife's sewing machine. Photographs on the wall—the children when they were very young—
Florence and himself—posed for Christmas cards a few years
ago. How fast the children grew! A miracle. He loved them tenderly, fiercely . . . he could feel a warm, blinding haze of love

for them in his own body, located in his chest . . . or in the base of his skull? . . . He thought of Len. A healthy, husky boy. Vicky: that cap of dark close-cropped hair, her thin arms and legs, her thin face. Len was handsomer. Golden-tanned, curly hair lighter than his father's, energetic arms and legs, a sudden smile that could break his father's heart. When he confessed to stealing a bicycle from school, years before, Matthew had been the one to break down. Unashamed to cry before his oldest son. The two of them in the basement of the house, talking quietly, a father and his son. Matthew was unashamed to cry. Unashamed.

If he cried now the tears would run down sideways, comically on his cheeks. No need to cry. Florence did not cry. . . . One day he stood in the doorway of the bedroom, watching her at the sewing machine, the rapid tonguelike flicking of the needle, her skillful hands guiding the cloth, the rattling noise, the vibrations he could feel beneath his feet, the look of danger, of relentlessness about her bent head and narrowed, skillful eyes. . . . She had been unaware of him.

Dr. Crane was talking to him suddenly. The door stood open. Florence in the doorway, a blur. Where were the children? Dr. Crane was talking to him, asking him something, and he felt his parched lips cracking into a smile. Must smile. Must communicate. Dr. Crane was wrapping something about his upper arm, tighter and tighter. The pressure was enormous. Matthew tried not to notice it. He must not seem too sensitive. What should he say to Dr. Crane? It was important to communicate. Communication was the first step in sales, in civilization itself. Nothing happened between people unless there was communication first. You could have a miraculous product but it would not sell itself. It would sit there, inert. The three enormous cars in the showroom—the sedan, the convertible, the station wagon—would remain there forever, unsold, unacknowledged, until they were explained to the customer. All their energy, their godliness inert for centuries! Unless they were explained, translated, sold. The product and the customer had to be brought together by a hand shake and certain words, which were magical and very powerful. Each word was extremely important. . . . Last winter, when things had gone so slowly, the salesmen were advised to telephone old customers: "Hello. This is ——— ——— of Overmeyer Ford. I was wondering how you are. . . ." No: "I was wondering if you might happen to be in the market for a new car this winter." No, too direct. "Hello, this is ——— ——— of Overmeyer Ford. I hope I'm not disturbing you? I was wondering. . . ." But no, it was a poor idea to apologize and to suggest that the telephone call might be a disturbance. Poor psychology. Begin again: "Hello. This is ——— ——— of Overmeyer Ford. Maybe you remember, in 19— you bought a car from me, and I was just wondering if. . . ."

Something was decided at the bedside, Dr. Crane and his wife conferring, and he felt suddenly very relieved. He would not have to explain himself tonight, then. Evidently they had decided to let him alone. He would rest. Sleep. In the morning everything would be back to normal and perhaps when he got to the agency he would come across Mr. Yates himself, that mischievous mysterious Mr. Yates!

Eleven o'clock already. One of us turned on the news. We had forgotten about the whole evening, suddenly it was eleven o'clock. Mother heated up some chicken gumbo soup from cans. Tommy looked feverish but wouldn't go to bed. Mother's face pale and lined. We will all go to bed at once, we said. All fall asleep at once. Make a vow: we will all fall asleep at the same minute.

In the morning, a peculiar stillness to the house. A foreign stillness. He woke from troubled dreams, dreams that did not belong to him. They must have been someone else's dreams, infecting him. Diseases were spread by germs, and bad dreams could be spread by germs. Why did he dream about flesh that was rosy turning to lard? About handshakes falling away to nothing, a hand coming loose in his own grip? He refused to think about these dreams. Maybe they belonged to Peter. Or Gardie. Maybe they belonged to Florence herself. They lay together at night, every night, side by side in the same bed, and between them there was an enormous distance of inches. . . . They never spoke of this distance. They would have had to shout across it. He would have had to telephone her from the agency, an impersonal voice: "Hello. Mrs. Brown? This is ———— ———— of Overmeyer Ford. I came across your name in my files and I was wondering if. . . ."

Maybe he was dreaming his wife's dreams?

But they were such ugly dreams! Himself in bed. Matthew Brown himself, still and cold in bed, wrapped up in blankets like a mummy. Ugh! How could she dream such dreams about her husband? His face flabby and old, the color drained out of it, wormy, grainy, pale, aged, no longer a handsome man, his hair plastered close to his skull. . . .

Len said to Vicky and Ronnie: "One of us better stay home today, it better be me." Ronnie agreed at once. He wanted to get out of the house. All A's at school. Father was very proud of him, but we all knew that he loved Len best. Vicky said, "I feel sick but I want to go to school. . . . I'm afraid to stay home here. . . ." "You're crazy!" Len said, reddening.

. . . Or maybe the dreams were Mr. Overmeyer's? He was a plump, big-voiced man of about five feet eight, fat grown on the outside of his body from too much drinking, alcoholic flab, soft wrinkles in the face and neck that seemed to gesticulate like Mr. Overmeyer's hands. Matthew was his best salesman. Mr. Overmeyer liked him best because Matthew did not ask for any favors. And he sold the most cars: a fact. Statistical fact. But sales were down, the economy was crazily inflated, who could pay such interest rates? . . . In the past no one noticed the interest rates, but now they did. The younger customers, college educated, scanning the figures Matthew gave them, their young foreheads wrinkling as they saw what the car would really cost. . . . "Jesus Christ," one of them whispered the other day. . . . Mr.

Overmeyer lived out in Hanley Park, along the river. He had three daughters, all taller than himself.

Mr. Overmeyer came out on Saturday, four days after Father had gotten sick. Stood eye to eye with Len and shook hands gravely. "You've got to be the man of the house, until your father gets well."

"Exhaustion," someone was saying to him. "Sick leave." "Busy period." "Too much strain." It sounded like Mr. Overmeyer. But why would he be here, at Matthew's bedside? Was Florence pushing the two of them together, urging Mr. Overmeyer to get closer, to get in bed with Matthew? A crowded bed! Matthew had a sudden idea: he would telephone customers from this bed. Very simple. Gardie could bring his files over, he could prop himself up with pillows, and use the telephone. An excellent idea. He would suggest it to Mr. Overmeyer, as soon as Mr. Overmeyer stopped talking and stopped moving his hands. Why did that man always move his hands!—it marked him as common. Matthew's mother had always noted gestures that marked people as *common*, even if they had money. As soon as Mr. Overmeyer stopped talking Matthew would tell him about his plan: telephoning from bed. That way he would still be at work. It would be quite an experiment, to see how many cars he could sell like that, over the telephone. Maybe it would be written up in the *Ford Times*.

The mess in the bed. The smell. Vicky imagining she carried it with her to school. Mother had to go to a medical supply store and buy a bedpan. The youngest of us were kept out of the sick-room. We hung around downstairs and watched cartoons on television all day long. Loud enough to hear all over the house. At school, Vicky thought of that pasty face, the strange dark pockets of his eyes, the flabby lips, the raspy breathing, the bedpan emptied in the bathroom, the whispering, Mother's vague hands and eyes, the television set and the endless cartoons, the smell that was in her own clothes and wouldn't come out . . .

she had to excuse herself and run to the rest room, where she was sick to her stomach for the second time that day.

Ronnie hated collection day. By now many people knew about Father: stray sly little questions, holding the money in their hands so that Ronnie couldn't escape, always asking if "things were any better at his house? . . ."

The hell with them all, Ronnie thought.

The hell with his sister Vicky puking in the bathroom.

The hell with the little kids, always giggling or bursting into tears.

The hell with Len, bossing everyone around.

The hell with Mother.

The hell with Father: let him stink.

His mother came to see him, that noble ravaged face, that harsh gray hair. She must have had some news to tell him. But he could not make sense of her words. Why didn't Florence come closer, why didn't Florence make his mother speak up? He could not make sense of her words, no. All his life he had been hearing them: *Matthew! I own you! My son!* But now they eluded him. She was only inches away. She might have come here to remind him that he was not just a father but also a son, he had been a son for forty-six years and could not escape that fact, hiding in his smelly cocoon. No. But he could not hear her. He wanted to weep: why was she leaning so close?

Mother, Len, and Vicky fed him. The doctor showed them how. The rest of us were kept downstairs. Bickering. Tommy throwing himself around. Ronnie yelled: "Goddamn you little bastards! I could kill you!" Father upstairs, drooling. The best thing to feed him, Dr. Crane said, is baby food. Why not? He did not spit the food out, but sometimes it came back out by itself.

Ronnie said: "I'm going to set that bed on fire. Get that big worm up and moving fast!" Len punched him in the chest. They wrestled together, falling back against the wall, Ronnie giggled and sucked blood from his bleeding nose and began to choke.

Sounds of battle in the distance. Beyond the range of his bed the world was in perpetual twilight and turmoil. Struggle—arguing—vibrations from angry footsteps—weeping—the ringing of the telephone. Two figures standing at the foot of his bed, speaking gravely. Was that his wife? Was that the doctor? The world was filling up with strangers, people whose names he did not know. Hands he could not shake. His customers were being taken away from him . . . perhaps his files had already been divided up among the salesmen at the agency. . . . What were these two saying, were they talking about him? He strained to hear, he tried to lift himself up on one elbow. . . .

One of us was waiting out on the verandah. Dr. Crane said: "There's nothing else to do. You'd better take this opening while you can. Yes, he did move, he seemed about to get up, but then he fell back again. . . . But it isn't enough. He's very sick." Mother stumbled over something of Tommy's on the porch. She was crying again.

Mother, why did you cry so much!—small pale rivulets worn in your cheeks—it took months of sunlight to erase them—

The doorway had widened. The whole world was trooping through it, into his room, trying to get into bed with him. Over the years the children had run in here, jumping in bed with him and Florence, what a noisy giggling bunch!—but now there were strangers coming in. They gripped him hard, skillfully. Eased him up. His body ached, his spine flashed pain. Someone was saying, "Come on. That's it. Okay. Fine. Get his feet. Hold steady."

He wondered if they would let him drive his own car. Why was he being put in the back of someone else's car? A small truck? The car he drove was not really his own, but it was given to him for his use; he always had a new car. But now his legs were strangely shortened, very limp. What had happened? Maybe if he were placed in his car, behind the wheel, he would be able to reach the accelerator and the brake. His heartbeat quickened at the thought of driving his car himself. Even if it was the last time he was allowed to drive. He was proud of that car. His sons had always been proud of the new cars he drove, because their friends' fathers did not have such expensive cars. Would they think of letting him drive, would they be that kind? Or would he have to request this favor himself?

We all watched. The stretcher, the blankets still wrapped around him, that face. Tommy, who hadn't seen him for a while, screamed: "That's not Daddy!" Len helped the attendants with the stretcher. Mother had to get out of the way, she looked vague and confused, as if she were having difficulty making sense of the scene before her.

The ambulance was driven away like an ordinary car. No siren, no red light. Down to the end of our street and onto Claremont Boulevard and out of sight. It did not seem right that Father should be taken away so quietly.

We kept waking up at night. Was somebody in the room? In bed with us? We kept running in to Mother, Tommy and Sally especially. Tommy screamed until his eyes filled up with blood. Wanted to kick at the rest of us. He pounded at his own face with his fists. Mother took him in with her every night, in the new bed. Everything new about it: a shiny smooth headboard, a new mattress, new pillows, new box springs, new sheets. Even there Tommy would wake up, frightened. "Was somebody here in bed?" Mother said, "No." "Wasn't there somebody?" Tommy cried. Mother said, "No."

One day one of us came home from school and couldn't find Mother. He walked through the house calling, "Mother? . . ." and then saw her out the back window. He ran out, back to the fence. Mother was digging in the weeds. A hot weedy garden the smell of earth and sunlight and plants and Mother's warm dress, all yellow and purple streaks. . . .

"Mother? Mother?" She let the hoe fall back against the fence and opened her arms for an embrace.

Where I Lived, and What I Lived For

I ran

I was running with great confidence: size 13 shoes, heavy soles, heels hard as rocks beating hard on the dirt path so that, behind me, there were sharp indentations in the ground.

I was running in short jagged swerves. Sweat on my forehead, my hair wet on my forehead, salty sweat running into my eyes. . . It began to rain and I thought *Will I be renewed?*

I was running and the sudden rain passed back to me, a moving cloud of light prickling rain, scattered and abrupt as *his* panic. There was no prediction of rain but only the rain itself. Today was July Fourth. I ran inside the rain and through it and out the other side, already forgetting it, the muscles of my calves and thighs enormous with energy—

I ran in a spasm of terror

My heart pounded steadily, with confidence: I could see in the mud alongside the highway his footsteps, anxious and stumbling, the footsteps of a terrified man. The rain would not renew him but only weigh him down—his clothes wet and smelly—mud splattered up on his face—If I ran on tiptoe I might see him up ahead—that terrified back, that head, the soles of his shoes—

My body was a cage, my ribs a cage, and inside, my heart was pounding to be let out! to get free! The rain had passed and it had not renewed me. The pores of our human skin, coated over with a film of grease, do not take in moisture; we are impenetrable.

The horizon is out of sight—my instinct tells me he is no more than a mile ahead—

Already a few headlights on the highway, distant traffic—human beings are very cautious as night approaches. The rain had passed and it had not renewed me. I did not have time to think of the life I had left behind, it dwindled in my memory, dwindling and tinkling like traffic lights in the distance, fading. I ran. Caution slows you down, but terror speeds you up. It was an ordinary evening for you who were not running, that July Fourth, perhaps your entire bodies were reduced to one body, one sense, one organ for delight. I imagined you—you who are not running—as creatures whose organs are refined to a single tempestuous thing, an essence, an idea. Do you exist at all? Did you exist then? You do not exist until you begin to run. . . . This was not even a maze, but open country. There were no little black painted-on arrows to guide my way, no signs to proclaim EXIT in red lights. . . .

I had to eat on the run. My teeth tore at the bread, thick crusty white bread, my mouth watered with the violence of hunger, I was savage with hunger, as if it was his body I had seized and was devouring, raw—On the run you pound your way through lifetimes. Your heart enlarges. It gets the size of a big man's fist, and then the size of a valentine box of candy, that fake shiny red satin. You think of your own father running upstairs after something—the old house in the country, the frightened creak of the stairs, those very steep, dangerous steps of farmhouses—you think of the child, who was yourself, looking up at the noise of his father's running, wondering why his father has run. Fathers rarely run. Why did his father run upstairs? If an answer is given, after a few minutes, it is never the right answer. A father's sudden running upstairs, the thump of his shoes on the stairs, is a catastrophe.

Running through someone's footsteps, overtaking and destroying the footsteps—your shoes at least two sizes larger than his—you fall into the rhythm of his running, dreamy and brutal with your duty. You begin to think: *He would like to dramatize this story.* A big man, running, size 13 shoes, a little dissatisfied that, at his age, he must still eat on the run, your head is bouncing too much to contain complex thoughts. But you sense this: *He would like to dramatize this tragedy.* You call it tragedy because it is *his*, his death, you are only being generous. You are sharing his thoughts as you overtake him. You are sharing his bewilderment, as he shares the bewilderment of his childhood, hearing his long-dead father running upstairs in one of the houses in which he lived, in his life. The pursued always has had a life, going back to a childhood. It is part of his tragedy. You, pursuing him, with your good hearty perspiration crystallizing around you, you have had no childhood, nothing to clutter the present. You, or someone like you, has always been running like this—tramping over a bridge, along an empty path, at the side of a highway, disturbing owls, loons, the sound of freight cars rattling along the tracks somewhere, the baying of dogs, the murmur of distant cities, *his* panicked thoughts—

Years later, a father myself, I did something to surprise my son, but it was on purpose—rolling a great boulder down a hill to make a lot of noise, childish noise, to surprise him—instead, it frightened him and angered his mother. *I should have known better.* To comfort him I took off my watch and held it up to his ear. My watch was still on my wrist as I ran, the time was 9:25. What did that mean? What did those numbers mean? I moved out of my parents' house and, some years later, moved into a house of my own, with a woman, and the two of us kept touching each other, bumping into each other, bodies and heads, because the house in which we lived was too small. Small rooms. Too many walls. We embraced each other, as people do, in order to ignore the walls of their houses. Up and down the length of her handsome body she was bruised, mysteriously. I remember her undressing—staring sullenly down at herself, just out of a patch of late-afternoon sunlight that fell harmlessly on the wall, staring down at her body, an ordinary female body, except for the bruises —gentle orange-blue bruises—immense pinches—Silence. I could have reached into the back of her skull and come out with nothing. She hid the bruises again, dressing quickly. She walked slowly ahead of me, out to the car—our battered station wagon—and I sensed that she wanted to run, to run for her life away from me. The taut, shivering, tanned muscles of her bare legs told me everything, and if I had loved her without anger I would have whispered to her: *You can leave, you're free.* But husbands and wives don't say that to each other.

In the old times hunters like myself were happy to do their duty, to get their pay, to please people. They brought maps to life. They crossed the wild dim stretches of a map with the exertions of their bodies, panting, mouths watering with hunger. But now, in our time, I am happy with the running itself, the hunting, the knowledge of my man up ahead, who cannot escape me---I know that the universe culminates in this moment and that he and I, the stranger and myself, are sharing a map together, are divine together.

My ankles ached. I ran doubled over with pain. Deep in the belly a pain, an unfamiliar pain. It was always there but I never felt it before. On either side of me animals crashed away into the thicket, frightened by me, by a man out here in the country. The horizon was at my elbow. Branches slapped my face, something stung my eye. . . . Behind me he was coming closer. I could hear him. I imagined his grabbing me and, with a sudden skillful jerking of his arms, snapping my backbone in two; it was a very dry backbone, the parts worn out and uncooperative. That backbone was once sweet and white and gristly and moist, the vertebrae moved together soundlessly. . . .

He ran in terror, stumbling.

I exaggerated my wife's strangeness. She was not strange, she was an ordinary woman. I was an ordinary man. The bruises on her body were real bruises—not from me, not from the density and vexing boredom of our love—but from the ocean. A large wave had picked her up and dragged her along the rocky bottom of the water near shore, one day, one summer. I wanted to make up strange memories, terrible memories, in the style of my own terror, but really everything before this was ordinary and domestic, like the accident in Maine, my wife's bruised body, her bruised accusing eyes. . . .

He ran in terror, making up memories, lies—he was becoming a kind of lie himself—I did not plan to break his backbone, but to seize him by the back of the neck, my big hand firmly closed upon the bottom of his skull, which will fit to my hand as if the two of us had rehearsed this scene many times. And, with my knife, which is always very sharp, I will make an incision at the top of his head and, with five or six swift precise strokes, loosen the scalp and the skin, and I will peel his skin off in segments, filmy and sticky segments, until his skin lies down about his feet like the pink opened useless petals of a flower.

Alongside me a stretch of water, suddenly—a river, a creek? The land here had buoyancy. My ankles were weak but my feet seemed springy; the moss was springy underfoot, unless I was imagining everything. Did I imagine this chase? The fist inside my chest, the hot pounding eyeballs, the knowledge that I am the hero of a story that will end with death? It was true that I told lies. I made up "lies" because I had to fill my life with something, all those tiny lines that marked off seconds on my wrist watch, I had to talk to myself, to argue with myself, to speak lovingly and teasingly to myself. It was true that I became fiction. But lies and stories and dreams and fiction all come to a final, honest end, people come to an end whether they are entirely real or half real or entirely made up, whether they lie to themselves most of the time or all of the time, everything runs out, everything dies. Therefore nothing exists that is not true, nothing that is entirely fiction. When I began this run I thought I would be renewed, I would never be caught, I thought it was in the nature of the pursued to outwit the millions of people pursuing him, all those people who want to take his place, his possessions, the food he has left uneaten, his wrist watch, his very skin. I thought I was running because I wanted to run. Because I wanted to. Because a certain bell had rung that I had goaded into ringing, because one segment of my life seemed to be over anyway and I was bored, because for thirty years I had not been happy, because I had disappointed certain people and they had disappointed me, because I was bored with the buildings, the towers, the steeples, the clouds, this *technological civilization*, because I had seen all the movies, acted in all the movies, taken all the parts, I had imagined all the dialogue, everything.

Eating on the run is no good—I'm still hungry—I could seize him and sink my teeth into his throat, why not? Suck his blood so that it runs down my chin, my chest; why not?—I had to stop to brush my teeth in a mud puddle. Ugh! I spat the water out again. I brushed my teeth with my fingers and with my fingernails I dislodged particles of food. I spat into the puddle. My gums began to bleed slightly.

He thought of me only as a thing, an object. His prey. He thought of getting me finished. Getting me over with. That irritable, guilty relief I felt when my parents died, when I *got them over with.* They withered and died, within four months of each other. An April death, and then a July death. They flickered. Faltered. My image on their retinas flickered, faded, became miniature, finally went out—I could have cried out, *What have you done to me? Where is my soul now?* But I showed nothing except ordinary grief. Domestic grief. My wife was watching me closely, watching for a breakdown, so that she could mother me—I wanted to elude her. They knew I was their son, yet they forgot me in their own hurry to die—I was only an object to them, a thing they were leaving behind, and then I wasn't even a thing. They forgot.

I could see him now—he was about my own height, at least six feet tall—he looked very lonely—the space between us was a confusion of wild grass and tree stumps and bushes—he ran with his arms loose and bobbing at his side, his head bobbing—

Can I imagine myself out of this? Imagine myself somewhere else? In bed, in any of the beds I have owned, even in a hospital bed, even in a crib? In a hospital crib, all set to begin my life anew? I would be willing to start over again! . . . There was always a certain mystery about me, about my skin. It was real to me and yet it did not contain me, not exactly. Thoughts and emotions and processes took place inside my skin, but I was able to stand a few feet away and watch myself, as remote from that body as I might be from any stranger's body. That presence was always beside me, encouraging me, teasing me, scolding me, murmuring to me in baby talk, in secret slang—how it loved me, when no one else knew me at all! The love of that other self was the only love that meant anything to me! It did not share this experience, it was not running with me, it was not about to collapse. A spectator, only. Waiting for a sequence of events to end. When it ends, the spectator will walk calmly away.

No you don't! Almost fooled me—swerved to the side, toward the water—but that water is only waist-high, look at the cattails growing there—no, way out on that side—the water is hardly deep enough to drown in—

Did he yell at me?

He thinks he is the hero of a certain story, but he is wrong. I am the hero of that story. It is not a story that is coming to an end when he dies. It takes a break, a pause, because he is one event in the sequence of my life. Only a pause. And then it goes on again when I stumble to the lake, wash my face, sigh heavily, get the blood off my hands and forearms, walk calmly back to the city and back to my own bed, my lair, where I will sleep for fifteen hours. And when I wake, heavy and enormous with sleep, I will be puzzled, as if a question had been put to me in that terrible sleep, in language not my own, a style not my own, I will jump out of bed and think wildly: *What was that question? Who asked it? What happened to him?*

But nothing—

He would like to shiver in his sleep and wake up safe in a bed, between human sheets. Clean white sheets. Clean white sheets at the back of his brain, nothing else satisfies, nothing else is so basic. He would like to jerk awake suddenly and find himself anywhere at all, so long as it isn't here—even in a hospital bed, his wife and son nearby where they've waited for hours to see this flutter of his eyelids, this gurgling of mysterious liquid in his throat—a woman of thirty-seven with eyes dark and bewildered from lack of sleep, a sullen, frightened, accusing face, and a child of eight, breathing nervously through his mouth, the two of them playing their roles the way ordinary people play their roles, not very convincingly, because they are so dazed by what is going on. They have no time to invent interesting dialogue. For *interesting dialogue* you must go somewhere else, to fiction. . . . But he will not wake there, safe with the nurses and the doctors who are always thinking ahead to an afternoon's game of golf, no, not even to the crib he slept in as an infant, the crib that stank so because of the stained wood, and embarrassed him, years later, when he came across it in the attic—no, none of these beds, not one of these beds, no human bed at all—

Is this the beginning—or have we come almost to the end? Looking back you can always make shrewd, swift assessments. *I should have been able to see it coming, obviously. A mental collapse. Cardiac arrest. The end of a marriage.* But when you are in it, running in it, you know nothing at all. It might be nearly over. I am so tired, so tired, it might be nearly over. . . . I thought my life had come to an end years ago, I was thirty-four then, my son fell outside playing and his forehead was torn so that blood poured down his face, and I screamed: *Your eye! Your eye!* But no, it wasn't his eye, both eyes were safe, only a cascade of blood, only a screaming child, a father about to faint, to give up, to go down. . . . You endure the ending a certain number of times, bouncing back elastic and manly, amazing your friends and making your parents proud, and then, then one day . . . you sigh, you are unaccountably tired . . . you are sick of bouncing back, sick of being manly and brave, you are bored with the awful endings, the treachery of life . . . you whisper to yourself, your old secret friend from boyhood: *All right, that's it.*

No more than six careful strokes of the knife—razor-swift, clean, gleaming—the skin unpeeling, the shudder of the slimy flesh left intact—the drone of insects—the sigh that will come from my lips: *All right, that's it.*

A rise in the land—railroad tracks and moist dark earth, a man-made hill—moist earth flowing down—is it my terror, or do I really see those shapes? Strange, marvelous shapes in the clay—flowing down the side of the hill, sand of every degree of fineness, clay of a dark, satiny, elegant texture, flowing downward like lava—Little streams overlap and interlace one another, flowing into the forms of sappy leaves or vines—I am seeing coral, I am seeing leopards' paws or birds' feet, brains or lungs or bowels, and excrements of all kinds—Architectural foliage more ancient than ivy, vine, leaves, everything the brute color of iron—the deepest earth colors, red, yellow, brown, gray, orange, all smeared together like oil, my eyes are lost in these streams as they run together as if whispering their secret, their meaning; I have forgotten what is behind me, if anything is behind me, if anything will happen when I stop—There is a meaning to all this—

No time to begin at the beginning, but only at the end. The end. Why did his father run upstairs in the old farmhouse one Sunday, why didn't his father instruct him more carefully in the snares and delights of this world, why did his mother turn selfish and coldly physical—yes, physical, turning all lard-colored, mottled flesh, too busy with her meals and her bowels and her ailments to pay much attention to *him*—why did everything remain mysterious to him? Disappointing to him? Why was he always reconstructing conversations, facial expressions, clothing, background music, skies, his wife's love for him, his son's love for him, his own doubleness, his presence as a spectator at certain dramatic moments in his own life? Why was he always diagramming a way out of a relationship after he had labored to diagram a way in? Why had he been in such a hurry? Now he is hypnotized by slithering, soft, grotesque shapes in the earth, sand and

ay in a maze of gentle eroded earth, on an ordinary hill in the
ountry. But there is no time to make sense of it.

am hypnotized—

le will die hypnotized—

will die—

The Lady with the Pet Dog

1

Strangers parted as if to make way for him.

There he stood. He was there in the aisle, a few yards away watching her.

She leaned forward at once in her seat, her hand jerked up her face as if to ward off a blow—but then the crowd in the aisle hid him, he was gone. She pressed both hands against her cheeks. He was not there, she had imagined him.

"My God," she whispered.

She was alone. Her husband had gone out to the foyer to make a telephone call; it was intermission at the concert, a Thursday evening.

Now she saw him again, clearly. He was standing there. He was staring at her. Her blood rocked in her body, draining out of her head . . . she was going to faint. . . . They stared at each other. They gave no sign of recognition. Only when he took a step forward did she shake her head *no—no—keep away*. It was not possible.

When her husband returned, she was staring at the place in the aisle where her lover had been standing. Her husband leaned forward to interrupt that stare.

"What's wrong?" he said. "Are you sick?"

Panic rose in her in long shuddering waves. She tried to get to her feet, panicked at the thought of fainting here, and her husband took hold of her. She stood like an aged woman, clutching the seat before her.

At home he helped her up the stairs and she lay down. Her head was like a large piece of crockery that had to be held still, it was so heavy. She was still panicked. She felt it in the shallows of her face, behind her knees, in the pit of her stomach. It sickened her, it made her think of mucus, of something thick and gray congested inside her, stuck to her, that was herself and yet not herself—a poison.

She lay with her knees drawn up toward her chest, her eyes partly open, while her husband spoke to her. She imagined that other man saying, *Why did you run away from me?* Her husband was saying other words. She tried to listen to them. He was going to call the doctor, he said, and she tried to sit up. "No, I'm all right now," she said quickly. The panic was like lead inside her, thickly congested. How slow love was to drain out of her, how rigid and sticky it was inside her head!

Her husband believed her. No doctor. No threat. Grateful, she drew her husband down to her. They embraced, not comfortably. For years now they had not been comfortable together, in their intimacy and at a distance, and now they struggled gently as if the paces of this dance were too rigorous for them. It was something they might have known once, but had now outgrown. The panic in her thickened at this double betrayal: she drew her husband to her, she caressed him wildly, she shut her eyes to think about that other man.

A crowd of men and women parting, unexpectedly, and there he stood—there he stood—she kept seeing him, and yet her vision blotched at the memory. It had been finished between them, six months before, but he had come out here . . . and she had escaped him, now she was lying in her husband's arms, in his embrace, her face pressed against his. It was a kind of sleep, this love-making. She felt herself falling asleep, her body falling from her. Her eyes shut.

"I love you," her husband said fiercely, angrily.

She shut her eyes and thought of that other man, as if betraying him would give her life a center.

"Did I hurt you? Are you—?" her husband whispered.

Always this hot flashing of shame between them, the shame of her husband's near failure, the clumsiness of his love—

"You didn't hurt me," she said.

2

They had said good-by six months before. He drove her from Nantucket, where they had met, to Albany, New York, where she visited her sister. The hours of intimacy in the car had sealed something between them, a vow of silence and impersonality: she recalled the movement of the highways, the passing of other cars, the natural rhythms of the day hypnotizing her toward sleep while he drove. She trusted him, she could sleep in his presence. Yet she could not really fall asleep in spite of her exhaustion, and she kept jerking awake, frightened, to discover that nothing had changed—still the stranger who was driving her to Albany, still the highway, the sky, the antiseptic odor of the rented car, the sense of a rhythm behind the rhythm of the air that might unleash itself at any second. Everywhere on this highway, at this moment, there were men and women driving together, bonded

ogether—what did that mean, to be together? What did it mean
o enter into a bond with another person?

No, she did not really trust him; she did not really trust men.
He would glance at her with his small cautious smile and she felt
a declaration of shame between them.

Shame.

In her head she rehearsed conversations. She said bitterly,
"You'll be relieved when we get to Albany. Relieved to get rid of
me." They had spent so many days talking, confessing too much,
riven to a pitch of childish excitement, laughing together on the
each, breaking into that pose of laughter that seems to eradicate
the soul, so many days of this that the silence of the trip was like
the silence of a hospital—all these surface noises, these rattles
nd hums, but an interior silence, a befuddlement. She said to
him in her imagination, "One of us should die." Then she leaned
ver to touch him. She caressed the back of his neck. She said,
loud, "Would you like me to drive for a while?"

They stopped at a picnic area where other cars were stopped
—couples, families—and walked together, smiling at their good
ick. He put his arm around her shoulders and she sensed how
ley were in a posture together, a man and a woman forming a
osture, a figure, that someone might sketch and show to them.
he said slowly, "I don't want to go back. . . ."

Silence. She looked up at him. His face was heavy with her
vords, as if she had pulled at his skin with her fingers. Children
in nearby and distracted him—yes, he was a father too, his chil-
ren ran like that, they tugged at his skin with their light, busy
ngers.

"Are you so unhappy?" he said.

"I'm not unhappy, back there. I'm nothing. There's nothing to
ie," she said.

They stared at each other. The sensation between them was
itense, exhausting. She thought that this man was her savior,
aat he had come to her at a time in her life when her life de-
anded completion, an end, a permanent fixing of all that was

troubled and shifting and deadly. And yet it was absurd to think
this. No person could save another. So she drew back from him
and released him.

A few hours later they stopped at a gas station in a small city.
She went to the women's rest room, having to ask the attendant
for a key, and when she came back her eye jumped nervously onto
the rented car—why? did she think he might have driven off
without her?—onto the man, her friend, standing in conversation
with the young attendant. Her friend was as old as her husband,
over forty, with lanky, sloping shoulders, a full body, his hair
thick, a dark, burnished brown, a festive color that made her eye
twitch a little—and his hands were always moving, always those
rapid conversational circles, going nowhere, gestures that were at
once a little aggressive and apologetic.

She put her hand on his arm, a claim. He turned to her and
smiled and she felt that she loved him, that everything in her life
had forced her to this moment and that she had no choice about
it.

They sat in the car for two hours, in Albany, in the parking lot
of a Howard Johnson's restaurant, talking, trying to figure out
their past. There was no future. They concentrated on the past,
the several days behind them, lit up with a hot, dazzling August
sun, like explosions that already belonged to other people, to
strangers. Her face was faintly reflected in the green-tinted curve
of the windshield, but she could not have recognized that face.
She began to cry; she told herself: *I am not here, this will pass,
this is nothing.* Still, she could not stop crying. The muscles of
her face were springy, like a child's, unpredictable muscles. He
stroked her arms, her shoulders, trying to comfort her. "This is
so hard . . . this is impossible . . ." he said. She felt panic for
the world outside this car, all that was not herself and this man,
and at the same time she understood that she was free of him, as
people are free of other people, she would leave him soon, safely,
and within a few days he would have fallen into the past, the
impersonal past. . . .

"I'm so ashamed of myself!" she said finally.

She returned to her husband and saw that another woman, a shadow-woman, had taken her place—noiseless and convincing, like a dancer performing certain difficult steps. Her husband folded her in his arms and talked to her of his own loneliness, his worries about his business, his health, his mother, kept tranquilized and mute in a nursing home, and her spirit detached itself from her and drifted about the rooms of the large house she lived in with her husband, a shadow-woman delicate and imprecise. There was no boundary to her, no edge. Alone, she took hot baths and sat exhausted in the steaming water, wondering at her perpetual exhaustion. All that winter she noticed the limp, languid weight of her arms, her veins bulging slightly with the pressure of her extreme weariness. *This is fate,* she thought, to be here and not there, to be one person and not another, a certain man's wife and not the wife of another man. The long, slow pain of this certainty rose in her, but it never became clear, it was baffling and imprecise. She could not be serious about it; she kept congratulating herself on her own good luck, to have escaped so easily, to have freed herself. So much love had gone into the first several years of her marriage that there wasn't much left, now, for another man. . . . She was certain of that. But the bath water made her dizzy, all that perpetual heat, and one day in January she drew a razor blade lightly across the inside of her arm, near the elbow, to see what would happen.

Afterward she wrapped a small towel around it, to stop the bleeding. The towel soaked through. She wrapped a bath towel around that and walked through the empty rooms of her home, lightheaded, hardly aware of the stubborn seeping of blood. There was no boundary to her in this house, no precise limit. She could flow out like her own blood and come to no end.

She sat for a while on a blue love seat, her mind empty. Her husband telephoned her when he would be staying late at the plant. He talked to her always about his plans, his problems, his business friends, his future. It was obvious that he had a future.

As he spoke she nodded to encourage him, and her heartbe
quickened with the memory of her own, personal shame, th
shame of this man's particular, private wife. One evening at din
ner he leaned forward and put his head in his arms and fe
asleep, like a child. She sat at the table with him for a whil
watching him. His hair had gone gray, almost white, at th
temples—no one would guess that he was so quick, so careful
man, still fairly young about the eyes. She put her hand on h
head, lightly, as if to prove to herself that he was real. He slep
exhausted.

One evening they went to a concert and she looked up to s
her lover there, in the crowded aisle, in this city, watching he
He was standing there, with his overcoat on, watching her. Sh
went cold. That morning the telephone had rung while her hu
band was still home, and she had heard him answer it, heard h
hang up—it must have been a wrong number—and when t
telephone rang again, at 9:30, she had been afraid to answer
She had left home to be out of the range of that ringing, but no
in this public place, in this busy auditorium, she found hers
staring at that man, unable to make any sign to him, any gestu
of recognition. . . .

He would have come to her but she shook her head. *No. S*
away.

Her husband helped her out of the row of seats, saying, "
cuse us, please. Excuse us," so that strangers got to their fe
quickly, alarmed, to let them pass. Was that woman about
faint? What was wrong?

At home she felt the blood drain slowly back into her he
Her husband embraced her hips, pressing his face against her,
that silence that belonged to the earliest days of their marria
She thought, *He will drive it out of me.* He made love to her a
she was back in the auditorium again, sitting alone, now that
concert was over. The stage was empty; the heavy velvet curta
had not been drawn; the musicians' chairs were empty, eve
thing was silent and expectant; in the aisle her lover stood a

niled at her—Her husband was impatient. He was apart from
er, working on her, operating on her; and then, stricken, he
hispered, "Did I hurt you?"

The telephone rang the next morning. Dully, sluggishly, she
nswered it. She recognized his voice at once—that "Anna?"
ith its lifting of the second syllable, questioning and apologetic
nd making its claim—"Yes, what do you want?" she said.

"Just to see you. Please—"

"I can't."

"Anna, I'm sorry, I didn't mean to upset you—"

"I can't see you."

"Just for a few minutes—I have to talk to you—"

"But why, why now? Why now?" she said.

She heard her voice rising, but she could not stop it. He began
talk again, drowning her out. She remembered his rapid con-
rsation. She remembered his gestures, the witty energetic cir-
ing of his hands.

"Please don't hang up!" he cried.

"I can't—I don't want to go through it again—"

"I'm not going to hurt you. Just tell me how you are."

"Everything is the same."

"Everything is the same with me."

She looked up at the ceiling, shyly. "Your wife? Your chil-
en?"

"The same."

"Your son?"

"He's fine—"

"I'm glad to hear that. I—"

"Is it still the same with you, your marriage? Tell me what you
el. What are you thinking?"

"I don't know. . . ."

She remembered his intense, eager words, the movement of
s hands, that impatient precise fixing of the air by his hands,
e jabbing of his fingers.

"Do you love me?" he said.

She could not answer.

"I'll come over to see you," he said.

"No," she said.

What will come next, what will happen?

Flesh hardening on his body, aging. Shrinking. He will grow old, but not soft like her husband. They are two different types: he is nervous, lean, energetic, wise. She will grow thinner, as the tension radiates out from her backbone, wearing down her flesh. Her collarbones will jut out of her skin. Her husband, caressing her in their bed, will discover that she is another woman—she is not there with him—instead she is rising in an elevator in a downtown hotel, carrying a book as a prop, or walking quickly away from that hotel, her head bent and filled with secrets. Love, what to do with it? . . . Useless as moths' wings, as moths' fluttering. . . . She feels the flutterings of silky, crazy wings in her chest.

He flew out to visit her every several weeks, staying at a different hotel each time. He telephoned her, and she drove down to park in an underground garage at the very center of the city.

She lay in his arms while her husband talked to her, miles away, one body fading into another. He will grow old, his body will change, she thought, pressing her cheek against the back of one of these men. If it was her lover, they were in a hotel room, always the propped-up little booklet describing the hotel's many services, with color photographs of its cocktail lounge and dining room and coffee shop. Grow old, leave me, die, go back to your neurotic wife and your sad, ordinary children, she thought, but still her eyes closed gratefully against his skin and she felt how complete their silence was, how they had come to rest in each other.

"Tell me about your life here. The people who love you," he said, as he always did.

One afternoon they lay together for four hours. It was her birthday and she was intoxicated with her good fortune, this prize of the afternoon, this man in her arms! She was a little giddy, she talked too much. She told him about her parents, about her husband. . . . "They were all people I believed in, but it turned out wrong. Now, I believe in you. . . ." He laughed as if shocked by her words. She did not understand. Then she understood. "But I believe truly in you. I can't think of myself without you," she said. . . . He spoke of his wife, her ambitions, her intelligence, her use of the children against him, her use of his younger son's blindness, all of his words gentle and hypnotic and convincing in the late afternoon peace of this hotel room . . . and she felt the terror of laughter, threatening laughter. Their words, like their bodies, were aging.

She dressed quickly in the bathroom, drawing her long hair up around the back of her head, fixing it as always, anxious that everything be the same. Her face was slightly raw, from his face. The rubbing of his skin. Her eyes were too bright, wearily bright. Her hair was blond but not so blond as it had been that summer in the white Nantucket air.

She ran water and splashed it on her face. She blinked at the water. Blind. Drowning. She thought with satisfaction that soon, soon, he would be back home, in that house on Long Island she had never seen, with that woman she had never seen, sitting on the edge of another bed, putting on his shoes. She wanted nothing except to be free of him. Why not be free? *Oh,* she thought *suddenly, I will follow you back and kill you. You and her and the little boy. What is there to stop me?*

She left him. Everyone on the street pitied her, that look of absolute zero.

A man and a child, approaching her. The sharp acrid smell of fish. The crashing of waves. Anna pretended not to notice the father with his son—there was something strange about them. That frank, silent intimacy, too gentle, the man's bare feet in the water and the boy a few feet away, leaning away from his father. He was about nine years old and still his father held his hand.

A small yipping dog, a golden dog, bounded near them.

Anna turned shyly back to her reading; she did not want to have to speak to these neighbors. She saw the man's shadow falling over her legs, then over the pages of her book, and she had the idea that he wanted to see what she was reading. The dog nuzzled her; the man called him away.

She watched them walk down the beach. She was relieved that the man had not spoken to her.

She saw them in town later that day, the two of them brown-haired and patient, now wearing sandals, walking with that same look of care. The man's white shorts were soiled and a little baggy. His pullover shirt was a faded green. His face was broad, the cheekbones wide, spaced widely apart, the eyes stark in their sockets, as if they fastened onto objects for no reason, ponderous and edgy. The little boy's face was pale and sharp; his lips were perpetually parted.

Anna realized that the child was blind.

The next morning, early, she caught sight of them again. For some reason she went to the back door of her cottage. She faced the sea breeze eagerly. Her heart hammered. . . . She had been here, in her family's old house, for three days, alone, bitterly satisfied at being alone, and now it was a puzzle to her how her soul strained to fly outward, to meet with another person. She watched the man with his son, his cautious, rather stooped shoulders above the child's small shoulders.

The man was carrying something, it looked like a notebook. He sat on the sand, not far from Anna's spot of the day before, and the dog rushed up to them. The child approached the edge of the ocean, timidly. He moved in short jerky steps, his legs stiff. The dog ran around him. Anna heard the child crying out a word that sounded like "Ty"—it must have been the dog's name—and then the man joined in, his voice heavy and firm.

"Ty—"

Anna tied her hair back with a yellow scarf and went down the beach.

The man glanced around at her. He smiled. She stared past him at the waves. To talk to him or not to talk—she had the freedom of that choice. For a moment she felt that she had made a mistake, that the child and the dog would not protect her, that behind this man's ordinary, friendly face there was a certain arrogant maleness—then she relented, she smiled shyly.

"A nice house you've got there," the man said.

She nodded her thanks.

The man pushed his sunglasses up on his forehead. Yes, she recognized the eyes of the day before—intelligent and nervous, the sockets pale, untanned.

"Is that your telephone ringing?" he said.

She did not bother to listen. "It's a wrong number," she said.

Her husband calling: she had left home for a few days, to be alone.

But the man, settling himself on the sand, seemed to misinterpret this. He smiled in surprise, one corner of his mouth higher than the other. He said nothing. Anna wondered: *What is he thinking?* The dog was leaping about her, panting against her legs, and she laughed in embarrassment. She bent to pet it, grateful for its busyness. "Don't let him jump up on you," the man said. "He's a nuisance."

The dog was a small golden retriever, a young dog. The blind child, standing now in the water, turned to call the dog to him. His voice was shrill and impatient.

"Our house is the third one down—the white one," the man said.

She turned, startled. "Oh, did you buy it from Dr. Patrick? Did he die?"

"Yes, finally. . . ."

Her eyes wandered nervously over the child and the dog. She felt the nervous beat of her heart out to the very tips of her fingers, the fleshy tips of her fingers: little hearts were there, pulsing. *What is he thinking?* The man had opened his notebook. He had a piece of charcoal and he began to sketch something.

Anna looked down at him. She saw the top of his head, his thick brown hair, the freckles on his shoulders, the quick, deft movement of his hand. Upside down, Anna herself being drawn. She smiled in surprise.

"Let me draw you. Sit down," he said.

She knelt awkwardly a few yards away. He turned the page of the sketch pad. The dog ran to her and she sat, straightening out her skirt beneath her, flinching from the dog's tongue. "Ty!" cried the child. Anna sat, and slowly the pleasure of the moment began to glow in her; her skin flushed with gratitude.

She sat there for nearly an hour. The man did not talk much. Back and forth the dog bounded, shaking itself. The child came to sit near them, in silence. Anna felt that she was drifting into a kind of trance while the man sketched her, half a dozen rapid sketches, the surface of her face given up to him. "Where are you from?" the man asked.

"Ohio. My husband lives in Ohio."

She wore no wedding band.

"Your wife—" Anna began.

"Yes?"

"Is she here?"

"Not right now."

She was silent, ashamed. She had asked an improper question. But the man did not seem to notice. He continued drawing her, bent over the sketch pad. When Anna said she had to go, he showed her the drawings—one after another of her, Anna, recognizably Anna, a woman in her early thirties, her hair smooth and flat across the top of her head, tied behind by a scarf. "Take the one you like best," he said, and she picked one of her with the dog in her lap, sitting very straight, her brows and eyes clearly defined, her lips girlishly pursed, the dog and her dress suggested by a few quick irregular lines.

"Lady with pet dog," the man said.

She spent the rest of that day reading, nearer her cottage. It was not really a cottage—it was a two-story house, large and un gainly and weathered. It was mixed up in her mind with her family, her own childhood, and she glanced up from her book, perplexed, as if waiting for one of her parents or her sister to come up to her. Then she thought of that man, the man with the blind child, the man with the dog, and she could not concentrate on her reading. Someone—probably her father—had marked a passage that must be important, but she kept reading and reread-ing it: *We try to discover in things, endeared to us on that ac-count, the spiritual glamour which we ourselves have cast upon them; we are disillusioned, and learn that they are in themselves barren and devoid of the charm that they owed, in our minds, to the association of certain ideas. . . .*

She thought again of the man on the beach. She lay the book aside and thought of him: his eyes, his aloneness, his drawings of her.

They began seeing each other after that. He came to her front door in the evening, without the child; he drove her into town for dinner. She was shy and extremely pleased. The darkness of the expensive restaurant released her; she heard herself chatter; she leaned forward and seemed to be offering her face up to him, listening to him. He talked about his work on a Long Island newspaper and she seemed to be listening to him, as she stared at his face, arranging her own face into the expression she had seen in that charcoal drawing. Did he see her like that, then?—girlish and withdrawn and patrician? She felt the weight of his interest in her, a force that fell upon her like a blow. A repeated blow. Of course he was married, he had children—of course she was mar-ried, permanently married. This flight from her husband was not important. She had left him before, to be alone, it was not im-portant. Everything in her was slender and delicate and not important.

They walked for hours after dinner, looking at the other strollers, the weekend visitors, the tourists, the couples like them-selves. Surely they were mistaken for a couple, a married couple. *This is the hour in which everything is decided,* Anna thought.

They had both had several drinks and they talked a great dea
Anna found herself saying too much, stopping and starting gi
dily. She put her hand to her forehead, feeling faint.

"It's from the sun—you've had too much sun—" he said.

At the door to her cottage, on the front porch, she heard he
self asking him if he would like to come in. She allowed him
lead her inside, to close the door. *This is not important, s*
thought clearly, *he doesn't mean it, he doesn't love me, nothin*
will come of it. She was frightened, yet it seemed to her nece
sary to give in; she had to leave Nantucket with that act co
pleted, an act of adultery, an accomplishment she would ta
back to Ohio and to her marriage.

Later, incredibly, she heard herself asking: "Do you . . .
you love me?"

"You're so beautiful!" he said, amazed.

She felt this beauty, shy and glowing and centered in her ey
He stared at her. In this large, drafty house, alone together, th
were like accomplices, conspirators. She could not think: how
was she? which year was this? They had done something unf
givable together, and the knowledge of it was tugging at th
faces. A cloud seemed to pass over her. She felt herself smili
shrilly.

Afterward, a peculiar raspiness, a dryness of breath. He
silent. She felt a strange, idle fear, a sense of the danger outs
this room and this old, comfortable bed—a danger that would
recognize her as the lady in that drawing, the lady with the
dog. There was nothing to say to this man, this stranger. She
the beauty draining out of her face, her eyes fading.

"I've got to be alone," she told him.

He left, and she understood that she would not see him ag
She stood by the window of the room, watching the ocean
sense of shame overpowered her: it was smeared everywhere
her body, the smell of it, the richness of it. She tried to re
him, and his face was confused in her memory: she would h
to shout to him across a jumbled space, she would have to w

her arms wildly. *You love me! You must love me!* But she knew he did not love her, and she did not love him; he was a man who drew everything up into himself, like all men, walking away, free to walk away, free to have his own thoughts, free to envision her body, all the secrets of her body. . . . And she lay down again in the bed, feeling how heavy this body had become, her insides heavy with shame, the very backs of her eyelids coated with shame.

"This is the end of one part of my life," she thought.

But in the morning the telephone rang. She answered it. It was her lover: they talked brightly and happily. She could hear the eagerness in his voice, the love in his voice, that same still, sad amazement—she understood how simple life was, there were no problems.

They spent most of their time on the beach, with the child and the dog. He joked and was serious at the same time. He said, once, "You have defined my soul for me," and she laughed to hide her alarm. In a few days it was time for her to leave. He got a sitter for the boy and took the ferry with her to the mainland, then rented a car to drive her up to Albany. She kept thinking: *Now something will happen. It will come to an end.* But most of the drive was silent and hypnotic. She wanted him to joke with her, to say again that she had defined his soul for him, but he drove fast, he was serious, she distrusted the hawkish look of his profile—she did not know him at all. At a gas station she splashed her face with cold water. Alone in the grubby little rest room, shaky and very much alone. In such places are women totally alone with their bodies. The body grows heavier, more evil, in such silence. . . . On the beach everything had been noisy with sunlight and gulls and waves; here, as if run to earth, everything was cramped and silent and dead.

She went outside, squinting. There he was, talking with the station attendant. She could not think as she returned to him whether she wanted to live or not.

She stayed in Albany for a few days, then flew home to her

husband. He met her at the airport, near the luggage counter
where her three pieces of pale-brown luggage were brought to
him on a conveyer belt, to be claimed by him. He kissed her on
the cheek. They shook hands, a little embarrassed. She had come
home again.

"How will I live out the rest of my life?" she wondered.

In January her lover spied on her: she glanced up and saw
him, in a public place, in the DeRoy Symphony Hall. She was
paralyzed with fear. She nearly fainted. In this faint she felt her
husband's body, loving her, working its love upon her, and she
shut her eyes harder to keep out the certainty of his love—some
times he failed at loving her, sometimes he succeeded, it had
nothing to do with her or her pity or her ten years of love for him
it had nothing to do with a woman at all. It was a private act
accomplished by a man, a husband or a lover, in communion
with his own soul, his manhood.

Her husband was forty-two years old now, growing slowly into
middle age, getting heavier, softer. Her lover was about the same
age, narrower in the shoulders, with a full, solid chest, yet lean
nervous. She thought, in her paralysis, of men and how they love
freely and eagerly so long as their bodies are capable of love, love
for a woman; and then, as love fades in their bodies, it fades from
their souls and they become immune and immortal and ready to
die.

Her husband was a little rough with her, as if impatient with
himself. "I love you," he said fiercely, angrily. And then
ashamed, he said, "Did I hurt you? . . ."

"You didn't hurt me," she said.

Her voice was too shrill for their embrace.

While he was in the bathroom she went to her closet and took
out that drawing of the summer before. There she was, on the
beach at Nantucket, a lady with a pet dog, her eyes large and
defined, the dog in her lap hardly more than a few snarls, a few
coarse soft lines of charcoal . . . her dress smeared, her arm
oddly limp . . . her hands not well drawn at all. . . . S

tried to think: did she love the man who had drawn this? did he love her? The fever in her husband's body had touched her and driven her temperature up, and now she stared at the drawing with a kind of lust, fearful of seeing an ugly soul in that woman's face, fearful of seeing the face suddenly through her lover's eyes. She breathed quickly and harshly, staring at the drawing.

And so, the next day, she went to him at his hotel. She wept, pressing against him, demanding of him, "What do you want? Why are you here? Why don't you let me alone?" He told her that he wanted nothing. He expected nothing. He would not cause trouble.

"I want to talk about last August," he said.

"Don't—" she said.

She was hypnotized by his gesturing hands, his nervousness, his obvious agitation. He kept saying, "I understand. I'm making no claims upon you."

They became lovers again.

He called room service for something to drink and they sat side by side on his bed, looking through a copy of *The New Yorker*, laughing at the cartoons. It was so peaceful in this room, so complete. They were on a holiday. It was a secret holiday. Four-thirty in the afternoon, on a Friday, an ordinary Friday: a secret holiday.

"I won't bother you again," he said.

He flew back to see her again in March, and in late April. He telephoned her from his hotel—a different hotel each time—and she came down to him at once. She rose to him in various elevators, she knocked on the doors of various rooms, she stepped into his embrace, breathless and guilty and already angry with him, pleading with him. One morning in May, when he telephoned, she pressed her forehead against the doorframe and could not speak. He kept saying, "What's wrong? Can't you talk? Aren't you alone?" She felt that she was going insane. Her head would burst. Why, why did he love her, why did he pursue her? Why did he want her to die?

She went to him in the hotel room. A familiar room: had they been here before? "Everything is repeating itself. Everything is stuck," she said. He framed her face in his hands and said that she looked thinner—was she sick?—what was wrong? She shook herself free. He, her lover, looked about the same. There was a small, angry pimple on his neck. He stared at her, eagerly and suspiciously. Did she bring bad news?

"So you love me? You love me?" she asked.

"Why are you so angry?"

"I want to be free of you. The two of us free of each other."

"That isn't true—you don't want that—"

He embraced her. She was wild with that old, familiar passion for him, her body clinging to his, her arms not strong enough to hold him. Ah, what despair!—what bitter hatred she felt!—she needed this man for her salvation, he was all she had to live for, and yet she could not believe in him. He embraced her thighs, her hips, kissing her, pressing his warm face against her, and yet she could not believe in him, not really. She needed him in order to live, but he was not worth her love, he was not worth her dying. . . . She promised herself this: when she got back home, when she was alone, she would draw the razor more deeply across her arm.

The telephone rang and he answered it: a wrong number.

"Jesus," he said.

They lay together, still. She imagined their posture like this, the two of them one figure, one substance; and outside this room and this bed there was a universe of disjointed, separate things, blank things, that had nothing to do with them. She would not be Anna out there, the lady in the drawing. He would not be her lover.

"I love you so much . . ." she whispered.

"Please don't cry! We have only a few hours, please. . . ."

It was absurd, their clinging together like this. She saw them as a single figure in a drawing, their arms and legs entwined, their heads pressing mutely together. Helpless substance,

heavy and warm and doomed. It was absurd that any human being should be so important to another human being. She wanted
to laugh: a laugh might free them both.

She could not laugh.

Sometime later he said, as if they had been arguing, "Look. It's
you. You're the one who doesn't want to get married. You lie to
me—"

"Lie to you?"

"You love me but you won't marry me, because you want
something left over—Something not finished—All your life you
can attribute your misery to me, to our not being married—you
are using me—"

"Stop it! You'll make me hate you!" she cried.

"You can say to yourself that you're miserable because of *me*.
We will never be married, you will never be happy, neither one
of us will ever be happy—"

"I don't want to hear this!" she said.

She pressed her hands flatly against her face.

She went to the bathroom to get dressed. She washed her face
and part of her body, quickly. The fever was in her, in the pit of
her belly. She would rush home and strike a razor across the inside of her arm and free that pressure, that fever.

The impatient bulging of the veins: an ordeal over.

The demand of the telephone's ringing: that ordeal over.

The nuisance of getting the car and driving home in all that
five o'clock traffic: an ordeal too much for a woman.

The movement of this stranger's body in hers: over, finished.

Now, dressed, a little calmer, they held hands and talked.
They had to talk swiftly, to get all their news in: he did not trust
the people who worked for him, he had faith in no one, his wife
had moved to a textbook publishing company and was doing
well, she had inherited a Ben Shahn painting from her father
and wanted to "touch it up a little"—she was crazy!—his blind
son was at another school, doing fairly well, in fact his children
were all doing fairly well in spite of the stupid mistake of their

parents' marriage—and what about her? what about her life? She told him in a rush the one thing he wanted to hear: that she lived with her husband lovelessly, the two of them polite strangers, sharing a bed, lying side by side in the night in that bed, bodies out of which souls had fled. There was no longer even any shame between them.

"And what about me? Do you feel shame with me still?" he asked.

She did not answer. She moved away from him and prepared to leave.

Then, a minute later, she happened to catch sight of his reflection in the bureau mirror—he was glancing down at himself, checking himself mechanically, impersonally, preparing also to leave. He too would leave this room: he too was headed somewhere else.

She stared at him. It seemed to her that in this instant he was breaking from her, the image of her lover fell free of her, breaking from her . . . and she realized that he existed in a dimension quite apart from her, a mysterious being. And suddenly joyfully, she felt a miraculous calm. This man was her husband truly—they were truly married, here in this room—they had been married haphazardly and accidentally for a long time. In another part of the city she had another husband, a "husband," but she had not betrayed that man, not really. This man, whom she loved above any other person in the world, above even her own self-pitying sorrow and her own life, was her truest lover, her destiny. And she did not hate him, she did not hate herself any longer; she did not wish to die; she was flooded with strange certainty, a sense of gratitude, of pure selfless energy. It was obvious to her that she had, all along, been behaving correctly; out of instinct.

What triumph, to love like this in any room, anywhere, risking even the craziest of accidents!

"Why are you so happy? What's wrong?" he asked, startled. He stared at her. She felt the abrupt concentration in him, the focusing of his vision on her, almost a bitterness in his face, as if he feared her. What, was it beginning all over again? Their love beginning again, in spite of them? "How can you look so happy?" he asked. "We don't have any right to it. Is it because . . . ?"

"Yes," she said.

The Spiral

MATTER

What was the girl doing? He was afraid to come any nearer to
her. So he took a path that led off to the side, away from her. On
this day he had a great deal to think about—his life might be
changed, or it might not be changed. Everything might change.
Nothing might change. He was a man of thirty-five, a young
doctor, walking through the park on a Wednesday afternoon,
waiting for five o'clock and a telephone call.

On the other path, hidden by a screen of bushes, the girl went
on singing—or talking to herself—idly and vacantly. No music
to her voice, not even any self-consciousness. She was not on display. She was not aware of listeners. In her twenties, thin and
hollow-faced, with small staring blank eyes and a blank voice, she
had an odd face—it looked as if it shaped inward, starting from

bulbous, bumpy upper forehead and going slightly in. Her nose was very small, flat. Her chin seemed to melt away like a chin in a dream. He could not see her from where he stood, but he remembered being unpleasantly struck by her small, blank eyes, in dark hollowed sockets. . . . It was obvious to him that she was mentally disturbed or drugged or perhaps both.

At five o'clock Joanne was supposed to call him. It was possible that she would call earlier, but he dreaded the thought of returning to his apartment to wait. He had done too much waiting in that apartment. He had waited for her too long. She was not the most beautiful woman he had ever met—though he believed her to be beautiful—but he was obsessed by her, as if there were something supernatural about her. Yet she was quite normal, quite levelheaded. There was nothing strange about her; it was only his imagination. At times, alone, he was struck by a sense of impending disaster, of terror in his having fallen in love, as if nothing could make right this mistake. He did not understand his feeling. The two of them were happy when they were together. He thought about her constantly, even when she was not in the foreground of his thoughts, and he had given up trying to get rid of this obsession—it was not her fault, why should he blame her? He looked forward eagerly to the times when they were together; at such times he felt immense relief, not having to imagine her.

And yet if it came to an end? It was the first time in his life he had ever loved a woman, though he had tried to love various women. He was a kindly, pleasant, understated young man, with many friends. The violence of his love unnerved him because it was not a friendly sensation, it did not lead outward to other people, it was a phenomenon of his own body and irremediable. . . . Alone in the park this morning, he felt himself dangerously set apart from everyone he had known in his life, even from Joanne, even from his father; the park, which was familiar, was very silent. Anything might happen. He had never thought about that before, but in a public park, during these silent afternoon hours, anything might happen. He looked around nervously, behind him. Nothing. The demented girl had wandered off in another direction, maybe knowing her way around better than he did. . . .

And if Joanne did call and her answer was no? She would remain with her husband? At the back of his skull a puddle of blankness began to form, to shape itself, as if it were the shape of his existence without her, a premonition. He had counted too much on her. Too much energy, too much pressure, too many hours of longing. . . . He had the idea that if she refused him his life would have no meaning. What meaning could it have? His father, the other night, had lectured him enthusiastically about photography—his father at the age of sixty-five had taken up a new hobby, photography, and his first pictures had seemed to Wendell very beautiful—and Wendell had had the feeling listening to him, that his father had somehow become younger having retired, having skipped back past his son to a kind of timeless and weightless style of living, a clean, well-dressed widower a handsome white-haired gentleman with money, a minor man about town and now an amateur photographer with a little talent and everything to live for.

"Every day there is something surprising, something to justif that day a hundred times over," the old man said, stabbing a fore finger into the air. Grown philosophical too, grown speculativ and sentimental? Wendell knew that his father was right, as a ways, but at the same time it seemed to him that he could no continue living if Joanne refused him; too many years had gon into this love.

Disappointed, he found himself out of the park. He ha walked right through it. For a moment he stood in a kind of daz wondering what to do. Traffic passed slowly on the street. H hated to look at his watch again. The whole day was wasted, day he should have used . . . but his hands were shaking ar he could not meet his patients. A day off, a day lost . . . wh was the element in which he lived except time, only time? A he had wasted a day. . . . Suddenly he was very hungry. He bought a hot dog from a man with a pushcart, wondering what was in the meat, amused at the bright, dyed skin. Mustard and relish. A slightly stale roll. He paid the man thirty cents for this and turned away, dripping mustard. He was very hungry and his heart had begun to pound.

Sometimes he ate fatty meat, like this, with a sense of abandon. So what? Why not clog up the veins? Everyone had to die. Sometimes he knew himself to be angry and pure and would eat nothing except fish and chicken, no eggs, no butter, nothing fatty, nothing dangerous. And he believed he could feel his spirit, whimsically, lifting itself from his body. A sensation like mist lifting itself from a bog, detaching itself. Freedom or dissolution? His father had never encouraged religious belief in Wendell, the family had never gone to church, and so Wendell had grown up entirely free of such sentiment—but he could discover its yearnings in him. Everyone wanted to be good, to be pure. It was a way of managing life. He himself wanted only to be good, to be a good man. He thought of this as he ate the hot dog greedily, in three or four bites. His mouth watered with the sharp taste. He felt even hungrier. The puddle at the back of his brain did not spread, it seemed to have been conquered; for a moment he could not remember what he was avoiding in the dark . . . a girl, a woman? . . . no, the thought of Joanne calling him to say good-by, to refuse him again, to cancel out his life.

But he thought clearly yes: yes, she would marry him.

For a while the year before, in one of his bad, helpless periods, he had followed her and her husband around. The husband was a minor county official, a very disturbed man. Joanne described his sicknesses constantly. Yet his social behavior was faultless, even impressive. He gave no indication of being disturbed. Joanne told Wendell, weeping angrily, of her husband's nighttime yelling, his accusations, his drinking, his . . . the various secrets of a disintegrating marriage, obscene secrets . . . his fear of death, of pain, of going mad. "It's life itself he's afraid of, the coward!" Joanne said in contempt. Yet the man's outward manner was controlled, even gracious. Wendell was jealous of him. He had felt that the whole relationship was a misunderstanding on his part, that this woman did not love him and did not even know him, would not acknowledge him if he were to approach her in public, and that the husband, the minor official, a mediocre lawyer from a locally famous and rich family, was the man she really loved and had never stopped loving, while Wendell could only watch from the outside. Ashamed, he confessed to his father this adulterous love, but his father only said, "You've chosen well. She's a marvelous woman, very fine. Yes, you've chosen well." What could you get out of a father like that? And he would say to Joanne, shyly and uncertainly, feeling his face get tight with apprehension, "I'm putting you through such a strain, I might be ruining your life . . . I'd understand if you wanted to say good-by." But she would only embrace him silently. In this way she assured him of everything. What had seemed to him lost the night before was returned, in a woman's silence, in her fragrant gentle arms. She did love him, he knew. She did love him and she would marry him.

Wendell threw the napkin into a wire container. Spotted with mustard, a white napkin. His eye was nervously alert to color this afternoon, to things strewn about the park, even to items stuck in the overflowing garbage container. Each of those objects had its meaning. They were man-made, and had had meaning. Why weren't there more people here? Had the park become dangerous, like parks closer to the city's core? The city was changing in all its neighborhoods, but the change was gradual as the passing from one season to another, and Wendell, like most men, did not feel real danger. He could take care of himself. Black children mysteriously free from school at this hour of the day, ran around and did not glance at him. They were not aware of him at all. A few very old men sat about, at park tables, reading newspapers, playing cards. Older than his father, these men. Or at least they

looked older. Not having his money they looked older, they bab-
bled in foreign languages, tossed their cards down bluntly onto
the picnic tables, scooped them up again, tossed them down,
everyone intent upon the cards' faces as if these faces had important news to tell.

He thought of Joanne's face and yet he could not see it in his
mind's eye. It was pressed too close to him. With a pang of lust
he thought of her, of the way she moved in his arms with anguish, a stately, cool, passionate woman, disturbing his most private being. He was certain that she loved him; he thought feverishly that it was obvious, why did he doubt it? But he was sick
with love for her and if she refused him? . . . Turning nervously, he saw the girl with the pushed-in face again. She had
wandered along a broad, flat path strewn with leaves, coming out
of the park's interior, toward him. She was barefoot and her steps
seemed accidental. She was in a daze, drugged, sleepwalking; it
was ugly just to see her. Around her thin shoulders she wore
what looked like a blanket or a rug, in festive but faded colors,
vaguely Mexican. It could have been a cheap throw rug from a
bargain-basement store. Her skirt was long and shapeless. Her
legs were bare, covered with very noticeable dark hairs, and her
feet were dirty. . . . Wendell looked away, alarmed. He should
do something about her. She should be picked up, cleaned up,
treated. . . . She was singing or chanting to herself, rubbing
her dry fingers together as if trying to calculate something, figure
something out. It eluded her. She was now only a few yards
away, stumbling right toward him as if she had no idea he was
here. He hurried away.

Back in his apartment he waited. He had begun to sweat, feeling sick. The telephone rang once but it was only his answering
service. He waited. A few minutes after five the doorbell rang
and he ran to the door, feeling how young he had become. His
teeth were chattering. Joanne took hold of his hand, of both
hands, and stared at him; she too was very frightened. She said,
'm leaving him. It's over. . . ."

So the day came to an end and his life was changed: it had happened as he had expected, after all.

ANTIMATTER

In a park, a field. The horizon is limitless. He is sitting on a park bench reading a book about tissue. What is tissue? What works to turn the pages of this heavy textbook, what guides his fingers? The very tips of his fingers are miraculously sensitive. He is most himself at his fingers' tips. . . . His mother used to say, *You had the smallest, most perfect fingers and toes!*

Between bone and tissue, tissue was more miraculous; you couldn't lose bone, it couldn't rot. Not exactly. Tissue disappeared and where were you then, where were you without a face?

He is reading with great interest. All the secrets of life are in his books—he is a student in medical school—he has only to keep on reading, keep on reading, in order to discover everything. Years to go. He will learn everything eventually and he will go out into the world and heal people. He wants to heal people. His father is a successful though not very dedicated businessman who gives money to charities and educational programs because he also wants to help people, to make them slightly less wrong. He does not want to heal them, exactly. He likes people at a distance as statistics; he does not want them in the same room with him. The sick should be put in hospitals. Wendell is impatient with his father, who only wants to make people slightly less wrong; he himself wants to raise them from the dead. Jesus had raised people from the dead, according to that lovely unbelievable story, and so history had stopped. The unviolent stopping of a watch. Wendell knows that he cannot raise the dead but he could snatch the living away from death at the very last second, stirring their limbs, breathing his own life into them. . . . He is twenty-three years old and perhaps that accounts for his enthusiasm.

Not in love yet. Peaceful in spite of his schedule at the hospital. A hard-working boy who understates his own exhaustion. H is to fall in love in a decade. It will happen. All his youthful energy will lead to this, to a happy ending. A man must love and must be loved or he himself cannot be healed, cannot heal others. Every scratch will bleed eternally. Life will leak out of him. But Wendell senses a secure future, trusting in his good luck, not like the dour, cynical medical students he knows who expect the worst. Wendell expects to be happy in his lifetime. He is not worried except, vaguely, about tissue and the precariousness of tissue. And if tissue is loosed from bone, its form? . . .

Someone approaches him. Silence. He stares at her, expecting to see Joanne, but it is not Joanne—instead it is the girl from the park, homely and vacant. Now he knows he is dreaming. What a relief! The girl from the park approaches him in her bare soiled feet, silently. Her eyes are fixed upon his. Her mouth is slightly open, her lips parted, her teeth are yellowish—uneven and yellow—he had evidently caught a glimpse of them in the park. So he knows with a spring of joy that he is only dreaming, that he is not twenty-three years old any longer but an adult, thirty-five, he is his own self, a certain self composed of a twenty-three-year-old but gone beyond that. He jumps to his feet, tosses the book aside. The girl stumbles toward him . . . her hair is long and greasy, falling into stiff strands . . . he is frightened, he feels pity, he feels excitement. Why is the park so empty? The girl shakes her head slowly, dazed, as if about to tell him something.

Suddenly she staggers. He has seen people stricken like this, falling heavily in hospital corridors, slumping over in wheelchairs. It is a mysterious and sacred moment, the moment of their being stricken. The girl falls to the ground and Wendell kneels beside her. "Don't stop breathing!" is his cry. He seizes her by the shoulders and shakes her, as if reprimanding her. Her head rolls lifelessly. He sees the white of an eyeball, slightly yellow. He puts his mouth against hers and forces his breath into her. He seizes her head in his hands, forcing air into her. Slumped and thin, sullen, her body lies without resistance beneath him. He feels the stirring of her pulse. Her lungs are being forced to receive air. On her thin, prematurely lined throat his hands are active, forcing the pulsations of the giant vein. Like forcing liquid through a tube. Up, up! He leans with all his weight on her heart, then tears open her clothing and seeks out the heart again, grinding the palm of his hand against it. *You are not going to die,* he thinks angrily. He manages to start the heart. It is like the top of a valve, clumsy to move. Its vibrations are feeble and he dreads their stopping. . . . *You are not going to die!* he thinks.

MATTER

They love each other during the night, even when they are asleep. He loses himself in her warmth, in her hair. He sleeps with his face pressed against her throat, waking to embarrassment—there is a thin trickle of his saliva on her, from his sleep. She laughs. She embraces him and presses herself against him, with passion.

"Oh, I love you, I love you!" they cry happily to each other. They are continually amazed. The curtains blow outward, toward them. He wakes for the first time that morning at about six, accustomed to waking at six and thinking of her; then he remembers that they are married. No office, no hospital, no city. They are on their honeymoon. He presses his face against her body, all the parts of her body, overcome with her beauty and the love that is so ready in her. Before they were married she had loved him with restraint, a little shyly; now it is clear that she is his wife.

Of her first husband they sometimes speak, casually and without emphasis.

At breakfast they smile continually. The coffee shop is a little pretentious, very expensive. But breakfast is a ceremony! A little dazed with love, they allow their fingers to brush together, as if by accident. She reaches for the salt, he anticipates her and hands the shaker to her. She smiles. She is very young again, as she must have been before her marriage of eleven years. He sees her mistily, sensing her, almost afraid to look into her eyes. So much has passed between them. . . . His love for her is no complete; he is her husband; everything has become perfect.

Out on the beach they talk. Their conversation evaporates, then shapes itself again and continues. It has lasted for about three years like this. "I never expected happiness. I was trying to survive," she says. She is telling the truth. There is something humble, wondering about her. She is still young. Other women yearn a lifetime for love, which never comes, but this woman has had in her short lifetime two men, two marriages, one that went sour and a second that is fated to be happy. . . . She has a small, supple body, a body that has never given birth, a flat stomach, beginning to tan. She wears a two-piece bathing suit, white. She sifts sand through her fingers and looks shyly at him. "Will we have children? Really?" she says.

"Of course."

He takes her hand, overwhelmed with emotion. A child, children? He loves them already. He considers Joanne pregnant already, her eyes moist with love for him, for him.

"I love you so much. . . ."

ANTIMATTER

A plastic radio disturbs his sleep, planted in the sand. Music and static. The sun is brilliant, too strong. He runs down the beach on the burning sand, the soles of his feet burning. In the waves near shore a crowd of people are bathing, their bodies splashing and turning in the sun. It is noon. It is late afternoon. It is dawn, very cold. He runs down the beach (which has become a beach north of Chicago, familiar to his boyhood) and his chest swells with the joy of being alone, of being alone on the beach at dawn. . . . Why had he thought he wanted other people, when his secret is this—alone on a cold beach at dawn, in sneakers and a sweatshirt, a college boy who has slipped away from his parents, he has everything, alone like this he possesses everything?

Why medical school? says his father. Ready to accept any decision his son will make, yet quietly questioning, doubting. (Home on vacation Wendell is shrewd, studying the old man: signs of age? a growing paunch? breathlessness?)

I want . . . I want to do good. . . .

He loves his father but must escape. He pretends he must return to college a day earlier than he really does; he stops off at this beach, needing to feel himself alone. Why does he need other people except to do good for them? Except to heal them? He does not need other people except as bodies.

Waking

he is on a beach, in the sun. Music as if miles away, confusing him. His head aches. An extreme depression moves upon him though he understands he is happy, safely awake and with his wife, a man of thirty-five and perfectly happy. His wife is looking out toward sea, sitting. She is so slim, her stomach so flat, that, though she is sitting, there is only the smallest fold of flesh, hardly more than a wrinkle, around her abdomen. His mouth goes dry with the thought of her. Her neat slender warm flesh . . . her magical tissue, diffuse with the blood of love for him, stiffened with that blood. . . . Or is he not quite awake? His head aches, he is perhaps still dreaming. He knows himself married yet he is somehow running along a beach at dawn, north of Chicago. The sand is hard-packed beneath his feet, very satisfactory. There is joy in running on a crusty hard-packed beach, alone. He thinks that all human beings are alone, doomed to be one self and one self only, alone, without love, without children or parents, alone on a cold beach with a self that will always be private and savage. . . .

MATTER

"It's beautiful," Wendell says slowly, staring at the photograph. "Where did you take it?"

"Along the river. The child walked out of the building just as came by. He must have been exploring, wandering around. D you really think it's beautiful?"

"Yes. I do."

A photograph of a black child, a boy of about eight. A delicate face, a beautiful face. Wendell stares at it. Behind the boy is an old building, a warehouse with the word QUIST on it, on a shabby sign. A mystery, QUIST. Wendell turns the photograph slowly in his hands, staring at it. There is a mystery here he cannot quite understand.

His father smiles, pleased. His face, in the harsh light from the office window, is gentle like the boy's face—the two of them pondering something, transfixed by the magic of a camera. Wendell feels a stirring of love for his father, and is tempted to touch him. He remembers his father touching him, embracing him, many years ago. (Once he heard his father arguing with a friend, over drinks—*Children need to be touched, they need their father's physical contact; I see to it that I embrace Wendell every day.*) He would like to touch his father now but does not.

"I wish I had time for lunch," Wendell says, glancing nervously at his watch, "but at twelve-thirty a patient is due here . . . she has to drive all the way from Flint. . . ."

"Oh, that's quite all right, I just thought I would drop in for a second," his father says at once. "I don't eat lunch anyway."

Wendell thinks that he, himself, is the one who does not eat lunch; but his father is the one who is saying it.

Standing, his father takes the photograph back from Wendell and puts it into a manila envelope. Something precious about that photograph, the way he handles it. Wendell feels a stab of jealousy—the black boy is so much a child, so young! His father says, "And how is Joanne?"

"Very well, wonderful! The baby is due in September, the last week. Oh, she's very well, she's very happy—we both are—Do you have to leave right now? I have a few more minutes," Wendell says, also standing, looking at his watch.

"I only dropped in to show you this," his father says. "It's nothing important. Nothing at all."

He walks with his father to the door, out the door. Betty, the receptionist, glances up at them and smiles. She is reading *Time*. Wendell says, suddenly afraid his father will leave too soon, "How are you feeling these days? Is everything all right?"

"Yes, the breathlessness seems to have gone away. It's a mystery," his father says with a smile. "Maybe your good news about the baby? . . . Anyway, it's all gone away. And no pains when I lie on my right side, either."

"That's wonderful. . . ."

"Yes, I feel fine, I've never felt better. Never felt better."

"Please drop in at noon anytime you can," Wendell says, as his father walks away, appearing now to be in a hurry and to have another destination to get to. "I'm free every day, at noon, because I don't eat lunch. . . ."

ANTIMATTER

This really happened, now it is a dream. Wendell is having lunch with an ex-patient of his, a lawyer whom he knows socially, distantly. The man is divorced from his wife. There is a heaviness about him that makes his shoulders slump forward . . . a man in his forties, with a heavy, handsome head, graying hair, slight pouches beneath his eyes. As Wendell's patient he told of many symptoms—frequent nausea, a sense of double vision, headaches, rapid heartbeat, shortness of breath, mysterious pains in the chest and the upper stomach. Wendell had him examined, tested, he had him hospitalized for a week . . . and nothing was uncovered, nothing. Perfect health, apparently. Years of drinking had not damaged that football player's physique, years of smoking, of working with high-level crooks had not worn him down.

He works hard, ten or twelve hours a day, though he does not need to work—he is of the Matthews family and does not need to work.

They are having lunch in the Statler Hilton, in a dark, dungeonlike restaurant, very expensive. The man says to Wendell "Without work a man is nothing, not even an existing thing. He doesn't exist. Without a wife, a man is nothing. . . ." Wendell looks at the menu. He is not hungry but he must eat. It is expected, it is a ceremony. He thinks, "My wife is pregnant; I must eat." But why is he here? He tries to remember who made this date, what the reason behind it is . . . did they have something to talk about? Why aren't they talking about it? It is too dark to read the menu and Wendell lays it down again, bewildered.

The man across from him is smiling. His smile is out of control. He says, "I feel free of all my pain for the first time now. I owe it to you. I'm going to tell everyone how excellent a doctor you are."

He reaches across the table to touch Wendell's arm and the moment is immortalized: someone has taken a picture of them from across the room. The flashbulb has dazzled Wendell's eyes —he laughs and tries to wipe away its glare with his fingers.

No explanation. The darkness becomes lucid again. A few people are milling around at the doorway, but no photographer comes forward to explain himself. People resume their luncheons. The man across from Wendell is grinning without control. Their food has arrived, although Wendell does not remember having ordered it. A large steak, twelve ounces at least, lying across his plate. Blood is oozing from it. So dark in the room is it that Wendell cannot be quite sure that his steak is dead. He picks up a knife, a fork. He begins to eat, cautiously. His friend, across the table, picks up a knife, a fork, and also begins to eat; grinning, he is mimicking Wendell's gestures, as if he were a reflection in a mirror.

Waking

he is very tired, his head aches. Slight nausea from the steak. Joanne sits on the edge of the bed. "I tried calling you earlier but you wouldn't wake up," she says. "Did you take some pills last night? I heard you get up to go to the bathroom."

His head aches violently. He cannot think.

"What is it? Are you worried about something?"

She cradles his head in her arms. She rocks gently with him,
his wife, a woman with a soft, full, pregnant body, a body pregnant in every cell, his wife. Yet he senses in her a desire to escape, to get out—better leave this sick man while she is still
healthy! Lately he has been seized by moods of depression, unaccountably. Never in his life has he been like this. It is not like
him, not natural for him. Everything in his life is excellent, his
marriage and his job are excellent, only good things have been
happening to him . . . and yet he cannot be equal to them.

How to be equal to a world of marvels?

MATTER

He hurries back from having seen the baby, a boy. A nurse is
smiling at him. He walks as if intoxicated, as if unfamiliar with
this hospital. Joanne is sitting up. She has put some make-up on
her face and it is too dark for her pale skin—but she is lovely to
him, luminous at every pore, at every cell. He speaks to her. She
closes her eyes. They hold hands, thinking of the baby, which is
more present to them now than it has been during those many
months she carried it. It is in another room now, living! Wendell
wonders if he should run back to check, to see if it is still living.
But instead he kneels beside the bed and buries his face against
his wife. She cradles his head, leaning over him as if over a baby,
smoothing his damp hair, murmuring, "Oh, I love you . .
only you . . . I love you so much. . . ."

ANTIMATTER

What is this, the smell of a hospital? He discovers himsel
kneeling on a floor. The bed is a high hospital bed, he has t
stretch his back to reach the woman he is embracing and who i
embracing him. His back aches with this effort. He cannot re
member why he is in the hospital, he suspects it is a day he doe
not belong here, he cannot remember who this patient is, wha
she wants from him. The odor of a hospital—familiar. The clea
comfortable antiseptic feel of hospital sheets—good, familia

What is unfamiliar is a woman's embrace, her warm panting nearness, her arms around his head. . . .

She has come from hours of bloody, warm, aching darkness, to tell him certain secrets. He can smell these secrets.

"Now things will be better," she says. "I've been so worried about you these last few months . . . your father is terribly worried. . . . But now, now I feel that everything will become perfect, the baby will make everything perfect. . . ."

MATTER

He and his mother, hunting bugs. Ants. A strange kind of ant, small, very black, with tiny wings. It looks as if they have wings. They have infested the kitchen cupboards!

He and his mother hunt the ants down, killing them grimly. His mother: a sweet woman, large and graceless in the hips. After having Wendell, people said, she stopped her girlhood and became a woman, a matron, grandmotherly and distracted. Not like the father, who spends too much time away from home, who will never become grandfatherly, who is an *adulterer,* should that word be uttered, a shallow sophisticated handsome man with too many friends. She is not like the father. She is intent upon killing ants on this afternoon twenty years ago, because they have infested her kitchen and must be killed, she and Wendell grim with killing, squashing the ants with paper napkins and brushing them into the sink. A light film of sweat gathers on Wendell's face and on his mother's face.

How sweet, to be killing ants! He will remember this afternoon all his life.

ANTIMATTER

A theater? . . . But an old one, not modern and sleek like theaters in the suburbs, at prosperous shopping malls. No, this is an old neighborhood theater, ready to be torn down. A smell of age, shabbiness, futility. Why is he here? . . . He is sitting with Joanne and a bachelor friend of theirs, an intern from Pakistan, very brilliant but friendless here in the United States. They have him over to the house often, and sometimes he even cooks dinner for them—superb, exotic dinners. Tonight they have evidently gone out to see a movie together. It is a movie both Joanne and Wendell have wanted to see for years but have always missed, *Jules and Jim*. It is playing at a theater near the university, in a slummy section of the city.

Jules and Jim. Two men and a woman. There are bones at the end of the movie—the bones of a man and a woman who have been in love. A surviving lover, the woman's husband, examines the bones . . . picks them up, stares at them without expression. Could you tell the bones apart? Is he unhappy over this, the turning of human beings into bones, or is he happy? Why does his face show nothing?

MATTER

Wendell stares at the man staring at the bones. Seconds pass in silence. The theater is nearly empty . . . beside him sits his wife, who is rather surprised by the ending of the movie. On her other side sits the Pakistani doctor, thin, dark, worried, gentle, a man who can always be counted on to smile quickly. If Wendell cries out in terror at the sight of those bones, will this man smile and reassure him? Will Joanne turn to him with love, touching him? Or will the two of them stare at him as if staring at bones, mere bones, seeing no value in him, now that he has succumbed to nothingness, now that he is no longer a man?

He wants to weep for all he has lost.

Doctor
     what is the diagnosis? what has been lost?

ANTIMATTER

The theater's lights come on but are not very strong. Feeble lights. Joanne shakes her head, moved. "What a strange ending, after all that . . . all that passion," she says slowly. She is wearing a suede coat with a fur collar. She has not taken the coat off because the theater is chilly. Wendell glances sideways at her, overwhelmed with her beauty and her assurance. Yet she has given birth to a child, has survived fifteen hours of labor . . . where is all that pain? Why did he feel none of it? Is pain sucked up into a woman's unconscious bones? She is a beautiful, calm woman, and her body is still slim. An ageless body. Was he not drawn to art museums, to paintings of all centuries, searching for an ideal body, an ideal face? And isn't this woman the woman he has always yearned for, now sitting beside him, his wife?

"Very strange movie!" says their friend with a laugh, shaking his head. He implies that such foolishness is beyond his understanding.

Wendell feels himself paralyzed.

MATTER

"What's wrong? Why don't you want to leave?" Joanne says.

He is staring at the blank screen. Disappointing—gray and not black, as one might wish. One might wish for total blackness. But a pale-gray screen is nothing . . . and one can see that it is only paper or some common material, unimportant. Nothing tragic can happen on such material.

Joanne is touching his arm. She pleads with him to look at her.

Beyond her anxious face is another face, a foreign man. Who? Some intern, a friendless friend from the hospital. Friends are to be good to. No matter. He cannot recall his friend's name or his wife's name.

"Are you sick? Do you feel faint? What . . . why are you sitting there?" Joanne whispers. All women become nurses, exposed to dying men. It takes a woman to see a man into life and to see a man out of life. Birth and death.

"Your father will wonder where we are, what's keeping us," Joanne says desperately, wisely, "and . . . don't you want to come home? Don't you want to see Stephen?"

Stephen?

That is not his father's name. His father is sitting with a baby, staring into a baby's face, seeking something. Once his father sat on a porch in Maine, by the ocean, in a rocking chair. Wendell came up behind him quietly and tried to see what his father was looking at.

ANTIMATTER

A cab. Slow shuffling walk. His wife's weeping, his friend's silent presence. The cab's radio squawks, a woman's voice reports something, shuts off. Their arms around him. "I don't understand," Joanne is saying slowly, helplessly. She has been betrayed but does not yet understand. "For months he's been strange . . . he seems tired. . . . But his patients have been doing well, everyone says he's doing so well, they praise him all the time, and he loves Stephen so much. . . . Why is this happening, what is happening?"

He can feel the madness in her. She would like to turn to him and beat him with her fists. Her coat smells of suede, a rich smell. He loves that smell. Instead she turns to him, embracing him. She weeps. It is a hopeless weeping, the weeping of any woman, discovering in a man no man but nothing, a nothingness. And so, after all, do women marry *nothing*? Is there never anything there?

MATTER

At home, asleep. Unnatural to be home at this time of day. His bones feel odd, resting in bed, and he can sense someone listening for him—his wife in another part of the house, listening anxiously for him. He will make no sound.

He sleeps again.

Walking in a park. Fearful. Something is going to happen. Today he will change his life or he will not change his life. What will happen? He recognizes the park, a park near the hospital . . . and he is wearing his dark summer suit, so evidently it still summer. . . . He is walking anxiously along. In a hurry

He is a young man whose terror lies in the future. It is necessary to change one's life at a certain point. He is thirty-five years old and his many friends, men his own age, have put their lives in order years ago. He is going to get married. His heart pounds in fear, in anticipation, of what will happen that day. What is he afraid of? Being refused? He is afraid of the park, of walking, of his body, of the mechanical swinging of his arms, of dark places, of sunny places, of the body of his father (which is aging), of the body of his mistress (which he loves with a lust that makes him tearful), of the body of his mother (now dead from cancer). He is afraid of failing, of being a failure, of having someone die in his arms. He is afraid of report cards, of x-rays, of all photographs. Certainly he is afraid of cancer. Of breathing, of breathlessness, of lonely dark beaches where anything can happen, of what one may see through a microscope, and of what one may see through the scope of a high-powered lens turned to the moon or just to another apartment building. Someone is arguing with him: *Don't stop breathing!*

He is on a path. It is a familiar path, leading out to St. Louis Avenue and all that monotonous traffic. If he continues, he will walk right out of the park. To his left is an area of scrubby grass, a few picnic tables. A bench angrily overturned. To his right someone is standing . . . a stranger, a girl he has never seen before. Why is she looking at him like that?

She has stopped him. She stands in his way and he can't brush past. He is paralyzed, frightened, and yet relieved. . . . Is the dream coming to an end now? Will she carry his burden for him, lift it from him? He wants only the weightlessness of a perpetual sleep, without bad dreams. No human being wants anything more. He is eight years old. He is three years old. The voices cry out, *Don't stop breathing!* but he ignores them. There comes to him a conviction, which he had felt fiercely as a young man, that there is reserved for everyone in this world a special fate—a fate no one else has the right to be jealous of, no one has any right to alter.

The girl is singing in a hoarse, breathy voice. Her voice is childlike but her face is not. She wears a strange outfit—a kind of blanket slung over her shoulders with a hole for her head. Or maybe it is a cheap rug, with red and yellow stripes. Seeing him, face to face with him, she still sings, but her voice is tense and self-conscious. She lifts one hand in an intimate gesture. . . . He takes off his coat at once. He begins to unbutton his shirt, stops and yanks at his necktie, loosening it. His hands don't know what to do next, his fingers are clumsy with the buttons on his shirt. *His bride. She is his bride.* He could weep, he is so clumsy! And now his belt, his trousers. . . .

She stares at him with her dark blank eyes, comprehending nothing. She wants nothing from him, fears nothing. Her body is angular and hollow, empty of life, a vessel that would echo only his own shouts and cries. Without energy, mechanically, she opens her arms to him. *His true bride. She knows him.* She is a dancer not dancing. He can see the bony ridge of her forehead. He can imagine her bony shoulders, her emaciated chest. Kneeling suddenly, he seizes her legs, her ankles, and kisses her feet. He presses his face against her feet and kisses them, weeping.

*T*he Turn of the Screw

FOR GLORIA WHALEN

Tuesday, July 6.

A wide stony beach. Pebbles big as hands. Here the sky is bluer than it is at home. Got out of the hotel before anyone could say hello—need to be alone after last night. Uncle and his hacking cough! Stayed up most of the night with him. His coughing is like the noise of the earth, its insides shifting. I imagine the earth splitting to draw the old man down, his body tumbling into the crater, into Hell. . . .

(Curious about Hell: will the flames make much noise?)

Tuesday, July 6.

Alone here, hidden, sick at heart. Away from that horrible numerosity. The oppression of the London sky, terraces bathed in evil light, the tonnage of history, too many horizons brought up short. . . . Chimneys that mock, beckon. Stained and weathered like cheeses. . . .

The stern demanding sea. It, too, mocks. But it does not know me. *Idle now for weeks, for a month and a half.*

Dying by the sea. Wearing the same two or three sets of clothes

Had to read the Bible to him
while he lay there coughing
and spitting. Didn't pay attention to me. Finally he slept—
around five. I fell onto my bed
fully dressed and slept until
seven. Sleep like death. In the
morning I got out fast, my head
echoing with Uncle's awful
noises . . . so glad to be alone!
And then a strange thing happened. . . .

A mile from the hotel. Me walking fast, enjoying the air, the
smell of the sea. Great gulping
breaths of air. My new boots
slick with mud, my eyes fixed
on the ground before me . . .
glancing up I saw a girl, hardly
more than a child. Twelve, thirteen years old.

Staring at me!

She called out something to me,
a stranger. A high wheedling
voice. Words I couldn't hear.
My senses rushed together,
stinging. I was deaf. A pull to
my insides. Pain. Ah, that girl!
—not pretty but full-faced,
full-bodied, her eyes gleaming
slits above her coarse pinkened
cheeks—eyes gleaming as if

—no need to change—anony-
mous gentleman dark-ringed
about the eyes with failure—
afraid of new arrivals at the
hotel: but they are all strangers.
This morning I nearly collided
with the young man I had noticed last night—he and an
older man, probably his father,
arrived yesterday, the old man
apparently quite ill—Saw him
walking along the beach, alone.
Rather finely dressed and yet
with a look—how strange that
I should feel so certain of this!
—of being doubtful of his
clothes, as if they belonged to
someone else. A waistcoat of
pale satin. Excellent boots. Hat
less, dark red hair, very strong
features—the eyebrows are especially dark and firm—the
eyes downcast as if searching
out his fate *there*, on the
ground. Something heraldic
about him—a figure for art—
My senses stung at the sight of
him—

Then I saw, standing farther
up the bank, near a thicket,
that poor little girl who runs
loose in the town sometimes—
"not right in the head"—she

there were already a secret between us! A dress of some green
material, shapeless over her full
hips and thighs; her plump
little feet in boots, splattered
with mud; her cheeks red as if
pinched, very excited, strange
dark eyes gleaming. . . . A
head of curls—dark blond,
depths of blond and shadow,
enough to make my body ache.
Licking her lips. One foot extended slightly as if in a dance.
Cried out to me—a question—
her voice tilting upward shrilly
—but the noise of the waves
drowned her out, my blood
drowned her out, pulsing in my
ears. Her gleaming eyes. The
mist seemed to thicken and
cloak us both. My eyes filmed
over, filmed over. . . .

Bell-like tone to her voice. I
could see now the veins in her
throat.

Behind her, half a mile from
the beach, a building like a for-
tress—is it a church? A barn?
Stinging film over my eyes
. . my heart is pounding vio-
ently. . . . Around us on the
beach: no one. Empty. Heart
pounding, temples pounding, a

was beckoning to the young
American. Some shy instinct
made me halt, back up—what
would happen? I wanted to
turn and hurry away. Befuddlement everywhere about us
—the crashing of the waves—
the young man's agitation—
His smart clothes suddenly the
clothes of an actor. *I must
leave, must leave!*

Flushed face—the girl's frizzy
blond hair—my own strange
elation—*She is putting her
hand out to him, she is calling
to him,* but I am too far away
to hear.

He will touch her, take hold of
her arm. He will approach her
and touch her. The three of us
stand on the beach in total
silence.

Waiting.

It is too late for me to turn and
hurry away—my own face
flushed and dangerously heated
—something churns in my
brain and fixes me here to the
spot—*His back is to me: what
does his face show?*
She is staring up into his face—
she *sees*—what words are pass-

dense dewlike moisture on every part of my body, cold and slick as fog, my insides in pain. . . . Suddenly I thought of my uncle back in the hotel: *he might be dying.*

A thicket for us. Giant bushes, spongy ground. The pebbles fade. The girl backs away from me. Wide staring smile. Her face protruding, plump. Something about her wet mouth that is fearful . . . but I cannot stop, it is too late, I cannot stop my hand from reaching out to her . . . There! Her arm, her elbow. My fingers close about her elbow. Giggling, backing away . . . a branch catches in her hair and then snaps away again, snaps straight . . . my fingers sliding up her arm to the shoulder and she is laughing faintly, breathily, the down on her upper lip is gleaming as if with cunning, she is very young, no more than twelve or thirteen years old . . . her chest rising and falling . . . little body stumbling backward, drawing us both backward into the thicket. . . .

She gave a jump. A little scream. Jerked away from me

ing between them? What words are spoken at such a time?

He approaches her. His stiff back. She draws away, teasing. Giant bushes will hide them from me. Panting, dizzy. I will be sick. He has taken hold of her now—yes, he has touched her—the two of them drawing back, back, almost out of my sight—they will hide themselves from me—it is going to happen, it is going to happen—

The girl screamed suddenly. Leaped back.

Must have seen me.

I hurry up the bank, must hide. Must get out of their sight. Heart sickened with fear, pani . . . I must not stumble. . . .

Reddening terrible face.

The dowdy room I have taken its small charms and beguilements, etched glass, lace curtains, the dust of sorrow, sorrow, sorrow. . . .

In the mirror my face surprise me. So pale, so frightened! I thought it to be, for one confused moment, the face of tha young man.

—pointed somewhere behind
me—what was it? I couldn't
see anything. What? Overcome
with panic—*I have made a
terrible mistake. My uncle has
followed me.* The girl ran
away. Behind me on the beach
there was nothing, no one, I
stood there trembling and staring back up the beach, no,
nothing, no one, and yet I had
the idea that someone had been
standing there watching us
only a few seconds before. . . .

Not my uncle? . . .

slick with sweat. Oh, reeking.
My head is still pounding. If
anyone had seen . . . if anyone. . . . Uncle would abandon me, like the rest, if he had
seen. . . .

od, held me to get through
each day.

Wednesday, July 7.

papers still filled with Victoria's
Jubilee. Uncle Wallace at
breakfast, robust and scornful,
in excellent mood. Eggs, ham,
toast, marmalade, buns.
snatches up the paper to read

Wednesday, July 7.

Sleepless. Preoccupied. Idle
now for a month and a half.
My life: turned over and over
as I turn this paperweight in
my hand, something to be
flung down, forgotten.

me an item; snorts with disgust. Breakfast takes an hour and a half. The dining room has a high cavernous ceiling: everything echoes. The room is not much used, the hotel not much used. Everyone looks English except us. Cold mealy independent faces.

A woman in her early fifties at a near table . . . dull red-blond hair, brusque mannish gestures . . . but her face is attractive as she glances toward me, past her husband. Uncle does not see. Reading the third newspaper, grunting, coughing up something into his napkin. . . . By the seaside windows an English family with three children—the oldest a girl about ten. A child. Alone at another table is a middle-aged man in a rough tweedy jacket, too big for him, sipping tea. Reading a paper. Very British. Lifting the paper to turn it, he glances toward Uncle and me —our eyes meet—then he looks away. A large rigid face. Eyes piercing.

With Uncle at the seaside. Grunts, clearing his throat vigorously, staring out at the sea.

Breakfast. Careful not to stare at *him*. Hot, hot tea. There is a delightful family at a window table—rather hazy light—rain today? No matter.

I will bicycle out into the isolation.

My heart has been turning inside me, tugging to one side. A leaden sickish tug. I surrender. . . . He is sitting with the old gentleman, wearing clothes that fit him splendidly. Yet somehow not *his*. I turn my paper very briskly, neatly, to draw his attention. . . . An instant of our exchanging a glance . . . perhaps he recognizes me from yesterday?

His eye wanders away from me

Close-curling red hair. Handsome, pale, American face. Sit erect at the table like a son. I imagine he is perhaps twenty-five years old, and most dreadfully bored in the company of that old man, somehow throw in with him for a trip, yet I don't believe that they are father and son. . . .

Absurdly sad: they are leavin the dining room. Yet an elati

It disappoints him. Spits something up in his handkerchief. *What if he dies?* . . . My first trip to Europe; three months of travel ahead; what if he sickens and dies and leaves me alone? No. Behind him is my father. His brother. Dying also, dying very slowly. Decades of it. In Boston they take decades. *Quarles Ltd., Dry Goods.*

Loosed, what would my body do? . . . Run from this wreck of a man. Run. Noble wreck, ruined noble face. Cascades of wrinkled shriveled flesh on his neck! Back in Boston they are frowning sourly over us—two of a kind, two failures. Uncle and nephew. When Uncle Wallace was my age he was already a father. . . . Then the children died. First the boy, then the girl. Then the wife. Now I am his son, maybe. Two failures.

Uncle in a chair below the hotel. Attendants eager to please. Cool for July, they talk the chance of clearing by this afternoon, always squinting at the sky and making prophecies. The middle-aged lady greets us doubtfully; yes, it is cool for

—the prospect lies ahead of further meetings, accidental meetings. Is there a mysterious and perhaps incomprehensible alliance here?

Subdued. A solitary breakfast. The family has left the dining room now—I hear excited talk of a carriage, an excursion—two girls and a boy, beautiful children. The boy is by far the youngest and walks with a bold stride. To be a father, a father of that particular boy. . . . What would that mean? How could it be experienced, so deep and terrifying a condition? Beautiful children!

Idle. Yet a small fever begins in me, as if I were about to start work. Idle and nervous. But I see that I am not heading for my room, no, I am walking quite reasonably headlong into a kind of hush—postbreakfast solemnity in this droll old hotel, all a kind of hush, the fixtures overdone and pompous and hushed, a held breath, as in that eerie moment when something gathers or crouches in preparation for an attack. . . .

Ah, the beach. Poor helpless eyes bobbing about—from hori-

July, she says. I am bored, bored. In a canvas chair beside Uncle. Staring at the sea. More blue here than back home— choppy distances—I cannot stop thinking of that girl of yesterday, that child on the beach. My body tries to shrivel. I think of my cousin Madeline —that face of hers. Accusing me. *He said things to me! Said things!*

Like a girl of twelve herself. But she was twenty-four.

Next week I will be thirty.

Uncle clearing his throat loudly, spreading a blanket across his knees; more newspapers. Brings the edge of his fingers hard across his mustache. Someone pauses near him. Cane in hand, jaunty for a man his age, his beard trimmed to a spadelike shape. Dark. Neat. He is a gentleman but nervous—wears a polka-dot bow tie and a golfing cap. Heavyset in the thighs and torso.

Uncle Wallace and he are talking—". . . north of Boston? . . ." ". . . the Clintons, Arnold Clinton, finance . . .

zon to shore—there they are, seated. The old man humped and tyrannical. The young man with legs crossed; white trousers, handsome high-button shoes, an air of indolence and impatience. The son of a wealthy father, certainly.

Approaching the old gentleman. His sudden raised face— querulous watery eyes—yet I introduce myself quite easily. Ah, yes, they are Americans; should I seem surprised? From Boston. It turns out that we know someone in common. I chat quite happily, quite easily with the old man. My agitation seems to have subsided. Ignore the young man's stare—it is good to hear my own voice again—too conscious of Self, too haunted, driven by Self, always Self. I must overcome myself.

Patrick Quarles II. His name.

I think of Dickens—for we are near David Copperfield's country—no, I think of Stendhal: young man lounging idly, restlessly, ambitious and yet not strong enough to direct the progress of the story he is in.

imports? . . ." ". . . crowds in London? . . . awful!"

My eye is drawn out to the edge of the sea.

Women: the girl of yesterday. Eyes secretive as slits. Her foot —the mud—the ankle—the pale stockings—the calf of the leg inside the stocking—the knee—the thigh—

Old men chattering: of London, of crowds, *this screaming, clumsy overdoing of a fine thing,* the man in the golfing cap says.

Ah, the cords of her little throat were taut with concentration! Cheap material of the dress drawn tight across the small bosom, tight as the veins of the throat, the tense arteries of the stomach, the loins . . . blue-veined thighs, the shadowy soft insides of thighs. . . . *London defaced: an atrocious sight. Miles of unsightly scaffolding . . . a sudden, new vision of our age, an unwelcome perspective of the century that lies ahead. . . . Machinery . . . that infuriates and deflowers and destroys. . . .*

Condemned almost and never to be quite *real,* quite sympathetic. *He seems to be listening as I speak of London. . . .* He is a man marked for some strange destiny. For women? Yes, but more. He does not know what his fate will be. *Nervous, I am beginning to be nervous. . . .*

He is like a young animal: no history.

The old man contains all their family history. Draws it up into him. We chatter wonderfully, two Americans, he seems to be impressed with my denunciation of the Jubilee nonsense. Can understand best harsh abrasive words.

The young man gets to his feet suddenly, unaccountably, and strolls away. . . .

The old man is a large monument: the nephew a small mark. In a flash I see their family gravesite. Yes. I, standing here so helplessly and timidly, cane tucked through my arm, smiling and smiling, a gravestone of too fragile a substance: the wintry gusts from this sea would destroy me.

Walking slowly down the
beach. Why do I want to run,
run away from the chatter
of old men!—a root is alive
in me, stirring in me. Trembling. Ugh. I am alive and the
old men are dying or are dead,
if I glance over my shoulder at
them I would see only two
aging gentlemen—one in a
canvas chair, bundled up for a
cool July morning, the other
with a cane thrust through his
arm, words that do not matter,
a flow of words that do not matter the way the pebbles of this
wide wet beach matter—and
behind them, in America, my
own father stands like a monument, his shadow rooted to him
at his base, unshakable. Can
you shake them? You walk
away from them.

I light a cigar.

Thursday, July 8.

Was informed of a letter for
me—took it from the clerk,
surprised, for who would write
to me?—having left home as I
did—could not recognize the
handwriting—walked confused
out the front of the hotel, almost slipped on the steps that

Thursday, July 8.

Walking quickly along the
shore. Unable to think. *Must
think.* Not fit for company now
—my face a mask of grimaces,
taunts, smirks, bewilderments,
small pains and pleasures, fea-
tureless as the sea. Not human
now. Not human. To have

were wet from the morning's rain—tore open the envelope nervously—

My Dear Boy,
I am anxious for this letter to do nothing except soothe you, encourage you, insist upon the simple joy you have given me by existing so innocently and so nobly as yourself. From my timid post of observation, your future strikes me as rich and enormously open, wide as the ocean—and I beg that you do not destroy it by any impulsive act—for, you see, I was a most reluctant and helpless witness to Tuesday's small episode—or by any systematic and perhaps more wasteful surrender of your youth to another's age. Be free: I rejoice in your very being. But: Caution!

No signature.

I stumbled along the street—cobbled street—row upon row of small blank houses, shops, the tower of the church and its crumbling ivy wall—mind in a whirl—panic—must tear up his letter and get rid of it—

Went into a pub. Seated, my eyesight blotched. Din inside

dared what I did! . . . A sleepless night, palpitating heart. Absurd attempts at prayer. Godless prayer. But something, something must aid me, must beguile me out of myself . . . out of the memory of what I have done . . . memories of Father's fits of madness, the Imaginary seizing his throat, the Demon always beside him, squatting, leaping up when he did not, could not, have expected it. . . . Am I my father's son, after all?

Heroism: acquiescing to that madness.

At the bottom of my soul it squats, like that dwarf of a demon: the fear that I am mad, evil, reckless, sick, corrupting, contaminating, loosed, form-less, sucking like the waves here upon the packed sand, desolate, inexhaustible, damned. . . .

Why did I write him that letter?

Yet—the joy of this morning! The utter abandoned joy of the writing, the sealing of the envelope, the very slow, slow, firm addressing of a name that my head. Last night Uncle kept me awake again, reading the Bible to him. Words kept rising in my head: *Why doesn't he die!* My fear of him, my love for him. *Why don't they all die, die!* I order a small beer and drink it at once and in the instant in which I close my eyes I can see their bodies bobbing and ebbing in a tide, the bodies of the old, old men, tossed up toward an anonymous shore that is neither American nor English, just a shore, just bodies of the dead. *Why don't they die and free us from them? —free us to life?*

Spent the afternoon. Seagoing men here—retired men—noisy in their greetings—"What ho!" they call out to each other when they meet—then fall into silence—but the silence is not awkward. Women. Moving about. They glance at me and my heart feels enormous, suffocating. One woman stares openly at me. A broad smile, straggly hairs on her forehead . . . skin not pale like Madeline's but opaque, blunt . . . *easing the stocking from her muscular leg, heavy flesh, dark*

suddenly seems to have been my own invention, to have been known to me all my life: *Patrick Quarles II.*

What is he? A disinherited son —so I have gathered. He has the look of a London urchin grown and clothed splendidly —an actor—a nervous flitting consciousness that no clothes can define—*I will clothe you.*

What will happen when our eyes meet? That fateful terrifying instant of our common *knowledge!* I will bow to him, I will acknowledge everything meekly. . . . Breath in ragged spurts. Aging. My best work is behind me. Now, ahead of me, is work of another kind. . . . He is so young, he is pure instinct. The old man, the uncle, wants to suck his energy. Ignorant old man!

I am mad to have such thoughts . . . sharp pain in my chest as I climb the hotel steps, which seem suddenly steep, mountainous. . . . Is h here, waiting? The letter in hi hand, waiting?

*hairs growing out of the flesh
. . . but I stand suddenly,
hurry away. Must get back to
the hotel before Uncle is angry.*

I tore the letter up into small
pieces and threw it away.

Friday, July 9.

Excursion by carriage. Out
along the country roads in spite
of the drizzle. Uncle's sour
cough. Forgave me for leaving
him yesterday: his heir.

Women. Foul and sluggish in
their evil. Mud on my boots,
scummy feel of my own skin.
My cousin's tears and red-
rimmed eyes. The woman in
the tavern: the veins of her
flesh would have been hidden
deep inside that opaque fatty
skin.

Afternoon tea: Uncle gorges
himself. Buns, jam. Beer.
Whisky. Coffee. Small
meat pie. My duty to rise
obediently as a son, to seek out
more food. Which village are
we in? What is its name? The
map I studied is marked with
names of places I had wanted
to explore—Blundeston, Great
Yarmouth, Bournemouth itself

Friday, July 9.

Sleepless. Feverish and very
happy. Three letters composed
for him, and I hardly know
which to select. All of them?

The chambermaid listens with
her good plain worried gaze
upon me. I begin explaining
carefully, but end by stammer-
ing, my eyes filled with moisture—"Mr. Quarles is an extremely sensitive gentleman
. . . and he would be dis-
tressed to be told that he
walked off with my letters this
morning . . . he quite simply
picked them up by accident,
when we paused to chat together. . . . I called after him,
of course, but, as you may
know, he doesn't hear quite so
well . . . and . . . and I
would actually prefer not to
bring the matter up to him, and
certainly I would prefer never
to see the poor letters again if it

—but everything passes now before my eyes in a mist, my senses sting, the machinery of my brain races ahead to what, to what?—

Caution, the letter advised.

What does that mean?—why caution?—Am I about to do something I must be urged against? *Uncle's piggish grunts. The Royal Park Hotel. Will I outlive him?* Sat in the pub with him, a lonely pub. Thought of hell. Spirits brushing against us in daylight, the damned. What could they tell us about hell if they could speak?

Dutiful nephew to a sick man.

Nothing more.

were a question of . . . a question of insulting him, however indirectly. . . ." Nods in sympathy with me. Grimly. Out of her mild gaze I think I see something growing—sharp and deadly and cunning—but no, I must be imagining it. Imagining it. She replies that it is out of her control. Only the manager, perhaps. . . . Very hard for her to know what to do. . . . But no, no, I say at once, the manager must absolutely not be bothered; I will surrender the letters—gaily I tell her this, ready to back away —She frowns, blinks slowly and stupidly at me—Suddenly she consents.

Ah, she consents! And within five minutes we are *there,* in that room! The Quarleses have taken a rather grand suite of rooms. A sitting room of really lavish proportions—excellent furniture—a carpet in much finer condition than the one in my sad little room—a balcony that stares out wonderfully at the sea and sky. There is a little old antique of a writing desk that I approach, under the chambermaid's watchful eye,

for my letters would be here if
Mr. Quarles had really walked
off with it—and humbly, timidly I bend over the desk, in
that good lady's sight, and do
not touch anything on it. Only
yesterday's *Times*. A letter
tucked into its envelope, post-
marked Boston. I shake my
head—nothing here—and,
with a slight questioning rise of
my eyebrows, indicate that I
will take just one step inside
this bedroom—

Staring at me impassively.
What is she thinking? Can she
guess? The forbidden rises to
one's face in the presence of
such women, they positively
draw guilt out, expose everything—But though I am nervous, extremely nervous, I smile
rather bravely back at her—
how she stands watching me!—
And so I open the door to one
of the bedrooms and simply
lean inside—my heart is
pounding—It is *his* room.

Scent of pomade. Tobacco.

For a long icy moment I stand
there—my body rigid with the
necessity of showing nothing,
absolutely nothing, as if the

hunters and their dogs will be upon me if I flinch—I feel his strange heedless presence everywhere about me, rushing upon me. So much closer and dearer than he might ever be in his own person—

"No luck, sir?" the chambermaid calls out.

Saturday, July 10.

Three letters.

That dark demanding hand—not a lady's hand—it is someone like myself, shouting at me—trying to make me hear—

A young woman and her mother brush past me with a scent of something harsh and flowery about them—my nerves are jumping—people are beginning to notice me. An elderly man is staring quite openly at me—did he write these letters?

I walk out quickly. Must be alone.

My Dear Boy,
Understand only that I wish
you well—only well!—and that
I should not communicate so
strangely and so secretively if

Saturday, July 10.

Another sleepless, aching night. The chambermaid's face hovering in my private darkness—witness of my folly!—this morning I will press upon her a small sum, hopefully not a bribe—or have I come to that? A gift, a sign of my gratitude for her kindness, her—

No breakfast this morning. My stomach is so weak, I am so preoccupied . . . I am terrified. . . . Must imagine *him. Him.* I stand on the balcony and think of him, envision him, only him. The sea is choppy and leaden today. Everything disappoints us that is not human.

Few people strolling out. Ladies with their long dresses, so drastically protected. Gentle *other means were open to me. . . .*

The last sentence is crossed out, I can't make out anything. No signature.

My Dear Boy,
You are generous to allow me to write, knowing that it is the only manner in which I may hold you close, lay upon you— oh, so soothingly!—the most respectful of hands—I see in your face a terrible need. I fear for you. Will you stand on the shore and accept these frail words of mine, will you accept the only gift I dare give you— words, prophecies—

For a long moment I cannot think. What is happening? It is as if a secret Self—my own Self —were writing to me like this, hinting at a terrible knowledge —*prophecies*: what does that mean?—Are there spirits, ghosts? Is there a future Self —a future Patrick Quarles— gazing back upon me, seeing me, from the future—the 1900's, when we may all be free!—and reaching back to bless me—

men. Hats, gloves, pipes. *Must imagine him. No freedom.* Fallen upon evil days, sick days —signs of vastation all around me, inside me—

Ah, he is there!

Wooden steps. The boardwalk. Ah, he is reading . . . he is reading my letters. . . . He is reading what I have written to him, in such anguish!

Disgust? Shame? Or can he sense the human wish behind it, the wish to speak kindly to another soul, a solitary soul? . . .

Feverish. The wind inside my head, not cooling it. Wind. Fever. My head is swimming. He is standing there with his back to me—his figure blurs and swims in my vision—I want to cry out to him, "Must I grow old? Must I die? If you walk away from me I will die—"

No—he is turning—

His figure against the somber water. Unimagined—such splendor! He is looking toward me but I draw back at once,

And so I stand on the shore, yes. I accept. In this dour chilling breeze I am very happy, and I turn slowly to look back at the hotel—that monster of a hotel!

Who is watching me?

He must be gazing at me from one of the windows. But I dare not wave. What does he think? Is he there? Is there really anyone there? I stare into space, smiling.

Across the distance something passes into me, like a breath.

Lighting a cigar, I stroll down the beach and open the third letter. A letter from a friend, one who wishes me well and knows me, knows me.

My Dear Boy,
You are without history and so you must free yourself from it. But caution. Am I speaking madness? Am I offending you? Or can you understand how I should, if I dared, quite openly invite you to lean upon me as a kindly father? . . . The sense that I cannot speak to you, cannot reveal myself to you—this torments me, makes me ache at the bitterness of

into the shadow of the room— my eyes brimming— . . . . .

Across that space he seems to bless me. I must put my hands out against the French doors, I must steady myself or I will fling myself forward, outward, to my death—

Yes, he looks at me. It has happened. The distance between us is holy. A hush. . . . He is my living Self: I see that now. Living as I have never lived. He is magnificent. I am alive in him and dead, dead in myself, but alive in him, only in him—

In a lifetime there are few moments of such bliss.

Trembling, hiding, in the shadows of my room . . . safe. Saved. My heart lunges backward into safety. Must hide. Must remain hidden. I am growing old, yes, soon I will be as old and as ugly as his uncle —yes, and it is right, we must be pushed aside, we must die— must acquiesce to darkness— Our heirs demand the future. They demand that history be turned over to them.

*things. I reach out toward you
—I let go—I abandon you—*

More words crossed out.

Something tries to come
through those X-ed out words.
A command. Angry urgent
words. *Utter caution.* A voice
has spoken. I know there are
ghosts. I understand them. I
feel them in this medieval
town, on all sides of me, harsh
and innocent with their cold
piercing eyes and their victories
—their terrible victories—

I will kill him.

No. The words are not mine. I
will never lay hands upon him.
The mark of my hands would
show upon him, it would
scream out that I was his mur-
derer—*I will suffocate him, I
have been given permission to
suffocate him, to destroy him—*
I will not come near him, no.
No. I will sit quietly at his bedside as he strangles in his own
phlegm—the poison that bubbles up out of his ugly soul—

Will I sit at his bedside? Will
I watch him die? Will I dare to
do what those letters instruct?

In this moment of joy I am
transformed.

He, he is myself: walking
away! Free to walk away! I
must strain to see him, his
handsome figure about to fade
into the low heathery bareness
of the country, that shy purple
and gold that runs nearly to
the edge of the sea. . . .

A moment too deep for any
utterance.

It takes me an hour to dress. I
am still shaky. A little feverish.
Soon I will be working again—
I will work through *him.* He
will possess me. I am ready to
work, ready even to return to
the coal-gray skies of London,
that sky that encloses and en-
traps the mind—

He has understood my mes-
sage. My love. I will live
through him and he through
me: born again in my writing,
in something I will, must write,
something I will begin soon in
honor of his youth and the perfect power of his face. . . .

I hurry downstairs. I must feed
the birds in the garden—I have

Will I outlive him? Will I outlive all these old men?

forgotten them for days—The garden is deserted, hushed. Everyone is elsewhere. Only *he* is with me, his presence close to me, our minds beating with the beauty of this somber garden and its wide gravel paths and its pinched roses and weathered walls—

In a lifetime there are few moments of such bliss.

*T*he Dead

*seful in acute and chronic depression, where accompanied by
xiety, insomnia, agitation; psychoneurotic states manifested by
nsion, apprehension, fatigue. . . .* They were small yellow
psules, very expensive. She took them along with other cap-
les, green-and-aqua, that did not cost quite so much but were
aker. *Caution against hazardous occupations requiring com-
te mental alertness.* What did that mean, "complete mental
rtness?" Since the decline of her marriage, a few years ago,
na thought it wisest to avoid complete mental alertness. That
s an overrated American virtue.

For the relief of anxiety and the relief of the apprehension of
xiety: small pink pills. *Advise against ingestion of alcohol.* But

she was in the habit of drinking anyway, always before meeting strangers and often before meeting friends, sometimes on perfectly ordinary, lonely days when she expected to meet no one at all. She was fascinated by the possibility that some of these drugs could cause paradoxical reactions—fatigue and intense rage, increase and decrease in libido. She liked paradox. She wondered how the paradoxical reactions could take place in the same body, at the same time. Or did they alternate days? *For the relief of chronic insomnia*: small harmless white barbiturates. In the morning, hurrying out somewhere, she took a handful of mood-elevating pills, swallowed with some hot water right from the faucet, or coffee, to bring about a curious hollow-headed sensation, exactly as if her head were a kind of drum. Elevation! She felt the very air breathed into her lungs suffused with peculiar dazzling joy, worth every risk.

Adverse reactions were possible: *confusion, ataxia, skin eruptions, edema, nausea, constipation, blood dyscrasias, jaundice, hepatic dysfunction, hallucinations, tremor, slurred speech, hyperexcitement.* . . . But anything was possible, after all!

A young internist said to her, "These tests show that you are normal," and her heart had fallen, her stomach had sunk, her very intestines yearned downward, stricken with gravity. Normal? Could that be? She had stared at him, unbelieving. "The symptoms you mention—the insomnia, for instance—have no organic basis that we can determine," he said.

Then why the trembling hands, why the glitter to the eyes, why, why the static in the head? She felt that she had been cheated. This was not worth sixty dollars, news like this. As soon as she left the doctor's office she went to a water fountain in the corridor and took a few capsules of whatever was in her coat pocket, loose in the pocket along with tiny pieces of lint and something that looked like the flaky skins of peanuts, though she did not remember having put peanuts in any of her pockets. She swallowed one, two, three green-and-aqua tranquillizers, and a fairly large white pill that she didn't recognize, found in the b

tom of her purse with a few stray hairs and paper clips. This
helped a little. "So I'm normal!" she said.

She had been living at that time in Buffalo, New York, teach-
ng part-time at the university. Buffalo was a compromise be-
ween going to California, as her ex-husband begged, and going
o New York, where she was probably headed. Her brain burned
dryly, urging her both westward and eastward, so she spent a
year in this dismal Midwestern city in upstate New York, all
lighted elms and dingy skies and angry politicians. The city was
n a turmoil of excitement; daily and nightly the city police
rowled the university campus in search of troublesome students,
nd the troublesome students hid in the bushes alongside build-
ngs, eager to plant their homemade time bombs and run; so the
ampus was not safe for ordinary students or ordinary people at
ll. Even the "normal," like Ilena, long wearied of political ac-
vism, were in danger.

She taught twice a week and the rest of the time avoided the
niversity. She drove a 1965 Mercedes an uncle had willed her,
n uncle rakish and remote and selfish, like Ilena herself, who
ad taken a kind of proud pity on her because of her failed mar-
age and her guilty listlessness about family ties. The uncle, a
dge, had died in St. Louis; she had had to fly there to get the
r. The trip back had taken her nearly a week, she had felt so
naccountably lazy and sullen. But, once back in Buffalo, driving
r stodgy silver car, its conservative shape protecting her heav-
, she felt safe from the noxious street fumes and the darting,
citable eyes of the police and the local Buffalo taxpayers—in
ite of her own untidy hair and clothes.

The mood-elevating pills elevated her several feet off the
ound and made her stammer rapidly into the near, dim faces of
r students, speaking faster and faster in the hope that the class
riod would end sooner. But the tranquillizers dragged her
wn, massaged her girlish heart to a dreamy condition, fingered
nerve ends lovingly, soothingly, wanted only to assure her
t all was well. In her inherited car she alternately drove too

fast, made nervous by the speedier pills, or too slowly, causing
warlike sounds from the rear, the honking of other drivers in
American cars.

In the last two years Ilena had been moving around constantly,
packing up the same clothes and items and unpacking them
again, always eager, ready to be surprised, flying from one coast
to the other to speak at universities or organizations interested in
"literature," hopeful and adventurous as she was met at various
windy airports by strangers. Newly divorced, she had felt virginal
again, years younger, truly childlike and American. Beginning
again. Always beginning. She had written two quiet novels, each
politely received and selling under one thousand copies, and then
she had written a novel based on an anecdote overheard by her at
the University of Michigan, in a girls' rest room in the library,
about a suicide club and the "systematic deaths of our most valu-
able natural resource, our children"—as one national reviewer of
the novel said gravely. It was her weakest novel, but it was
widely acclaimed and landed her on the cover of a famous magazine, since her *Death Dance* had also coincided with a sudden
public interest in the achievement of women in "male-dominated
fields." Six magazines came out with cover stories on the women's
liberation movement inside a three-month period; Ilena's photograph had been exceptionally good. She found herself famous
and fame made her mouth ironic and dry with a sleeplessness
that was worse than ever, in spite of her being "normal."

The pills came and went in cycles—the yellow capsules favored for a while, then dropped for the small pink pills, tranqui-
lizers big enough to nearly knock her out taken with some gin
and lemon, late at night. These concoctions were sacred to her,
always kept secret. Her eyes grew large with the prospect of
those "adverse reactions" that were threatened but somehow
never arrived. She was lucky, she thought. Maybe nothing adverse would ever happen to her. She had been twenty-six years
old at the start of the breakup of her marriage; it was then that
most of the pills began, though she had always had a problem

with insomnia. The only time she had truly passed out, her brain gone absolutely black, was the winter day—very late in the afternoon—when she had been in her office at a university in Detroit, with a man whom she had loved at that time, and a key had been thrust in the lock and the door opened—Ilena had screamed, "No! Go away!" It had been only a cleaning lady, frightened off without seeing anything, or so the man had assured Ilena. But he had fainted. Her skin had gone wet and cold; it had taken the terrified man half an hour to bring her back to normal again. "Ilena, I love you, don't die," he had begged. Finally she was calm enough to return to her own home, an apartment she shared with her husband in the northwestern corner of the city; she went home, fixed herself some gin and bitter lemon, and stood in the kitchen drinking it while her husband yelled questions at her. "Where were you? Why were you gone so long?" She had not answered him. The drink was mixed up in her memory with the intense relief of having escaped some humiliating danger, and the intense terror of the new, immediate danger of her husband's rage. Why was this man yelling at her? Whom had she married, that he could yell at her so viciously? The drinking of that gin was a celebration of her evil.

That was back in 1967; their marriage had ended with the school year; her husband spent three weeks in a hospital half a block from his mother's house in Oswego, New York, and Ilena had not gone to see him, not once, being hard of heart, like stone, and terrified of seeing him again. She feared his mother, too. The marriage had been dwindling all during the Detroit years— 1965–1967—and they both left the city shortly before the riot, which seemed to Ilena, in her usual poetic, hyperbolic, pill-sweetened state, a cataclysmic flowering of their own hatred. She had thought herself good enough at hating, but her husband was much better. "Die. Why don't you die. *Die*," he had whispered hypnotically to her once, as she lay in bed weeping very early the morning, before dawn, too weary to continue their battle. Off and on she had spoken sentimentally about having children,

but Bryan was wise enough to dismiss that scornfully—"Yo
don't bring children into the world to fix up a rotten marriage,
he said. She had not known it was rotten, exactly. She knew tha
he was jealous of her. A mutual friend, a psychiatrist, had tol
her gently that her having published two novels—unknown a
they were, and financial failures—was "unmanning" to Bryan
who wanted to write but couldn't. Was that her fault? Wha
could she do? "You could fail at something yourself," she wa
advised.

In the end she had fallen in love with another man. She ha
set out to love someone in order to punish her husband, to r
venge herself upon him; but the revenge was forgotten, she ha
really fallen in love in spite of all her troubles . . . in love wit
a man who turned out to be a disappointment himself, but a
other kind of disappointment.

Adverse reactions: *confusion, ataxia, skin eruptions, edem
nausea, constipation, blood dyscrasias, jaundice, hepatic dysfun
tion, hallucinations*. . . . Her eyes filmed over with bri
ghostly uninspired hallucinations now and then, but she believe
this had nothing to do with the barbiturates she took to sleep,
the amphetamines she took to speed herself up. It was love th
wore her out. Love, and the air of Detroit, the gently waftin
smoke from the manly smokestacks of factories. Love and smol
The precise agitation of love in her body, what her lover and h
husband did to her body; and the imprecise haze of the air, of h
vision, filmed-over and hypnotized. She recalled having lov
her husband very much at one time. Before their marriage
1964. His name was Bryan Donohue, and as his wife she h
been *Ilena Donohue*, legally; but a kind of maiden cunning h
told her to publish her novels as *Ilena Williams*, chaste Ilena, t
name musical with *l*'s. Her books were by that Ilena, while l
nights of sleeplessness beside a sleeping, twitching, perspiri
man were spent by the other Ilena. At that time she was n
famous yet and not quite so nervous. A little insomnia, t
wasn't so bad. Many people had insomnia. She feared sleep

cause she often dreamed of the assassination of Kennedy, which was run and rerun in her brain like old newsreels. Years after that November day she was still fresh with sorrow for him, scornful of her own sentimentality but unable to control it. How she had wept! Maybe she had been in love with Kennedy, a little. . . . So, sleeping brought him back to her not as a man: as a corpse. Therefore she feared sleep. She could lie awake beside a breathing, troubled corpse of her own, her partner in this puzzling marriage, and she rehearsed her final speech to him so many times that it became jaded and corny to her, out of date as a monologue in an Ibsen play.

"There is another man, of course," he had said flatly.

"No. No one."

"Yes, another man."

"No."

"Another man, I know, but I'm not interested. Don't tell me his name."

"There is no other man."

"Obviously there is. Probably a professor at that third-rate school of yours."

"No."

Of course, when she was in the company of the *other man*, it was Bryan who became "the other" to him and Ilena—remote and masculine and dangerous, powerful as a nightmare figure, with every right to embrace Ilena in the domestic quiet of their apartment. He had every right to make love to her, and Gordon did not. They were adulterers, Ilena and Gordon. They lost weight with their guilt, which was finely wrought in them as music, precious and subtle and prized, talked over endlessly. Ilena could see Gordon's love for her in his face. She loved that face, she loved to stroke it, stare at it, trying to imagine it as the face of a man married to another woman. . . . He was not so handsome as her own husband, perhaps. She didn't know. She only knew, bewildered and stunned, that his face was the center of the universe for her, and she could no more talk herself out of

this whimsy than she could talk herself out of her sorrow fo
Kennedy.

Her husband, Bryan Donohue: tall, abrupt, self-centered
amusing, an instructor in radiology at Wayne Medical School
with an interest in jazz and a desire to write articles on science
science and sociology, jazz, jazz and sociology, anything. He wa
very verbal and he talked excellently, expertly. Ilena had alway
been proud of him in the presence of other people. He had
sharp, dissatisfied face, with very dark eyes. He dressed well an
criticized Ilena when she let herself go, too rushed to bother wit
her appearance. In those days, disappointed by the low salary an
the bad schedule she received as an instructor at a small unive
sity in Detroit, Ilena had arrived for early classes—she was give
eight-o'clock classes every semester—with her hair bare
combed, loose down to her shoulders, snarled and bestial from
night of insomnia, her stockings marred with snags or long di
figuring runs, her face glossy with the dry-mouthed euphoria
tranquillizers, so that, pious and sour, she led her classes in tl
prescribed ritual prayer—this was a Catholic university, ar
Ilena had been brought up as a Catholic—and felt freed, on
the prayer was finished, of all restraint.

Bad as the eight-o'clock classes were, the late-afternoon class
(4:30–6:00) were worse: the ashes of the day, tired undergrad
ates who needed this course to fill out their schedules, hig
school teachers—mainly nuns and "brothers"—who needed
few more credits for their Master's degrees, students w
worked, tired unexplained strangers with rings around their ey
of fatigue and boredom and the degradation of many semesters
"special students." When she was fortunate enough to have o
or two good students in these classes, Ilena charged around
excitement, wound up by the pills taken at noon with bla
coffee, eager to draw them out into a dialogue with her. Tl
talked back and forth. They argued. The other students
docile and perplexed, waiting for the class to end, glancing fr
Ilena to one of her articulate boys, back to Ilena again, tak

notes only when Ilena seemed to be saying something important. What was so exciting about Conrad's *Heart of Darkness*, they wondered, that Mrs. Donohue could get this worked up?

Her copper-colored hair fell in a jumble about her face, and her skin sometimes took a radiant coppery beauty from the late afternoon sun as it sheered mistily through the campus trees, or from the excitement of a rare, good class, or from the thought of her love for Gordon, who would be waiting to see her after class. One of the boys in this late-afternoon class—Emmett Nolan—already wore his hair frizzy and long, though this was 1966 and a few years ahead of the style, and he himself was only a sophomore, a small precocious irritable argumentative boy with glasses. He was always charging up to Ilena after class, demanding that she explain herself—"You use words like 'emotions,' you bully us with your *emotions!*" he cried. "When I ask you a question in class, you distort it! You try to make everyone laugh at me! It's a womanly trick, a *female* trick, not worthy of you!" Emmett took everything seriously, as seriously as Ilena; he was always hanging around her office, in the doorway, refusing to come in and sit down because he was "in a hurry" and yet reluctant to go away, and Ilena could sense by a certain sullen alteration of his jaw that her lover was coming down the hall to her office. . . .

"See you," Emmett would say sourly, backing away.

Gordon was a professor in sociology, a decade or more older then Ilena, gentle and paternal; no match for her cunning. After a particularly ugly quarrel with her husband, one fall day, Ilena had looked upon this man and decided that he must become her lover. At the time she had not even known his name. *A lover. She would have a lover.* He was as tall as her own husband, with married, uncomfortable look about his mouth—tense apologetic smiles, creases at the corners of his lips, bluish-purple veins on his forehead. A handsome man, but somehow a little gray. His complexion was both boyish and gray. He did not dress with the self-conscious care of her husband Bryan; his clothes were tweedy, not very new or very clean, baggy at the knees, smelling of tobacco and unaired closets. Ilena, determined to fall in love with him, had walked by his home near the university—an ordinary brick two-story house with white shutters. Her heart pounded with jealousy. She imagined his domestic life: a wife, four children, a Ford with a dented rear fender, a lawn that was balding, a street that was going bad—one handsome old Tudor home had already been converted into apartments for students, the sign of inevitable disaster. Meeting him, talking shyly with him, loving him at her finger tips was to be one of the gravest events in her life, for, pill-sweetened as she was, she had not seriously believed he might return her interest. He was Catholic. He was supposed to be happily married.

When it was over between them and she was teaching, for two quick, furtive semesters at the University of Buffalo, where most classes were canceled because of rioting and police harassment Ilena thought back to her Detroit days and wondered how she had survived, even with the help of drugs and gin: the central nervous system could not take such abuse, not for long. She had written a novel out of her misery, her excitement, her guilt, typing ten or fifteen pages an evening until her head throbbed with pain that not even pills could ease. At times, lost in the story she was creating, she had felt an eerie longing to remain there permanently, to simply give up and go mad. *Adverse reactions: confusion, hallucinations, hyperexcitement. . . .* But she had not gone mad. She had kept on typing, working, and when she was finished it was possible to pick up, in her fingers, the essence of that shattering year: one slim book.

Death Dance. *The story of America's alienated youth . . . shocking revelations . . . suicide . . . drugs . . . was . . . horror . . .* $5.98.

It had been at the top of the *New York Times* best-seller list for fifteen weeks.

Gordon had said to her, often, "I don't want to hurt you, Ilena, I'm afraid of ruining your life." She had assured him that her life was not that delicate. "I could go away if Bryan found out, alone

I could live alone," she had said lightly, airily, knowing by his grimness that he would not let her—surely he would not let her go? Gordon thought more about her husband than Ilena did, the "husband" he had met only once, at a large university reception, but with whom he now shared a woman. Two men, strangers, shared her body. Ilena wandered in a perpetual sodden daze, thinking of the . . . the madness of loving two men . . . the freakishness of it, which she could never really comprehend, could not assess, because everything in her recoiled from it: this could not be happening to her. Yet the fact of it was in her body, carried about in her body. She could not isolate it, could not comprehend it. Gazing at the girl students, at the nuns, she found herself thinking enviously that their lives were unsoiled and honest and open to any possibility, while hers had become fouled, complicated, criminal, snagged, somehow completed without her assent. She felt that she was going crazy.

Her teaching was either sluggish and uninspired, or hysterical. She was always wound up and ready to let go with a small speech on any subject—Vietnam, the oppression of blacks, religious hypocrisy, the censorship haggling over the student newspaper, any subject minor or massive—and while her few aggressive students appreciated this, the rest of her students were baffled and unenlightened. She sat in her darkened office, late in the afternoon, whispering to Gordon about her classes: "They aren't going well. I'm afraid. I'm not any good as a teacher. My hands shake when I come into the classroom. . . . The sophomores are forced to take this course and they hate me, I know they hate me. . . ." Gordon stroked her hands, kissed her face, her uplifted face, and told her that he heard nothing but good reports about her teaching. He himself was a comfortable, moderately popular professor; he had been teaching for fifteen years. "You have some very enthusiastic students," he said. "Don't doubt yourself, Ilena, please; if you hear negative things it might be from other teachers who are jealous. . . ." Ilena pressed herself gratefully into this good man's embrace, hearing the echo of her mother's words of years ago, when Ilena would come home hurt from school for some minor girlish reason: "Don't mind them, they're just *jealous*."

A world of jealous people, like her husband: therefore hateful, therefore dangerous. Out to destroy her. Therefore the pills, tiny round pills and large button-sized pills, and the multicolored capsules.

There were few places she and Gordon could meet. Sometimes they walked around the campus, sometimes they met for lunch downtown, but most of the time they simply sat in her office and talked. She told him everything about her life, reviewing all the snarls and joys she had reviewed, years before, with Bryan, noticing that she emphasized the same events and even used the same words to describe them. She told him everything, but she never mentioned the drugs. He would disapprove. Maybe he would be disgusted. Like many Catholic men of his social class, and of his generation, he would be frightened by weakness in women, though by his own admission he drank too much. If he commented on her dazed appearance, if he worried over her fatigue—"Does your husband do this to you? Put you in this state?"—she pretended not to understand. "What, do I look so awful? So ugly?" she would tease. That way she diverted his concern, she bullied him into loving her, because he was a man to whom female beauty was important—his own wife had been a beauty queen many years ago, at a teachers' college in Ohio. "No, you're beautiful. You're beautiful," he would whisper.

They teased each other to a state of anguish on those dark winter afternoons, never really safe in Ilena's office—she shared the office with a nun, who had an early teaching schedule but who might conceivably turn up at any time, and there was always the possibility of the cleaning lady or the janitor unlocking the door with a master key—nightmarish possibility! Gordon kissed her face, her body, she clasped her hands around him and gave herself up to him musically, dreamily, like a rose of rot with only a short while left to bloom, carrying the rot neatly hidden, deeply hidden. She loved him so that her mind went blank even of the euphoria of drugs or the stimulation of a good, exciting day of teaching; she felt herself falling back into a blankness like a white flawless wall, pure material, pure essence, a mysterious essence that was fleshly and spiritual at once. Over and over they declared their love for each other, they promised it, vowed it, repeated it in each other's grave accents, echoing and unconsciously imitating each other, Ilena carrying home to her apartment her lover's gentleness, his paternal listening manner. Maybe Bryan sensed Gordon's presence, his influence on her, long before the breakup. Maybe he could discern, with his scientist's keen heatless eye, the shadow of another personality, powerful and beloved, on the other side of his wife's consciousness.

Ilena vowed to Gordon, "I love you, only you," and she made him believe that she and Bryan no longer slept in the same bed. This was not true: she was so fearful of Bryan, of his guessing her secret, that she imitated with her husband the affection she gave to Gordon, in that way giving herself to two men, uniting them in her body. *Two men. Uniting them in her body.* Her body could not take all this. Her body threatened to break down. She hid from Bryan, spending an hour or more in the bathtub, gazing down through her lashes at her bluish, bruised body, wondering how long this phase of her life could last—the taunting of her sanity, the use of her rather delicate body by two normal men. *This is how a woman becomes prehistoric,* she thought. *Prehistoric. Before all personalized, civilized history. Men make love to her and she is reduced to protoplasm.*

She recalled her girlhood and her fear of men, her fear of someday having to marry—for all her female relatives urged marriage, marriage!—and now it seemed to her puzzling that the physical side of her life should be so trivial. It was not important, really. She could have taken on any number of lovers, it was like shaking hands at a party, moving idly and absent-mindedly from one man to another; nothing serious about it at all. Why had she feared it so? And that was why the landscape of Detroit took on for her such neutral bleakness, its sidewalks and store windows

and streets and trees, its spotted skies, its old people, its children
—all unformed, unpersonalized, unhistoric. Everyone is protoplasm, she thought, easing together and easing apart. Some touch
and remain stuck together; others touch and part. . . . But
though she told herself this, she sometimes felt her head weighed
down with a terrible depression and she knew she would have to
die, would have to kill her consciousness. She could not live with
two men.

She could not live with one man.

Heated, hysterical, she allowed Gordon to make love to her in
that office. The two of them lay exhausted and stunned on the
cold floor—unbelieving lovers. Had this really happened? She
felt the back of her mind dissolve. Now she was committed to
him, she had been degraded, if anyone still believed in degradation; now something would happen, something must happen.
She would divorce Bryan; he would divorce his wife. They must
leave Detroit. They must marry. They must change their lives.

Nothing happened.

She sprang back to her feet, assisted by this man who seemed
to love her so helplessly, her face framed by his large hands, her
hair smoothed, corrected by his hands. She felt only a terrible
chilly happiness, an elation that made no sense. And so she
would put on her coat and run across the snowy, windswept
campus to teach a class in freshman composition, her skin rosy,
radiant, her body soiled and reeking beneath her clothes, everything secret and very lovely. Delirious and articulate, she lived
out the winter. She thought, eying her students: *If they only
knew.* . . . It was all very high, very nervous and close to hysteria; Gordon loved her, undressed her and dressed her, retreated
to his home where he undressed and bathed his smallest children
and she carried his human heat with her everywhere on the coldest days, edgy from the pills of that noon and slightly hungover
from the barbiturates of the night before, feeling that she was
living her female life close to the limits, at the most extreme
boundaries of health and reason. Her love for him burned in

ward, secretly, and she was dismayed to see how very soiled her clothes were, sometimes as if mocking her. Was this love, was it a stain like any other? But her love for him burned outward, making her more confident of herself, so that she did not hesitate to argue with her colleagues. She took part in a feeble anti-Vietnam demonstration on campus, which was jeered at by most of the students who bothered to watch, and which seemed to embarrass Gordon, who was not "political." She did not hesitate to argue with hard-to-manage students during class, sensing herself unladylike and impudent and reckless in their middle-class Catholic eyes, a *woman* who dared to say such things!—"I believe in birth control, obviously, and in death control. Suicide must be recognized as a natural human right." This, at a Catholic school; she had thought herself daring in those days.

Emmett Norlan and his friends, scrawny, intense kids who were probably taking drugs themselves, at least smoking marijuana, clustered around Ilena and tried to draw her into their circle. They complained that they could not talk to the other professors. They complained about the "religious chauvinism" of the university, though Ilena asked them what they expected—it was a Catholic school, wasn't it? "Most professors here are just closed circuits, they don't create anything, they don't communicate anything," Emmett declared contemptuously. He was no taller than Ilena herself, and she was a petite woman. He wore sloppy, soiled clothes, and even on freezing days he tried to go without a heavy coat; his perpetual grimy fatigue jacket became so familiar to Ilena that she was to think of him, sharply and nostalgically, whenever she saw such a jacket in the years to come. The boy's face was surprisingly handsome, in spite of all the frizzy hair and beard and the constant squinting and grimacing; but it was small and boyish. He had to fight that boyishness by being tough. His glasses were heavy, black-rimmed, and made marks on either side of his nose—he often snatched them off and rubbed the bridge of his nose, squinting nearsightedly at Ilena, never faltering in his argument. Finally Ilena would say, "Emmett, I have to go home.

Can't we talk about this some other time?"—wondering anxiously if Gordon had already left school. She was always backing
away from even the students she liked, always edging away from
her fellow teachers; she was always in a hurry, literally running
from her office to a classroom or to the library, her head ducked
against the wind and her eyes narrowed so that she need not see
the faces of anyone she knew. In that university she was friendly
with only a few people, among them the head of her department,
a middle-aged priest with a degree from Harvard. He was neat,
graying, gentlemanly, but a little corrupt in his academic stand-
ards: the Harvard years had been eclipsed long ago by the stern
daily realities of Detroit.

The end for Ilena at this school came suddenly, in Father
Hoffman's office.

Flushed with excitement, having spent an hour with Gordon
in which they embraced and exchanged confidences—about his
wife's sourness, her husband's iciness—Ilena had rushed to a
committee that was to examine a Master's degree candidate in
English. She had never sat on one of these committees before.
The candidate was a monk, Brother Ronald, a pale, rather obese
pleasant man in his thirties. His lips were more womanish than
Ilena's. The examination began with a question by a professor
named O'Brien: "Please give us a brief outline of English literature." Brother Ronald began slowly, speaking in a gentle, faltering voice—this question was always asked by this particular professor, so the candidate had memorized an answer, perfectly—
and O'Brien worked at lighting his pipe, nodding vaguely from
time to time. Brother Ronald came to a kind of conclusion some
fifteen minutes later, with the "twentieth century," mentioning
the names of Joyce, Lawrence, and T. S. Eliot. "Very good," said
O'Brien. The second examiner, Mr. Honig, asked nervously,
"Will you describe tragedy and give us an example, please?"
Brother Ronald frowned. After a moment he said, "There's
Hamlet . . . and *Macbeth*. . . ." He seemed to panic then. He
could think of nothing more to say. Honig, himself an obese good-

natured little man of about fifty, with a Master's degree from a local university and no publications, smiled encouragingly at Brother Ronald; but Brother Ronald could only stammer, "Tragedy has a plot . . . a climax and a conclusion. . . . It has a moment of revelation . . . and comic relief. . . ." After several minutes of painful silence, during which the only sounds were of O'Brien's sucking at his pipe, Brother Ronald smiled shakily and said that he did not know any more about tragedy.

Now it was Ilena's turn. She was astonished. She kept glancing at O'Brien and Honig, trying to catch their eyes, but they did not appear to notice. Was it possible that this candidate was considered good enough for an advanced degree, was it possible that anyone would allow him to teach English anywhere? She could not believe it. She said, sitting up very straight, "Brother Ronald, please define the term 'Gothicism' for us." Silence. Brother Ronald stared at his hands. He tried to smile. "Then could you define the term 'heroic couplet' for us," Ilena said. Her heart pounded combatively. The monk gazed at her, sorrowful and soft, his eyes watery; he shoook his head *no*, he didn't know. "Have you read any of Shakespeare's sonnets?" Ilena asked. Brother Ronald nodded gravely, *yes*. "Could you discuss one of them?" Ilena asked. Again, silence. Brother Ronald appeared to be thinking. Finally he said, "I guess I don't remember any of them. . . ." "Could you tell us what a sonnet is, then?" Ilena asked. "A short poem," said Brother Ronald uncertainly. "Could you give us an example of any sonnet?" said Ilena. He stared at his hands, which were now clasped together. They were pudgy and very clean. After a while Ilena saw that he could not think of a sonnet, so she said sharply, having become quite nervous herself, "Could you talk to us about any poem at all? One of your favorite poems?" He sat in silence for several seconds. Finally Ilena said, "Could you give us the *title* of a poem?"

A miserable half minute. But the examination was nearly over: Ilena saw the monk glance at his wrist watch.

"I've been teaching math at St. Rose's for the last five

years . . ." Brother Ronald said softly. "It wasn't really my idea
to get a Master's degree in English . . . my order sent me
out. . . ."

"Don't you know any poems at all? Not even any titles?" Ilena
asked.

"Of course he does. We studied Browning last year, didn't we
Brother Ronald?" O'Brien said. "You remember. You received
B in the course. I was quite satisfied with your work. Couldn'
you tell us the title of a work of Browning's?"

Brother Ronald stared at his hands and smiled nervously.

"That's my last duchess up there on the wall. . . ." O'Brien
said coaxingly.

Brother Ronald was breathing deeply. After a few seconds h
said, in a voice so soft they could almost not hear it, *"My la
duchess? . . ."*

"Yes, that is a poem," Ilena said.

"Now it's my turn to ask another question," O'Brien sa
briskly. He asked the monk a very long, conversational questic
about the place of literature in education—did it have a plac
How would he teach a class of high-school sophomores a Shak
spearean play, for instance?

The examination ended before Brother Ronald was able to a
swer.

They dismissed him. O'Brien, who was the chairman of t
examining committee, said without glancing at Ilena, "We w
give him a B."

"Yes, a B seems about right," the other professor said quick

Ilena, whose head was ringing with outrage and shame, p
her hand down flat on the table. "No," she said.

"What do you mean, no?"

"I won't pass him."

They stared at her. O'Brien said irritably, "Then I'll give l
an A, to balance out your C."

"But I'm not giving him a C. I'm not giving him anythi

How can he receive any other grade than F? I won't sign that paper. I can't sign it," Ilena said.

"I'll give him an A also," the other professor said doubtfully. "Then . . . then maybe he could still pass . . . if we averaged it out. . . ."

"But I won't sign the paper at all," Ilena said.

"You have to sign it."

"I won't sign it."

"It is one of your duties as a member of this examining board to give a grade and to sign your name."

"I won't sign it," Ilena said. She got shakily to her feet and walked out. In the corridor, ghostly and terrified, Brother Ronald hovered. Ilena passed by him in silence.

But the next morning she was summoned to Father Hoffman's office.

The story got out that she had been fired, but really she had had enough sense to resign—to write a quick resignation note on Father Hoffman's memo pad. They did not part friends. The following year, when her best-selling novel was published, Father Hoffman sent her a letter of congratulations on university stationery, charmingly worded: "I wish only the very best for you. We were wrong to lose you. Pity us." By then she had moved out of Detroit, her husband was in San Diego, she was living in a flat in Buffalo, near Delaware Avenue, afraid of being recognized when she went out to the drugstore or the supermarket. *Death Dance* had become a selection of the Book-of-the-Month Club; it had been sold for $150,000 to a movie producer famous for his nodding, "socially significant" films, and for the first time in her life Ilena was sleepless because of money—rabid jangling thoughts about money. She was ashamed of having done so well financially. She was terrified of her ability to survive all this praise, this publicity, this national good fortune. For, truly, *Death Dance* was not her best novel: a hectic narrative about college students and their preoccupation with sex and drugs and death,

in a prose she had tried to make "poetic." Her more abrasive colleagues at the University of Buffalo cautioned her against believing the praise that was being heaped upon her, that she would
destroy her small but unique talent if she took all this seriously,
etc. Even her new lover, a critic, separated from his wife and
several children, a fifty-year-old ex-child prodigy, warned her
against success: "They want to make you believe you're a genius
so they can draw back and laugh at you. First they hypnotize you,
then they destroy you. Believe nothing."

The flow of barbiturates and amphetamines gave her eyes a
certain wild sheen, her copper hair a frantic wasteful curl, made
her voice go shrill at the many Buffalo parties. She wondered if
she did not have the talent, after all, for being a spectacle. Someone to stare at. The magazine cover had flattered her wonderfully: taken by a Greenwich Village photographer as dreamily
hungover as Ilena herself, the two of them moving about in slow
motion in his studio, adjusting her hair, her lips, her eyelashes,
the tip of her chin, adjusting the light, altering the light, bringing out a fantastic ethereal glow in her eyes and cheeks and forehead that Ilena had never seen in herself. The cover had been in
full color and Ilena had looked really beautiful, a pre-Raphaelite
virgin. Below her photograph was a caption in high alarmed
black letters: ARE AMERICAN WOMEN AVENGING CENTURIES OF
OPPRESSION?

Revenge!

Death Dance was nominated for a National Book Award, but
lost out to a long, tedious, naturalistic novel; someone at Buffalo
who knew the judges told Ilena that this was just because the
female member of the committee had been jealous of her. Ilena,
whose head seemed to be swimming all the time now, and who
did not dare to drive around in her Mercedes for fear of having
an accident, accepted all opinions, listened desperately to everyone, pressed herself against her lover, and wept at the thought of
her disintegrating brain.

This lover wanted to marry her, as soon as his divorce was

final; his name was Lyle Myer. He was the author of twelve
books of criticism and a columnist for a weekly left-wing magazine; a New Yorker, he had never lived outside New York until
coming to Buffalo, which terrified him. He was afraid of being
beaten up by militant students on campus, and he was afraid of
being beaten up by the police. Hesitant, sweet, and as easily
moved to sentimental tears as Ilena herself, he was always telephoning her or dropping in at her flat. Because he was, or had
been, an alcoholic, Ilena felt it was safe to tell him about the pills
she took. He seemed pleased by this confidence, this admission of
her weakness, as if it bound her more hopelessly to him—just as
his teen-aged daughter, whose snapshot Ilena had seen, was
bound to be a perpetual daughter to him because of her acne and
rounded shoulders, unable to escape his love. "Drugs are suicidal,
yes, but if they forestall the actual act of suicide they are obviously beneficial," he told her.

With him, she felt nothing except a clumsy domestic affection:
no physical love at all.

She was so tired most of the time that she did not even pretend
to feel anything. With Gordon, in those hurried steep moments
back in Detroit, the two of them always fearful of being discovered, her body had been keyed up to hysteria and love had made
her delirious; with Bryan, near the end of their marriage, she had
sometimes felt a tinge of love, a nagging doubtful rush that she
often let fade away again, but with Lyle her body was dead, worn
out, it could not respond to his most tender caresses. She felt how
intellectualized she had become, her entire body passive and ob-
servant and cynical.

"Oh, I have to get my head straight. I have to get my head
straight," Ilena wept.

Lyle undressed her gently, lovingly. She felt panic, seeing in
his eyes that compassionate look that had meant Gordon was
thinking of his children: how she had flinched from that look!

The end had come with Gordon just as abruptly as it had come
with Father Hoffman, and only a week later. They had met by

accident out on the street one day, Gordon with his wife and the
two smallest children, Ilena in a trench coat, bareheaded, a leather
purse with a frayed strap slung over her shoulder. "Hello, Ilena,"
Gordon said guiltily. He was really frightened. His wife, still a
handsome woman, though looking older than her thirty-seven
years, smiled stiffly at Ilena and let her gaze travel down to
Ilena's watermarked boots. "How are you, Ilena?" Gordon said
His eyes grabbed at her, blue and intimidated. His wife, tugging
at one of the little boys, turned a sour, ironic smile upon Ilena
and said, "Are you one of my husband's students?" Ilena guessed
that this was meant to insult Gordon, to make him feel old. But
she explained politely that she was an instructor in the English
Department, "but I'm leaving after this semester," and she no
ticed covertly that Gordon was not insulted, not irritated by his
wife's nastiness, but only watchful, cautious, his smile strained
with the fear that Ilena would give him away.

"In fact, I'm leaving in a few weeks," Ilena said.

His wife nodded stiffly, not bothering to show much regret
Gordon smiled nervously, apologetically. With relief, Ilena
thought. He was smiling with relief because now he would be rid
of her.

And so that had ended.

They met several times after this, but Ilena was now in a con
stant state of excitement or drowsiness; she was working out the
beginning chapters of *Death Dance*—now living alone in the
apartment, since her husband had moved out to a hotel. Her life
was a confusion of days and nights, sleepless nights, headache
days, classes she taught in a dream and classes she failed to meet
she spent long periods in the bathtub while the hot water turned
tepid and finally cold, her mind racing. She thought of her mar
riage and its failure. Marriage was the deepest, most mysterious
most profound exploration open to man: she had always believed
that, and she believed it now. Because she had failed did not
change that belief. This plunging into another's soul, this pr

sure of bodies together, so brutally intimate, was the closest one could come to a sacred adventure; she still believed that. But she had failed. So she forced herself to think of her work. She thought of the novel she was writing—about a "suicide club" that had apparently existed in Ann Arbor, Michigan—projecting her confusion and her misery into the heads of those late-adolescent girls, trying not to think of her own personal misery, the way love had soured in her life. Her husband. Gordon. Well, yes, men failed at being men; but maybe she had failed at being a woman. She had been unfaithful to two men at the same time. She deserved whatever she got.

Still, she found it difficult to resist swallowing a handful of sleeping pills. . . . Why not? Why not empty the whole container? There were moments when she looked at herself in the bathroom mirror and raised one eyebrow flirtatiously. *How about it? . . . Why not die?* . . . Only the empty apartment awaited her.

But she kept living because the novel obsessed her. She had to write it. She had to solve its problems, had to finish it, send it away from her completed. And, anyway, if she had taken sleeping pills and did not wake up, Gordon or Bryan would probably discover her before she had time to die. They often telephoned, and would have been alarmed if she hadn't answered. Gordon called her every evening, usually from a drugstore, always guilty, so that she began to take pity on his cowardice. Did he fear her committing suicide and leaving a note that would drag him in? Or did he really love her? . . . Ilena kept assuring him that she was all right, that she would be packing soon, yes, yes, she would always remember him with affection; no, she would probably not write to him, it would be better not to write. They talked quickly, sadly. Already the frantic hours of love-making in that place had become history, outlandish and improbable. Sometimes Ilena thought, *My God, I really love this man,* but her voice kept on with the usual conversation—what she had done that day, what he had done, what the state of her relationship with Bryan was, what his children were doing, the plans his wife had for that summer.

So it had ended, feebly; she had not even seen him the last week she was in Detroit.

Bryan called her too, impulsively. Sometimes to argue, sometimes to check plans, dates. He knew about the pills she took, though not about their quantity, and if she failed to answer the telephone for long he would have come over at once. Ilena would have been revived, wakened by a stomach pump, an ultimate masculine attack upon her body, sucking out her insides in great gasping shuddering gulps. . . . So she took only a double dose of sleeping pills before bed, along with the gin, and most of the time she slept soundly enough, without dreams. The wonderful thing about pills was that dreams were not possible. No dreams. The death of dreams. What could be more lovely than a dreamless sleep? . . .

In late April, Bryan had a collapse of some kind and was admitted to a local clinic; then he flew to his mother's, in Oswego. Ilena learned from a mutual friend at Wayne Medical School that Gordon had had a general nervous collapse, aggravated by sudden malfunctioning of the liver brought on by malnutrition— he had been starving himself, evidently, to punish Ilena. But she worked on her novel, incorporating this latest catastrophe into the plot; she finished it in January of 1968, in Buffalo, where she was teaching a writing seminar; it was published in early 1969, and changed her life.

Lyle Myer pretended jealousy of her—all this acclaim, all the fuss! He insisted that she agree to marry him. He never mentioned, seemed deliberately to overlook, the embarrassing fact that she could love him only tepidly, that her mind was always elsewhere in their dry, fateful struggles, strung out with drugs or the memory of some other man, someone she half remembered or the letters she had to answer from her agent and a dozen other people, so many people inviting her to give talks, to accept awards, to teach at their universities, to be interviewed by them, begging and demanding her time, her intense interest, like a hundred lovers tugging and pulling at her body, engaging it in a kind of love-making to which she could make only the feeblest of responses, her face locked now in a perpetual feminine smile. . . . With so much publicity and money, she felt an obligation to be feminine and gracious to everyone; when she was interviewed she spoke enthusiastically of the place of art in life, the place of beauty in this modern technological culture—she seemed to stress, on one national late-night television show, the tragedy of small trees stripped bare by vandals in city parks as much as the tragedy of the country's current foreign policy in Vietnam. At least it turned out that way. It was no wonder people could not take her seriously: one of the other writers at Buffalo, himself famous though more *avant-garde* than Ilena, shrugged her off as that girl who was always "licking her lips to make them glisten."

She did not sign on for another year at Buffalo, partly because of the political strife there and partly because she was restless, agitated, ready to move on. She sold the Mercedes and gave to the Salvation Army the furniture and other possessions Bryan had so cavalierly—indifferently—given her, and took an apartment in New York. She began writing stories that were to appear in fashion magazines, Ilena's slick, graceful prose an easy complement to the dreamlike faces and bodies of models whose photographs appeared in those same magazines, everything muted and lightly distorted as if by a drunken lens, the "very poetry of hallucination"—as one reviewer had said of *Death Dance*. Lyle flew down to see her nearly every weekend; on other weekends he was with his "separated" family. She loved him, yes, and she agreed to marry him, though she felt no hurry—in fact, she felt no real interest in men at all, her body shrinking when it was touched even accidentally, not out of fear but out of a kind of chaste boredom. So much, she had had so much of men, so much loving, so much mauling, so much passion. . . .

What, she was only twenty-nine years old?

She noted, with a small pang of vanity, how surprised audi
ences were when she rose to speak. *Ilena Williams looks so
young!* They could not see the fine vibrations of her knees and
hands, already viciously toned down by Librium. They could not
see the colorless glop she vomited up in motel bathrooms, or in
rest rooms down the hall from the auditorium in which she was
speaking—she was always "speaking," invited out all over the
country for fees ranging from $500 to a colossal $2000, speaking
on "current trends in literature" or "current mores in America" or
answering questions about her "writing habits" or reading sec
tions from her latest work, a series of short stories in honor of
certain dead writers with whom she felt a kinship. "I don't exist
as an individual but only as a completion of a tradition, the end
of something, not the best part of it but only the end," she ex
plained, wondering if she was telling the truth or if this was all
nonsense, "and I want to honor the dead by reimagining their
works, by reimagining their obsessions . . . in a way marrying
them, joining them as a woman joins a man . . . spiritually and
erotically. . . ." She spoke so softly, so hesitantly, that audi
ences often could not hear her. Whereupon an energetic young
man sitting in the first row, or onstage with her, would spring to
his feet and adjust the microphone. "Is that better? Can you all
hear now?" he would ask. Ilena saw the faces in the audience
waver and blur and fade away, sheer protoplasm, and panic
began in her stomach—what if she should vomit right in front of
everyone? on this tidy little lectern propped up on dictionaries for
her benefit? But she kept on talking. Sometimes she talked about
the future of the short story, sometimes about the future of civili
zation—she heard the familiar, dead, deadened word *Vietnam*
uttered often in her own voice, a word that had once meant
something; she heard her voice echoing from the farthest corners
of the auditorium as if from the corners of all those heads, her
own head hollow as a drum, occasionally seeing herself at a dis

tance—a woman with long but rather listless copper-red hair, thin cheeks, eyes that looked unnaturally enlarged. *Adverse reactions: confusion, edema, nausea, constipation, jaundice, hallucinations. . . .* Did that qualify as a legitimate hallucination, seeing herself from a distance, hearing herself from a distance? Did that qualify as a sign of madness?

During the fall and winter of 1969 and the spring of 1970 she traveled everywhere, giving talks, being met at airports by interested strangers, driven to neat disinfected motel rooms. She had time to write only a few stories, which had to be edited with care before they could be published. Her blood pounded barbarously, while her voice went on and on in that gentle precise way, her body withdrawing from any man's touch, demure with a dread that could not show through her clothes. She had been losing weight gradually for three years, and now she had the angular, light-boned, but very intense look of a precocious child. People wanted to protect her. Women mothered her, men were always taking her arm, helping her through doorways; the editor of a famous men's magazine took her to lunch and warned her of Lyle Myer's habit of marrying young, artistic women and then ruining them—after all, he had been married three times already, and the pattern was established. Wasn't it? When people were most gentle with her, Ilena thought of the tough days when she'd run across that wind-tortured campus in Detroit, her coat flapping about her, her body still dazzled by Gordon's love, damp and sweaty from him, and she had dared run into the classroom, five minutes late, had dared to take off her coat and begin the lesson. . The radiators in that old building had knocked as if they might explode; like colossal arteries, like her thudding arteries, overwhelmed with life.

In the fall of 1970 she was invited back to Detroit to give a talk before the local Phi Beta Kappa chapter; she accepted, and a few days later she reecived a letter from the new dean of the School of Arts—new since she had left—of her old university, inviting her to a reception in her honor, as their "most esteemed ex-staff member." It was all very diplomatic, very charming. She had escaped them, they had gotten rid of her, and now they could all meet together for a few hours. . . . Father Hoffman sent a note to her also, underscoring the dean's invitation, hoping that she was well and as attractive as ever. So she accepted.

Father Hoffman and another priest came to pick her up at the Sheraton Cadillac Hotel; she was startled to see that Father Hoffman had let his hair grow a little long, that he had noble graying sideburns, and that the young priest with him was even shaggier. After the first awkward seconds—Father Hoffman forgot and called her "Mrs. Donohue"—they got along very well. Ilena was optimistic about the evening; her stomach seemed settled. As soon as they arrived at the dean's home she saw that Gordon was not there; she felt immensely relieved, though she had known he would not come, would not want to see her again . . . she felt immensely relieved and accepted a drink at once from Father Hoffman, who was behaving in an exceptionally gallant manner. "Ilena is looking better than ever," he said as people crowded around her, some of them with copies of her novel to sign, "better even than all her photographs. . . . But we don't want to tire her out, you know. We don't want to exhaust her." He kept refreshing her drink, like a lover or a husband. In the old days everyone at this place had ignored Ilena's novels, even the fact of her being a "writer," but now they were all smiles and congratulations—even the wives of her ex-colleagues, sturdy dowdy women who had never seemed to like her. Ilena was too shaky to make any sarcastic observations about this to Father Hoffman, who might have appreciated them. He did say, "Times have changed, eh, Ilena?" and winked at her roguishly. "For one thing, you're not quite as excitable as you used to be. You were a very *young* woman around here." She could sense, beneath his gallantry, a barely disguised contempt for her—for all women—and this knowledge made her go cold. She mumbled something about fighting off the flu. Time to take a "cold tablet." She fished

in her purse and came out with a large yellow capsule, a tranquil-
izer, and swallowed it down with a mouthful of Scotch.

Father Hoffman and Dr. O'Brien and a new, young assistant
professor—a poet whose first book would be published next
spring—talked to Ilena in a kind of chorus, telling her about all
the changes in the university. It was much more "community-
oriented" now. Its buildings—its "physical plant"—were to be
open to the neighborhood on certain evenings and on Saturdays.
The young poet, whose blond hair was very long and who wore a
suede outfit and a black silk turtleneck shirt, kept interrupting
the older men with brief explosions of mirth. "Christ, all this is a
decade out of date—integration and all that crap—the NAACP
and good old Martin Luther King and all that crap—the blacks
don't want it and I agree with them one hundred percent! King is
dead and so is Civil Rights—just another white middle-class
week-night activity the blacks saw through long ago! I agree with
them one hundred percent!" He seemed to be trying to make an
impression on Ilena, not quite looking at her, but leaning toward
her with his knees slightly bent, as if to exaggerate his youth.
Ilena sipped at her drink, trying to hide the panic that was beginning. Yes, the NAACP was dead, all that was dead, but she didn't
want to think about it—after all, it had been at a civil-rights rally
that she and Bryan had met, years ago in Madison, Wiscon·
in. . . . "I haven't gotten around to reading your novel yet,"
the poet said, bringing his gaze sideways to Ilena.

Ilena excused herself and searched for a bathroom.

The dean's wife took her upstairs, kindly. Left alone, she
waited to be sick, then lost interest in being sick; she had only to
get through a few more hours of this and she would be safe. And
Gordon wasn't there. She looked at herself in the mirror and
should have been pleased to see that she looked so pretty—not
beautiful tonight but pretty, delicate—she had worked hard
enough at it, spending an hour in the hotel bathroom steaming
her face and patting astringent on it, hoping for the best. She
dreaded the cracks in her brain somehow working their way out

to her skin. What then, what then? . . . But beauty did no
good for anyone; it conferred no blessing upon the beautiful
woman. Nervously, Ilena opened the medicine cabinet and
peered at the array of things inside. She was interested mainly in
prescription containers. Here were some small green pills prescribed for the dean's wife, for "tension." Tension, good! She
took two of the pills. On another shelf there were some yellow
capsules, perhaps the same as her own, though slightly smaller;
she checked, yes, hers were 5 mg. and these were only 2. So she
didn't bother with them. But she did discover an interesting
white pill for "muscular tension," Dean Spriggs's prescription
she took one of these.

She descended the stairs, her hand firm on the bannister.

Before she could return safely to Father Hoffman, she was
waylaid by someone's wife—the apple-cheeked Mrs. Honig, a
very short woman with white hair who looked older than her
husband, who looked, in fact, like Mrs. Santa Claus, motherly and
dwarfed; Mrs. Honig asked her to sign a copy of *Death Dance*
"We all think it's so wonderful, just so wonderful for you," she
said. Another woman joined them. Ilena had met her once, years
before, but she could not remember her name. Mr. Honig hurried over. The conversation seemed to be about the tragedy of
America—"All these young people dying in a senseless war,"
Mrs. Honig said, shaking her white hair; Mr. Honig agreed
mournfully. "Vietnam is a shameful tragedy," he said. The
dean's wife came by with a tray of cheese and crackers; everyone
took something, even Ilena, though she doubted her ability to
eat. She doubted everything. It seemed to her that Mrs. Honig
and these other people were talking about Vietnam, and about
drugs and death—could this be true?—or was it another hallucination? "Why, you know, a young man was killed here last
spring, he took part in a demonstration against the Cambodia
business," Mrs. Honig said vaguely; "they say a policeman
clubbed him to death. . . ." "No, Ida, he had a concussion and
died afterward," Mr. Honig said. He wiped his mouth of cracker

crumbs and stared sadly at Ilena. "I think you knew him . . . Emmett Norlan?"

Emmett Norlan?

"You mean—Emmett is dead? He died? He died?" Ilena asked shrilly.

The blond poet came over to join their group. He had known Emmett, yes, a brilliant young man, a martyr to the Cause—yes, yes—he knew everything. While Ilena stared into space he told them all about Emmett. *He* had been an intimate friend of Emmett's.

Ilena happened to be staring toward the front of the hall, and she saw Gordon enter. The dean's wife was showing him in. Flakes of snow had settled upon the shoulders of his gray coat. Ilena started, seeing him so suddenly. She had forgotten all about him. She stared across the room in dismay, wondering at his appearance—he wore his hair longer, his sideburns were long and a little curly, he even had a small wiry brown beard— But he did not look youthful, he looked weary and drawn.

Now began half an hour of Ilena's awareness of him and his awareness of her. They had lived through events like this in the past, at other parties, meeting in other groups at the university; dangerous, nervous sensation about their playing this game, not wanting to rush together. Ilena accepted a drink from a forty-year-old who looked zestful and adolescent, a priest who did not wear his Roman collar but, instead, a black nylon sweater and a medallion on a leather strap; Ilena's brain whirled at such surprises. What had happened? In the past there had been three categories: men, women, and priests. She had known how to conduct herself discreetly around these priests, who were masculine but undangerous; now she wasn't so sure. She kept thinking of Emmett dead. Had Emmett really been killed by the police? Little Emmett? She kept thinking of Gordon, aware of him circling her at a distance of some yards. She kept thinking of these people talking so casually of Vietnam, of drugs, of the death of little Emmett Norlan—these people—the very words they used turning flat and banal and safe in their mouths. "The waste of youth in this country is a tragedy," the priest with the sweater and the medallion said, shaking his head sadly.

Ilena eased away from them to stare at a Chagall lithograph, "Summer Night." Two lovers embraced, in repose; yet a nightmarish dream blossomed out of their heads, an intricate maze of dark depthless foliage, a lighted window, faces ghastly-white and perhaps a little grotesque. . . . Staring at these lovers, she sensed Gordon approaching her. She turned to him, wanting to be casual. But she was shaking. Gordon stared at her and she saw that old helplessness in his eyes—what, did he still love her? Wasn't she free of him yet? She began talking swiftly, nervously. "Tell me about Emmett. Tell me what happened." Gordon, who seemed heavier than she recalled, whose tired face disappointed her sharply, spoke as always in his gentle, rather paternal voice: she tried to listen. She tried to listen but she kept recalling that office, the two of them lying on the floor together, helpless in an embrace, so hasty, so reckless, grinding their bodies together in anguish. . . . They had been so close, so intimate, that their blood had flowed freely in each other's veins; on the coldest day they had gone about blood-warmed, love-warmed. Tears filled Ilena's eyes. Gordon was saying, "The story was that he died of concussion, but actually he died of liver failure. Once he got in the hospital he just disintegrated . . . he had hepatitis . . . he'd been taking heroin. . . . It was a hell of a thing, Ilena. . . ."

She pressed her fingers hard against her eyes.

"Don't cry, please," Gordon said, stricken.

A pause of several seconds: the two of them in a kind of equilibrium, two lovers.

"Would you like me to drive you back to your hotel?" Gordon said.

She went at once to get her coat. Backing away, always backing away . . . she stammered a few words to Father Hoffman, to the dean and his wife, words of gratitude, confusion. Good-by to Detroit! *Good-by, good-by.* She shook hands. She finished h drink. Gordon helped her on with her coat—a stylish black coat with a black mink collar, nothing like the clothes she had worn in the old days. Out on the walk, in the soft falling snow, Gordon said nervously: "I know you're going to be married. Lyle Myer. I know all about it. I'm very happy. I'm happy for you. You're looking very well."

Ilena closed her eyes, waiting for her mind to straighten itself out. Yes, she was normal; she had gone to an internist in Buffalo and had been declared normal. *You are too young to be experiencing menopause,* the doctor had said thoughtfully; *the cessation of menstrual periods must be related to the Pill or to an emotional condition.* She thought it better not to tell Gordon all that. "Thank you," she said simply.

"I'm sorry they told you about Emmett," Gordon said. "There was no reason to tell you. He liked you so much, Ilena; he hung around my office after you left and all but confessed he was in love with you . . . he kept asking if you wrote to me and I said no, but he didn't believe me . . . he was always asking about you. . . ."

"When did he die?"

"Last spring. His liver gave out. Evidently it was just shot. Someone said his skin was bright yellow."

"He was taking heroin? . . ."

"God, yes. He was a wreck. The poor kid just disintegrated, it was a hell of a shame. . . ."

He drove her back downtown. They were suddenly very comfortable together, sadly comfortable. Ilena had been in this car only two or three times in the past. "Where is your wife?" she asked shyly. She watched him as he answered—his wife was visiting her mother in Ohio, she'd taken the children—no, things were no better between them—always the same, always the same —Ilena thought in dismay that he was trivialized by these words: men were trivialized by love and by their need for women.

"I've missed you so much . . ." Gordon said suddenly.

They walked through the tufts of falling snow, to the hotel. A gigantic hotel, all lights and people. Ilena felt brazen and anonymous here. Gordon kept glancing at her, as if unable to believe in her. He was nervous, eager, a little drunk; an uncertain adolescent smile hovered about his face. "I love you, I still love you," he whispered. In the elevator he embraced her. Ilena did not resist. She felt her body warming to him as toward an old friend, a brother. She did love him. Tears of love stung her eyes. If only she could get her head straight, if only she could think of what she was supposed to think of . . . someone she was supposed to remember. . . . In the overheated room they embraced gently. Gently. Ilena did not want to start this love again, it was a mistake, but she caught sight of Gordon's stricken face and could not resist. She began to cry. Gordon clutched her around the hips, kneeling before her. He pressed his hot face against her.

"Ilena, I'm so sorry . . ." he said.

She thought of planets: sun-warmed planets revolving around a molten star. Revolving around a glob of light. And the planets rotated on their own private axes. But now the planets were accelerating their speed, they wobbled on their axes and the strain of their movement threatened to tear them apart. She began to sob. Ugly, gasping, painful sobs. . . . "Don't cry, please, I'm so sorry," Gordon said. They lay down together. The room was hot, too hot. They had not bothered to put on a light. Only the light from the window, a dull glazed wintry light; Ilena allowed him to kiss her, to undress her, to move his hands wildly about her body as she wept. What should she be thinking of? Whom should she remember? When she was with Lyle she thought back to Gordon . . . now, with Gordon, she thought back to someone else, someone else, half-remembered, indistinct, perhaps dead. . . . He began to make love to her. He was eager, breathing as sharply and as painfully as Ilena herself. She clasped her arms around him. That firm hard back she remembered. Or did she remember? . . . Her mind wandered and she thought suddenly of Bryan, her husband. He was her ex-husband now. She thought of their meeting at that civil-rights rally, introduced by mutual friends, she thought of the little tavern they had gone to, on State Street in Madison, she thought of the first meal she'd made for Bryan and that other couple . . . proud of herself as a cook, baking them an Italian dish with shrimp and crabmeat and mushrooms . . . yes, she had been proud of her cooking, she had loved to cook for years. For years. She had loved Bryan. But suddenly she was not thinking of him; her mind gave way to a sharper thought and she saw Emmett's face: his scorn, his disapproval.

She stifled a scream.

Gordon slid from her, frightened. "Did I hurt you? Ilena?"

She began to weep uncontrollably. Their bodies, so warm, now shivered and seemed to sting each other. Their hairs seemed to catch at each other painfully.

"Did I hurt you? . . ." he whispered.

She remembered the afternoon she had fainted. Passed out cold. And then she had came to her senses and she had cried, like this, hiding her face from her lover because crying made it ugly, so swollen. . . . Gordon tried to comfort her. But the bed was crowded with people. A din of people. A mob. Lovers were kissing her on every inch of her body and trying to suck up her tepid blood, prodding, poking, inspecting her like that doctor in Buffalo—up on the table, naked beneath an oversized white robe, her feet in the stirrups, being examined with a cold sharp metal device and then with the doctor's fingers in his slick rubber gloves—checking her ovaries, so casually—*You are too young for menopause,* he had said. Was it the pills, then? The birth-control pills? *This kind of sterility is not necessarily unrelated to the Pill,* the doctor had conceded, and his subtlety of language had enchanted Ilena. . . .

"Don't cry," Gordon begged.

She had frightened him off and he would not make love to her. He only clutched at her, embraced her. She felt that he was heavier, yes, than she remembered. Heavier. Older. But she could not concentrate on him: she kept seeing Emmett's face. His frizzy hair, his big glasses, his continual whine. Far inside her, too deep for any man to reach and stir into sensation, a dull, dim lust began for Emmett, hardly more than a faint throbbing. Emmett, who was dead. She wanted to hold him, now, instead of this man —Emmett in her arms, his irritation calmed, his glasses off and set on the night table beside the bed, everything silent, silent. Gordon was whispering to her. *Love. Love.* She did not remember that short scratchy beard. But she was lying in bed with an anxious, perspiring, bearded man, evidently someone she knew. They were so close that their blood might flow easily back and forth between their bodies, sluggish and warm and loving.

She recalled her husband's face: a look of surprise, shock. She had betrayed him. His face blended with the face of her student, who was dead, and Gordon's face, pressed so close to her in the dark that she could not see it. The bed was crammed with people. Their identities flowed sluggishly, haltingly, from vein to vein. One by one they were all becoming each other. Becoming protoplasm. They were protoplasm that had the sticky pale formlessness of semen. They were all turning into each other, into protoplasm. . . . Ilena was conscious of something fading in her, in the pit of her belly. Fading. Dying. *The central sexual organ is the brain*, she had read, and now her brain was drawing away, fading, dissolving.

"Do you want me to leave?" Gordon asked.

She did not answer. Against the hotel window: soft, shapeless clumps of snow. She must remember something, she must remember someone . . . there was an important truth she must understand. . . . But she could not get it into focus. Her brain seemed to swoon backward in an elation of fatigue, and she heard beyond this man's hoarse, strained breathing the gentle breathing of the snow, falling shapelessly upon them all.

"Do you want me to leave?" Gordon asked.

She could not speak.

Nightmusic

Perched on a chair. My feet in tiny stiff boots. My arms at my sides, my fingers deliberately still, held still. The melodies in my fingers silent. I am at attention.

My clothes are being adjusted, my sleeves tugged down tightly, impatiently; though I rarely grow, never more than an inch or two in many months, this jacket seems too small for me already. And the expense of it, this silk and handmade lace! . . . I am being instructed in the need to be absolutely fearless. The valet's long, mournful, grayish-pink face is so familiar to me that I hardly need to look at it. But closing my eyes would be impolite; it would show fear. I stand at attention and listen.

It is necessary to endure all things, all sounds, to cringe before nothing. It is not necessary to live. But if you live, then it is necessary to endure all things.

The valet is telling me that the single instrument I fear, the one sound I despise, is my only weakness and must be eliminated. How else to be immortal?—to be equal to my destiny? "So you won't cry as you did last time, you won't be reduced to a hysterical infant. . . ." My little shoulders hold themselves firmly, in spite of the fear that is gradually beginning. Maybe my tight-fitting jacket will encase the trembling so that the valet will not notice. And if I press my lips together firmly enough I will not whimper.

I am centuries old.

No, I am five years old. The sharp crease in the valet's bony forehead belongs to my fifth year: when I almost died of pneumonia. That was the year of the many carriage trips, the windy rainstorms, the air that sucked away my breath. But I never died.

". . . the trumpet isn't a delicate instrument, no. It isn't beautiful. Nobody argues that it is beautiful. But it belongs to life; it belongs to the world. What portion of the world is beautiful? You must harden yourself. You must realize that the world will always try to blast itself into you. . . ."

The day of my final "trumpet lesson."

The valet is eye-to-eye with me; he must be crouching slightly. His jacket, too, has grown tight, but only because he is tensing his body, his muscles straining the frayed black material. He adjusts me, my head. Seems to be balancing me in place. His two wide, familiar hands frame my face, the way you hold a mirror up to your face, with an affection and yet a dissatisfaction you display to no one else.

Perfectly balanced. Proud. At attention. Not trembling so that anyone can see. He stoops to pick up the trumpet from the floor. He raises it to his lips, and still his mournful subdued face is no changed; even with the gleaming instrument brought to his mouth, the upper part of his face remains the same. But no— there is a slight reflection on it, an almost imperceptible glow from the metallic surface of the instrument, glancing up onto the bridge of his nose and his bony, frugal forehead to emphasize the severity of that crease.

There is no sound that the mind of man has devised, no music that can be foreign to me.

2

The trumpet is blown into my face.

3

You and I are children, perhaps six years old. But we look younger. We are traveling, not here and not there. Past the window of our carriage flows the backward kingdom, where everything flows back, behind us, in a steady bumping stream. The carriage rocks with a certain comfortable rhythm, but sometimes there is an irregularity in the road and the wheels bounce; sometimes one of the horses falters or shies away from an object we can't see. You and I are drawn forward into the future, and behind us the world turns into yesterday and last year and the last century. Beyond that, a blur. We are too young to think about it.

You are puzzled at this journey, but I, who am accustomed to carriages much worse than this, am quite content. I am almost happy. You don't know where we are going and this worries you. But I can see the shape of our destination, though of course I haven't been there either—it is perhaps like other cities I've visited; it will play itself out on a day like other days I have experienced. So I am content, I am almost happy.

For the trip, a new outfit of scarlet and lace. New white gloves. My father is sitting beside me in his regular traveling clothes, with his booted feet on one of our valises. He is reading a musical score, turning the pages slowly. The inside of the carriage is so cold that he is wearing his gloves.

Though you are a little stronger than I, a larger child, you seem more affected by the cold; you are shivering openly. I try not to shiver, because once I begin I can't stop—it's like coughing—and

also because my father will notice. But he seems to notice anyway. He looks at me and says, "Tonight a hot bath, a bed with
goose-feather pillows and quilts, and tomorrow morning absolute
good health. This is not too much to ask."

No.

At the inn a sign is creaking in the wind. It hangs from a
hook. My father smooths his clothing, adjusts his hat, walks carefully a few paces behind me, carrying the valises. He is watching
the back of my head; he does not dare walk beside me. He is too
common, his clothes are the clothes of a valet, his long, narrow,
mournful face is the face of an ordinary man.

You and I walk bravely before him: princes.

4

Do you love me?

Do you know enough to love me?

God daily works new wonders through our child: a message
sent home to my mother. She is a fact, my mother. But she is
distant, unclear, as remote in time as the farthest reaches of my
kingdom, ugly barbaric tidelands and marshes where the only
music is that of sea birds.

But it is possible to imagine her: inside the face and heavy
yards of cloth of one of the women at the court, not the queen
or the empress or an obvious favorite, but a smiling, unquestion-
ing woman at the periphery. She smiles at me because I am so
small.

My toylike sonatas fly out beneath my toylike fingers, impro-
vised after everyone has finished eating. One of the gentlemen
has commanded: "Play us a song inspired by the word *truite*—it
has such a musical sound!" But one of the ladies protests and
amid laughter the gentleman amends his request: ". . . the word
amour, then!" And so I am playing this song.

It is a secret code, a song that says *Do you love me?* But: *Do
you recognize me, appreciate me, do you know enough to love
me?*

Afterward I must be carried out, away to my room, my warm bed. My father weeps with joy. He pulls off my new black suit and lays it carefully aside. I can see in his face a joy that is almost blinding: he worships me.

. . . *love?*

My fingers twitch to improvise a new song. But I am beneath the heavy quilts, I am sunk into the warm dark bed. Helpless here, beginning to drift into sleep. . . . A keyboard rises to me and my fingers take their place and so I am saved. . . .

5

In Frankfurt I performed in a powdered wig, I wore a sword fashioned of the most delicately engraved silver, and the boy Goethe stared at me and thought: *Another immortal!*

But afterward my valet took away the sword so that I wouldn't hurt myself; he took away the other gifts also, laying them aside with care, tenderly, and drew me away from the mirror I was gazing into, to kneel beside him as he offered thanks to God for the success of the evening.

. . . *help us to hurry onward with firm strides across all of Europe . . . help us to avoid the smallpox . . . fever . . . other shapes of death. . . .*

Help us into immortality.

6

You wince at my happy endings, you wince as you realize that this, too, has a happy ending, rounds off to the usual sprightly ending that is a habit of mine. But you get into such habits as a child—the habit of satisfying people, which then becomes satisfying and is its own ending.

Am I loved, am I saved . . . ? is a song people don't want to hear. Even you don't want to hear it. Well, maybe at a distance: across centuries. You listen for it in my music, sly and clever as my music is, so powerful it can't be measured; like ordinary sunlight. But you wouldn't want to hear it close up, face to face, a face mirror-close to yours, would you? What answer could you give?

So the happy ending is really for you, for your guardedness. And if you are anaesthetized. . . . After all, that is a kind of rehearsal.

7   THEORY OF THE HAPPY ENDING

As I walk out onto the stage, the applause begins. I am accustomed to applause, but this is almost overwhelming, almost frightening. Wave after wave of applause! I pause, staring out at the great assembly. Rows and rows of people, the flash of handsome, gleaming armrests, an illusion of enormous distance—and from that distance there come several lights shining on me and around me, singling me out. I am in a very large hall of a kind new to me: the floor seems to slope upward. Can this be right? Or is it another illusion? The rows of spectators seem to rise and to recede. There is an odor of newness here, new cushions, new wood, new carpeting; and the audience seems new, very anxious to applaud. As I grow somewhat calmer, I can see individual faces in the first several rows. They are wild in their applause— some of them are crying—I can see tears running down their healthy cheeks. But why? Astonished, I notice something else about them—their teeth are so even, so white!

Who are these strange people?

I walk to the piano, which is extremely large, a monster. Made of excellent wood. But it is very large and I can hardly sit before it, my legs are so short. They seem to have shrunk. My fingers are childishly optimistic, though, and if I spread them wide enough —like this—so wide that the weblike folds between them almost split, I can reach the necessary number of keys with my left hand and almost that many with my right hand. Perhaps I will be able to reach it after I begin playing . . . perhaps, if I play fast enough, I can split a chord and no one will notice. But my legs My legs are far too short.

And now, behind me, the members of the orchestra are taking their seats. They move quietly, humbly. Some coughing, some rearranging of chairs, an odd sense of uneasiness about them. If I turn to look at them, they don't meet my gaze. The conductor wanders in, unnoticed. He is not an old man, but his face is lined and pale; he carries what appears to be a handkerchief made of paper, crumpled in one hand. And he is dressed quite ordinarily, in a black outfit with a white shirt and a white tie. He is very mortal.

So I begin. The fear ebbs, is forgotten, I concentrate on my hands and wonder how, this time, they will vary my song. The piano stool is too high for me, the piano is too high, but other people know best how to exhibit me . . . other people, like the orchestra, know when it is time for them to accompany me and when to falter and fall off into silence. . . . I have never played more beautifully, in spite of my small aching hands and the strangeness of this place.

The music emerges out of my fingers note by note, as the cells of any man's blood emerge one by one out of his bleeding, no miracle to it. The miracle would be to stop the process. Childlike the manipulation of my fingers, the innocent runs and jumps of those fingers, and childlike also the astonished gasps and scattered applause of the audience. Why? What is wrong? I notice that some of the spectators have risen, some are out in the carpeted aisles; a few are even approaching the stage. A woman hurries at me, stumbling, her face smeared, the fleshy colors smeared . . . clapping, clapping . . . her hands are brought together in rough violent sweeps that agitate the air. . . . Now a man pushes ahead of her, to get to me. He is weeping. And someone else pounds against the piano, he is too excited to be restrained. . . . I keep on playing, toward that ending. It will be a closed, perfect ending, a happy ending.

But someone grips me hard, from behind, as if to stop me . . . now a man tries to force the keyboard cover down onto my fingers. . . . But no. No. The song inside the music insists upon its ending. I can't be stopped! I can't even be understood by people like you!

You wince at the ending I have imagined, because you prefer tears. You are piggish in your appetite for other people's sorrows; you are pigs, really, wallowing and snorting around me—pitying me!—imagine, pitying me!

No, I won't tell you you're happier than I am.

8   *ALTERNATE THEORY OF THE HAPPY ENDING*

Childlike the manipulation of my fingers, the innocent runs and jumps of those fingers, and childlike also the astonished gasps and scattered applause of the audience. You must imagine your hands here, your fingers springing out of mine, suddenly adult and powerful. There is no other way to know my music.

And your legs replace mine, long enough to reach the pedals, of course. Long, powerful adult legs. The heel of your right foot is firmly on the floor, the rest firmly on the pedal.

Enormous power in us!

The audience grows silent as we approach the sacred ending: one last spasm of clapping, then silence. You might almost imagine that there is no audience. You might be playing in an absolute emptiness, in a purity of silence, a listening silence, in which every note of your music is registered. To make a mistake at such a time—! Your heart contracts with the terror of it, but there is no need for terror, no need to imagine that you are heading into an unrehearsed future. I, who have been dead so long, have perfected these notes, these exertions of your brain, and there is no terror left for you. . . . Even the exertion of dying: that too has been explored and perfected and rehearsed—endlessly rehearsed—and it is only another kind of performance for you.

Therefore the happy ending: which you now realize is unavoidable. Your audience waits anxiously, row upon row of people waiting, listening. If you glance out into the darkness you can perhaps catch a glimpse of someone—a face—yes, there is a face, several faces. If you weren't concerned for the propriety of such a gesture, you might turn your head openly to stare, to count the rows of seats, to multiply, to calculate. . . . But out of respect for the occasion, and perhaps out of respect for the difficulty of my composition, you don't dare look around.

And now, as you begin the ending, which is so perfect that no other ending is imaginable, as you feel the shape of my music closing in upon you, with the rigor of my skull closing in upon your brain, you are teased suddenly out of yourself and you are now myself, we are fused together with a grace that must be godly, it is so obvious.

And then—

Then the silence is broken by applause. The music is over. The audience applauds wildly, unrestrained now, as if such applause is somehow necessary, or a part of what they have bought with their tickets. And the members of the orchestra applaud as well, at first not so enthusiastically, and then with more strength—those professional rivals who resist until the very end, who believe they must despise all happy endings except their own.

But why resist?